"If you get on the back of my bike, I can keep you alive."

Petrified, she connected with a pair of jade green eyes. Gorgeous. Absolutely the type of man she wanted to be with at any other time.

The stranger held out his hand. "We really need to go now, sweetheart. You coming?"

She straddled the back of the motorcycle. The bike sprang to life and her arms shot around him. There wasn't any give to his body when her fingers locked together across his hard abs. She closed her eyes and buried her face against his black jacket. She wanted to see nothing, especially the gruesome picture the shooting had left in her mind.

"Hold on tight."

Had she left the safety of the house for a dangerous daredevil?

BULLETPROOF
BADGE

BY
ANGI MORGAN

MILLS &
BOON®

First Published in Great Britain 2016
By Mills & Boon, an imprint of HarperCollins*Publishers*
1 London Bridge Street, London, SE1 9GF

© 2016 Angela Platt

ISBN: 978-0-263-91895-3

46-0216

Our policy is to use papers that are natural, renewable and recyclable products and made from wood grown in sustainable forests. The logging and manufacturing processes conform to the legal environmental regulations of the country of origin.

Printed and bound in Spain
by CPI, Barcelona

Angi Morgan writes Mills & Boon Intrigue novels "where honor and danger collide with love." She combines actual Texas settings with characters who are in realistic and dangerous situations. Angi and her husband live in north Texas, with only the four-legged "kids" left in the house to interrupt her writing. They recently began volunteering for a local Labrador retriever foster program. Visit her website www.angimorgan.com, or hang out with her on Facebook.

Tim, thanks for doing the dishes.

A special thanks to Cindi D & Tamami
for bouncing ideas around.

Another to Janie for all the late nights.
Always to my pal Jan (you know why).
And a special shout-out to Brenda R for the
constant reader support over the last five years!

Chapter One

Garrison Travis caught the kick with both his hands before it slammed into his chest. How had he given himself away? Why was this guy so dead set that neither of them get to that bedroom? He'd eventually find out during the interrogation. This moment though— He pulled the leg with him as he fell backward, rolling and placing his opponent under him.

Screams came from downstairs. Shots, upstairs and down, had started this mess. His opponent swung and missed. Garrison retaliated, sending a hard elbow to the guy's chin. It ripped the tuxedo across his shoulders. Always a good reason to rent. The company could reimburse the bridal shop. He popped to his feet. His opponent did the same.

Right cross. Uppercut. Double jabs to the ribs. He blocked them all and retreated. He was unarmed, having gone into the private event undercover as one of the waitstaff.

Where are the damn security guards or men from downstairs? Hadn't they heard the shots?

More screams. Pleading through the closed door off of the upstairs landing. He rolled across the plush carpet struggling to get free. He'd been heading to that bedroom with a tray of sangria when he'd heard the shots from the back of the house. He'd sent the text message to his captain from the staircase that shots had been fired. He didn't have backup, but where were Tenoreno's men?

The three glasses were crushed across the white carpet, leaving dark red stains. If he could get to the door…

"Come on, man. Somebody's in trouble." Why was this guard trying to prevent him from getting to those women?

Right jab. Right jab. His opponent's face flew back along with his feet. A give-it-all-he-had left to the belly doubled the guy in half. Muffled cries and threats from inside the room. He had to end this and get inside. He raised his knee into the guy's chin. Eyes rolling back in his head, his opponent sank to floor. One more kick to his jaw guaranteed he was out cold.

Two succinct pops behind the solid oak door. A blood-curdling scream. He checked the downed guard for a weapon. Nothing. Last pocket had the key to the door. He got it in the lock, turned and burst inside.

Two women lay dead. Executed.

The intruder had a fistful of hair in one hand and a gun pointed at a third woman's head. He sported the same rent-a-monkey tux, but had added a face hood to conceal himself.

Slamming the door into the wall was enough to divert the direction of the barrel and make the bastard let the blond hair go. Garrison dropped and rolled, the monkey suit fired, missed. The woman picked up a metal case, swung, connected. The pistol flew under the bed. The case burst open spraying makeup supplies in every direction.

The monkey suit focused his attention on Garrison. Outweighed by forty pounds, Garrison locked his fists and swung them like a bat against a jaw as solid as rock. The bigger man barely staggered back a step.

But he did stagger, giving Garrison enough time to pounce. A double punch connected with ribs. His knee jabbed the man's thigh. Once. Then twice. And then the gunman threw a punch that hit Garrison square in the chest like a battering ram, slamming his head into the solid door.

The hooded monkey suit left through the balcony doors while Garrison was momentarily stunned. Tingling on his cheeks. A faraway plea for him to wake up. Both brought him fully to his senses.

"Get up. We've got to go," the woman whispered. Her makeup had smeared from the tears running down her face. "Come on."

Garrison took in the room. The lady of the house and her guest were lying holding hands on the floor. Both shot execution style in the back of the head. The other shots from downstairs must have been this guy's cue to take care of the extended family.

Top Texas organized crime boss wives. Dead instead of extracted. The captain was going to have his head on one of these silver platters.

"What are you waiting for? They're coming up the stairs, and I don't know what to do."

He got to his feet. "Close and lock the door."

There was nothing he could do for either woman. While the one left alive did as she was told, he reached under the bed with the hankie from his tux pocket and retrieved monkey suit's gun. The man had been in gloves, but maybe they'd get lucky.

Then again, they had a witness. He swiped the business card from the dresser. Kenderly Tyler, hair and makeup. Long multicolored golden or ash-blond hair past her shoulders, oval face and dark chocolate eyes. She was a little taller than his shoulder. He memorized the way she looked, every shapely curve covered in shiny sequins.

The doorknob shook. Shoulders slammed against the wood. His eyes fell to the gun in his hand. The Tenoreno men wouldn't ask questions. They'd shoot first.

"Kenderly?" He'd ask her why she'd waited for him once they were safe. Teary eyes questioned what he wanted. He jerked his head toward the balcony.

Following the gunman's path, they ducked into the cooling Texas sun. He kept her back against the brick, blocked her from anyone's view on the ground with his body. He could see down the open roads that his backup was nowhere in sight. The gunman was next to the pool house. Unless he wanted both crime families coming after him forever, he'd eventually need something to prove there was another person in the house. He dug into his front pocket, swiped the phone and took a series of pictures.

Heading the opposite direction next to the garage would take them to his bike. And right next to an older Volkswagen Beetle where two armed guards stood. They weren't waiting for them. At least not yet.

Which way? Follow the killer or protect his witness? Not a real question.

If the family got hold of her, he'd never find her again. They may even think she'd pulled the trigger or that he had. That settled which direction they'd run. He swung his legs over the side, dangling like a baited worm on a hook before he dropped and sprang up from the grass.

He looked up at the blonde who tossed him a small jeweled box, then a purse. She shook her hair away from her face as soon as she hiked a leg over the banister. He pointed to her shoes, which she flicked off, hitting the ground next to him. He scooped them up and shoved them in his pockets along with the box.

"Grab the bottom with your hands. Then lower, and I'll catch you." He tried to shout in a whisper. He kept looking over his shoulder expecting a gun in his kidney at any second.

Kenderly Tyler wasn't exactly ladylike coming down. At least she stifled her short scream the two feet she fell into his arms. There wasn't any type of special moment or slow-motion feel as she slid through his grasp to the grass. She pushed back, picked up her purse and ran.

The men breached the room right behind her escape. Moans, cries, questions shouted to God... Garrison caught up with her before she darted across the driveway. He tucked her behind him, gave her a shush signal and evaluated their position.

They hugged the house, avoiding the guards. All pointing their guns around corners and opening car doors. Taking their time. Didn't they want to find the gunmen? It was one thing to sign up to fight in Tenoreno's army. It was much different when that army went to war. Shoot. His job would be easier if he could just shout at them to search for the killer by the pool.

The guards were armed to the teeth and outfitted better than the Secret Service. How the hell had they allowed the gunmen on to the property in the first place? Why had the gunman executed the women? Had the shots fired downstairs taken out the rival organized crime bosses, too?

Just as he thought they'd be in the clear, his witness darted around him and headed straight to the Volkswagen. Too many questions had distracted him. He needed to secure Kenderly Tyler and hightail it back to Company F.

ONE STEP AT a time and she'd make it. Kenderly's hands shook, rattling the keys as she tried to push one into the car door. She just needed inside. She saw the man who had let her in the gate earlier. He held up his hand for her to stop.

No way. She couldn't stay with all the guns and… death. She ignored him and sat behind the wheel. He put his finger in his ear, then looked at her again and began running. His rifle bounced across his chest until he held it against his ribs.

The keys rattled. Her body was shaking now. Isabella and Trinity were dead. She would have been next. They were going to kill her. If she hadn't been cleaning up in the bathroom, she would already be faceless and…and…

The man with a rifle yanked the door open and grabbed a fistful of her hair, tugging. She'd forgotten to lock the door, but somehow she'd already put on her seat belt so she was stuck. He reached across and popped the lock, then yanked again. All she could do was grab his wrist to keep her hair attached to her head.

The image of the dead women fixed on the back of her eyelids. Every time she blinked she saw the blood and gore. He pulled her hair to get her to move, but she was about to be terribly sick.

With blurred vision, she leaned forward and lost what little was in her stomach. The man hopped out of her way. Hearing more fighting above her head, she continued to retch. Someone pulled back her hair, put an arm around her waist and helped her stand. He led her off the white gravel drive. Past the man who had yanked her hair, now unconscious on the green grass. Its cool shaded lushness registered under her bare feet.

"Water?" she squeaked out.

"Can't help you with that," a deep Texas twang answered. "But if you get on the back of my bike, I can keep you alive."

As weary as she was, that popped her head up. Petrified, she connected with a pair of jade-green eyes, sandy short brown hair and a casual self-confident smile that didn't belong in her surreal afternoon.

Gorgeous. Absolutely the type of man she wanted to be with any other time. He dangled her shoes in front of her, and she slipped them on.

The stranger held out his hand. "We really need to go now, sweetheart. You coming?"

Yes. But she didn't think she said it out loud. She straddled the back of the motorcycle in her short skirt and heels. Two large, strong hands grabbed her thighs, pulled her closer and placed her feet on two metal rods. Her sequined skirt was up as high as it could be without revealing anything, but now wasn't the time to care.

The motorcycle sprang to life, and her arms shot around him. There wasn't any give to his body when her fingers locked together across his hard abs. She closed her eyes and buried her face against his black jacket. She wanted to see nothing, especially the gruesome picture the shooting had left in her mind.

The motorcycle screeched to a halt, sliding sideways in the gravel. Her rescuer slowly took off across the field, avoiding the closed front gate.

"Hold on tight."

She didn't think she could hold tighter until her bottom was airborne over the first incline. Had she left the safety of the house for a dangerous daredevil? Had it been safe at the house? Absolutely not. And how did she know for certain this man wasn't a part of the…the…

Go ahead and say it. Murders! The man dressed in black had murdered two people right in front of her, then stared openmouthed as she'd screamed. This wasn't the killer. His dark green eyes proved that. The man she'd fought with was just as tall, but his eyes were black with hatred.

She'd never forget those eyes.

They flew over the next small hill, landing hard on both tires.

"Slow down before your kill us!" she shouted in his ear.

"Can't. They're following. May start shooting."

She turned behind them, her hair whipped across her face. Sure enough, a black SUV bounced over the rolling hills of the Texas lake country. The motorcycle skidded, and she held tighter. If the men shot at them, she'd be dead. Period.

Her rescuer turned sharply, heading toward a tree line. "Where are you going?"

"Where they can't."

The trees were so thick she didn't think they could get through, either. He slowed a little, but zigzagged, tilting them from side to side, making her want to put her feet out to drag along the ground. She kept them secured and kept her body smooshed against the stranger's back, moving like a second layer with him.

Bushes whacked at her legs as they zoomed past. The branches stung but suddenly stopped. The first thing she saw was the perfectly smooth carpet of green. She looked behind them, and no one followed. The SUV turned and followed on the other side of the trees for a few seconds before turning away.

"Hey!"

Someone shouted, making her look forward. They were on a golf course, bouncing yet again over the greenway to a cart path. Once there, the ride was smoother, but her hero didn't slow. If anything, he went even faster. It was a Friday night at dusk, and the golfers were finishing their rounds. So they were few and far between on the earlier holes they'd zipped past.

Kenderly only relaxed a little. This time when her eyes closed, they were burning with tears for Isabella. No one deserved to die that way.

He was right. Her hero. They couldn't stop. Her unnamed rescuer popped over curbs, into a parking lot and on to the street. He ran stop signs, passed other cars as if they were standing still and just kept going.

Once on Highway 71 leading back to Austin, he wrapped his long fingers around her thigh and gently tugged her close again. His subtle message was that their wild ride wasn't over. She moved, resting her head once more on his back. They rocketed through the wind, which didn't allow for talking.

She couldn't have answered any of his questions or any of the thousands running through her mind. Isabella had given her a small jewelry case and told her not to open it for three days.

Oh no! The case! She'd dropped it somewhere. She'd been so out of it by losing her cookies all over the guard's feet that she'd forgotten. What had Isabella not wanted anyone to know? Why was she supposed to wait three days? Kenderly wasn't sure she'd ever know now.

Her hero stroked her frozen forearm, slowly warming it back to life against his chest. When she cried harder, he held on to her hands tighter.

It didn't matter who he was. He'd probably saved her life. Okay, he'd definitely saved her life. But that was only one reason she was thankful. The stranger's actions in the past few minutes were more intimacy and kindness than she'd felt in years.

Chapter Two

The arm under Garrison's hand was no longer frozen. Early spring in Texas was fine with lots of sunshine on you, but once it got dark—and speeding in excess of seventy miles per hour—you could get chilled to the bone.

"You can let me off anywhere," she said as he slowly merged with city traffic near the university hangouts.

"I don't think so, sweetie. No discussion necessary." He sped up again to limit the conversation.

"But I need to go back. I have to."

Darting between stopped cars, the horns blared as he pushed safely through red lights. He had to keep moving, so she couldn't jump off. Go back? She was the ranger's big break, and he couldn't let her disappear.

"Let me go at the next corner, or I'll start screaming my head off," she shouted, piercing his ear.

"We have a head start, but we're still being followed." It was logical to think so. There was only one road back to Austin from the crime scene. It didn't make sense that Tenoreno's men would give up because of a row of trees. He slowed the bike to a more normal speed. "After I rescued you and everything, screaming just wouldn't be cool."

"Neither is kidnapping."

"Come on, Kenderly. We both know I'm not kidnap-

ping you. I saved your a— I got you out of there safely,"
he amended. "Why the hell do you want to go back?"

"I appreciate it. I really do. But there's something I...
I just want to go home." She sat straighter, pulling away
from him.

He immediately missed her soft breasts pushed against
his back. He needed both hands to control the bike, or
he'd pull her closer again. Instead he pulled into a parking lot, darted to the side of the building and cut the engine. He twisted a bit on the seat to face her and reached
into his pocket.

"Is this what you need to go back for?" He held up the
smaller case he'd picked up from her seat. "The purse
strap got stuck on the gear shift. I couldn't get that. You
tossed this to me at the balcony."

"Oh my God, thank you so much." She reached for it,
but he kept it high above her head.

"I'm thinking I should have a look inside."

"No. You don't understand. It isn't mine."

"Then I especially need to look inside."

"Just who do you think you are? A hotshot waiter with
a fast motorcycle has no right—"

"Lieutenant Garrison Travis, Company F, Texas Rangers. Temporarily on assignment in Austin." He wanted to
pop whatever lock was on that case, but he didn't have
anything with him. "I'm sorry that you can't go home.
They'll be waiting there. They know who you are."

"But I didn't do anything." She grabbed his upper
arm. Her hand shook a bit. She was either shivering in
her short sleeves or from the shock of everything that
had happened.

"They don't know that. Plus, you saw the killer." He
shrugged out of his split jacket and flipped it around her
shoulders, holding it until she slipped her arms through

the sleeves. "You're coming home with me. It's your only option."

"Are you crazy? I don't know you. Where's your ID? Just take me to the nearest police station, and we can tell them what we saw." She swung her leg over the back of the bike and took off. "They'll protect me if I need it."

"I can help you," he called after her. "And that's smart, asking for my ID. But I don't carry it while I'm undercover."

"You did help, and I thank you. But the police need to know what I witnessed. I'm sure I broke a law or something leaving the scene of a crime." She backed up across the run-down parking lot in a short fancy skirt and his torn tux jacket. She might trip in her heels. "Why are you shaking your head at me?"

"Come on, get back on the bike." He threw one of his best smiles at her, attempting to make his witness feel more comfortable. But she wasn't reacting like the rest of the women in his life.

Maybe because she'd just seen two of her friends executed, and someone was trying to kill her. Maybe he should change tactics.

"No."

"Well, I'll need my jacket. It's a rental." Fortunately, he'd dropped the murder weapon in the cycle's saddlebags, so it was safe. He dug his cell from his front pants pocket. "I'm going to dial a number, and you can confirm my identity. Then I'm taking you to my place."

Garrison was afraid she'd break her neck running away from him if he got off the bike and chased her. He stayed put, got the number and pressed dial. He heard his captain answer, pressed speaker and told him, "Hang on." Then he extended the phone to his witness.

For some crazy reason, she walked back to him and took the phone. "Hello?"

"This is Captain Aiden Oaks, Texas Rangers. Who is this? Why do you have Travis's phone?"

She shrugged, searching him for answers. Garrison pointed to it and made a talk symbol with his hand.

"Someone handed it to me. Are you really a Texas Ranger? Is he?"

Garrison took the keys, opened the saddlebag, dropped the case inside and locked it. What was coming next would be pleasant for Kenderly, but not so much when Garrison confronted the captain.

"Is the smart-ass who handed you the cell riding a motorcycle, wearing a tuxedo and got a smart-alecky grin on his face?"

"I think so."

"Lieutenant Garrison Travis didn't have identification with him, miss. Did he call to assure you of something?"

She hung up and walked the phone back to him. "He says you have a smart-alecky smile. He's right."

"Ouch. I've been told this smile was reassuring. Ready to come home with me now?"

Kenderly had been through a sick ordeal and needed a lot more help than he could provide. The first step was getting her under the protection of the Rangers. And for that to happen, he had to find out exactly what she'd seen and what was in that case.

He braced the bike while she hopped on the back again. He moved his hand to bring her closer, then thought better of it, speaking over his shoulder. "You can trust me, Kenderly."

"No more running red lights."

"Not a prob."

"And you promise that I'll be safer with you than with the police?"

"You've got my word as a Texas Ranger. Nothing'll happen to you while you're with me." He started the bike and rejoined traffic before she realized he was a complete stranger and decided to yell for help. She didn't yell. She only cooperated.

Kenderly was too trusting. Or playing him.

Witness or perpetrator? He had a lightbulb moment of his own. He hadn't seen the actual shooting. He couldn't swear who pulled that trigger. The makeup artist could have unlocked the balcony doors and let the monkey-suit guy inside.

Maybe he was protecting an accomplice?

Not a chance. There was no blood spatter on her clothes. She couldn't have been near the fatal shots. He'd find out all the details when they got to his house. Just a couple of minutes and they'd be safe.

The small jewelry box would have to wait until he was at his place. He needed to ask her about everything, but was certain Captain Oaks would want to be there for the questioning.

Turning down Forty-first, he replayed the scene in his head, searching through his memory for what the murderer looked like. Approximately the same height as him, so the guy had to be six-one, maybe more. Brown eyes, huge nose that protruded under the hood. He didn't have much to go on, but the man's shoes weren't from a rental company like the tux.

Garrison had rented enough times to know how unforgiving a new pair of rental dress shoes were. Or how the older ones looked scuffed no matter how hard you shined. This guy was wearing his own.

He pulled to a stop in his driveway. Then he mentally

brought up the image of the man in black. He'd turned to him—surprised someone had entered Mrs. Tenoreno's bedroom—guilty.

Blood. Bright dark spots that couldn't be mistaken for anything else shone all over the black tux. He was confident he'd interrupted the gunman before he pulled the trigger on a third victim. Kenderly was a state's witness.

Kenderly was off the back of the bike before he'd cut the engine. He popped the kickstand, tugging her to him. He might be confident she wasn't the murderer, but he wasn't so sure she wouldn't run down the street hollering for help.

"Mind if I take the jacket back?"

Delicately, treating the ripped tux like an expensive designer jacket, she folded it in half and handed it to him. He tossed open the saddlebag and removed the gun, wrapping it protectively in the jacket's folds, then setting it on the bike seat along with the case. The evidence couldn't be out of his line of sight, and this was the best he could do. He unlocked the detached garage and lifted the heavy door, then rolled his bike inside and reversed the procedure.

"I think I have a couple of sodas inside and maybe a frozen pizza."

"I can't possibly eat." Her hand covered her lips.

"How about some soup, then? I got a cabinet of the stuff."

"Really, I'm fine." She shook her head and preceded him up the steps. "What I really need is a toothbrush."

"Got you covered. My aunt has extras from visits with her dentist. She's visiting my mom." If he could remember where she'd put them.

"Oh." She tugged at her hair, trying to smooth tangle upon wind-massacred tangle.

His Aunt Brenda's house was on the small side. What most people might call cozy. Just right for one bachelor ranger who wasn't home half the time. That is, if he really lived in Austin. He was on temporary assignment and shared a place in Waco. He opened the door and prepared for the assault.

"Hey, I forgot to ask. Do you like dogs?"

Both his monsters slid across the old linoleum, tongues out, ready to jump on their visitor, expecting a treat. Before he could yell at them to get down, Garrison set the coat-wrapped gun on the counter. He knelt at the pups' level, taking one dog under either arm.

"I adore dogs. Are they Labs? What are their names? They're so sweet." Kenderly brightened and dropped to her knees with him.

"Diabolical is more like it. Don't turn your back on them for a minute. This big black boy is Bear. The chocolate pup is his half sister, Clementine." He reached up and pulled treats from a jar, handing them to his guest. "They'll do tricks for these."

She sat at the kitchen table, patiently petting the panting Labradors. "Clementine isn't exactly what I'd call a puppy."

"Sit, Clem. Bear, you know better than that." He used hand signals to get them to sit, wanting to show them off. "She's barely a year old. Already seventy pounds of love. I didn't know how long I'd be here, and these two sort of go berserk if I don't check in every day. Excuse me while I make a phone call."

He dialed, then retrieved a new Ziploc from the cabinet while he waited for the captain to answer. "Travis? I guess the party blew to hell?"

"Yes, sir. So you've heard. The beautician, Kenderly Tyler, witnessed the whole thing. I stopped the murderer

from blowing—" He darted a look at the woman he'd rescued to see if she'd heard his slip. "I stopped him from
having a third victim. We came straight here. I didn't
think you'd want anyone to know we have her in custody."

Kenderly got the dogs another treat and repeated his
hand commands to them.

"You think she's reliable?"

"As far as I can tell. I also have the murder weapon."
He placed the gun inside the bag. "It should take you about
forty minutes to get here, sir. See you then." He dropped
his phone on the counter, and Clementine nudged the back
of his knee. "Oh no, you don't. Christy fed you an hour
ago."

"Where's the bath, and do you have a first-aid kit?"

"You okay?" During the call, she'd taken a paper towel
from the roll he left on the table and started dabbing at her
legs. "Obviously not. Those from the trees we brushed
through?"

"Yes. My legs started stinging on the golfing green."

"Let me get something."

The house really was super small. Keeping the medicine cabinet mirror open, he could still see the kitchen
table. Bear was spread-eagle on the floor waiting for
some more attention. Kenderly was staring at the gun
and not moving. He dug through the antibiotic creams,
looking for something without an expired date. No luck.

"I found some cotton, alcohol and peroxide. Best I
can do." He knelt and took a look at the long scratch at
the top of her thigh.

"It'll be fine." Kenderly's soft voice matched her
dainty frame and manner.

"Need a belt to bite down on?"

She looked a bit confused. Instead of explaining, he

poured the bottles over the scratches. Her tanned thigh used to be completely smooth, not even a freckle.

The deep scratches would cause the peroxide to sting—a lot. Garrison fanned at her leg, and she shut her eyes. He leaned in close and blew across the peroxide bubbles, hoping to ease the pain.

"How could I have gotten into this mess?" She fanned her cheeks in a motion his sister used years ago when trying not to cry. "When I woke up this morning, I never imagined I'd have two dogs at my feet, be sitting in a funny little kitchen with peroxide dripping down my thigh and have a complete stranger blowing up my skirt."

"I don't really know what to say after that." He choked to keep from busting out laughing. Two Band-Aids across the deepest scratch and they were done.

She covered her face, looking embarrassed. "I didn't mean to complain about a scratch when Isabella... She's... Oh, gosh, I can't stay here."

Garrison lifted her to her feet, against his chest and into his arms. "Go ahead and cry. I won't stop you. You're safe here." He couldn't just tell her she would be okay. He had to make her feel as though she was safe, and he didn't know another way.

She shoved at his shoulders, and he let her go. "What am I doing here? If they're following us, how can we possibly be safe?"

"You witnessed a murder, and we need to get your statement. The captain will be here soon, and we'll have some decisions. Until then, let's wait in the other room."

He led the way to the living area, just big enough for a small couch, arm chair and a television that covered most of the end wall. He loved that television and would be hauling it back to Waco after this assignment.

"Why did he shoot them?" Kenderly sat and dropped her head in her hands. "He was going to kill me, too. Wasn't he?"

"I think so."

"Why did he kill them?"

"That's what I'm hoping you can help us with, Kenderly."

"Why were you there?" She looked up quickly, accusing him of something without a word.

He flattened his lips shut and shook his head. He couldn't tell her that he was undercover tonight after an anonymous tip let them know there'd be trouble. He should have gotten the women extracted earlier instead of waiting for the cover of darkness. They'd been hoping to turn one of the families against the other. Instead, both had been hit.

"Let's start with how you knew Isabella Tenoreno."

"She came once a week into the shop where I have a chair. Wednesday she said she was having a party today and asked if I could come. I do hair and makeup for private events. This was a little different since she invited me to attend. I ended up doing her friend Trinity's hair, too."

Trinity Rosco, the wife of the rival crime family. Garrison noticed how stiff Kenderly had become. She was a terrible liar. So there was more to her story than she was letting on. "What happened after that?"

"I was gathering my things and cleaning my brushes in the bathroom. I heard something break, and Trinity screamed. At least I think it was her. The man, he already had the gun out and told them both to get to their knees."

"What language?"

"English."

"Why didn't he see you?"

"I saw the gun first thing, so I didn't open the door all the way. I should have. I should have done something. Maybe they'd still be alive." She covered her face with her hands again, crying this time.

"Don't doubt for a minute that you'd be dead now."

"I… I thought it might be a…a joke. You know? The gun didn't look real at first. But then he…he shot them. He just…shot them."

She jumped up and stood at the window. He let her. What could he say? Two women had been brutally murdered. There was nothing that would take the image away from her. He was just lucky she wasn't falling apart. She could be a hysterical mess.

"Then he found you?" he prompted.

"There were noises coming from the sitting room. I thought about calling out, but I didn't. I must have moved backward, hit something or made a noise. He found me and was pulling me over their bodies when you came into the bedroom."

"So you're a hairstylist?"

She nodded, rubbing under her eyes, smearing the mascara that had run from her tears. Personally, he didn't care for a lot of makeup on a woman, but he did appreciate her long multicolored hair and bare legs.

"I know my aunt used to talk to her hairdresser all the time," he prodded. "Did Isabella happen to mention what this special occasion was about?"

"Isabella was never at my work alone. Her bodyguard was never more than five feet away and could always hear what we were saying. This time she locked them out of the bedroom, while she changed her clothes."

"She didn't mention…anything?"

"I'm not sure I know what you're getting at. Isabella

had lots of money. Why wouldn't her husband's enemies just kidnap her?"

"That's one of the things I'm trying to find out, Kenderly."

Was there something too innocent in her wide eyes? Something she was holding back? Or was he too paranoid, after losing not one, but two women to an assassin? Naw, she was holding something back. She'd said "husband's enemies," and that meant she knew. She just didn't trust him yet.

"Is that horrible man going to try and kill me again?"

If we're lucky he'll be after us both. It was easy to think that. As a Texas Ranger he wanted the guy to find him.

It would be harder to involve an innocent woman. He'd held Kenderly's hair away from her face as she lost her cookies in the driveway. He couldn't afford to have a personal attachment.

Yeah, the sensitive guy inside him winced at the thought of using her as bait. The investigative ranger didn't have a choice. If his captain ordered it, he'd have to act.

Chapter Three

One of the most gorgeous male specimens Kenderly had ever encountered had choked while laughing at her. She wished she knew what he and his captain were talking about outside. The captain seemed to have brought news Garrison didn't really want to hear.

She'd been introduced while the murder weapon was locked away in the captain's trunk. Now she was eating toast at the kitchen window and watching the men talk.

Captain Oaks was calm, watching her from where he stood in the backyard. His hands were behind his back, as stoic and sturdy as his name. But her rescuer waved his hands, disagreeing or in disbelief. She could make out the words no and no way. Just a few minutes before he'd said "hell, no" loud enough to be heard in the next county.

Garrison adamantly refused whatever his new assignment required. The only movements that were relaxed at all were reaching down to pet Clementine or take her ball and throw it again. Such a normal action that he performed without thinking.

He hadn't broken a sweat saving her life today. Confident. Cocky. Extremely good-looking. A little arrogant. And sweet, sweet Thelma, he rode a motorcycle like it was nobody's business.

Her fingers tangled in the mess that was now her hair.

The long extensions were so matted that she couldn't unclip them from her head. The wind had done permanent damage, and it would take hours of combing to make them wearable again. She headed to the bathroom to see if she could get them loose. Bear followed and sat in the doorway, then slid to his belly.

"I suppose you're used to the door staying open," she said gently to him, stroking the old boy on the head. She looked in the mirror and almost screamed. "I look like a middle-aged drug addict."

The slate liner was smudged under her eyes and halfway down her cheeks. She had no way to repair the damage, other than removing all the makeup. She had nothing except her cell. Her makeup case, purse, keys and car had all been left at the Tenoreno estate.

How was she going to get to work? Or work without her supplies, for that matter? Everything was in that bathroom or her Beetle. Her ID, debit card, checkbook…how would she even eat until they could be replaced?

But she couldn't feel sorry for herself. Isabella and Trinity had lost much more than supplies or money.

Much more.

The men hadn't opened the jewelry case yet. It had also been locked in the captain's trunk almost immediately. Neither of them asked what was inside. They'd just assumed it was important. Probably because she'd asked to go back for it.

She took a deep breath and tried to slow her racing heart. Turning the water off, the men's voices drifted in through the slightly open window.

"You have your choice. Protect her or be the bait."

"I appreciate your confidence in me, sir. I don't think I have a choice. I don't have the skills or patience to sit and wait. And isn't it against some type of regulation or something? Don't we need to involve a female DPS officer to be on her protection detail?" Garrison was marching back and forth across his grass.

"You're the one insisting that she needs protection without evaluating if what she saw is admissible in court. Or what's in that case you locked away. How dangerous do you think the threat to her is?"

Garrison stopped pacing. His smile was gone, and he suddenly looked grown up. The white teeth he'd flashed all evening put her at ease, but it made him look much younger.

"From everything you've told me about these two families, they shoot first and never bother to ask if it's the right person. If they find her, they will kill her, sir."

"You're right, and she'll be safe. I'm giving you the option, son. Keep your word and be a part of her detail. Or you nail these bastards once and for all. As I said before, the Tenoreno family released a blurred picture of you both to the media. They're going to find the fake background information we set up for you to get the job. It won't take them long before they track down your cover phone. We need a decision and need a plan."

Kenderly wanted to crawl through the tiny window and shout at both the men. They were making decisions about her life without asking her anything. She wasn't running off with Garrison Travis to hide. But she also wasn't stupid enough to go home. Without money or a place to live, the Texas Rangers were her best chance to stay alive.

"That ID got me on the grounds. The pictures will get me back inside. Regarding Kenderly, there isn't a choice here," Garrison said so seriously it scared her. "Without me, you don't have a connection to the shooter. If Kenderly comes forward, it will blow the entire operation. It's the closest we've been to bringing these crime families down in years. If they join forces, we might never get the chance again."

"As of today, the Tenorenos and Roscos were falling behind the cartels. Together…" Captain Oaks shook his head with the implication. "They'll either kill each other, taking a lot of other people along the way. Or they'll be strong enough to control seventy percent of organized crime in Texas."

"There's only one choice, then. I go back inside. Try to convince them I was just running for my life when the shots started. It would help if I had something of value to trade. I don't see anyone making an identification from the pictures. I've got my fingers crossed there's something in that jewelry box that Isabella thought was worth smuggling out with Kenderly."

She couldn't see the captain's face, but she did have a good look at Garrison's dissatisfied expression. He shoved his hand through his sandy-blond hair. He'd changed into jeans and a button-down shirt. She'd seen his badge ready to go on the kitchen table before he slid it into his back pocket.

"We'll do the initial Q and A here. We both need to hear her answers firsthand. You could come to headquarters but—"

"Got it. The fewer who know about Kenderly Tyler, the better." Garrison looked more relaxed.

Why he should be…she had no idea. He was planning on returning to the Tenoreno house surrounded by men with guns…and more guns.

"I'll make a call and get a video camera here. Then we'll get started. You okay with your cover story about why you left in such a hurry?" Captain Oaks asked.

"Easy to explain. Shots start flying, and I'm not hanging around. It might take longer to wrap my head around officials thinking I might have something to do with the murders. I'm not usually the one being hunted. I'm more the hunter type. But I can fake it."

"You're our best bet to discover the true reason for the assassinations. We can assume they don't know about the real murderer." The captain bent down to pet Clementine. "But he knows about you."

"And Kenderly. We both saw him."

"That was quick thinking to get the pictures. Maybe something will come from it. Having evidence of the murderer is your best way to get back in to see Tenoreno. He should be extremely interested in your photos."

"I don't understand why the wives were killed and not the crime bosses. It doesn't make sense. I heard shots at the back of the house, but couldn't get to both."

The captain clamped a hand on Garrison's shoulder, stopping him. The younger man didn't flinch or try to get away. It seemed friendly enough, fatherly in fact. "It's not your fault, Garrison. No one predicted they would be murdered."

"If I'd only been a couple of minutes earlier."

"According to what you told me, more lives would have been lost if you were a couple of minutes later."

"But—"

"No buts in this line of work. It was out of your control. We move on."

Kenderly liked Captain Oaks. She had no idea what some of the things they were talking about meant, but she liked him just the same. Taking his wise words to heart, she also needed to move on. There wasn't anything she could do about the past. She couldn't go back and change time or rush in and save Isabella.

All she could do was help find her friend's murderer.

"WHERE DO WE START?" Kenderly sat at the kitchen table, her hands clasped together so tightly her knuckles were turning white. "Do you need for me to write out my statement? I looked for a tablet. Oh, but I didn't go through anything. Sorry, I promise I wasn't looking through your things."

"It's okay." Garrison wanted to hug her and calm her down again. But that wasn't happening in front of his captain.

"Miss Tyler," Oaks began, "we've sent for a video camera and plan on recording your statement here. If I take you downtown, too many people will know we have you in protective custody. We'd rather continue without spreading that knowledge. That okay with you?"

Kenderly nodded and moved her hands to her lap until she swiped at a tear with the back of her knuckle. She'd washed her face. Gone was the heavy makeup he'd become used to in a very short time. Without it she looked younger.

"I have to confess... I didn't mean to eavesdrop, but the bathroom window was open. I could hear a few things."

"Like what?"

Garrison let the captain lead the discussion. He tried to keep a solemn look on his face out of respect for the two women who had died and the seriousness of the current situation. But just sitting there, Kenderly had a way of making him smile. Or the way she tugged at the stretchy skirt jerked him back to the memory of his hand on her thigh.

"I'm not sure I know what you meant by extracting. Who? Were you there to get Isabella away from that horrid man she was married to?"

She'd turned to Garrison, looking for an answer. He

popped away from leaning on the wall next to the living room. Taken totally off guard, his mind had been on the soft flesh that had been beneath his fingers. The question had him staring straight back at his commanding officer.

"Oh, my gosh, you were. Is that why you want to open her jewelry box?" She turned back to Oaks. "You see, I honestly don't know what's inside. Isabella told me to open it in three days. I thought it might be another letter to mail."

"Why do you think she said three days? And you'd mailed letters before?" Oaks brought out his pocket notepad, something he was never without.

If Garrison wanted to take notes, he'd have to get a pad from the hall closet. No way. He wasn't going to miss any part of this interview.

"I don't know why she said three days. I've been doing her hair for several years. Like I told Garrison—" Her hair flew over her shoulder when she turned toward him. "Oh wait, should I call you Lieutenant?"

"I don't mind being called Garrison." There it was again…the urge to smile.

"Like I told Garrison, it had gotten to the point that I had to ask her bodyguard to move back while I washed her hair. And they absolutely refused to let her come on her own. But I did pass notes to Trinity and mail an occasional letter."

"You passed notes for her?"

"Right. Isabella whispered to me that her husband was mad at one of her friend's husband. And he was being very strict about even allowing her to talk with her friend. So she wondered if I'd mind holding a note for her. It was very secretive. She wanted to pay me to do it, but I said no. I was getting a new customer out of the deal."

"So both Mrs. Tenoreno and Mrs. Rosco had their hair done at your shop?"

"Yes. Although, they never got to come in at the same time or the same day because of their husbands."

Garrison moved forward so Kenderly could look at him and Oaks at the same time. "Did you know what their husbands did for a living?"

She shrugged, and he realized that her hair was just above her shoulders. He could have sworn it had been longer.

"Not at the time. I looked them up online after somebody mentioned it one day." She tugged nervously at her skirt again. "I know they weren't the best of men, but that didn't have anything to do with Isabella and Trinity. After their husbands got mad at each other, they couldn't see each other."

"Did you ever read any of the notes or keep the address of something you mailed?"

"Of course I didn't read them. They were private." Kenderly looked at her lap where her hands had dropped again.

The reaction was one of embarrassment, not indignation.

"You didn't happen to keep copies of the addresses where Mrs. Tenoreno sent letters?"

She looked up, connecting with him on a level he didn't understand.

"Yes," she whispered. "Their husbands were—are—frightening. I sort of wanted to...well, to have some proof in case something went wrong."

"I could kiss you, Kenderly. This is sure to be a break we've been needing," Garrison said, receiving a cross look from Oaks.

"It might help us determine why they were murdered.

What are the addresses?" Oaks's pen was poised in one hand, and he pulled his cell out of his shirt pocket with the other. "We'll get units over there ASAP before Tenoreno discovers they exist. If we can get the original letters… Is that the video crew?"

Garrison saw the headlights pull into the driveway and stay lit. He went to get the kitchen door for the TDPS video crew and to signal them to kill the lights.

"No offense to the video crew, but have you ever seen any that are over six feet and two hundred and thirty pounds of muscle?" he threw over his shoulder. Every nerve he had jumped to alert.

Was it the same guy from the murder scene? He sure had the same build. He pulled his weapon and hit the switch closest to him.

Oaks immediately moved Kenderly into the bathroom, closing the door behind her. Garrison saw the machine pistol outlined from the streetlight as the guy moved closer to the shrubbery on the far side of the drive. Garrison dove, knocking Oaks to the floor. They turned the ancient wood table to its side just before his aunt's house began to be cut in half.

Chapter Four

"How many?" Oaks asked, covering his head, protecting it from the breaking glass raining on them.

"Just the one son of a bitch from Tenoreno's estate."

"How the hell did he find you here?"

Garrison didn't have an answer. Kenderly didn't have a phone on her. He had no landline, so she couldn't have called anyone. She seemed as though she wanted to co-operate, so her betraying their position didn't make sense. And he knew that Oaks didn't do it.

Or did he?

"What if they believe Isabella was communicating with authorities, sir? Is that a possibility? Is another agency involved? They could have waited for a call or followed you."

"However it happened, you've got to get her out of here. We'll wait for him to reload, then move. Toss me that dish towel," Oaks commanded. "He winged my leg, or your aunt's gravy boat cut me."

Garrison tossed the towel and admired the captain's attitude. The force of the bullets ripped through the paper-thin walls of the side of the old house. Dishes shattered inside a cabinet, and the doors burst open. Thank God for the solid table his aunt had squeezed into the tiny kitchen. Though she was clearly going to kill him when she saw what was left.

"I'll get Kenderly."

Garrison belly-crawled to the bathroom, covering his head more often than not. Just as he passed into the short hall, the gunfire stopped. He didn't wait for the captain to begin firing. He kicked open the door and pulled Kenderly from the tub.

"Out the front as soon as I give you the go-ahead."

They moved. She was silent. Oaks fired through the shattered kitchen window. The assassin ceased firing a moment longer.

"Take mine," Oaks shouted, throwing his keys to Garrison. "Phone's busted. Call it in. I'll keep him pinned down."

Garrison had a split second to follow or disobey orders. The small feminine hand latched on to his biceps reminded him they had a witness to protect. That was his first duty.

Not to mention that no one normally argued with Aiden Oaks, captain or otherwise.

Moving Kenderly's hand to his belt, he pointed at her shoes. "Take those off and run beside me. We both get on the driver's side in the street. Take these." He handed her the keys. "Unlock the door while I cover you. I'll drive. You're in the back. Unless something happens to me."

She nodded.

"Go!" Oaks shouted and fired.

Garrison jerked open the door, searching for any accomplices. No shots this direction. They were still on the side of the house. He touched Kenderly's hand, then they moved across the porch. He kept as wide a view as possible, turning, scanning. Then he saw the Tenoreno assassin to his left.

"Run. Hit the unlock button."

She did, the alarm sounded, then he heard door clicks. They got to the far side of the car before shots were fired, but it was the captain out the front door firing at their pursuer.

Both men took cover in the yard. The keys were very steadily placed in his free palm, then Kenderly got inside and lay across the floor. Oaks had their backs covered. He started the engine and got out of there as fast as he could. He tossed his phone in the back.

"Dial 911."

He turned a corner, hitting the brakes to slow the car to a below normal speed and then hearing an "ow" from Kenderly.

"What are you doing?" she asked leaning close to his shoulder. "Oh, the cops." She could see the flashing lights heading past them and skidding around the corner. "Still want me to call?"

With no more flashing lights in sight, he sped up and headed for downtown Austin. "Not if we don't have to. Oaks will be fine. No reason to give the cops my number."

"What now?"

If they were being followed, more traffic would help them get lost. He drove the car as fast as he safely could.

"That's a very good question. I can contact Oaks in a couple of hours to find out what story he spun." *And hope that he has a plan.*

"Maybe they caught Isabella's murderer." She sounded a bit frightened.

He couldn't see her face in the rearview mirror. He couldn't hold her hand, needing both of his on the wheel. She might be scared. She should be, and he had to tell her straight.

"It's more likely he's right behind us." Garrison searched all the mirrors again but couldn't see anyone following. "You should put on a seat belt."

Again with the silence, but she did as he'd suggested. Just ten minutes ago she might have been white-knuckled at his kitchen table, but she'd been talking faster than he was driving. Ready to help with a statement and volunteering new information.

Statements? Where had the video tech crew gone? They should have been there about the time the assassin showed. Another question for Oaks.

"I guess we can't call your captain to find out what happened. Didn't he say his phone was busted?"

"Yeah. They'll try to take him to the hospital. Don't know which one, though." Oaks would be okay. He was their only shot at keeping this operation alive. They just had to hang on until he could contact them.

"Are we going to just drive around until he calls us?"

He shrugged. He hadn't decided where to go. He didn't know of any rangers who were a part of this undercover operation. And then there was the leak. Somehow the assassin had found them. Garrison couldn't believe it was on his department's side of things, but he'd been taught not to rule out any possibility until he had proof.

"I don't think anyone's following, but I still have no clue how that guy found us."

He stopped at a red light and the back door opened. He was ready to yell and his hand was on the handle, but in the blink of an eye Kenderly sat next to him.

"Or how he did it so quickly? Do we still need to record my statement and open the box? Do we wait until your office can do that? Or can you use your phone?"

"We can't wait. I should get hold of a digital recorder and do this thing right. That includes a reliable witness."

"I have a friend who has several cameras. He's an amateur photographer. Don't cameras have a record button now? Will that work?"

"As long as it embeds date information, stuff like that. It's definitely better than doing nothing. He'd have to be willing to testify that we opened the case in front of him."

She waved him off like he was being silly. "No problem. He lives a boring life like me. I bet he's hanging out somewhere on Sixth Street. All we have to do is hit a couple of bars with good music, and we should find him."

"Sixth Street?" Clubbing on a Friday night on the busiest street in Austin was a fate worse than… Okay, not as bad as death. "Can't we wait for him to go home?"

"Sure. He lives across the breezeway from me," she said flippantly, knowing exactly what his reaction would be.

There was no way he was parking this car in Kenderly's lot. Between Tenoreno's men, the police and their assassin all searching for them…that wasn't going to happen. And Kenderly knew it without him saying a word.

"Looks like we're bar crawling."

"I KNOW I'M going to regret this, but I am super hungry." Kenderly hated bar food. It was greasy, normally cold and completely overpriced, but she was totally starving.

"This is the fourth place we've been inside. Do you think he went home?"

"Can I order something?" She hated to beg, but she was getting close to being that desperate.

"I'd rather find this guy and not hang around here too long."

The toast at Garrison's house had only reminded her stomach that it was empty. "Fine." She shoved her hair away from her face.

The bar was crowded and hot. A huge neon sign flashed "Keep Austin Weird" against a mirror, making her want to shade her eyes.

It was hard to breathe at armpit level. For people who were tall, they never had a problem finding each other in a crowd. For someone just over five feet two inches, it was terrible. The last thing she needed was to become light-headed, but that's exactly how she felt.

Shutting her eyes for a second brought the gory image of Isabella and Trinity. She covered her stomach with one hand and clutched her mouth with the other.

"Are you turning green or is it the lights from the dance floor?" Garrison tried to pry her hand away, and she stopped him. "Okay, that's you. Bathroom is...this direction."

Her hero excused himself with each gentle shove to part the crowd. He got her to the ladies' room in record time, cutting straight across the dance floor. And he didn't stop there. Making more excuses, he cut in front of everyone, then flashed his badge when he waltzed through the door with her.

"I've got this part on my own." She tried to push him away before the bile rose.

"Can't let you out of my sight. Sorry, miss. Give us five, will you?" Even though he sounded polite, he wasn't really asking. He guided the last person out before she could use the hand dryer.

"Seriously, Garrison, I'm okay now. Let's just leave." She tried to open the door, and he stopped it with his toe.

"You're still as white as a sheet, Kenderly. Dammit, why don't they have paper towels anymore? Can you splash your face or something?"

The image in the mirror was sort of scary-looking. No makeup, seriously pale. Cooling her skin was actually a good suggestion. "Just getting away from all the people helps tremendously."

She wet her hands and patted her cheeks, cooling her hot flesh. She took a deep breath of semiclean air. The need to throw up no longer registered, so she stood straight and faced Garrison.

"You really okay?" He placed both hands on her shoulders and searched every inch of her face. "Still think you can eat something? Will you keep it down?"

"Yeah, I'm sure. I'm sorry we haven't found my friend."

There was a knock on the door. "Management. Do we have a problem?"

Garrison flattened his lips and raised his eyebrows, sort of shrugging in the process of reaching for the door handle. He flashed his badge before they got a close look, sort of gave an explanation, and they were out on the street without the help of a bouncer after a couple of minutes.

"The cool air feels great." She twirled on the sidewalk as they headed back to their borrowed car, thankful for the crisp feeling in her lungs. "Where do we go from—"

Garrison jerked her in the opposite direction. "Stay close."

She had no idea what was happening. But after having her life threatened twice, she completely trusted the man at her side. He'd tell her when he could. They walked at a very fast pace away from the car.

"What about Isabella's jewelry case?"

"Oaks will have to take care of it. Right now the cops are too close for us to get back to his car." He cursed under his breath.

She looked up and saw the red, white and blue reflections in the windows. "Can't you explain to them who you are?"

"Not unless I want to completely blow my cover and not find the murderer." He slowed a little after they turned a corner. "Right now we're both wanted for questioning."

"So the cops don't know you're a Texas Ranger?" Kenderly looked up and saw a fast-food restaurant. "Can I borrow five dollars?"

"Right. Sure. We'll get something and sit in the back corner." Garrison ushered her through the doors and stood outside checking the street for something. He backed in the door and pulled out his wallet, handing her a twenty. "Bacon cheeseburger, ketchup, no pickles and any soda."

She placed their order and watched him at the front window looking at his phone. He was texting one minute, then talking furiously the next.

No matter what he was currently doing, Kenderly decided to follow his original instructions and sit at the back booth.

"Hey, we're closing in fifteen minutes," the teenager behind the counter called out. "You'll have to leave by then."

"No problem," Garrison let him know.

Kenderly ate her small, dry burger and fries alone. Her hero texted, made more calls and popped outside the door another time. She had no idea if he was leaving messages or holding conversations about her future. His food sat in its bag.

The drink gathered sweat and made a ring around the bottom of the medium cup. She was mesmerized with the droplets.

It kept her from wondering what might have happened if Garrison hadn't been there today. She would be dead. No question about it. She felt helpless. She dipped a fry in the ketchup, and a red drop hit the table. She froze. Even though she knew it was ketchup, she couldn't eat another bite.

The clock over the front door indicated three minutes until they closed. She should quickly use the restroom before they were kicked out. She locked the door behind her and almost immediately heard Garrison yelling on the other side.

"Kenderly, are you there?"

"Give me a second, please? I promise, I can't get away. There aren't any windows."

"We have to get out of here."

"I know, they're closing."

"Listen to me, Kenderly. Cops are gathering outside. The kid must have called us in. Our status changed from wanted for questioning to wanted for murder. It's scrolling on the television. Tenoreno has a bounty on our heads."

Chapter Five

"Do you have any idea where you're going?" Kenderly had lived in Austin most of her life, but she was getting disoriented. Garrison had turned down almost every street and doubled back and then doubled back again. She tugged him to a stop not only to get her bearings but also to catch her breath.

"I'm certain of one thing. We have to keep moving." Garrison reached for her hand, but she took a step away from him.

"I can see that you believe you're right. But I can't keep this up all night." She glanced at her watch. They'd been walking just over an hour since the burger she'd choked down. "Don't you have a plan?"

They'd blended in with college students for a while, but were alone again on the corner of Brazos and Eighth Street. It was late enough that hardly anyone was around in this area.

The thought of being scared fleeted across her mind. She certainly had good reason to feel that way, but she didn't. The Rangers had convinced her they were legit and wanted to protect her. It was hard to get used to having someone else make the decisions. Limited choices as she had, every path she'd taken was completely hers.

He flashed that perfect smile at her and tilted his head like he was actually curious about something. "Sweetheart—"

"Stop right there. Your wicked gorgeous smile might work on the girls you're trying to pick up and sway back to your tiny little house." She caught her hand shaking as she pointed in the direction they'd come from. She quickly wove her fingers together. She might be upset, but she didn't need to show the world. Or him. "I have no choice except continue wherever you go. I know that. So you don't need to convince me of anything."

"Wicked gorgeous?" He winked.

She had to turn away from him. Appreciating his cavalier attitude was one thing, falling for the charm he oozed with every movement was quite another.

"Just give it to me straight. Bottom-line it."

"I like you, Kenderly Tyler. I really do." He sent another text and then removed the battery from his phone before sliding both back into his pocket. "Our odds aren't very good. Truth is… I didn't think we'd make it this far."

"Well, that's reassuring." If she'd had any choices she might have turned around and run from him. But there weren't any other choices.

She stood beside a set of stairs leading to a church. Sitting on the cold concrete she leaned back only to jolt forward. She'd forgotten that her heels were hooked into her skirt at the small of her back. It might have looked normal for a college student, but she felt silly.

"So, what now?"

For a split second the confident young smile disappeared, and the thoughtful Texas Ranger who had absentmindedly petted his dogs stood there. Maybe he was as lost as her?

"Oh my gosh! Clementine and Bear! Are they okay?"

"They were in the bedroom at the back of the house. I don't think the bullets penetrated that far."

"Those poor puppies. What will happen to them?"

"They have a regular dog walker. She lives across the street. But I sent a message to my buddy, Jesse, to come get them."

Disappointed that they didn't have a way to find out, she rubbed her bare feet and wasn't about to complain. Captain Oaks had been shot, and that man was trying to kill Garrison because he'd helped her.

"Can he come get us, too?" she mumbled.

But he'd heard and grinned. He casually leaned against the corner of the building. Or he tried to look casual. His body was tense. His eyes darted a different direction with each tilt of his head.

"Trouble is, no one really knew that I was at Tenoreno's place. This operation is sort of…" He shrugged.

"Off the record?"

"More like last minute and hasn't gone through all the proper channels."

Kenderly jumped up and ran across the street. "Great. This is just absolutely great. And so in character for my life."

She spun around midintersection to see her escort picking up her shoes, so she continued jogging across the road.

"Kenderly," he said sternly, running after her. "Come on. You know we have to stay together."

"So you have any idea when this is going to end?"

"Look. You're a smart gal. You know life isn't going to be the same. You might want to think about relocating."

"You aren't serious?" His lips pressed firmly into a straight line, and she knew that he was very serious. "What am I going to do?"

Placing both hands on her shoulders, one heel dangling from each, he looked at her for a good thirty seconds. If they'd been at her apartment door… If they'd been on a date or had met at the party Isabella said she could attend…

If. If. If. If things had been different, the moment might have been full of nervous anticipation instead of emotional dread.

"One step at a time, Kenderly. Just one small step. Our first is to find someplace out of the way to hang out for a while. We've got to give Oaks a chance to straighten this manhunt out."

Headlights shone on them as a car turned onto the street where they stood. Garrison ducked his head and curled her into his side. Whoever it was kept going. Loud, happy music poured from the open windows along with the laughter of the young people inside.

Why did she suddenly feel so old? She was only twenty-three, dammit.

The music faded as she watched the taillights disappear. Her fingers curled around the folds of Garrison's T-shirt. The tears came before she could completely bury her face in the soft, dark cotton.

As hard as she tried, she just couldn't stop them. Mournful tears for Isabella and Trinity. Frightened tears for herself. Angry tears that everything she'd worked for was gone.

She didn't know if he was patient about it, but her Texas Ranger wrapped his arms around her and didn't crack a joke. He didn't try to stop her. No attempts to rush things along.

His arms gave her the illusion of being secure. It was a strange feeling, with her body relaxing while her mind raced because she was so frightened.

"Sorry. I didn't mean to cry again." She tilted her head back to look up at him, expecting to see frustration or at least disappointment. There was neither.

"Ready to move out?"

She nodded. He dropped to one knee, sliding his hands down her calf and tapping on her foot.

"Oh, wow. You don't have to do that."

"Lift your foot. I'm down here all ready."

Off balance, she clung to his strong shoulder and let him slip her impractical high heels back into place.

GARRISON HAD SEEN the scrapes on Kenderly's feet. She couldn't move fast in the ridiculous heels, but she wouldn't be able to walk at all if she cut her foot. Putting them on was easier than her trying to accomplish it in the skirt he'd appreciated more on his bike.

What should he do?

"I need to check on Oaks." He stood and guided his witness up the street. He recognized where they were. The capitol wasn't too far away.

"Well, we can't walk into the hospital. Not with our faces splashed all over the TV."

"Right."

"You don't even know which one they took him to."

"Right again." He kept watch. Kept expecting the cops around every corner. They didn't have time for explanations. Should he just take Kenderly to Rangers headquarters and let them straighten the mess out? Or stick with her until the captain was giving orders again?

"And I hate to be a wimp, but I'm really tired. I don't know how much longer I can stay awake. Let alone move my legs to walk."

"Got it."

"You wouldn't happen to have an emergency credit

card, do you? I have one, but it's at my apartment. I leave it there since, of course, it's only for emergencies."

Garrison halted and checked his back pocket. He was an idiot. All this time he'd been worried about the police tracking any transactions or his phone. He didn't have to worry about that with his real name. Just his under-cover identity.

"Don't worry. Your time walking the streets is over."

"If I wasn't so relieved, I'd make you correct that street-walking phrase. But I am very grateful not to walk another step. Are we grabbing a cab?"

He wouldn't mention aloud that he'd had his own wal-let the entire time. He hadn't had a chance to switch them after Oaks decided to send him back to Tenoreno's.

"Are you going to call or something?" Kenderly asked, giving her skirt a habitual tug.

Her eyes looked as exhausted as she claimed. Her hair wasn't nearly as tangled as when she'd first arrived at the house. He really liked how it was so many differ-ent colors. Every place they'd been she looked like a dif-ferent woman.

There were other things he liked. Of course, being responsible for her, he couldn't tell her how good she looked in sequins and silk. Or how the unrealistic heels made her legs look four inches longer.

His hands itched to touch the smooth skin of her thigh again...

"We should get a cheap motel room until I receive some orders. And maybe pick up some sweats for you."

"Sweatpants? Couldn't we just get me some jeans? But you're not talking about right now. Or are you?" She grabbed his wrist and flipped it to see his watch. "It's almost three in the morning."

"Okay. Got it." He partly listened, partly searched for

their enemy and tried to keep thinking about their options. Nothing seemed to be going their way. Not even a cab. "Where can we catch a ride?"

"Oh, good grief. We need to head back to Congress Street." She laced her fingers through his. "Just so you know. I'm not really a sweatpants type of girl."

Holding hands was standard practice. Along with dragging him across the street, heading west again. She leaned into his arm, using his body to steady the fast pace. He was proud of her for hanging in there so well. He almost opened his mouth to tell her but thought again. It somehow felt intimate to tell her.

Shoot. He needed sleep himself if he was having this type of debate in his head. More importantly, he should be making plans. Deciding where they could stay, someplace a manager wouldn't call the police.

"Would calling the police be so bad?"

"Huh? How did you know…?"

"You were mumbling. So, would it? Would calling them be so bad?"

"It would ruin our chances of catching Tenoreno."

"Well, then we're definitely not going to the police. I want that horrid man to spend the rest of his days rotting in jail. Even if he didn't pull the trigger, he was responsible."

Garrison felt Kenderly's determination through her fingers squeezing his biceps. Yep, he liked her. He felt himself smiling without anyone looking.

Nice. Wait. Not nice. She's my witness.

They spotted the cab at the same time. Their hands separated, and Kenderly's earsplitting whistle got the cabbie's attention.

"Evening."

"Hi," Kenderly responded to the driver, then looked at Garrison. "Where to?"

"I...um... I'm not sure."

The driver tapped his finger against the steering wheel, flipped the meter on, then tapped again. At least he wasn't listening to local news. Their descriptions were accurate enough, and the burger shop probably let the police know what they were wearing. At least, if Garrison was the cop assigned to their case, he would have gotten a description.

"Hey, buddy, I need to get going. So where to?"

"Take us south on I-35."

"Got a particular place in mind?" the cabbie asked.

"I can't remember the name, but I'll tell you when I see it."

"Sure," the driver said.

"You have no clue where, do you?" Kenderly whispered.

He crossed his fingers and showed them to her. She covered her mouth, but he heard the giggle.

Fifteen minutes later, there was no laughter. He checked them into a semisleazy motel. Sheets in hand, he unlocked the door facing the highway and wished he hadn't flipped on the light. It wasn't the worst place he'd stayed in, but it was far from the best.

A long sigh escaped from Kenderly next to him. "At least they didn't assume we needed it by the hour."

Chapter Six

"Coffee."

Garrison smelled his favorite morning aroma before he pulled his nose from the pillow. He raised his head, squinting as the light bounced from the metal part of a car parked in front of their room.

"Good morning." Kenderly carefully crossed her legs while sitting in the one chair in the corner of the room.

"Where'd you get a grande?" At least that's what he hoped he asked. He wasn't really sure his mouth was working at the same rate as his brain. He sprang up. "What the hell, Kenderly? You went out for coffee?"

"Well, I was desperate for food. The coffee came with."

"You're missing the point. You left this room on your own? What if you'd been seen? Our pictures are probably everywhere this morning."

Didn't say a whole lot for his skills if a hairdresser left and returned without him waking up. He might just have to leave that out of the final report.

"Well, first, I was really hungry and thought you would be, too." She pointed toward a plastic bag and a Styrofoam cup. "And second, I was very careful. I avoided cameras and wore your T-shirt."

"I can see that." She looked good in his clothes. Or partially in his clothes. She still had the dressy short skirt.

He stretched his arms above his head, tracking Kenderly's reaction. She sipped the hot drink a little too quickly, swallowing extra hard as she watched him.

"Breakfast doesn't make up for you leaving on your own."

"It was probably safer since they're looking for a man and woman traveling together. Of course, they think we're long gone from Austin and haven't connected us to the shoot-out at your house." She pushed the paper—neatly sitting under his breakfast—across the small, rickety nightstand. "At least according to the *Austonian*, which covered both stories."

"Still…"

"You were out. I really did try to wake you. I mean, just trying to get off that bed. It rocks more than my grandma's rocker."

They laughed. And she sipped again. Coffee was coffee, and he needed his morning ration. Just as he reached for the cup, his stomach growled loud enough to be heard through the thin walls.

"Goodness. I'm glad I got you the deluxe breakfast."

"I thank you for that." He pulled a biscuit off the plate and shook it at Kenderly. "But don't leave my side again until you're told. I can't protect you if you aren't there."

"Any idea how long that will be? And for the record, you could have asked politely instead of commanding."

"Do you think the person trying to kill you will ask politely?" He tried to shock some sense into her, but had a feeling that commanding Kenderly to do anything was going to be a challenge.

"You have a point."

"Of course I have a point. This isn't a game." He

scooped his cell and the battery from the top of the television—for which they'd been charged extra to have in the room. He admired Kenderly's shapely legs while waiting for it to boot up. Then he forced his eyes to scan the phone. "There's plenty of reception here, but nothing from Oaks. At least Jesse has my dogs."

"That's such a relief. I assume they're okay?"

"He didn't say otherwise." Just as a precautionary measure, he removed the battery and shoved both into his pocket. He dove into the take-out breakfast, inhaling the scrambled eggs in two bites. "I am thanking you for this because I was hungry. Just don't do it again, okay?"

"I promise. But I really did try to wake you up."

"That I'll never believe. You were up early. Did you manage to get any sleep?"

"Me? Sure. I was snug all wrapped up in the clean sheets you rented from the manager."

"Did I snore?" He shoveled in the last bite and dropped his back to the bedspread, taking a deep breath.

"Not really." She twisted her finger in the hem of his shirt. "I suppose you need this back."

"It'll probably be easier to get into a store. You know, no shirt, no service. That sort of thing." He sat and reached for his boots.

"Isn't that risky? I mean, you were worried about me getting coffee. Won't stores have security cameras? Where will we go after that?"

"We'll avoid showing our faces. But if we want to stay put somewhere, we'll need supplies. Food, clothes—"

"A toothbrush," she added.

They needed practical items to hide out. Kenderly would need things no matter who babysat her. If he was going to finish his assignment, he'd still need a way to defend himself...and a toothbrush wouldn't hurt.

"You also need out of those four-inch monsters. How were you cutting hair like that? I don't see how any woman walks around on stilts."

"Isabella hired me to *fix* their hair, not cut it. I did that Wednesday. And I told you this, she said I could come to the party afterward. But I was just going to sit by the wall and watch. Maybe have a glass of champagne, try some of the food." She shrugged her shoulders that were swallowed by his T-shirt.

He hadn't noticed how petite she was yesterday. The heels threw off her real height—like they were supposed to do. Thinking about it, she hadn't acted small. Everything about her was strong. She might have cried a couple of times, but she hadn't fallen apart.

Her words finally hit his brain. Were their sources wrong? Was it just a social gathering for the two families or had they intended to merge? "She invited you to a Tenoreno-Rosco meeting?"

"Wasn't it a party?"

"Not according to our sources. Then again, they could have been covering something up by inviting more people."

"Something like the murder of two women?"

"Yeah." He fingered the fading curtains to the side and checked the perimeter. He also noticed that Kenderly's hands tightened into fists, and there wasn't a tear in sight. "You might be right about that. Sure would be nice to know what was in that jewelry case Isabella gave you. Still no idea why she'd trust you with it?"

"I told you, she was my friend."

"And you really didn't know her husband is head of one of the biggest crime syndicate families in the South?" Garrison watched her closely.

She covered her lips with the tip of her finger and

shook her head. She was hiding something. He could feel it. Knew immediately that she was trying to lie. All the classic tells were there. She looked away, bit her lip, brought her hands closer into her body and stopped talking.

"Finished?" She began gathering the trash.

He reached across the stool-sized table and stopped her hand. "You don't have to clean up after me."

"I just need to *do* something. Anything. Did Isabella die because she gave me some letters?"

"I doubt it was that simple. It might have been what was in those letters. Or what her husband thought was in them. It could be because he was afraid of another divorce splintering the family. His son's wife left him last year. Made the news cycle for a while."

"Isabella mentioned they were petitioning the church for an annulment. Of course, even if the annulment went through, they don't know where she disappeared to."

"I believe she disappeared because she was afraid they'd take matters into their own hands."

"As in kill her so an annulment wasn't necessary?" Her entire body shook with the recognition. "Do you think Isabella was planning to leave, too? It just doesn't seem anything like her. She was more upset about the sin of divorce than her son being unhappy."

"Oh, I think he was happy. We have a file of all the women he was sleeping around with."

"So, you've been watching the Tenorenos for a while then?" Kenderly's eyebrows lifted in an arch. The sun brightened her brown eyes to the same color he liked his coffee.

"I think we'd be better off developing a definitive plan for us today. We can't stay here."

"What about Mr. Oaks? Are you worried? I know I

would be." She tapped a manicured nail at a picture of the ranch house they'd fled from. "At least he's not dead, or it would have been in the papers."

It didn't matter if he were worried about his captain or not. He had a job to do before personal feelings or distractions. Long legs or shiny pink nails or eyes the color of his coffee.

"True. First things first. We need a car."

KENDERLY CLOSED HER eyes and took another deep breath. It was necessary to keep the tears tucked away until she could hide her face in her pillow later. She'd cried after they'd gotten situated in the room. Partly feeling sorry for herself, but mainly because she couldn't get the images of Isabella and Trinity out of her mind. No movie could ever compare to the reality of their deaths.

The amount of detail she kept recalling frightened her. Seriously frightened her. The wind had caught the outside door to the rental car building, making the same sound as when the balcony doors had burst open in Isabella's room. She'd barely made it to a bench with her shaky knees.

Garrison had left the counter and helped her. He hadn't spoken, thank goodness. She wouldn't have been able to keep it together if he'd asked her anything.

He was waiting on the keys. She was waiting on her stomach to stop rolling. She jumped out of her skin when he touched her shoulder.

"Oh, God, you scared me."

"Sorry. You ready to go?"

"Sure." She accepted his outstretched hand and was surprised when he laced his long fingers through hers.

She was noticing all sorts of things about Garrison. During their conversation that morning, he'd compressed his lips when she'd mentioned Isabella's ex-daughter-in-law was missing. As if he had more information he couldn't share or knew the answer to her questions.

Noticing him was a nice distraction. It was hard to miss the way his muscles flexed with every simple movement. He had a strong, firm grip. Confident that she wouldn't shake her hand free. It made her feel safer—even if she knew it was just a pipe dream. Paul Tenoreno would never let her live. Not if he thought she had anything to do with his wife's murder.

"What if—" She grabbed Garrison's arm with her free hand, pulling them to a stop. Lowering her voice as soon as she heard it echo in the hallway, she started again. "What if they think I let that man inside the room? Is that why…" Her eyes filled, and she reached up to swipe them dry. "Dammit. It's a good thing I don't have any makeup. I doubt there's a mascara in the world that could weather this amount of tears."

"It's okay. Come on." He pointed her through the doors, urging her to walk a little faster by placing his hand in the small of her back.

"I'm right, aren't I?" She heard her nervous laughter and couldn't stop it. At least they were outside now, and it didn't bounce around the empty walls of the airport rental center.

"Hold it together until we're inside the car, will you?"

"I'm good." *Or hysterical.* "I can handle this. I've handled tough situations before. Not as tough as this, of course. But at least I thought they were tough at the time."

Garrison turned her toward him and tilted her chin up with his index finger. Their eyes met, and he held her gaze. She couldn't look away. She didn't want to.

"Don't fall apart on me now, Kenderly," he whispered.

She managed a nod. He smiled and tucked her into his side.

The car appeared, and he calmly drove them away from the airport, back toward the city. They went through another fast food drive-through. He ordered something for her and set the sack in her lap. Then a bank to make a withdrawal. And then they were on the highway.

"Do you have a plan now?" she asked, unable to keep the shakiness from her voice.

"You should eat so you'll feel better."

"I don't think a bacon cheeseburger will do much good."

"Fries might." He winked and smiled. Then he realized what he'd done and drew his brow in concentration. "Okay, look, I'll have more of a plan after I know the captain is letting someone know we're not the murderers. But I need to get you out of this county, get a throwaway phone and call Jesse. He should have an updated status. Might have a couple of suggestions where I can take you."

"What if he's not? Conscious, that is. What if Captain Oaks is out of the picture? Is there anyone else we can ask for help? Will your friend Jesse hide us?"

"One step at a time, Kenderly." He tapped the top of the food sack. "Eat."

She bit into a burger identical to the one he'd already finished. Fortunately, she could barely taste the ketchup that she hated on any sandwich. She stared out the window, watching the cars and buildings they passed. People going about their business like any other ordinary day.

There was no room to fall apart while on the run from crime bosses and assassins. How insane was it that the thought even crossed her mind? Today was supposed to be ordinary.

"I wonder if anyone at the shop canceled my appointments? Barbara Baker has a color at one and will be severely ticked off when I don't show up. And I have a new perm at four."

"That's the least of your problems," he said, both hands gripping the steering wheel tightly.

"You're right. But that was my life, my livelihood, my reputation. I've worked too hard to watch it disappear in an instant." Her head collided against the glass as he swerved to change lanes. "Hey, um…aren't you going a little fast?"

"Someone's following us."

"That's impossible. How could they find us?"

"Hold on. We're making our own exit."

She dropped the burger and held on with both hands as Garrison cut in front of two lanes of cars and slid down an embankment. Horns blared. Cars skidded. Kenderly squeezed her eyes shut as the side of the rental headed on to the access road. There were a lot of cars on the frontage road. She had no idea how Garrison turned at the last minute, missing them all.

Before she could celebrate, the car following them slid down the incline, too. Garrison had to lose him. But how? His answer was to go faster. She braced herself, but with each swerve it was harder to maintain her grip.

Each second ticked by as a series of movements. One to judge if he could dart in front of a car. One to jump ahead of another. One to apologize for putting so many lives in danger. The next one to illegally U-turn between two pickups. Another to skid through a right turn. One long moment to fishtail into a used car lot, barely missing the iron post where the gate was swung open.

All she could do was pray that the man following didn't see them turn.

When he slowed, he pulled his cell and battery out of

his pocket and held them in his palm. "Dial 911. It's the only way to get you safe. This guy's not going to stop."

"But—"

"We don't have a choice. Do it!"

She threw the sack of food into the back and reached for the phone, but it went flying.

"Grab hold!" Garrison yelled as he hit the brakes.

Kenderly had kept calm and hadn't screamed...until then.

Chapter Seven

Garrison slammed on the brakes too late to avoid the drop-off. What he thought to have been an exit ramp was just a broken piece of concrete. The wheels of the car popped over the curb and shot them into the air.

The top of a building, then a light pole, then a parking lot sloped on a hill. He watched Kenderly slam sideways. Thank God it was only about a four foot drop. The rental's undercarriage caught on the retaining wall so the air bags didn't deploy.

"Stupid. Now what?" He hit the steering wheel once, then turned to Kenderly.

She was out cold.

The person following them would have them trapped shortly. Garrison checked Kenderly's head. No blood, just a huge goose egg on her temple. He had to get them out of there.

The car was still running. He stepped on the gas, smoke billowing from the front tires. But nothing budged. Men ran across the parking lot he'd crashed through, then scrambled out of the way of a speeding car. The murdering son of a bitch from the previous day was driving the car.

Garrison jumped from the car—really jumped since it was firmly stuck. He scrambled to the passenger side.

One of the garage workers was there prying the door open. Wordlessly, he gave Garrison a leg up so he could pop the seat belt. Kenderly slumped sideways with him, and they got her free.

"Thanks for the help." Garrison caught Kenderly over his shoulder.

"She okay? The cops are on their way."

"I've got no time to explain. She's dead if we don't—"

"We got it, man." He hit his palm with the pry bar he'd used on the door. "He won't follow you this way. 'Less he's a cop."

Garrison did a questioning turn trying to decide which way to run. "Not a cop. Thanks, but I can't let you do that. He's armed—"

"The dry cleaners has a back door that's always open. The lady's safety is more important. Let us help."

It was hard to walk away, but the stranger was right. He hoped that the man following them wouldn't draw his weapon.

Down the embankment and across the lot. Every second anticipating the worst. Would he feel the impact of the bullet or hear the fatal shot first? He made it to the propped-open front door of the cleaners.

Nothing. Not even shouting. Wheels peeled out.

The murdering son of a bitch had been kept in his car by the onlookers.

"Oh, Lord. What be happenin' out there? She dead?"

The woman behind the counter might help if he asked. But they couldn't stay. "Which way?"

She jerked her thumb over her right shoulder. He ran through the maze of baskets and steam. He couldn't turn, fearing he'd whack Kenderly's head on something else. She hadn't stirred. Once he saw the open door, he ran faster.

A slight pause to verify no madman was in the alley, then up a grassy slope and across another back drive of a gas station.

What now?

The words bounced around in his brain. He'd jumped from the car, forgetting to swipe up his phone and battery. How had that bastard found them? Right that moment, it didn't matter how. It mattered that the murderer had.

He adjusted Kenderly on his shoulder, tugging at her skirt to make sure she was decent. He had no clue where to go. Dumpster? Inside? Steal a car? Make a run for it?

But he crossed all the options off as soon as he listed them. Delivery truck. He tried the door. Open. It was their only chance. He climbed into the back and maneuvered Kenderly with him as gently as possible. No way to lock the door behind him.

There was no real place to hide and no weapon unless he threw cardboard boxes. Not much of a defense for an assassin with a gun. Packages on either side of them, a special roof kept it well lit on the inside so he could see how pale Kenderly was.

"Come on, sweetheart. Wake up." Completely out and probably needed a doctor.

Tires screeched to a halt—the murderer. Metal crashed into metal—the Dumpster lid. The door raised an inch or two. Men shouted.

"You ain't stealing from my rig, you son of a bitch. Somebody call the cops."

Garrison heard a scuffle. A short one.

"That's right, run, you big lug."

Tires squealed, then the car's engine noise grew fainter.

"I'm fine, everybody. Thanks for your help. Not the

first time I dealt with some loony tunes," the owner of the truck said.

The door shut. The driver got in the front, cranked the truck and pulled out. Garrison sat out of his line of sight, pulling Kenderly into his arms. This was the only way. If the delivery guy drove straight to the police, it would be better than getting shot between the eyes.

"Kenderly," he whispered as softly as he could. He was so close that his words were cupped by the curve of her ear. "I need you to wake up now, babe."

She stirred with a short moan that the driver didn't hear over the natural noise of the truck. Garrison didn't care if he did hear. Relief saturated him as thoroughly as when he'd gotten the news he'd been accepted as a ranger.

The color was coming back to her cheeks as her eyes fluttered open. He gently covered her mouth while pressing a finger to his own. When her eyes registered, he got back close to her ear.

"Just hang tight, and we'll get out at the next stop."

Her eyes shut, and she relaxed her head against his arm. Her hand found his and latched on tightly. He should take her to the hospital. A possible concussion, maybe worse. She should be observed by doctors. His gut told him they'd be sitting ducks in a hospital.

Which wouldn't be necessary if he hadn't thought his phone was safe to use. How the hell had they been found? Who was this maniac working for?

He didn't have long to think about it since the truck pulled over and stopped. The driver consulted his clipboard, then stood facing the back where the packages were.

"What the hell are you doing in my truck? Don't tell me. The SOB back at the station was after you and you hid inside?"

"I can explain."

"I don't need no explanation. That SOB was crazy-eyed. But I can't give you a ride back to your car. It's against regs."

"Thanks for the help."

"Okay. Fine. So go already." He backed into the built-in shelves, gesturing that they should pass.

Kenderly was apparently still a little stunned. It took her a second to realize she was sitting on his lap and needed to stand first. Garrison followed, squeezing by the rather large driver.

"Excuse me," Kenderly asked. "Is that Highway 183 back there?"

"Yes, ma'am, 183 and North Lamar."

"Sweet." She took their surroundings in at a glance and walked toward the street.

"Wait a minute. Where are you going?"

"I worked nights up here for a while. A restaurant near North Capital." She faced the driver again. "A couple of miles that way, right?"

The driver had a package in his hands ready to step from the truck. He looked at Kenderly and shrugged. "I'm going that way. Stay put while I get a signature." He ran down the sidewalk into the office buildings.

"Do you think he'll get in trouble? It shouldn't take us long to walk. I think I can get us a car, and you can call your friends."

He grabbed her by the arm and spun her around harder than he'd intended. "Wait just a damn minute. They might let us use one phone while they call our location into the cops."

"I know these people. They'd never do something like that. The cops are the last people they want there."

"Money does strange things to people. Are you forgetting about the reward Tenoreno put on our heads?" She tried to shake off his grasp, but he was determined she wouldn't get free. "Give it up. You aren't going anywhere 'til I get my bearings and think this through."

"So why don't you ask to borrow the driver's phone?"

"I don't think the man likes to share. You didn't hear him get the crazy bastard chasing us to back down." The delivery man was pretty good swinging that tire iron. "You shouldn't be walking a lot. We're taking him up on the ride offer."

She rubbed her temple and winced when her fingers crossed the lump. "We're lucky to be alive. You know that, right? How did that creep find us anyway?" She took a side step to lean on the door, either trying to break free or ignoring him.

"Kenderly. Wait. I need a minute to think." He pulled her next to him, backing up to the truck, watching around them as much as he could. If they'd been followed...

"Can't we think once we're inside a building where the sun isn't blaring and making this headache worse? Besides, what's there to think about? The big bad murderer found us and tried to kill us a—"

"Now you're with me. We know he's the murderer, and he's not going to give up just because a truck driver scared him off for a few minutes."

The driver emerged from the building whistling and waved at them to get inside. He looked around all the corners as much as Garrison had. Kenderly was already inside. Garrison followed just one step ahead of the driver jumping in and throwing the truck in gear.

"They have a tracker in the truck. I can't turn off my route or I'll have some explaining to do, which I don't want to do. Get me?"

"I'm sure wherever you can drop us is fine." Kenderly had to raise her voice over the truck noise. She had tried to keep standing, but ended up sitting on the floor.

His mind freed up and began working again. It finally sank in that the murderer had found them by tracking his real name, finding the rental, using it. That took connections.

The truck stopped once more. Kenderly thanked the driver over and over again, elbowing Garrison in the ribs several times. He took the hint and thanked him once or twice before holding her hand and running to the building's edge.

"I figured it out," he told her when she faced him. "In order to find us, he has to be working for one of the crime bosses. They're the only ones with connections that could have sent him looking for me."

"Somehow they found out who owned your house." Kenderly shaded her eyes. He hadn't noticed how bright everything was reflecting off the cement lots and cars.

"Yeah. After they knew my real name, it would be a cinch to search my credit card activity."

"Which led them to the rental car company."

"And my cell. They could have bribed or threatened someone to locate us via the GPS in the car." He blocked the sun from his own eyes and scanned the cars. None of them were black. None had dark tinted windows. But the murderer was out there.

The corner where they stood was visible from only two directions parallel to the highway. They needed to disappear. "Risking the restaurant is our only option. But just so we're clear. It's a bad option."

"Believe me, Joey Crouch does not want the police near him." She laughed and stepped away.

Garrison caught her arm. She turned to him with

brows raised, her brown eyes sparkling in spite of the headache she had. "Who is this guy to you?"

"An old friend and an old boss."

"Boyfriend? He the reason you don't work there anymore?"

"As a matter of fact, no. I finished up school and went to work full-time. I no longer needed to work nights. My life was in order, Ranger Travis. Was yours?" She walked and he let her.

Perfect timing as the delivery truck pulled by blocking anyone's view. They crossed with the light. He hurried her toward the patio of the building, scooping her over the short hedge and gently setting her on the other side.

The couple finishing their meal shot a couple of looks, but it didn't stall Kenderly. She wove her way through the tables, and he followed—one look to her and a complete spin to see if they were being followed.

"Hi, Jen. Is Joey here today?"

"Kenderly. What in the world happened to you?" The restaurant hostess with her arms full of menus laughed. "Have a rough night, hon?"

"Is he in the kitchen?"

"Where else would he be?" Jen set the stack down and took a step toward the door.

"That's okay," Kenderly said. "I know the way. I don't want to pull you away from your work."

Garrison wished he could have seen Kenderly's expression, because he caught a glance of Jen's. A cross between guilt and satisfaction. Kenderly's tone sort of implicated a love triangle. One more glance at the streets. No black sedan.

Garrison had to speed walk to catch up with Kenderly before she stopped short of the kitchen. She gave an exaggerated tug on her skirt, shoved her fingers through her hair and wiped her face with both hands.

She mumbled, "I wish I had my shoes," before pushing the swinging door aside and stepping through. Garrison looked at her bare feet. He'd been so busy rescuing her, he hadn't noticed he'd left her shoes back at the car.

The staff was light at this time of day. They all greeted his witness with welcome surprise. One tall dude stood near the stove, arms crossed, black hair pushed back from his naturally tanned face. He appeared to be over thirty, but if Garrison admitted it to himself, he was good-looking enough to probably attract a young woman like Kenderly.

Not that he'd readily admit that to anyone else.

There was a hard, resentful look. As his staff—it was obvious he was in charge—looked toward him, his sternness cracked with a broad smile. Shoot. He understood how Kenderly saw through him so quickly.

Ex-boyfriend Joey had the same smile as him. Of all the stinkin' luck.

"Kenderly, darling. It's been ages and ages." If Joey's smile wasn't wide enough, he opened his arms. Why? Expecting her to run into them? "Who's this?"

"A friend. Can we talk a minute?" She avoided his arms and led the way toward a door by the dish-washing station.

Outside. Potential targets again. Kenderly might have been wishing for shoes, but he was wishing for his side-arm. He wanted to gauge this character's reaction, but he watched the perimeter and listened.

"It's been a while, Kenderly."

"Yes. We both know why, and there's no need to dredge it up."

"This my replacement?" Gone was all pretense of a happy return. There was animosity in his voice. "Or did you bring muscle to get your way?"

Maybe he hadn't cheated on her, after all.

The sounds of the highway interfered with Kenderly's mumbled words, but not with Joey's "you owe me."

"Really, baby? You going to bring that up after all this time?" Joey's voice continued getting louder with a touch of anger mixed in.

Garrison forced himself to keep his back to the conversation. He searched each passing car for the guy who'd been chasing them. The look he'd gotten had been quick and blurred, but he'd recognize him again. It wasn't enough to look for the car. He might have ditched it. So he stared, growing angrier himself at each word Joey spat.

"I owe you nothing," Kenderly answered. "In fact, I'm here to collect on that little problem you have."

"Nobody will believe you, baby. It's been two years."

"You're right. Of course, you're right. But I don't think two years is long enough to avoid prosecution for tax evasion. And don't call me baby."

There was a quick movement in Garrison's peripheral vision. He spun and caught Joey's hand on the way toward Kenderly's face. "Not a good idea, buddy."

"I wasn't going to hit her. Just try to—" He yanked his arm. "Do you mind?"

"Yeah. A lot."

Kenderly smiled, but Garrison didn't let go. "I need to borrow your car and cell. And a couple of hundred cash would be nice."

"There's no way in hell I'm doing that, b—"

Garrison dropped the man's arm but stuck a finger in his face. "Watch it."

"It's okay, honey. I've got this," she said patting his shoulder. "Joey owes me big-time. Would it help if I promised to be careful? Oh, and never mention your little off-the-books business again."

"No way, baby. I can't do that." Joey shook his head and waved them off with his hands.

"Sure you can." Garrison wouldn't strong-arm the ex-boyfriend again. Not unless he threatened Kenderly. On the other hand, there was no harm letting the man think he would. They were desperate.

Chapter Eight

Kenderly tried calmly lacing her fingers together in her lap. It didn't work. She didn't feel secure and had almost bitten through the inside of her lip. Joey's sports car didn't help. With each shift in gears, her heart revved a little higher.

The built-in safety handle would be too obvious. It would make her look scared. Dammit, she was scared. What did it hurt if Garrison knew it? She reached up, latching on with a death grip.

She was so ready for a nice slow drive in the country. Barely missing cars at every juncture was beginning to take its toll. Not to mention being shot at, running, sleeping like a mummy—when she'd slept at all. Garrison was staying with traffic, but definitely pushing the speed limit and switching lanes like a maniac. The fast corners she could manage. Just no more parking lots.

"I know it's hard, but I want to get away from that area as fast as we can."

"Do you have a destination in mind?" Kenderly used her left hand to grip the console, wedging herself in place. If she'd been more prepared the last time, she may not have hit her head. "Any place with aspirin?"

"I'm delivering you to my company in Waco. It's the

safest place for you to be. They'll take care of you, and I can come back to sort through this mess."

"That doesn't work for me." The words were out before she realized the thought was there. She didn't want him to leave her anywhere. The panic rose faster than he was driving.

"Don't be naive, Kenderly. My first duty is to get you to safety. I can't investigate the murders or find this guy who's after you as long as you're in danger."

She knew about his assignment, knew he had a duty. She felt her eyes welling with tears. Frightened of starting over again, of trying to trust yet another person who had nothing to risk but their job.

"Us. He wants to kill you, too," she reminded him, blinking the moisture away.

Garrison gave her a quick sideways look. Did he think she was crazy? Did he really think he was invisible? Of course he did. He was a Texas Ranger. Maybe he was above being scared.

"What if he finds me wherever I am? What if whoever's behind this doesn't ever stop sending killers? What if we get stopped before you get to Waco, and we're arrested on the spot? What if—"

"Whoa. That's a lot of what ifs. How about trying *what if* you trust my judgment and experience?" He let off the gas. A car actually passed him. "Taking you to Waco is a risk I'm willing to take. The men of Company F know me. Know that I'm one of them. Know that a ranger would never commit murder."

"I'd rather find out what's in the jewelry box. Don't you want to know what happened to Captain Oaks?"

"Of course I do."

"Then why don't we take a breath, slow down and maybe talk some of this through?"

"Once you're safe in Waco." He relaxed a little, draping his wrist over the top of the wheel. "Why would you want to play detective and risk that SOB finding you again?"

"Isabella was my friend."

"Who would want you to stay alive."

"But also trusted me to finish something for her. What if she gave me evidence that would convict the person who ordered her death?"

"The Rangers can take care of this…even without us."

Did she really need this man to make all the decisions regarding her life? She was out of her mind if she thought she didn't. But there was a feeling that she needed to stay in Austin. Maybe because she'd always been in charge of her own life. She couldn't dismiss Isabella's faith in her as easily as Garrison could.

"Do you trust them?" she asked. "These men you work with."

"Only with my life."

"Then how come you're wanted for murder?" Why would anyone jump to the conclusion that an undercover ranger would murder two women? Was Mr. Tenoreno truly that powerful?

"I'm certain Company F is wondering the same thing." He slowed and stopped for a red light.

"That's not really an answer. I think I'll take this." She gathered the cell with shaking fingers, not knowing completely what she would do. But she couldn't run and hide. Isabella had depended on her.

"Who are you going to—"

She got out of the car, slamming the door and cutting his words off before she could change her mind. She ran between the cars, across two lanes to the right side of the road. It would take him a few minutes to make a U-turn and come back for her.

Or at least she thought it would. She turned around to find him following. On foot. The light turned green, and cars began honking. It was a busy street, but it didn't stop him.

"Leave me alone, Garrison!" She looked around for a place to run. She had picked the only street with no store or gas station around. Just a covered bus stop.

"No way. I have a job to do."

It didn't take him long to catch her. She was barefoot and wearing a ridiculous party skirt. Horns and shouts from other drivers didn't hide their exerted breathing as they faced each other. He held on to her arms, but it didn't frighten her. His grip assured her she wasn't going anywhere without him, but the look in his eyes was admiration. Not anger.

"Come on before somebody calls the police." He cocked his head back toward Joey's car and smiled. Genuinely. Only for her. Not part of a calculated plan.

Fingers laced, he led her quickly through the cars. It didn't go unnoticed that he pressed the auto-lock as soon as he was also inside. But she wasn't going anywhere. As soon as she'd made it to the sidewalk, she knew she was in trouble. She had no idea how to go about helping Isabella on her own.

Even more than that, she had no one to turn to for help. She would just be putting her friends in danger if she went to them. She needed the Texas Rangers as much as Garrison relied on them.

A mile or so up the road, he pulled over on a residential street and twisted sideways in his seat to look at her. "I admire you, Kenderly. I really do. But you have to be reasonable about this."

"I know you're right, but running away to save myself just feels so…wrong."

He reached out and cupped both of his hands around hers resting on the console.

Hold it.

"Wait a minute." She slipped her hand from his and leaned back against the door. "I've known you a little over twenty-four hours, but this comforting thing…it's not you. What happened to the overconfident Texas Ranger on the motorcycle?"

"That's a relief. I didn't know how long I could keep that up." He winked. "I need the phone."

She handed it to him, a little confused as to what that scene was about. Garrison was a mixture of arrogance and cocky. That was definitely appealing for a while, but those men never ever turned out to be the comforting type. He wasn't a jerk. At least she didn't believe he was. But it sure would have taken a lot to prove he wasn't. That is, if they'd met under different circumstances. Was it just an act?

"I'm looking up news footage. If they're reporting on the condition of Oaks, they'll be in front of… Gotcha. Brecken Ridge Hospital. If that don't beat all. It's right back where we were last night."

"Are you calling them? They won't give you any information."

"It can't hurt to try. Somebody might slip up and let us know something."

The car automatically connected to the phone, and she heard it dialing. Garrison put a finger across his lips.

"Brecken Ridge Hospital, how may I direct your call?"

"May I have the room for Captain Aiden Oaks?"

"I'm sorry, that information is restricted. May I help with something else?"

"No, thanks."

He disconnected. He could have taken it off speaker but hadn't. He could have driven straight to Waco without any other discussion. Instead he'd parked and included her. Now what was he up to?

"He's still there, still alive. He must have been shot more seriously than he let on. I admit that I wondered if he was the primary leak that left me out to dry. Then again, Tenoreno has so many dirty cops and politicians in his pocket that I don't think Oaks would have faked an investigation."

"Somehow I don't believe you were thinking of him like that."

"I might rule Oaks out simply because he's a ranger. But I don't think we're going to get close enough for a chat to verify our roles in yesterday." He continued to scan news about the shooting from the day before. "Thing is, we're out of the loop. I don't have a way of knowing if it's better to take you to Waco. As much as I want to jump in and clear my name, my orders were to keep you safe."

He flipped the phone toward her, and she saw the headline: State Manhunt for Rogue Ranger.

"Do you really think it's a good idea to leave Austin?" She genuinely wanted to know. If this man was willing to risk his career to protect her, that meant something. She should trust him completely. Right?

It was just so hard to do. No one had really been there for her to practice that particular skill. The situation was calling for her to quickly overcome big time therapy issues…without any therapy.

"We need to talk with Jesse. We'll call, and you can pretend that you're the dog sitter. Whoever's chasing us knows all about me, so they might be monitoring his phone. We'll see if it's safe."

"How do I do that? I don't know what to ask."

He dialed. "Let him do most of the talking. If I shouldn't come home, he'll find a way to let me know."

"Jesse Ryder."

"This is…um…the dog sitter for Bear and Clementine. I just wanted to see if things were okay."

"Sure. They're happy to be here."

Kenderly shrugged her shoulders not knowing what to say. "That's…um…great. Real good."

"I appreciate you checking up on them. But, yeah, there's really no telling when they'll be able to go back to Garrison's place. Not with all this mess."

"I heard someone was shot pretty badly." Kenderly watched Garrison mouth the word package, drawing a square with his fingers.

"Captain Oaks. He's still in ICU. No one's getting in to take his statement."

"There was a…um…a package left here. Should I forward it to you?"

"Don't rush it or anything. I won't be around for the next three days. Thanks for checking on these mutts. If you want, you can check again."

"Thanks." Kenderly searched Garrison's face for confirmation of what she thought she'd heard. If she was the package, then it wasn't safe. Not for either of them. "What do we do now?"

"We find a place to stay. Ditch this car and phone before your friend calls the police."

"He won't. He's afraid of what I might say." She heard him suck in a breath. He was about to ask a serious question. "We can't get into that. Not now. I promised I wouldn't tell you about him, but I didn't promise I wouldn't drop an anonymous call to the IRS. But one problem at a time. A bed for tonight. I don't suppose you have any friends in Austin."

He shook his head. "Do you?"

"As a matter of fact. How good are you at picking locks?"

Chapter Nine

Garrison was in total awe of this woman. The news from Jesse wasn't good. The fact that they were reporting a statewide manhunt for the first Texas Ranger wanted for murder was worse. There was no way he was going down in history with *that* title.

All things considered, Kenderly was holding it together and working with him.

Without shoes.

She had made a run for it, but he didn't think that was serious. Just a moment's hesitation. She'd come back to the car quick enough and been cooperative afterward.

Not to mention calling his bluff when he'd tried to comfort her. He wasn't that guy. He'd been way too busy over the past ten years to get where he was at. Naw, comforting wasn't his style. He was more the love 'em and get too busy to call back sort of fella.

If he heard that description out loud about someone, he might call them a jerk. Okay, there was no might in that thought. He *would* call them a jerk. It didn't happen all the time, though. Yeah, he could justify it. His work since transferring to the Rangers had been secretive and intense. It hadn't left time for serious—or even nonserious—dating.

"You take a left on the next street unless you want to go to the store before we stop."

They still hadn't bought a change of clothes. Had nothing except a couple hundred bucks and the change in the console. His stomach seemed to be a bottomless pit, and Kenderly hadn't eaten since breakfast. Their outlook wasn't good at all.

"This is the apartment of a coworker who you're sure is gone for the weekend?"

"Yes. Rose took off for a family emergency Thursday. I was supposed to take her four o'clock perm. Home is in California, so she didn't know when she'd be back in town. It'll be at least a week, giving us time until we check in with your friend again. Right?"

Fifteen minutes ago he'd agreed to break into an apartment because there was no other option left for them. Jesse's message to check back later meant just that. Stay out of sight and come up for air in three days. No hotels, motels or checking out the captain's hospital room.

"There it is. The corner one."

"With the light on?"

"I'm pretty sure."

"Dammit, Kenderly. You need to be more than just pretty sure."

"I'm going to let that outburst slide because I can understand your anxiety. I've only been here once. Coworker—not best friend. I remember it was on the corner because I could see the parking lot from two windows. I also remember climbing two flights of stairs. So, yeah, I'm sure now. And for the stupid record, I leave my lights on all the time." She mumbled the last sentence.

"Sorry. I'm not good at this."

"What? Breaking and entering or communicating?"

She had his number, unlike most people. "Let's just get it over with."

Maybe they got lucky with the time of day or maybe it was because they were on the third floor. No one caught him shoving or pulling at the door. And no one barreled up the outside staircase after he'd gotten it open. The complex hadn't bothered to install secure, safe locks, and Kenderly's friend had left without latching the dead bolt.

"It's very discomforting to see how easy it was for you to get in the door," Kenderly said as she walked through.

Once inside, to turn the dead bolt he lifted the door a little, making it slip into the slot. "Your friend needs to have maintenance rehang that door."

Kenderly dropped to the couch, spreading her arms wide, sinking into the cushions. "Oh, my gosh, this feels good. How long do you think we'll be here? Do you think I could take a shower?"

Garrison shrugged, pulling the cord to close the blinds. He looked around the parking lot that had one teenager walking a dog. Other than that, it was completely quiet. Kenderly looked comfortable. Her skirt had been through the wringer, with lots of bare spots where it had lost the sequins. Her feet looked just as bad.

"Think your friend has some practical shoes you can borrow?"

"I'll check." She sat forward, then fell backward again. "Right after a nap. I'm wiped out."

He secured the second window and curtain. "Sounds like a good idea."

"Do you think they'll find us here?"

"I didn't think they'd find us before. There's no sign anyone followed. But I need to get that car away from here. I don't trust your old boyfriend."

"I don't trust him, either." She yawned. "That's why he was never a boyfriend." Her eyes were closed by the time she rested her head on the arm of the old couch.

Garrison opened the fridge and cabinets. It wasn't his normal junk food, but he could do healthy for a couple of days. They could lie low and wait for Jesse to give them the all-clear. Or the captain could straighten out his involvement. He'd leave the car and take a bus back. No one would notice him on a bus, especially since they were flashing a ten-year-old academy picture of him on the screen. The Rangers must not have released his official white Stetson picture.

"Do you think your friend has an extra key?" He waited with the freezer open for a response, then looked around the corner. "Kenderly?" He crossed to her, took a blanket from the back of the couch and covered her legs.

As brave as she'd been since they'd been thrown into each other's lives, she finally met something she couldn't handle. Exhaustion. It had taken over and claimed some sleep time. He'd wait half an hour to make sure they were really safe and leave her a note. He could take care of Joey's stuff on his own.

GARRISON KNOCKED ON the door with one knuckle. It was as quiet as he could manage with plastic grocery bags looped over his arms. If Kenderly was still asleep he'd be lurking in the dark until she could open the lock.

The flimsy door was jerked wide. He nearly fell through as Kenderly grabbed his new T-shirt sleeve and yanked him inside.

"You went shopping?"

"I left a note."

"Be back soon. You call that a note?"

"It took a while to catch a bus."

"You can't blame it on public transportation. We're really going to have to work on your communication skills, Garrison." She took a few of the bags, glanced inside and led the way to the kitchen. "I've been out of my mind flipping channels to see if there were any reports about your capture."

"I brought dinner."

"Like I could eat anything after the past three hours." Kenderly used her hands, expressing her dismay or concern or panic.

"Three hours? You must have woken up right after I left."

Blocking his entrance into the tiny kitchen, she placed her cute little fists on her sequined-covered hips and tilted her chin up to look at him. There was something in her eyes he hadn't noticed before.

Fear. During their escape, she'd been in shock. Maybe they'd been running enough that it just hadn't sunk in until now. But she looked frightened.

"I would have known how long you'd been gone if you had left the time on your note."

"Yes, ma'am." He admitted it to very few people, but he wasn't great at resolving conflicts. He took them in stride, sidestepped as often as possible, and forgot them immediately. He wanted to sidestep here, but she kept returning directly to the problem…him.

"Seriously, you tell me never to leave your side. I close my eyes for a few minutes, and you're gone. I learned one thing, though. I'm glad you came after me when I got out of the car. If I was truly on my own, I'd have no clue what to do."

She threw her arms around his waist, smashing her cheek to his chest. He didn't have to make a decision whether or not to hug her back. His hands were still full of bags.

"Promise you won't abandon me. Okay?" she asked softly.

He flinched and she let go. "I can't make that promise."

"Sorry. I didn't mean to put you on the spot." She wiped at her eyes.

He'd seen her frightened, sad, mourning, unconscious and acting like she owned the world. He hadn't seen this. She'd used the word *abandoned*. This would have been the perfect time to plug her name and date of birth into a database and see what records were spit out.

Communication.

Quickly setting the bags on the floor, he caught her shoulders before she scooted by him. The silky shirt was cool and smooth under his fingers. The roundness of her shoulders fit perfectly in the palm of his hands.

"I can't make that promise, Kenderly, because I have to do what's best for you. Keeping you safe might mean leaving you. But I won't walk away until I guarantee you're safe. You can count on me. I can promise you that."

"Thanks," she whispered. "I was just so scared. Maybe if we had some sort of plan… Some way to figure out why all of this happened, I'd feel better."

"I really did bring dinner."

"I get it. Change the subject before the strange woman can get too emotional."

"Naw. I'm just hungry. I've been smelling this chicken since I got to the store. I snuck a piece on the bus and just made my stomach growl more."

He gathered the sack handles and set them on the counter. The kitchen was a tight fit while they worked together and put away the things he'd bought. The deli fried chicken and sides were opened by Kenderly while he set one sack in the corner. They fixed their plates without Kenderly seeing the sack that held her surprise.

The TV was muted. It didn't take much to decipher what the report was stating. National headlines about two women being executed by a Texas Ranger and his stylist accomplice.

"Want me to turn it off?"

"Does your friend have cable? Is there a movie or something?" he asked to take her mind off the news.

She pointed the remote, and the screen went blank. Guess that decided what they were watching. Sure, they needed to talk. He got it. He had been hoping for a moment to not do anything. Just a few minutes to decompress.

First day with the Rangers more than one of the men had told him to enjoy the days when nothing happened. He'd been in law enforcement long enough to realize that truth on his own.

You couldn't drive forever. You had to stop to refuel. He also realized that Kenderly needed him to—dang it—communicate. At least he could eat at the same time.

"What did you do with Joey's car?"

"Left it in a parking lot, took a bus five miles away, went to the store, ate a piece of chicken on the return bus, then knocked on the door. That's it. I didn't talk with anyone or get noticed. I didn't make eye contact with the deli person. I even went through the self-checkout to avoid another person seeing my face."

She pushed her mac and cheese around her plate.

"I thought everybody liked green beans and macaroni. Eat up."

"I'm not too hungry."

He shrugged. "Eat or don't eat. It'll be there when you're ready." He was on his second piece—third if he counted the appetizer on the bus.

Kenderly dropped her fork and sank into the couch cushions, pulling the blanket up to her chin. It was clear that she was attempting to be patient. If it had been him, he'd be pacing the floor demanding answers. He knew what she wanted to ask but didn't know to ask.

"There were a lot of patrol cops and Texas Highway Patrol." He swallowed his last bite and wiped his hands. "Joey might not have reported the car stolen, but I still don't trust him."

"Agreed and I understand why you didn't wait for me to wake up. But you reminded me this morning not to leave your side. So it seemed strange to me. I panicked and had no clue what to do if something did happen to you."

"Sorry 'bout that. If we're separated, you call Jesse. You can trust him. After these accusations, he knows not to turn you over to the police." He needed to make certain nothing happened. They needed a plan, and he needed time to think of one. "It was better to leave you here. They're looking for a couple and ignored a guy without a car buying groceries."

"Well, no one's busting down the door, so I guess you're right."

He laughed. He couldn't help it since she was so matter-of-fact about it. He'd taken great pains to guarantee no one followed and busted down the door.

"I don't see what's so funny about me being frightened to death. Or that someone's trying to kill me. Or that we're both wanted for murder. There's just not anything funny about it at all, in my opinion."

"I didn't mean—let's forget it and chill. How about that movie?"

Kenderly popped up from the old couch quicker than toast from a toaster. She shoved her fingers into her hair, sort of with a low, irksome long "ugh," followed by a short "ow." Her arm was bent at an awkward angle.

"Dang it, my ring's stuck." She yanked a couple of more times. It was stuck and getting worse.

"Come back over here and I can help."

"No." She tugged some more.

"Don't be a spoilsport." When she didn't budge, he stood and crossed the room with a couple of steps. "Hold on or you'll tear it out by the roots." He gently worked the tangled strands free. "I could have sworn that your hair was longer yesterday."

"Hair extensions."

He smoothed the multicolored blond strands. "It made you look different."

She covered her face. "I feel weird without my regular makeup on."

"I think you look better. Not that you didn't before. I mean… Hell, I think you're just as pretty without it."

"Thanks. I think." She rolled her eyes.

Not good, man. He opened his mouth to try to take his foot out, but she stopped him.

"I'll accept it as a compliment." She disappeared around the corner and came back with a yeast roll. "I know I look different. That's why I do it."

"I'll never get why a woman wants to look that different. Now, someone on the run using a disguise makes perfect—"

She whipped around, her mouth dropping open to match his.

"Do you think?"

"Could you?"

They spoke together.

"I'm sure Rose has everything I need here." Kenderly took lids off of boxes of supplies stacked against the kitchen wall. "What are you thinking? Would it be too obvious if we dyed our hair dark? Would they be looking for us like that? Do they teach you to expect changed appearances in Ranger school?"

Garrison let her chatter away with ideas and questions. She assumed they'd be running. It was a natural progression. But for him, it was natural to investigate. With a couple of calls he could find out where the captain's car had ended up. Or if it might still be on the street.

If it had been towed, it wouldn't surprise anybody if *Mrs. Oaks* showed up to drive it home. Looking at how excited Kenderly was, he knew she could pull this off. Easy. They could retrieve the jewelry box and maybe a major clue to help solve the murders.

And if she gets caught? Is that a risk worth taking?

Chapter Ten

"You're nuts. Completely and totally nuts. There's no way I'm going to walk into a police station that might be full of men who report to Paul Tenoreno. No way. No. You don't trust them. Why should I?"

"You won't go into the station. If the cops have the car, there's no way they'd let us inside the vehicle. It'll be evidence. No, odds are the car was towed and is at an impound lot. We'd need cash to pay the fee."

Kenderly had tried reasoning with Garrison. She'd presented what she thought was a solid debate about how she wasn't trained for undercover work or even pretending to be married for half an hour. He—in all his arrogant, self-confident glory—had said she could do it. Just like that, he'd turned her simple makeover into a secret agent plastic mask that would hide them from the world.

"I can't do the level of work you're expecting. They'll see right through it. If we get caught, it'll be all my fault."

Garrison sat backward in the little chair from the dinette. This time the smile on his face was at her—what he'd called an overreaction. Not once but at least twice.

Infuriating was putting it mildly. And now he was just smiling. Not saying a word and just smiling.

"How can I argue with you if you won't say anything?"

She put it out there, but she didn't really hope for an argument. She prayed he'd change his plans.

"I think you were doing okay there by yourself. Don't mind me at all."

Kenderly walked around the table, nervous as the caged white tiger she'd seen at the zoo when she was a kid. "Why don't I put makeup on you and *you* be Captain Oaks's wife? You're the one with all the experience."

He burst out laughing. "Not in heels," he managed to get out between heehaws. "I've never been undercover in heels."

"Oh good grief. You truly are serious about me doing this."

He stood and followed her to the couch. They were in close quarters, so she sat immediately, sinking on to the broken-down cushions. At least she was farther from him than if she'd remained standing. She was either going to grab his face between her hands and shake some sense into him or shower his face with kisses, thanking him for saving her life multiple times.

And how would she manage that? She slipped her fingers over her lips at the thought. No! She would not kiss him out of the blue like her body wanted to.

Not in a million years. Not innocently or passionately. He'd interpret the gesture as an invitation. It was the genuine laughter. He'd looked so real and relaxed and sexy. "No, no and no again."

"Hey, take it easy. I understand you're scared. There's no real reason to even think about it. The towing company for that part of Austin is closed, and I can't verify where the car is until the morning. So just relax." He dropped to the couch, remote in hand, finally flipping channels searching for that movie he wanted to watch.

Kenderly remained quiet, but not for the reasons he'd suggested. She needed some deep breaths and a few moments to catch her runaway thoughts. Why did she want to kiss him a half hour after believing he'd abandoned her? It didn't make sense. But of course, none of the past two days made much sense to her.

Garrison Travis was totally all wrong for her. They knew nothing about each other and probably would never have even met if he hadn't saved her life. She was grateful he had. And tremendously grateful that he hadn't just dropped her off to be dealt with by the police until he knew the entire story.

Danger. Vulnerability. Trying to solve the mystery. And if she allowed herself to think that way, excitement had brought them together. A relationship couldn't be built on adrenaline.

So, no. Kissing him wasn't an option or something she actually desired. Not really. She was exhausted. Her mind was just going down a familiar path while in the company of a handsome man. Even if she hadn't been in a man's company for a very long time. It didn't make a difference.

Then why were her insides doing a little dance? Okay, a very big dance. She drew in another deep breath, holding a throw pillow against her chest. Desire took over. The need to scoot across the cushions and have strong arms engulf her in their protection was tremendous. She curled her feet in the space between them and used the pillow for her head.

"You don't have to watch this. You could get a shower if you want. I'll take the couch tonight. You can take your friend's bed."

It would get her out of the room. Away from temptation.

Without a word, she hurried from his close proximity and locked herself in the bathroom.

Sweet, sweet Thelma…she was in big time trouble.

As soon as Kenderly left the room, Garrison remembered the surprises he'd brought from the store for her. Too late. He heard the shower and wasn't about to interrupt. He gathered the sack he'd dropped out of her sight and decided to put her things on the bed.

Pink, pink and twenty more shades of pink. The bedroom was covered in it and trimmed in more of it. Right down to a pink scarf with roses and beads covering the lamp shade. He clicked the switch, turning the bedside lamp on and then another to shut off the bright light from overhead.

Then he put the clothes he'd bought on the silky spread. Kenderly was correct that her friend had everything handy to change their appearances. There were a couple of wigs on the dresser, other hairpieces—they looked like long braids—pinned to a bulletin board, and some sort of makeup sat on every available inch of a mirrored table.

His plan would work if Kenderly let him coach her through a couple of techniques. If the car had been impounded, though, that was a different animal altogether. It wouldn't do any good to get inside the car. Everything would have already been taken and logged as evidence. If the car had just been towed, there'd be nothing to it. Just sweet-talk the attendant to get her purse out. No prob.

Maybe he could change her mind over an omelet. He fingered the short curly black wig on the Styrofoam head. The hair felt real to his untrained touch. It would look real to anyone watching. No one would suspect that she was Kenderly Tyler.

The shower cut off. Time for him to retreat to the couch before his witness went all weird on him again.

KENDERLY WASN'T ABOUT to show her face in the living room. Her adrenaline-filled veins wanted release like nothing she'd experienced before. The more she tried to downplay her desire for Garrison, the worse it became.

Cold showers might work for men, but all it had done for her aching body was give it the idea to warm up next to the man in the next room. She couldn't put her ratty clothes back on. What used to be her favorite satin shirt and skirt was trash can filler. She hoped Rose wouldn't mind her borrowing some things. Starting with pajamas.

With her head wrapped in a towel and another large comfy one around her body, she opened the hall door and barreled right into Garrison.

"Sorry." His hands caught her as she sort of bounced off his chest and tripped backward over her own feet. "Hey, you okay?"

The towel around her hair fell to the floor, and the one around her middle was barely secured by a pinch of her fingers. "I'm fine. What are you doing? Checking the windows?"

"No. I did that before I left you here alone."

"Okay. I should… If you'd excuse me." They did a little dance moving the same direction to let each other pass.

"Hold it." Garrison grabbed her shoulders, turning her sideways. He mirrored her. "There."

The palms of his hands burned her icy skin. A quick look up told her Garrison felt the fire as much as she did. For once there was no smile on his face. He smoldered as his hands tightened, moving her slightly against the hall wall.

"This is going to break at least fifty regulations."

She knew what *this* meant, and she didn't care about regulations. She'd been dying to get her lips next to his since waking up that morning. How many thoughts of consequences could she have in the amount of time it took him to crash into her mouth?

Garrison trapped her with a hand pressed against the wall to either side. He didn't need to worry about her going anywhere. She couldn't. Curiosity or hunger… neither would let her move a step away.

Then he was there. His lips covered hers. She tilted her head back, giving him full access to her mouth. He took it. Devoured it. Moist, hot heat saturated her…everything as his lips took control.

Thoughts were over. Pure unadulterated feeling took the lead.

Sounds from the back of her throat bubbled up, awakening something that had been dormant long before her past couple of boyfriends. Was it the feeling of finally being alive after coming so close to losing her life?

She had no idea and didn't want to think too hard about it. The sensation was more than a little wonderful.

Garrison lifted his head, gently sucking her bottom lip through his teeth and sending cold chills down her spine.

His hand had moved to pinch the towel just under her arm where she apparently had forgotten about it. He guided her fingers back to the spot and let go, taking a step toward the living room as he did.

"'Night, 'night, sweet Kenderly," he whispered like the breeze.

"Good night," slipped from her breathy voice before she could fully open her eyes again. She dashed into the bedroom, shutting the door and leaning her back against it as if Garrison was hot on her trail.

If he had been, she would have let him in. It was the simple truth. But he didn't follow. She was disappointed and didn't want to think about it. Of course that's all she could think about as she took a sheet from the top closet shelf, intending to wrap herself on top of the covers.

She turned to the bed and saw the clothes and a cute pair of white sneakers. She flipped them over, and they were only a half size too big. The underwear was remarkably accurate, as were the jeans.

Somewhere between opening the bikini panties and the simple beige sweater, she began crying. She skipped the PJs and cried into her friend's pillow.

Fitful sleep finally came as she twisted, turned and then twisted again.

THERE WAS NO way he was sleeping after that total surrender in the hallway. Garrison fought with himself to stay put on the couch.

"Stupid. Impulsive. Idiot. You're an idiot, Garrison Travis." He might have whispered the words into the dark, but he heard his best friend's voice screaming them at him.

They'd worked so hard to become rangers. Jesse, Avery and he had gone to college and the academy together. They'd all been accepted as TX DPS officers. All climbed the ranks, tested, learned more in every class they could manage on their schedule.

When his sister didn't make the final roster, things changed. They hadn't really been the same since. The last thing she'd said to him before trading her DPS badge for one as a small-town deputy was not to screw up.

Kissing a witness was a royal screwup.

None of his fellow rangers in Company F would look on it as anything else.

Captain Oaks would let him have it. One look from his captain and Garrison would be falling all over himself apologizing. He couldn't let it happen again. He glanced at the clock. It had only been twenty minutes, but he might as well get a shower. No way was he going to sleep for a while.

The frightening part of kissing Kenderly wasn't a reprimand. It wasn't breaking the rules. It was falling for her. He was on the edge, and it was a long way down.

When he tasted her kiss again, he'd be at her mercy. That was a place he couldn't afford to be. He needed to be at the top of his game.

He lifted the shade at the windows. It was late on a Saturday night, and nothing was moving. A door opened across the complex, and the same dog walker was slowing his dog, trying to keep the massive mutt from pulling him down the stairs.

A quiet neighborhood. He dropped his head against the wall thinking about what his family must be going through. Not to mention his aunt's house that might need to be demolished. Jesse would assure everyone that Garrison wasn't guilty. Would that be enough? They'd all thought he pushed things too hard and fast to meet his goals. Would they still have faith in him?

Shower. Then sleep. No thinking about Kenderly. A plan in the morning. And finding another place for them to stay or disappear for another couple of days. He turned the water as hot as he could stand.

Cold showers to relax were a myth in his mind, since they made his body tense. A hot hard spray normally had the desired effect of easing his tense muscles and nerves. Almost. He almost had a peaceful minute when he closed his eyes. But Kenderly's face was plastered on the back of his eyelids.

Once there, the tiny upturn to her nose, the perfect shape of her cheekbones and the cute arch of her eyebrows refused to leave. He relived every soft curve of her mouth. Each imperfection of her lips that he'd pulled under his own had him clamoring for more. Ultimate softness and a response that had him shaking to the tips of his Western boots, or bare feet at the moment.

Why couldn't it have been a kiss that he didn't want a second or third or fourth. He toweled dry and wrapped it around his hips. His new clothes were on the table. Stepping into the hall, he heard a whimper... Kenderly's. Mumbling. No one could have gotten into the apartment, but he had to be certain. He turned the bedroom doorknob slowly and pushed it open.

Kenderly was tangled in a sheet, lying on top of the bed. Dressed only in her undergarments, her smooth flesh called to him. He resisted. When he did touch her, it wouldn't be while she was sleeping. She'd be awake for every soft caress, every firm deliberate stroke.

He tugged the sheet free and covered her legs, adding the comforter to prevent a chill. With a finger, he hooked her long hair behind her ear and got a smile for a reward.

Yep. The next time their bodies were together...she'd definitely know and remember.

Chapter Eleven

Waco, Texas

Jesse Ryder tried to act as if he was comfortable instead of hanging off a cliff by his fingernails while he stood at the back of the room. No one asked if he'd had contact with his best friend. The major had given him a couple of looks, so it was just a matter of time before it happened. But Jesse keeping his mouth shut wasn't unusual. Garrison usually had enough words for the both of them.

The first question on everybody's mind was why Garrison was in Austin. The second was how the hell whatever operation he was involved with had gone so belly-up. The third was why he was running. No one had accused Garrison Travis of crossing the line. They wouldn't. He was one of them. A Texas Ranger.

Texas Rangers didn't cross that line.

Yet he'd run and taken a witness or accomplice or perpetrator. No one knew for certain. No matter how much they believed in him, they were in the dark.

As the rest of the company left their commanding officer's office with late night assignments, Josh Parker nodded in Jesse's direction. *Here it comes.* His loyalty would be questioned along with the rest of his life's direction.

He and Garrison were closer than a lot of brothers. How could he keep the man's secrets and not break his oath?

"You know the powers-that-be argued against allowing you and Travis to stay in the same company. They didn't think it was a wise decision. I wanted you both." Parker took his seat behind his desk. "I thought you were a good team. So, what's going on?"

A familiar sight was to see the major tip his chair back, prop his worn boots on the solid oak desk corner—heels off the edge so as not to scuff the wood—and doze. Thing was, no one cared. He was an outstanding ranger, wise beyond his years, and those cat naps normally resulted in an inspiring realization about cases.

There hadn't been any napping this afternoon, but that same look of awareness was apparent in his eyes.

"We appreciated it, sir, but I don't know what's going on."

"It says in both your files that you've been friends since grade school. Is that going to be a problem?"

"No, sir."

"So your loyalty to your best friend isn't going to put him in more danger or trouble?"

"I swore an oath to uphold the—"

"I know what the oath is, Ryder." The major gestured for him to take a chair. Then pointed to the frame hanging above the door. "I look at it every day."

Jesse sat. Attempting to appear as comfortable as possible, still feeling like each of his fingers was popping off that cliff's edge into an abyss. He didn't need to look behind him to know the major's deceased wife had embroidered the motto. "Of course you do, sir."

"I also know that you've had contact with Travis."

"No, sir, I have not. A woman called around two this

afternoon, claiming they were his dog sitter. I wasn't certain the caller was credible."

"You don't think it was the dog sitter. You didn't think that was necessary information to pass along to us?"

"I knew it would be relevant at some point, sir. Before Austin headquarters brought us in on the investigation, I didn't know if it was important or not."

"Skip it. What did she say? You think it was the hairdresser, Kenderly Tyler?" Parker took a plain yellow pencil and threaded it through his fingers.

"I can't be certain, sir. She didn't identify herself. She asked about the dogs. I said they were okay and we hung up. I drove to Austin and brought them back last night. They're with Travis's mom and aunt. Waco PD is watching the house for now."

"He cares about his dogs enough to risk burning a phone, and that's all that was said?" Parker sat forward, leaning on the formidable ancient desk. "This is where you make it or break it, Ryder. You know what I'm implying?"

Jesse knew exactly what his commanding officer asked. Where would his ultimate loyalty lie? If roles were reversed, he knew exactly what his best friend's decision would be.

"I indicated to the woman that it might be better to check on the dogs in three days."

"And that satisfied her? She didn't say anything else?"

"That was it, sir. I figured we'd have a direction by that time." He'd also hoped that Garrison could stay alive and avoid apprehension for that many days.

Parker slapped the desk's surface and grinned ear to ear. "They don't know squat in Austin. Oaks is still unconscious and might need a second surgery. So they're keeping him that way. Whatever the captain had going on wasn't being shared with headquarters. It happens sometimes when we're forced to move fast."

"What do you want me to do, sir?"

"You're to follow my exact orders. Got that? Travis is a smart man. It's clear to me that he wanted to know if it was safe to bring his witness here. Oaks must have a reason not to trust the men he's working with in Austin."

"I came to that same conclusion."

Jesse caught glimpses of men watching the office. The blinds weren't drawn, and anyone could see a calm conversation happening. They'd all be as curious as hell why, and none of them would hear a word. They may be watching through glass, but their major spoke in a low voice that just didn't travel well.

"Then make it safe. The Tenoreno family is a dangerous one. You heard me say the police believe they located Travis using his rental car, which he abandoned near I-35." He scratched his chin, rocking back in the desk chair. "When did they call?"

"My call was after that time frame. She didn't seem panicked. She was hesitating enough that someone may have been feeding her what to say."

"Good to know. If Tenoreno has Travis's name and information, they may go after his family for leverage. Might not care that he's a ranger." Parker stood.

Jesse stood half a second later, uncertain if he were a part of that family threat or if he were to handle it. He chose the latter. "I can arrange a protective detail. He… um…has a sister in the Panhandle. She's a deputy and won't want to be pulled from duty."

"Get it done. We can't give either crime family a way to threaten him further. You drove to Austin and back. You were up all night. I'd send you home for sleep, but need you close. You stay put. Understood? In the building until I say otherwise."

"Yes, sir." Relief went through him that he wasn't suspended. Grounded maybe, but not suspended.

Back at his desk, it took longer than he wanted, but Jesse made arrangements for the Travis family to be moved from Waco and protected. Avery wasn't as easy. He was waiting for verification her fellow officers had located her. It would be harder for the sheriff Avery worked for to keep her under wraps. Jesse suggested that she might be thrown in the Dalhart lockup for her own safety. Boy, he'd love a picture if it happened.

The files were thick on the Tenoreno and Rosco families and piled on the desk opposite his own. Bryce Johnson was the resident expert. Crimes over the past decade could be linked to them, but nothing ever stuck.

The family's representative had told police that Kenderly Tyler was there as Mrs. Tenoreno's hairdresser. In the photos of her escaping on the motorcycle with Garrison, she was wearing silk and sequins. A hairdresser wouldn't have been going to the dinner. He studied the crime scene photos of the two murdered women he'd left visible on his computer screen.

Their deaths were statements. Assassinations. The shooter had made them get to their knees, taken his time to pull the trigger. Maybe told them why. The hairdresser might have heard.

"But who ordered it?" he mumbled out loud.

"That's the million dollar question. Or billions. The families are worth billions." Johnson was neck deep in files. "A legitimate theory is that a new player wants them to take each other out by ordering their wives' deaths. They haven't yet, but a declaration of war might not be far off."

"But why was Garrison there?"

"The Austin PD is just as confused about Travis and Oaks's involvement. We're assuming they were working together. The police are assuming Travis went rogue. They are stretching that whopper as far as they can. I'm wondering if someone needs to drive down there and remind them we're on the same side."

"The media has it that Travis ambushed Oaks. After the first reporter posed it as a hypothetical, the rest began replaying it as an exaggerated fact." Jesse had explained to Garrison's mom and aunt that they couldn't believe anything about the case on television.

"I guess we're holding the information that Travis had a fake ID. Oaks put it in the system himself. That's why it didn't hold up long under scrutiny when Tenoreno's people looked into him." Bryce continued to type on his computer. "Do you think it's suspicious that Travis took a witness back to where he was staying?

"It was his aunt's house. Tells me that Oaks didn't trust someone along the way. Why he bypassed standard operating procedures… He must have needed a new face neither crime family would recognize as the law."

"Logical. It would be easier if we knew if Travis was at the meeting to eavesdrop or to extract." Johnson tapped away on his keyboard. "Things have been rocky with the Tenorenos since their daughter-in-law disappeared. Can't help but wonder if she's in hiding or buried in the desert across the border."

Jesse rolled his pen across his knuckles, imitating the major. He scrolled through the available photos again. The rental car threw him. It was perched across a cement retaining wall separating two parking lots that were different levels.

What the hell chased Garrison over the edge, and

where did he go from there? The image of Garrison joining a body in the desert kicked in Jesse's chest, making it hard to breathe or sit. He scrambled from behind his desk like a rat had scurried under it.

"Man, I need to do something instead of just sitting here staring at pictures. My best friend is out there with a price on his head."

"Working the evidence is doing something, Ryder. We figure this out, we'll nail them." He shut the file and handed it to Jesse. "For good."

"Yeah, but will we be burying the man I consider my brother along with it?"

"You've done what you can to protect them. Now we move forward, find the killer and clear Travis of the bogus charges."

Jesse wasn't one hundred percent certain he could accomplish that as an armchair investigator, but it was better than being suspended. He hoped Garrison wouldn't wait three days to call in. Now that the company was aware of the situation, they'd be there to protect him until his name was cleared.

They just needed to know where he was first.

Chapter Twelve

Kenderly adjusted the curly wig one last time on Garrison's head. He suggested the wig changed him more radically than dyeing his hair, and he was right. She had a scarf covering her hair and huge sunglasses to add to her costume when they went outside.

Both their styles might be a little retro '70s but were absolutely accepted in Austin. The wig changed Garrison's overall appearance. He'd been tall compared to her while she was barefoot, now he was ridiculously lofty.

Their complexions were more like beach lovers, four or five shades darker than they should be if properly applying makeup. It looked so fake to her. She was completely filled with doubts about being able to pull this off. She was bound to totally muck up retrieving the jewelry box.

"Do you really think this is going to work?"

He pointed to the mirror. "No one's going to recognize us. No way. I could pass my twin sister on the street, and she wouldn't know me."

"You have a twin? Seriously? That's so cool."

"Yeah, most people think so. Just imagine not ever celebrating your birthday alone with your friends. Believe me, it's demoralizing when you're an eight-year-old boy and forced to ask girls to your party."

"I bet that's not the case now."

They got to the front door where he kept his hand on the knob, delaying their departure. "I'll admit that Avery is sort of cool. You'll like her. She's nothing like me."

"I'm sure I will." A layer of the unknown disappeared between them. He'd made fun of himself but also shared. Progress, but they were still strangers. "You're sure the key you found in Rose's desk works on the door?"

Kenderly didn't have his confidence that everything would work out perfectly. She shouldn't have allowed him to talk her into trying to find the captain's car. If he touched her again he might just discover she was shaking down to the tennis shoes he'd bought her.

"Yes. I've checked it twice. Remember who to call if something goes wrong or we get separated?"

"Your friend Jesse at Company F in Waco. I'm to tell him I'm Christy, the dog sitter."

"Right. But nothing's going wrong since no one is going to recognize us looking like this."

And the police wouldn't expect two fugitives to return downtown. Or at least she hoped they wouldn't.

Maybe she was more willing to help than she believed. If it was possible to find the jewelry box and discover what Isabella wanted her to have, then she was definitely willing to try.

"You ready?" he asked.

The sincerity of his expression and deep concern in his eyes made her melt. She didn't totally understand the need he had to risk his life to keep a total stranger safe or recover the jewelry box that may or may not have evidence inside. But in that moment she understood the attraction of every fairy tale where a handsome prince rescued the maiden in distress.

"Wait." She latched her free hand on to his arm. "Garrison, I know why I'm taking this risk. But why should you? If you just stay out of sight for a few days, your ranger friends will clear your name. Now, don't laugh. You've told me they will, and I have to believe they will. So it's just a matter of time. Tell me. Explain why we shouldn't stay here and watch television until Rose gets back."

He leaned against the door instead of opening it. "When the murderer showed up at my aunt's house instead of the real videographer, the captain and I had doubts about who we could trust. The Rangers. Sure. It goes without saying that we'd never doubt them. But the others." He shrugged.

"One day you're going to have to explain that loyalty sentiment. I've never experienced it. Who else would have known?"

"Other agencies are involved trying to gather evidence against these two crime families. Local PD to the FBI. It's never been a secret. And somewhere along the line, the Tenoreno organization found a person who could be cracked...or bought. There goes our security. Why am I willing to go after your jewelry box? We don't know who this mole is. What if they breach the team that inventories the car? We can't take a chance that the box might disappear. We'd never know if it's important or not."

"You want to get to it before the people who betrayed you. All right, then. Thanks for explaining this time." She tried to open the door.

Garrison covered her hand with his, but he remained leaning against the thin door. "You don't have to do this if you're too scared."

"It's not that I'm scared as much as..." She lowered her voice to a whisper, almost afraid to admit the truth. "I don't want to mess up. I don't want us to get caught."

He shook his head, dismissing her fear as he pushed a

lock of her hair under the scarf, leaning forward slightly. "You have the most expressive eyes."

Was he about to kiss her? She loved the flutter of anticipation in her tummy and her racing pulse. Would it feel as good as last night? He leaned closer with a mischievous but genuine grin. He used his thumb to smooth her cheek.

"There was a weird spot of makeup," he whispered and continued his descent to drop his lips closer to her ear. "If I kiss you right now, you know we're not going anywhere. So I'm not going to kiss you. Not until I know we have time to finish."

The man was too sexy for words. And too darn practical. He also needed to be taught a very important lesson. He wasn't completely in charge…at least not about when they should kiss.

Kenderly slipped her hand from his, and before he could straighten to his full height, she stroked the back of his neck. His eyes brightened with surprise, and before he could finish arching an eyebrow, she pressed her lips to his.

He might be able to wait, but why should she? The sexual tension would distract her and make concentrating on his instructions impossible.

So she kissed him. His arms wrapped around her waist. His strength brought her chest into his body, her feet lifted from the carpet. Their mouths slashed against each other. Open. Closed. Noses softly bumping as they turned their heads, not caring about anything else.

The flutter in her belly spread across her shoulders and breasts. She paused half a second to look into the blazing fires that were now his eyes. His skin temperature grew. She could feel the heat, or maybe it was her own.

Her feet, snug in the new tennis shoes, floated to the

ground. Her hands drifted down his arms, stopping at the muscles under her fingertips. He was breathing hard and inching away, ready to stop.

So she kissed him again. And he kissed her back. Madly. Hungrily.

She might have touched him first with her lips, but he had total control. His nails gently grazed her scalp as he shoved the scarf from her head. His palms cupped her cheeks as he caressed her lips with one sensuous kiss after another. She untucked his shirt, needing more of his burning flesh under her hands.

"Dammit, you taste good," he said between their lips, continuing their exploration.

"You bought minty toothpaste," she answered between each new sensation.

"Yeah." Then he shook his head as his tongue tasted her again. "No. This is all you." Another taste. "Yep, all you."

No one had ever kissed her like this. Not. Ever.

Garrison kept her next to him, his lips firmly against hers as his knuckle grazed her breastbone. Even through her shirt she felt her skin sizzle with anticipation. The tension she'd felt since last night... Well, there wasn't a measurement she could put to it that would be accurate.

It was so intense, so fast, so...much.

His kisses moved close to her ear and then down the back of her neck where there wasn't any makeup.

"Wait," she panted. "The makeup. You were...you were right."

"About?" He nipped her at the curve where her shoulder met her throat.

"We need to take care of...you know that thing." She hoped he knew because she certainly didn't anymore. He sucked a little on her sensitive skin, and her knees went weak. His arm around her waist secured her next to him.

Take care of what?

He swung his mouth to hers again. She couldn't think…just feel. As quick as the last kiss began, it ended.

GARRISON STAGGERED BACK, catching himself with the door.

He could think enough to reach out and keep Kenderly from crashing in the opposite direction but not much past that. He stiffened his elbow at the last second to keep from bringing her supple body against him. Tempting him again.

Damn, he wanted her. He hurt, he craved her so badly.

At arm's length he was still tempted.

He didn't think she wanted to stop any more than he did. She'd continued to kiss him while she said wait. His lips had taken a different path. Given her a chance. She could have asked him to stop at any point. It would have been easier than forcing his body to back away on its own. He'd warned her that this would happen.

The pull between them was stronger than anything he'd experienced.

But somewhere in the backs of both their minds, they knew they had to put this on hold. The contents of the jewelry box were important. They needed to get to the car before anyone else realized it was there.

Kenderly's breasts rose and fell with her rapid breathing. He could feel her hand shaking in his. Or maybe his was shaking in hers. Didn't matter. He had a job to do, and she had to stick with him. She'd pass out or hyperventilate if she didn't slow her breathing down.

"How's my makeup?" He grinned at her, expecting the same reaction as always. A laugh and a scolding remark.

She took a deep, long breath, throwing her head back a little. Stretching her neck in a way that made him want to forget about retrieving the evidence and dive back into their kiss.

"Sweet, sweet Thelma. Is being flippant your reaction to every situation? Do you feel anything other than your smile splitting your face in half?"

"What about you? Can't you just enjoy the moment? I thought we had a pretty good one, so I smiled. What the hell's wrong with that?" He was lost.

Having avoided women who could potentially make him turn down this road, he'd never traveled to a place where it mattered what someone thought. Laughter and a smile had always worked before. Every situation.

"Nothing. It doesn't matter. Let's just go and get this over with." She covered her face with her hands, then dropped them before spoiling her makeup. "I'm messed up. It's not like we actually care about each other anyway."

Whatever it was, it probably mattered a hell of a lot more than he could figure out. The two of them had crossed so many lines in two days that his sense of direction was fouled up. Lost was a good word for what he was experiencing. Or maybe it was just plain inadequacy.

She pulled her scarf back into place, adjusting it and dabbing the dark black outline of her eyes. He twisted the dead bolt and opened the door a crack, then slammed it shut.

"Hold on a minute."

"What now?" Kenderly tilted her head back to look at him.

Bonehead of a move as it might have been, he stopped himself from bending toward her for another kiss. He stopped the action, but not the desire.

"I, um… I've never been around a woman like you. That's hard to admit. But I picked up on it real fast. So you might give me a break for the learning curve." God, he sounded like a wimp. "I've lost track of what we're really talking about."

She laughed, then reached up and straightened the wig sitting on his head. A curly black mess he'd forgotten all about.

"Then maybe we need to get back on track and take care of business." She placed her hands on her hips, acting proud of her work transforming his looks.

Ridiculous and lost. "Will I be a jerk if we leave now?"

"Not at all," she whispered.

That elusive remark was put on a hook in his mind. He had every intention of finding out what the hell they'd been talking about. Just not at this moment.

Right now, he had to put their lives in danger to see if he could eventually keep her safe.

Chapter Thirteen

The light blue sedan was still on the street where Garrison had parked it late Friday night. The key was in his pocket, and he'd seen Oaks punch in the code to the lockbox where he'd placed the jewelry box. So getting the jewelry box wouldn't be that difficult.

Unless the cops or anyone else following them was waiting for them to come back to it. The police might not know the significance of the car, but the SOB who had shot at them knew they'd left his aunt's house in it.

"Are we supposed to act like we don't know each other?" she asked behind her grande café au lait skinny extra foam.

The name of her coffee made him want to laugh, but he held back, draping his arm around her shoulders instead. "Sure we do. If anyone's watching, they saw us get coffee together and sit together. Yeah, we can talk."

"So the reason we're just not getting into the car and driving away—because that would be much more convenient than riding public transportation—is that someone might be watching the car."

"Right."

"And if they're not, why don't we take it?"

He and Kenderly had grabbed coffee and were sitting on a bench near the parked car. "One or both groups might have attached a tracker. We can't risk it."

"Aw, yes." She sipped. "The old tracking device ploy."

The bench they'd chosen didn't have a cover. His face itched from the sun shining in his eyes.

"We've been here half an hour, and I've barely seen anyone around at all. I feel exposed like this. Can't we just get this done and leave?"

"We agreed—"

"No. You dictated. I'm sitting next to you as a result. This is your decision."

"Whoa there. We're in this together. If you want to leave, then we will. There are better things at the apartment I'd like to…explore." Yeah, he looked her body over. Deliberately. Slowly. He was attempting to take her mind off their situation. He might have, but he also got a look that needed no interpretation.

"Please, take me seriously."

A couple of minutes later, a guy who looked like a regular Joe passed with his hands in his pockets. A couple left the bar across the street. The bar didn't seem open, so they might have worked there.

Little things caught his attention. Like Kenderly's shoes already had scuff marks on them. He'd noted that the jeans he'd purchased fit her, which meant the underwear worked, too. For some reason he'd never had a problem guessing a woman's size.

"I am so glad it's not hot out here. I feel like my face would melt off." She fanned her cheeks like a beauty queen.

"I feel the same way. So I can joke now?"

"I don't think you could stop if someone were sticking bamboo shoots under your nails."

"I think that's where I'd draw the line." Garrison's fingers curled into fists as he thought about what it might feel like. "I bet it's hard to laugh when you're screaming. Although, it might give the interrogators a shock if I did."

"I bet…" The words rolled around while she turned to him with a grin. "I bet you could pull that off. Laughing is the first place you go. Is there anything you don't laugh at?"

"There would have to be incentive to stop."

"I bet you couldn't do it."

"Do what exactly?" Although he turned his face slightly to her, movement in the bar window caught most of his attention. A guy wearing a ball cap low over his eyes kept darting close to the glass.

"I bet you can't go two hours without attempting to charm someone."

Easy as pie. There was no one around to charm. Except Kenderly. "What do I get when I win?"

"You mean when I win. Anything you want, no questions asked."

"I can think of quite a few things. Foot massage. Back massage. Foot massage again."

"Whatever you want for the rest of the day."

"It's a bet."

Their plan was to sit for an hour and observe the car. Sip coffee and take a look to see if anyone was watching the sedan. He could handle not smiling, or charming people. Right?

Laughter didn't equal charmer, did it? Was it cheating on the bet if he asked her? Aw, hell. He had to forget about it and concentrate.

If he were here as a ranger, he would have had backup to send into the bar and check out who seemed to be watching them. Or not watching them. He couldn't make a determination.

"I might…" he began, but the bar door opened, and the guy he'd noticed meandered slowly out, heading in the opposite direction. He staggered a bit from side to side. So maybe they'd both been watching for cops.

About to nudge Kenderly and share a staggering story of his own, he stopped himself. Would that be charming? Wait a second. Was everything he said really that predictable? Damn, it was going to be a long two hours until this bet was over.

Coffee gone, more tense than they'd been at the apartment before she kissed him—it was time to make a move. "You ready? Remember what we're going to do?"

"Sweet Thelma, it's about time. This has been the longest hour of my life. And, yes, I remember." She sprang from the bench, running straight to the sedan.

He ran after her. "Wait. Honey. I didn't mean it," he shouted and waved his arms.

She spun around, and the few contents she had in her borrowed purse fell to the street, rolling under the car, bouncing off the curb. He ran to her side. Better than they'd planned.

"Let me help." He crawled under the car, snagging the lipstick, but looking for anything unusual.

No one was around. No one rushed from a hiding place. No one paid them any attention.

Kenderly was on her knees, gathering some pennies, but looking at him. He nodded. By the time he was out from under the sedan, she had the car unlocked and was sitting in the passenger seat. He sat behind the wheel, and seconds later they were around the corner.

Another corner. He knew exactly where he wanted to go. They'd planned it. He drove straight to a parking garage, third floor, throwing the car into P in the back corner. He popped the trunk, and they were out the doors. At the trunk he keyed the entry code to the gun lockbox, and there was the case. Kenderly put it in her purse and slung the strap around her neck. She was turning to leave when he picked up the captain's Glock and extra magazine. He shoved the weapon into his belt and covered it with his shirt.

The whole episode took four or five minutes. Tops. It didn't look like they'd been followed, but he couldn't be certain. As Kenderly was about to fly through the outside door, he yanked her behind him.

"We walk to the bus stop. Very quickly, but we walk." He checked his watch. "It still has a couple of minutes. When I see it, we cross the street."

Kenderly bent and rested her hands on her knees, catching her breath. "I can see why you like this work."

"Huh?"

"Being undercover, all these getaways. They're addictive."

He took her hand when the bus stopped at the light on the corner. "Here we go."

"All right." She casually licked her bottom lip, still bright red from the garish lipstick.

He didn't care. He kissed her quick on the mouth, checked the street again—for whom, he didn't know—and pressed the bar to open the door. Her "ha" echoed behind them as they got on the bus.

A block later he was still looking around to see if they'd been followed.

"Oh, wow. That was awesome." Kenderly adjusted the scarf and pushed her sunglasses higher on her nose. "If someone wasn't trying to kill me," she whispered, "this would just be amazing. Don't you love it?"

"No. It's dangerous."

"Come on. Even just the tiniest bit?" She slapped his knee.

"I haven't had time to think about it. We've been thrown a lot of surprises."

"Is it always like this?"

"I wouldn't know."

"What do you mean?" she asked with a curious face that was cute even with the heavy makeup.

"I mean that this might, sort of be…like my first…" He nodded his head, hoping she'd catch on without him having to admit it out loud.

"What? Ooohhh. Really? You mean I'm your first?" she asked a little louder.

Heads turned. An older gentleman with a cane winked. A mom moved to the front with her child.

"No. Wait. That's not what I—you don't understand." He wanted to set the conversation straight with the passengers, but he couldn't.

"You don't have to explain yourself, young man," a white-haired lady said two rows back. "It takes courage to wait for anything in this day and age."

"Yes, ma'am. I mean, you misunderstood. She's not talking about sex."

"Oh my, is that what she meant?" The older woman feigned shock.

"You're just giving me a hard time." He smiled and did what came naturally…he took a few minutes of harmless flirtation to catch his breath and keep an eye on traffic behind the bus.

The woman—named Frankie—got off, and he turned back in his seat. Kenderly had an all-knowing grin.

"What?"

"I win."

Damn. He'd lost the bet. No question. For the rest of the day, he was hers to command. At least he was armed.

KENDERLY FELT LIKE a spy in a movie. Their plan had worked. Completely. Wonderfully. They had the jewelry box. And she'd won the bet. She could ask Garrison to do everything for the rest of the day.

After running in shoes that were a little too big, maybe she would ask for the foot massage he'd suggested. It would serve him right if she did. Actually, the idea of a full body massage wasn't so lame at all. As soon as they found out what was inside the case. She patted the rectangle safely in Rose's purse as they climbed the stairs to the apartment.

"Stay here." Garrison pointed to a step halfway up the last flight.

She did as she was told while he entered the apartment, checked things out and waved at her to come inside. He was looking through a crack in the shade when she turned the dead bolt into place.

"Still no sign of the bad guys?"

"Something is very wrong or we're very lucky."

"I'm going with lucky. Come on." She patted the seat next to her on the couch. "Do we need to document this or anything? Forget that I asked that. I'm not waiting."

The jewelry box sat in her lap. She couldn't be patient. Garrison stood in front of her, almost at attention. She hesitated and he gave a nod. She closed her eyes—either wishing or praying—and flipped open the lid.

"We need a computer."

She opened her eyes and found a flash drive. "Nothing else?"

"This is good news. That might be a money trail. Mind

if I keep this?" Without waiting on a response, he snatched it from the box. "Does your friend have a laptop?"

"If she does, which isn't likely, she probably took it with her. I haven't seen one here."

He wandered around the room. She had no clue what he expected to find now. He'd already been through the apartment and knew what was in every corner. He tossed the flash drive in the air, catching it like a baseball. "Looks like we have to wait to find out what's on this thing."

"We could go somewhere…"

"We risked a lot to get this today. I'm not putting you in danger like that again. Nope, we wait. We're safe here and should stick it out until we hear from Jesse."

"So we're stuck here for two more days, then we call Waco? Meanwhile, every person we know believes we're wanted for murder."

"Better that than in the hands of Tenoreno because we're too curious about what's on this thing." He tossed the flash drive, caught it and shoved it in his pocket. "The tech crew would remind me that it's better for them to take the first look at it anyway. But, yeah, I'm curious, and my body's pumped from outrunning them earlier. It's going to be hard to sit still for two days."

"It's sort of a letdown after finding it." She toed off her shoes and remembered the heavy makeup. "I'm going to get this stuff off my face. Be right back."

When she had finished washing her face, Garrison was in the kitchen. Wig on the table, button shirt on the back of the chair, face being scrubbed in the sink. She just stood there. Staring. So glad to be simply watching and not running from yet another man wielding a gun.

"Hey, you lost the bet." She handed him the dish towel to dry his face.

"I sure did," he mumbled behind the towel. "Ready to eat? As my first command, I'll make dinner."

"I've given it great consideration, you know."

"You have?"

"Yes. I really think I need that back massage you offered."

"That wasn't an offer, sweetheart. It was a request." He opened the freezer, taking a box down before it really registered that dinner would be from a frozen package.

"It was a good idea. I'm still stiff from bouncing on the back of your motorcycle."

"I'll put a pizza in the oven, and you get out of your shirt and pants."

"What?" She wasn't certain he heard her since he kept talking, issuing instructions.

"Grab that sheet you used last night. I think I saw some lotion on the dresser." He quirked an eyebrow in her direction while folding the pizza box to fit the trash can. "Do you expect me to massage you through your clothes?"

"Well, yeah. I thought you'd rub my shoulders a while."

"Trust me." He winked. "This'll be great."

She didn't feel in charge while grabbing the lotion, sheet and a towel. But before marching back into the living room and telling Ranger Travis a thing or two about flipping the tables…she changed clothes, borrowing a workout top and yoga pants from Rose.

Much more confident, she gathered the items and was ready to put Garrison in his place. He wouldn't be getting her out of her clothes unless she decided. And at the moment she hadn't decided.

Chapter Fourteen

The window blinds swung into the wall as Garrison turned to face her and dropped them, once again caught keeping watch over the parking lot. He tilted his head sideways and quirked a brow as if he knew something she didn't. Did he?

"Is this a problem?" She pointed to her borrowed outfit.

"Not for me. Lotion or oil?" His hands each held a bottle. "I found some on the counter."

The coffee table was pushed out of the way, now in front of the door. The couch cushions were on the carpet. He stood next to them ready to start. Her body tingled a little—okay, a lot—imagining his hands rubbing the kinks from her neck. "I brought sheets, so...um...oil."

"I'm at your service." He bowed and dropped to his knees, hiding his face. So if he was laughing at her, she couldn't tell. Or maybe not laughing, but absolutely commanding with his presence.

Why did she no longer think any of this had been her idea? She was so determined back in the bedroom that she could bring him down a peg or two. She wanted a massage. Her body ached and needed to relax after the rush from earlier.

Or did she need something more?

Could she allow his hands to touch her body and still keep him at a distance? Just how did that work with a heart?

It hit her like a sledgehammer to the side of her head. She could fall in love with Garrison Travis. Easily fall in love with everything about him. Of course he'd rescued her numerous times, and the adrenaline high probably had something to do with it, but she actually *liked* him.

If the average date was three hours, and they'd already spent forty-eight together… That would be…sixteen dates. Maybe it wasn't unrealistic to think she could be halfway in love with him already.

Of all the things she knew she'd have to give up in order to stay alive…her job, her friends, a career she was hopeful about. He would be the hardest.

When she'd walked into the room, she'd been uncertain of Garrison, uncertain that she could keep him in line. Why did she really want to?

"We going to do this?" he asked.

"You know what? This isn't going to make any sense to you at all." She spread the sheet open, concentrating on how it drifted across the cushions. It hid her from his view for a second. Long enough for the outline of a plan to set itself in her mind. His curious eyes locked with hers above the floating white cotton.

Garrison didn't need to say a word. He drew his breath in deep, straightened his shoulders so his chest stuck out a bit more. She could see that he knew what she was about to propose. His eyes asked exactly what had flashed through her mind. The ultimate question…was she certain?

She was. Sixteen dates or forty-eight hours hiding from an assassin. It didn't make any difference. She wanted this funny, slightly arrogant, very charming man.

But more than that, she needed to be wrapped in his arms and feel safe.

Not abandoned.

She swallowed hard and stretched her fingers. "I've never managed to pop my knuckles like other people."

He cracked his own and they laughed, but he remained silent. It left the decision with her. He stayed on his knees. She joined him but on the opposite side of the cushions.

"Lay down on your stomach, please."

He did without any hesitation.

"I should have said to pull off—"

His shirt quickly went over his head and landed near the wall.

Kenderly popped the cap and squeezed a generous amount of oil in her hands. She'd never given a man a massage—or anyone else, for that matter. Nothing more than using her nails on a customer's scalp during a hair wash.

The oil felt cool, so she rubbed her palms together before touching them to Garrison's shoulders. The muscles tensed and relaxed under her fingertips. She kneaded across the corded sinew, experiencing the restrained power within her touch. She formed a fist and twisted it gently down his spine, adding oil and keeping his skin shiny.

Garrison's arms were stretched out in front of him, crossed at his wrists. She tugged a little, massaging his upper muscles all the way to his fingers. She repeated the same with his other arm, then began his back again. If the short moans and sighs were an indication, she was catching on to the art quickly.

All the while, he kept silent, allowing her to guide their encounter any direction she wanted. She worked her way to his waist. He was still wearing his jeans and boots.

"Why were you so scared to be alone last night, Kenderly?"

"I… I just panicked for a minute."

"A minute?" he asked in a muffled sort of voice.

She continued to knead his tight shoulders. The muscles relaxed but not the feel of his strength. She was safe, and it was a wonderful, heady sensation. "I was abandoned when I was a child."

"How old were you?"

"Close to seven. At least I think I was. I had it in my head that it was my birthday."

"You didn't know for sure?"

"Not really. I couldn't read. All I had was a balloon and my sweater."

He lifted a shoulder attempting to sit up, but she pushed him back to the sheet. "Did they find your parents?"

"I knew that I'd been staying with my aunt Soppie for a couple of days. At least someone who let me call them aunt Soppie. The police searched the mall, but all they could really do was wait for someone to report me missing."

"And no one ever did?"

She didn't hear pity in Garrison's reaction so she plunged forward, with more oil on her hands. "No one. I went into foster care. There are horror stories out there, but mine's not bad. I was placed with a genuinely loving couple. Georgia died about three years ago. Wiley died shortly after I went to live with them."

Tired of leaning awkwardly over him to reach his far side, she straddled his jeans-covered thighs.

"You…um…consider yourself lucky, then?" he asked with a hitch in his voice.

"How lucky is a person who knows nothing about their parentage or where they came from? Or even what day their real birthday is?" She sat straight, arching her back in a stretch, then she pressed her palms into his flesh again. "But, yes, Georgia was nice to me. She didn't have any children of her own and didn't foster anyone else. There wasn't any jealousy or fighting. I mainly stayed to myself."

The cords in his muscles rolled under her fingers like cords in a thick rope.

"Where was this?"

"A little town near the Gulf called Victoria. Enough about me." She hadn't predicted this turn in the conversation. It wasn't exactly the sexy foreplay she'd envisioned.

"I like hearing about you."

She needed to forget her lonely past and now lonely future. Instead, she needed to celebrate the moment with Garrison.

KENDERLY'S RHYTHM AND deep massage changed as her nails barely scraped the skin on Garrison's back and shifted to his sides. Circle after circle got lower and lower—closer to his abs and sometimes dashing under his belt.

Being turned on seemed like a trickling creek compared to the rushing white water racing through his veins.

He'd watched the clock on the stereo slowly tick by. He gulped, trying to swallow with his dry throat. He wanted to flip over and give Kenderly the same torturous treatment she'd given him for the past half hour.

As good as her massage felt, he was sweating bullets from the sensuous overtures. There wasn't any mistake about where she wanted this to go.

His only question was when? She'd won the bet. She was commanding him for the rest of the day. He was close to taking the decision out of her hands.

"Think you could face me?"

She made no effort to move from where she sat on his thighs, so he didn't hesitate. He twisted, and she had enough weight on her knees that he flipped around, staying under her.

A little more oil on her palms, and his chest was covered…and on fire.

The thought of ripping her skimpy clothes from her body and rubbing their bare skin across each other entered his mind more than once. More like every other heartbeat. His hands gripped her hips, trying to maintain his sanity as she rocked across his manhood.

"Look at me," she whispered.

He forced his eyes open when she stopped massaging his chest. She took a lone fingernail and parted his chest hair from his neck to his navel. He thought he might bruise her. His grip was tight on her slender hips as she unbuckled his belt and reversed his jeans zipper. He bit his lip to stop from shouting.

But complete relief wasn't to be his. She took his hands in hers and guided them to her waist, then up to her firm rib cage.

He gave her the same feathery treatment. His thumbs brushed across her nipples, which fought to peak through the workout bra. She closed her eyes and threw back her head as she'd done several times over the past two days. This time he didn't hesitate. He dove forward, bending her backward just far enough to catch the delicate white of her throat with his lips. He limited his kisses to her collarbone.

Restraint. Patience. Two of his evils, not virtues.

Instead of helping himself to the delights of her swelling breasts like a man needing a drink in the desert, he held her closer by wrapping his arms around her completely. There was no hiding his desire. She still sat in his lap and could feel his erection.

The yoga pants did nothing to hide the shape of her body as it molded around him. If it weren't for the jeans, he would have been inside of her—that's how badly he wanted her.

Jeans were a good thing, or he wouldn't be able to wait for her to make the decision about what came next.

Aw, hell. He couldn't wait.

He let his lips give up their hard-won territory of her magnificent skin to make his move. He was one move away from setting her to the side and shucking the barriers between them when she smoothed one cheek with her palm.

Then Kenderly took his face between her hands and kissed him. She opened her mouth, inviting his tongue deep inside as their lips devoured each other, exploring the intimate warmth.

No explanations or reasoning. If they talked he might try to convince her it wasn't right, convincing himself again that it shouldn't happen. And making love to Kenderly—right or wrong—was going to happen without regrets.

His hands skimmed her sides and tugged at the bottom of her workout bra while her fingers clung to the back of his neck. He could have left it hanging around her neck when the perfect globes were released. Kenderly helped him out by pulling it off over her head while he leaned back against the pillows and stared.

Had he ever seen breasts before? He had, but not like these. Kenderly's were perfectly round with a dusky pink nipple. He barely outlined each one, cupping the undersides gently, extracting a deep moan as his thumb brushed across the center.

She shivered and he noticed. He watched each of her

reactions, her quick drawn breath when he tweaked her nipple to attention. The surprise as her eyes opened wide when his knuckle grazed her most intimate place, still resting near his.

"Let's move to the bed."

"Shhh." She leaned forward, laying her finger across his lips, dusting his abs with her breasts. "I won the bet, remember? I get to decide what happens when."

Stretching out against his body, she caught his hand intimately between them. He took care of the rest until she gasped with relief and her body calmed on top of him.

He stayed put. Unable to jeopardize what should come next. She was in command, after all, and might try to teach him a lesson.

"Now."

Barely a whisper or just the outline of the word with her lips. He didn't care if it was his imagination. He couldn't wait any longer and grabbed her waist, flipping their positions.

He supported them with one arm so he wouldn't crash down on her with all his weight, until he realized they still had clothes on. Her hands shoved at his jeans at the same time he tried to kick free of his boots. He thought he'd been smart keeping them on earlier. A layer of protection to keep from making love to her.

Kenderly was like no other woman. She tugged at the yoga pants. He helped.

Lying next to each other as intimate as two people could be, he'd learned at least one lesson. He couldn't keep his hands off her.

And drove into her body, which was completely ready for him. He doubted he'd ever be able to be hands-off with her. And he didn't want to be. That was the biggest surprise of all.

THE WONDERFUL SENSATION surrounded her completely. She closed her eyes and was consumed, completely safe. Each intimate stroke, each soft touch, each gentle teasing kiss kept the illusion that no one could hurt her again.

Garrison explored her everywhere. The light hint of the back of his hand flickered across her ribs. The slight graze of his scruff of a beard across her breast. Fluttering awareness overcame any hesitation she might have had that this was the right thing to do.

Her body and mind needed this release.

Their bodies fit tightly together. Garrison didn't leave any part of her untouched. The rhythm might be as old as the world, but newer than fresh raindrops for them. They rocked and strained, pushing themselves to their limits and enjoying every second of it.

Just when she didn't think she could take another wondrous second, she exploded like a string of firecrackers. The climax shattered her into fragments, and Garrison was there, holding her, pulling her back together. He kept her safe so she could do the same for him moments later when he reached his own pinnacle.

Chest pounding, gulping air through his mouth, eyes rolling slightly back in his head...he collapsed on top of her. She loved it. Every second of it. She ran her fingers through his sandy hair, super glad they hadn't dyed it black. She brushed a few beads of sweat from his brow with her finger.

She pulled another sheet over them and rested her head in the crook of his shoulder. She was completely content and refusing to think about men trying to kill them. "I hardly know anything about you."

"Sure you do. No one except Jesse knows my aunt's address. Hey, you've even met my dogs." He stroked her arm, then drew circles over her skin.

The simple gesture sent shivers down her spine. "Come on, Garrison. Spill something. Any little secrets hidden in there?" She tapped his forehead, then smoothed his wrinkled brow.

"I'm an open book."

"That's hard to believe." *Then again.* "Maybe you do believe that. So I'll just ask what I want to know. How did you get your name? Garrison is like a fort, right?"

"It's also a couple of famous Texas Rangers. Including one of the original commanders. My dad was a big history buff. I can't tell you how many times he stopped by the museum near our house." He continued to drag his fingertips across her hot body.

Kenderly wasn't certain if the gesture was calculated to turn her on again or if he was just comfortable with her. "And you grew up to be one? That's awesome. What's his name, your dad, I mean."

"William," he whispered. "He was shot and killed in the line of duty when I was fourteen."

"I'm sorry, I didn't mean to pry or bring up bad memories."

"No bad memories there. Besides, it was a long time ago. He worked with the Texas DPS. One day, making a routine speeding stop, he was shot. That's about all I know. About all that anyone knows. The shooter was never caught. Dad radioed dispatch, left his vehicle, and the next thing is a 911 call from a driver who saw him fall to the ground."

"That must drive you crazy. Not knowing why..." She'd thought about why she'd been abandoned at the mall. "Georgia always told me to imagine the good reasons. That my biological mother must have wanted a better life for me. I got it, but others don't."

"It was my dad's dream to become a Texas Ranger,

you know?" His hand wrapped around her upper arm. "After he died, I swore I'd do this for him. I sort of hauled Jesse right along with me. Everything clicked. It all made sense."

"That's a nice way to honor your father."

"Hey, it's something I wanted, too. My mom...not so much. She hates that I went into law enforcement."

"Have you been in trouble to make her worry? Good grief, I bet she's scared for you now. There's no way she hasn't seen the reports about us on TV, and I know you haven't called her."

"She knows I'm safe. Jesse would have taken care of things." He shifted to his side, head resting on his elbow now.

"I hope she does know. It must be crazy being worried about you all the time. I've only been a part of your life for a couple of days, and I can already see that."

The sheet drifted lower when Garrison moved to his side. When it continued to glide down to her hip, his hand floated across her bare skin.

Kenderly's body was hungry for his touch. There were so many emotions running through her. It was a constant mixture of excitement from their attraction and the fright of hiding. But what girl wouldn't want to be in the arms of a man protecting her? This adventure was surreal.

Something she'd never imagined would happen to her. And was still a mystery about how it would end.

"What's your next command, sweetheart?"

More commands? He was hers for the day. His skilled hand brushed her breast. The answer might have been hers to decide, but the hints of what he wanted were very plain.

"Well, at the Best Little Hair House in Texas where I work, we have a saying."

"Wait a minute." He paused, laughing under his breath and rolling on to his back. He pulled her on top of him, fitting his hands onto her waist. "You actually work at a place called the Best Little *Hair* House?"

"As I was saying." She swatted at his wandering hands. "Our policy is lather, rinse…repeat."

"Lather, rinse, repeat? I don't get—oh, repeat? That's your command?"

"That's…right." She smiled wide enough that Garrison Travis would be proud of her.

His hands cupped both her breasts, and she began the ascent to heaven again.

"If it's company policy…"

Chapter Fifteen

Garrison propped the blinds open just enough that he could see through them sitting on the corner of the couch. The parking lot was silent. No sign of the dog walker. The lamp pole was collecting some crickets at its base. He dug into his front pocket and snagged the flash drive, turning it over and sideways.

A regular flash drive. Nothing special. It could be bought at any checkout and probably had been. But Isabella Tenoreno wouldn't have made the purchase. Other people did her shopping.

"If you keep rubbing that thing like Aladdin's lamp, will it give up its secrets? Or maybe yours?" Kenderly leaned against the wall separating the room from the kitchen. She wore his T-shirt and the underwear he'd bought her. "Don't you still need a computer?"

Long blond hair—scratch that. Her hair was still every shade of blond he'd ever seen. Every time she turned her head, he saw a new color. It fascinated him. He'd never been fascinated by hair before.

He needed to concentrate on something—anything— or he'd take her back to bed. "It's hard to believe we have one crucial clue, and it has to be tucked away instead of turned over to clear our names." Garrison stuffed the drive back in his pocket.

Going back to bed might not be a bad idea. They were supposed to lie low another day before calling Jesse back. Then what?

"Whatever's on that drive started this entire mess. Didn't it?" She moved to sit in the middle of the couch.

Until he knew for certain, all he had was a theory—a strong theory—but nothing more than that. "I don't know, Kenderly." He slid off the arm to a spot next to her.

"Two women have been executed for no apparent reason. It had to be planned. Not random. So one of their husbands has to be responsible."

He pulled her into his arms, tucking her head under his chin, wanting to comfort her. It surprised him as much as the conversation. He couldn't have pictured this two days ago. "Who else would risk the wrath of the two biggest crime families in Texas?"

"No one? What good came out of killing them? What purpose did it serve?"

"Damn, I want a computer to find out what's on this thing."

She pulled back. "I know we're supposed to stay hidden, but I can't stand not knowing what's there. It's driving me crazy. What about the library?"

"What about it?"

"Garrison, we could read what's on the flash drive at the library's computer. Who would know?" She spread her fingers across his chest. "Even if plugging it into a computer activated a tracer or something, we could be gone before they find us."

He wanted to kiss her and twirl her around the room. It would let them know what they were dealing with. "That's right. Who would know?"

"Let's get dressed."

"Right after—"

He swooped in and let his lips have their way, putting his brain on hold.

GARRISON FOLLOWED KENDERLY into the library, keeping three or four people between them. He was wearing the curly black wig again, but this time without the heavy makeup. He didn't have the stamina to wash it off again. He'd already asked how women do that to themselves on a daily basis.

Kenderly had just laughed at him and kept getting dressed.

The plan was to sit next to each other at the library's computer center. She took a seat, and he had to wander for another ten minutes before the one next to her opened up. He glanced at her screen as he passed behind her. She was reading articles about the murders and about them as suspects.

"Don't push your luck," he whispered.

"The library will close in ten minutes. Please, bring your articles to the checkout." The voice through the speaker did one thing for them. It cleared out the area as the other patrons closed their notebooks and signed off.

Garrison plugged the flash drive into the slot. He was taking a huge risk by coming to the library and exposing them. Opening the files was just as risky. He clicked on the buttons, Kenderly moved to his side.

Several numbered files. Only one had a name. He double clicked "Kenderly."

My dear Kenderly,
Thank you for being such a wonderful friend to me and Trinity. I am sorry we won't meet again, but leaving in secret is the only way we can escape.

We decided that we want our freedom. We can no longer live this life knowing the horrible things about our husbands that we do. This is why we are leaving, never to return, and no one must know where we are.

Please, deliver the information from the files to the authorities. There is a list of information I copied from my husband's computer. We do not know who you can trust, but every name in that file has accepted bribe money. Many others have received money from our families to do illegal things. Some files involve the Roscos, but most are about Paul. The files should be enough to prosecute my husband for his sins.

We trust you to know what's right and to find someone to help you. Because, sweet girl, our husbands will come after you. Being the last person outside our home that we spoke with, they will suspect that you helped.

It is very important that you take the files to the police and get protection for yourself. I am begging your forgiveness for putting you in this situation.
Isabella

HE PROBABLY SHOULDN'T HAVE, but he opened one of the numbered files. Three names down, there was an easy one to recognize, then another…and another. He closed the file, stuck the drive deep in his pocket, grabbed Kenderly's hand and practically yanked her from the small study room. They wove their way through the library until Kenderly pulled her arm from his grasp.

Kenderly wiped her eyes. "Isabella's note had been so hopeful of a new life. Oh, God." She covered her mouth.

Of course she was upset. She hid her crying from

being heard by library patrons leaving with their books and videos. He pulled her closer, tucked under his arm.

"Come on, let's get out of here." Garrison's heart raced. This was exactly what they needed. "No reason to wait. We need to get to Waco. Pronto."

He didn't think that she knew what they'd just stumbled on. Hell, he didn't know much. Isabella Tenoreno hadn't just put together a list of names. She'd copied ledgers.

"What did you see?"

"This flash drive is the jackpot of jackpots for a prosecutor. A lot of important names are on the list."

They were in way over their heads. This information couldn't sit in his pocket. They couldn't take a chance that these files never made it to someone legit who could use it in court.

"How are we going to get to Waco?"

"Good question. We have about six bucks left."

"Should we just call your friend Jesse? Couldn't someone from Austin pick us up? We could go back and email it."

Lights at the back of the room flipped on and off. They had timed their visit perfectly in case the flash drive triggered some type of trace.

"I can't call just anybody."

"Why not? You've called Jesse before. Even if your friend can't help, he could find someone who can."

"If we wait around," he whispered, "Tenoreno's people will find us. I'll be honest with you, Kenderly. We've underestimated this crime family's reach. I wouldn't put it past them to be listening to conversations in and out of Company F. It's probably one of the reasons Oaks set up this operation limiting the people who knew. We need to get to my company commander. Major Parker will know how to handle things."

"And your certain his name isn't on the list?"

He nodded and grinned. For a hairdresser, Kenderly Tyler was fast catching on to the concept of trust no one. "I don't have any doubts about Parker. You ready?"

"I'm okay now. You don't have to squeeze so tight." She wiped another tear and turned her face toward him.

He gave her a quick kiss and knew exactly what they needed. "The quickest way to get this in Parker's hands is for us to get to Waco. We need transportation and my motorcycle will still be at my aunt's house. The police had no reason to confiscate it. We can take the bus nearby."

"What if they're watching?"

"I can sneak in the back. My bike will fit through the door on the side of the garage. You can stay about twelve blocks away. There's a supermarket by the bus stop."

"Garrison?" She was squeezing his hand this time. "I'm really afraid. Are you sure this is the right thing?"

"We don't have a choice," he whispered.

The bus was about two blocks away. He took a couple of steps, but she stopped dead in her tracks.

"What did you see when you opened that file? There were names, but what frightened you?"

He smiled. Yeah, this time it was calculated. She'd called him on it countless times in the past three days. This time she needed him to charm her. He needed her to believe that everything would be okay.

"Motive. Proof. Enough to clear our names, get you some real protection at a safe house and prosecute Paul Tenoreno and a lot of other people."

"How on earth did you ever think you were a good liar?" She laughed and pulled him forward. "Whatever is on that list and has you this motivated scares the living daylights out of me. I trust you, Garrison. You stay confident and cocky. It makes me feel safer."

She wouldn't feel safe at all if she knew he'd read a whole lot of dollar signs next to the name of the deputy first assistant attorney general of Texas. Walking into a police station was a death sentence for them.

Trust no one else. No police. No state trooper. No elected official. He hated to add Rangers headquarters to the list, but he did. He could trust two people with this information. Two rangers.

The entire bus ride had him looking over his shoulder, watching to see if any cars were trailing them. But no one was there. If the Texas mafia knew where they were, they wouldn't be riding on a city bus.

"I'll meet you in the fruit section in one hour. Got it?" He reluctantly left Kenderly at the store next to the market. He looked backward one time, saw the fear in her eyes and ran the blocks to the house, cutting through a few yards without back fences.

He was breathing hard and watched the light blue house belonging to his aunt. He'd told everybody he was staying here to get the yard ready for the next college student. The bushes were grown up, and he hadn't realized just how difficult it was to see into the yard or along the side of the house.

No cars parked on the street with an unknown person sitting there. No one walking the sidewalk. It was a quiet Sunday evening. Quiet, and the coast seemed clear for stealing his motorcycle from a crime scene.

The yellow tape was across the doors to the bullet-ridden house and garage. He hopped over the back fence and took his keys out. No alarms sounded. No police lights flashed. Maybe he was in the clear. Maybe something would go right, and he could get Kenderly to safety.

Darkness surrounded him. He let his eyes adjust, and the open door to the yard let in enough light to see. That feeling of something wrong crept up the back of his neck. He knew it before he saw it.

The beam was a motion detector. He'd seen a couple before. The police wouldn't have these resources. One guess who did. The murdering son of a bitch was as smart as he was big. He was probably nearby. Probably had a tracer on the bike. Would be on him as soon as he turned the corner.

He had to think. If it was just him, he'd face this guy without worrying about the consequences. But it wasn't him. The only thing on his mind was Kenderly. Her beautiful face lying lifeless like Isabella and Trinity made bile rise in his throat.

She'd be waiting on him. Pretending to look at veggies and fruit. Where would she go if he didn't get back to her?

"Dammit!" He fished the flash drive from deep in his pocket. He had to hide it. Had to keep it safe as much or more than either of them.

Aunt Brenda had cases of water stacked in the back. He slit the top plastic and emptied a bottle from the middle. It was a good hiding place, but he needed a plastic bag to keep the drive dry.

Drawers. Garden supplies. Plastic wrap.

The drive was secure as he switched the top case of water to the middle. If they were caught he'd know where it was. Staying alive to tell someone was his next goal.

Next split decision. Pick up Kenderly before she freaked and called the police. If the deputy first assistant AG was on the take, then the responding officers would be, too.

The sound of squealing tires got his attention. He straddled his bike, started the engine and pushed the door opener. The drive was clear. He had twenty feet of drive-way to clear before he could cut across the front lawn.

He ducked his head even with the bike handles, not waiting for the door to open completely. Headlights on the street. Five feet till the lawn. He barely heard the gun-fire before he fishtailed into the grass. He felt the second shot rip through his arm as he zigzagged into the street. The handgun at his back was useless. He couldn't fire. He needed both hands and was losing a bit of strength in his left. He had to shake this guy.

The yards without fences!

It would be tough but worth it.

After the first yard taken, he could at least drive in a straight line in the alley. If he'd been staking the scene, he would have placed a tracking device on his bike. If they had, he'd cross that giant obstacle when he got to the store. Find the device or ditch the motorcycle after all.

Second yard and back on the street. He blasted through the stop sign. Gunned the bike hoping this street would be as deserted as the rest. He passed the street for the store, seeing if he was followed. High beam headlights turned behind him. He watched for another house with-out a fence.

Took the turn. Back in the alley he darted forward, then spun to a stop and U-turned back to the same house. That maneuver might gain him an extra minute. He went back through the yard, passed somebody coming out the back door shaking his fist, turned right and hit the yard of another fenceless house in the direction of the store.

No sign of the murderer's car. He circled the block.

Two more streets, and he was in the shopping center. He parked across the street, giving his bike the once-over and locating the tracker. He'd seen enough movies to know he needed to keep it moving, so the piece of slime following him would be following someone else.

Spinning through the parking lot, he tossed the device into the back end of a pickup heading the opposite direction. He glanced at his watch. Late and light-headed, he sped to the back entrance of the market. There wasn't a way to hide the red stain on his arm, or the trail of blood running down it.

Might be a graze, but it still burned and bled like the devil. He needed his shirt, but not the bottom of it. He pulled it over his head, his left arm demanding a little more care now that he was off the bike and thinking about it.

Damn, the wound stung. Throbbed. Ached.

He ripped at the seam with his teeth. He was either weak from the shock of being shot, or T-shirts weren't as easy to rip apart as on TV. He found a nail close to the trash and finally got a strip of cotton. He tied it around his arm after wiping at the blood. Stained looked a lot better than dripping.

Then he ran—not as fast as he had after dropping his witness off—but he ran.

Veggies. Nothing visible from the front of the store, so he pushed his feet to the left. He darted in between carts and old gray-haired ladies begging forgiveness as she set them from his path. A stack of potatoes came into view. Lettuce, tomatoes, onions, but no Kenderly.

Quickly searching each row, he ran the back aisle of the store again. Swallowing the fear that threatened to stop him.

Then he saw her.

Grocery cart overflowing. Head down reading the label on a can of something. She put it back on the shelf and saw him. He looked past her to the opposite end.

The murderer was steps behind her.

"Run!" he shouted and pulled Oaks's weapon from his waist. He couldn't pull the trigger here, but the bastard now knew he was armed.

Kenderly's feet slipped a little, she started to fall, caught herself on the shelf and knocked cans to the floor. She made it to his side, steering clear of the gun. He pushed her behind the end of the aisle. Tenoreno's man disappeared.

"They found us?"

It was a rhetorical question, not needing an answer.

"Back door, sweetheart."

A decade of law enforcement and a lifetime of pretending to be the toughest kid around kept him calm. The wound to his arm slowed him. Kenderly's presence made him more cautious. He directed her to behind the refrigerated food displays and pointed toward an employees-only door.

Having his weapon drawn caused civilians to run in the opposite direction. After a few screams from those gray-haired ladies, Kenderly pushed through the swinging doors just as the intercom buzzed to life.

"Hey, Texas Ranger," a raspy bass voice said.

He jerked Kenderly to him and put his back to the wall, searching for a path outside. An exit sign caught his eye, and he pointed to it, giving her shoulder a nudge.

"I'm not leaving without you."

"You have to, babe. It's the only way. Get going and call Jesse for help."

"Garrison, you don't understand."

"You have to run. Go. I'll keep him here long enough for you to get—"

"I can't drive a motorcycle!"

"Texas Ranger dude, I know you're still in the store. I also know you don't want anyone to get hurt. If you give yourself up, I'll let these nice people at the front door leave."

"Dammit."

"I'll count to ten."

The countdown wasn't slow. He had a few seconds to make a decision. "All right!" he shouted through the door. "I'm coming out."

"I want the pretty lady, too."

"Hide, Kenderly. There's gotta be an office back here. Find it. Lock the door and hide. Call Jesse," he whispered. "Trust no one but him."

"I don't know if I can."

"Two…"

"Don't hurt anyone," Garrison shouted again. "We're coming." He turned back to Kenderly. "The drive is in the water at the house."

"You can't go out there. He'll kill you." She grabbed his arm and looked at the makeshift bandage. "God, are you shot? When did he shoot you? Oh my God."

He kissed her. As passionately as he could get during a situation like that, pressing the gun into her hands. Then he pushed through the swinging doors.

"Don't shoot."

"Now, buddy, what makes you think I won't?" the voice asked, still on the intercom. "You've seen me work."

Garrison ran down the aisle to the front. The intercom was still on. Screams echoed through the store.

A lone shot.

Chapter Sixteen

Kenderly stared at the gun in her hands. She jumped with the firing of a single shot and dropped the weapon. She knelt to the floor and couldn't get back up.

Garrison? Was he dead?

"Don't shoot."

At the sound of his voice, relief shot through her as fast as any bullet. Air rushed back into her lungs. She was weak at the thought of him lying on the cold linoleum floor. It seemed like an eternity and had only been a split second.

"Ranger Travis, words aren't necessary," the intercom voice said. His lips must have been too close to the microphone. He sounded as distorted as his mind must have been.

"Why don't you show your face, you ugly son—"

Garrison's voice sounded strained as he shouted. No more shots. No more screams. She once again was cradling the gun he'd handed her...this time tight between her breasts. She couldn't stay here. Where could she hide?

"Miss Tyler," the voice taunted, close to the microphone like a child playing, "it's no use hiding. You can't get away. Come on out, unless you want me to hurt some of these people, or I could just hurt your friend over and over. You know what will eventually happen."

If she went out there, no one would ever find the flash drive. But if she were honest with herself, she didn't hold out much hope that she could resist this killer's threats. How could she live with herself, knowing she'd caused anyone's death?

She ran for the phone inside the office, locking the door behind her. The number she'd memorized went to voice mail. "Jesse, this is Mr. Travis's dog walker. If you're in Austin, there are special instructions with the water."

"Where are you, my little pretty lady?" the voice sing-songed over the intercom.

She couldn't leave Garrison. He had gone out there to save innocent customers, but he would kill her himself if she walked out front and just gave up.

"This is 911. Please, state your emergency."

"I'm at the market on Forty-First Street. Someone has a gun and is threatening to kill everybody."

"I need you to stay on the line, ma'am. Can you do that?"

The doorknob rattled. The door shook.

"Please, let me in. Oh God, please, don't leave me out here to die. He's shooting people." A customer in a checkered shirt pounded with his palm on the door's glass. "Open up."

It wasn't the man chasing them. This man was slender, a slighter build, and his eyes were totally different. He looked as frightened as her.

"Hold on, I need to let this customer inside." With shaking hands, she left the receiver off the hook and unlocked the door. The man burst through, locking the door behind him. He threw his hands in the air when he turned and saw her gun.

"Oh no, wait." She set the gun on the desk, anxious to get back to the phone call. "I'm not going to hurt you."

"What a shame." He swiped the gun, tossed it to his other hand, like someone used to handling a weapon, and pointed it at her chest.

Isabella's murderer had a partner. Big surprise. But the cops should be on their way. The 911 operator was listening.

"So there are two of Tenoreno's men here with guns," she said for the operator's benefit. "Please, don't hurt the innocent people out there shopping."

"They want you alive. So no trouble, or the boyfriend gets it first. Let's go." He jerked the barrel toward the door and clicked a button on his cell. "Got her. Back. Got it."

He shoved her between her shoulders toward the door that should have taken her to safety. She wanted to slow down, but he didn't allow it. "Where's Garrison? What are you going to do with us?"

The question she wanted answered at any minute was *what are you going to do when the police arrive?* She searched reflections in windows...no flashing lights. She'd put in the call. They should be there any minute.

The black car that had followed them the day before was parked in a fire lane on the vacant side of the building. Her feet crunched broken glass. She took a real look at her surroundings.

The neighborhood wasn't as nice as she'd first assumed. Half of the parking lot lights around her were broken or out. It was doubtful the security cameras still worked. Less doubtful that anyone would help her.

She was alone.

Uncertainty consumed her. She didn't want to die. Especially not today. She'd just begun to live. Her knees grew weak. The man shoved her again. Apparently she'd stopped next to the Dumpster for a convenient shot to the back of her head.

"Remember what I said about cooperating. Not a peep. You got it?"

She nodded as she walked next to the dimly lit car. So they must really want her alive. At least for now. "Where's Garrison?"

He didn't have to answer.

She recognized the ski mask immediately. He had the same build, the same walk and the same confidence as the man who'd shot Isabella. Garrison walked in front of him with his hands behind his head. Once they were side by side, she saw the gun in the murderer's grip.

"You okay?"

She nodded without moving too much, completely unable to push a yes through her lips. She hadn't ever been this frightened. It was debilitating and far worse than escaping over the balcony on Friday.

This time she had a chance to contemplate what might happen. They handcuffed Garrison and shoved him face-first on to the back of the car.

Then the smaller man who had tricked his way into the office began patting her down. His hands took in every contour of her body. Every pocket, the inside of her bra. Garrison struggled to stand up, and the big man shoved his cheek against the trunk, lifting his wrists higher into the air, pinning him there.

"What the hell are you looking for?" Garrison said.

The man was about to descend into the front of her jeans when the murderer who killed Isabella waved him to a stop. They stood there, him behind her, arm wrapped around her waist, his fingers at the top of her jeans about to violate her.

Dim light or not, there was enough to see the sizzling hatred in Garrison's eyes as he pushed back again and again. The makeshift bandage slipped from his strong arm. His wound, raw and visible, bled and dripped to the dusty metallic paint.

"That isn't necessary," he gritted and stood.

"Please, stop. He's hurt."

"Shut up," the checkered-shirt jerk who'd fooled her said. He continued his search on the outside of her jeans.

It was humiliating, but it had almost been so much worse. As it was, tears sprang from her eyes and blurred her vision. She had no weapon for him to confiscate, or she would have used it on him inside the market. He nodded to the big man.

"It's going to be okay. No matter what—" Garrison tried to reassure her and received a blow to his temple with the man's gun.

Why weren't these men in a bigger hurry? Did they know the police would be delayed? She'd left the 911 operator on the line. Had Garrison been right not to trust the cops?

One more time she was shoved, tripping and falling to the pavement, only to be lifted by her arm. The murderer faced Garrison, but not before she saw the blackness in his eyes. He wanted to hurt people, and this time it was their turn.

The car door opened, and she was shoved into the backseat. Her arms were yanked behind her back and handcuffed. She'd barely scrambled to a sitting position when she heard the scuffling behind her. As she watched in the rearview mirror, the two men took turns throwing punches, hitting Garrison.

The car rocked as Garrison fell over and over. He was defenseless. Another punch took him to his knees and out of her sight. She could only see the top of his head.

Isabella's killer kicked him, grabbed a fistful of hair, keeping him upright, hitting him again. They bent over him, disappearing, then Garrison was thrown inside, his face landing in her lap.

Standing close to the door, the man who'd been chasing them took off his mask and handed it to the checkered-shirt liar. He placed the heavy wool ski mask backward over her head.

The men didn't talk. After the car turned a couple of times, the accomplice got out. She could tell it was him because he'd said "I'll find it" before slamming the door.

The mask over Kenderly's head smelled like a cheap aftershave. Why it was on his hair baffled her, but it was only a fleeting thought. She was getting sick from the odor, the rough car ride and wondering how badly Garrison might be injured.

Kenderly could barely see Garrison's face through the weave of the mask. He was still out cold in her lap and hadn't moved. She didn't think he could be faking such unconscious perfection. They hadn't bothered to blindfold him like they had her. The thought that he'd been drugged fleeted through her mind along with all the other details she was trying to rake in.

The longer he didn't move, the more it made sense. He would be much less trouble drugged. She fought back the tears and the feeling of total helplessness.

What could she do? Her wrists were bound by handcuffs. She was blind to her surroundings. Even if she could get out of the moving car, she wouldn't leave Garrison behind.

Think. Think. Think.

Yes, the Texas Ranger who had been protecting her with his life would want her to leave him behind and escape. She hated that option. But if she could, she would. It was their only chance at survival. If she could get out of there, she could bring someone back to help Garrison.

Back to where? For every answer, she had more questions spring up.

The man who had been chasing them wouldn't care about her personally, so attempting to reason with him wasn't an option. She'd already heard Isabella beg for her life, so that wouldn't work. The man had no heart and no soul. She couldn't bribe him. She had no money.

The sound of traffic disappeared. Their captor didn't play the radio or music. He didn't talk or even breathe hard. If she spoke to Garrison and tried to wake him up, the murderer would hear.

What was she supposed to do? She was only a hairdresser. Her training hadn't included escape artist techniques or hand-to-hand combat. Even after two days, her on-the-run skills weren't very good, either.

There were too many thoughts in her head, and she didn't know how to sort through them. Or maybe there weren't any ideas at all, and she was as helpless as she appeared.

Why not just kill them? Were they being taken to a location where their bodies would never be found? But they'd drugged Garrison instead of killing him.

Or had they? She could feel his warmth penetrating through her jeans to her thighs. She leaned forward and felt his chest rise. He was alive.

Why?

What did they want?

The flash drive. That's why they'd been searched so thoroughly. They wanted the flash drive.

Chapter Seventeen

Jesse Ryder played the phone message again. When he'd first arrived back at headquarters his hair had been dripping from his shower. He was surprised he'd gotten all the soap off after he heard the general ringtone.

"Something has happened. He must have found the evidence he was searching for."

"We're waiting on facts, Ryder," the major answered sternly.

Jesse noticed the differences, though. His superior was stiff in the chair, not flipping a pencil with one hand while he tapped his chin with the other. His feet were squarely under him, not propped up on the corner of his desk. This time he hadn't drawn a conclusion about the correct course of action.

"I do know it, sir. There's no logical reason to leave me a message like this if they weren't in danger. I told them three days. It's been two. Travis should check in tomorrow." He hesitated to say the next words, but what the hell. "If we wait until we know there's trouble, it'll be too late to get there. Sir."

"And you believe that the 911 call at the grocery store involved Travis and Tyler? Did you get a copy of the tape? You might recognize the gal's voice. Run it down for me." The major's finger began tapping his chin. He was ready to listen.

"Multiple witnesses on the news report said the masked man demanded that the Texas Ranger give himself up. Reports say the ranger looked like he was abducting a woman, and was safely in the storage area. The threat of shooting hostages got him to surrender to the man threatening customers out front. Witnesses didn't see the woman again. We're waiting on the security footage, but the police department didn't seem very forthcoming. The sergeant I spoke with might as well have accused me of trying to cover up for Travis."

"You think it would be any better if you were in Austin? What do you hope to find that the police can't?"

My best friend. Alive.

"I think Travis uncovered something important enough to get Kenderly Tyler to call me while he stalled at the front of the store. It's a cryptic clue, and we'll be lucky if we find it before Tenoreno's men do."

"Why not just tell you what's going on?" He looked at Jesse, expecting an answer.

"Perhaps they believe that two crime families might be listening. Even Johnson was surprised at how quickly the police and media began calling Garrison Travis a murderer. We already knew Tenoreno was paying officials. We just can't prove it."

"You don't believe the media jumped on the chance to sensationalize because of our Ranger history?" the major asked.

"Partly. Don't you think they were hasty?"

Jesse forced himself to stay at attention. Any other stance would have him anxiously drumming his fingers or performing some other tapping while waiting on permission. Didn't really matter. He was heading to Austin to help his best friend, no matter what his directive was.

He was done sitting here at his desk or trying to get shut-eye at home. Garrison's dogs were whining to get outside or whining to get into bed with him. Pets he could take, but waking up face-to-face with dog breath was pushing their friendship to the limit.

"We're losing time, sir."

"Take Johnson with you. Lights all the way. I know you aren't traveling at the speed limit anyway. Let me know when you arrive." He stood. "In fact, keep me apprised of every move you make."

Jesse was dismissed. "Thank you, sir."

"Don't thank me yet. You have to deal with headquarters. I'll be making that call after you've gone." Parker picked up the phone from his desk. "Easier to ask forgiveness than permission. Hit the road."

"Understood."

He did understand. He hadn't been in Company F all that long, but he knew that his commander was getting his head chewed off at regular intervals from the top brass.

He tapped Bryce's desk as he passed. "Grab your weapon, Johnson. We're heading to Austin."

"I thought the company had been ordered to stand down. That there would be consequences from Austin if we investigated." Johnson was correct.

There might be reprimands for their permanent records, but he had to find his friend. He wasn't getting any psychic message or anything. Far from it. Garrison Travis was the last person on earth Jesse would ever correctly predict. In all their escapades and adventures together, this was the first time he'd ever known his friend was in serious danger.

It was the first time Jesse knew he had to help.

"Orders change. I'll fill you in on the details when we hit the road."

Both men unlocked drawers, removed weapons and ammo, then left the building.

"Any idea what we're going to find? Or how to find Travis and the woman?" Johnson asked when they got to the parking lot.

"Not a clue. But we will. Even if we have to beat down Tenoreno's front door."

Chapter Eighteen

Garrison's skull pounded harder than on the day after he'd graduated from the police academy. This hangover was the absolute worst. He tried to grab his aching head, but his arms were pinned behind him.

He cracked one eye open. At least there was darkness. Light would have been too much to handle. He was already sitting upright. That was a start. Or a really bad sign.

"Damn, that must have been some good tequila."

"Garrison? Are you really awake this time?"

This time?

He knew that voice. Remembered his hands on her perfect body. Then his hands were replaced by a guy in a checkered shirt. Was this a dream? His hands were pinned again, he couldn't do anything. There was pain. Everything hurt. Things went black.

Memory or imagination?

"Kenderly?" he croaked through a dry, odd taste in his mouth. *Handcuffs.* He recognized the feel of the metal bracelets. It wasn't his imagination.

"Thank goodness. I don't know how much longer I could take being alone in here."

He had a vague memory of being caught in the soup

aisle of a grocery store. That made for a weird dream. "Where's here?"

"I'm not sure, but I think we're back at Isabella's house. At least somewhere on the estate. They covered my eyes with a ski mask, but we didn't drive far, so it seemed logical to assume they'd take us here. Right?" She must have been shifting.

He heard metallic noises, but couldn't focus on anything. Or feel much either. "Why aren't we dead?"

"I'm fine. Thank you very much for asking. No one's done anything except lock my hands to a chain on the floor and slap me once or twice."

"My head's a bit foggy regarding some details. More like all the details. Are you really okay? Or are you just staying strong?"

"I think he split my lip. Other than that, I'm fine. Sorry for taking your head off."

"Sweetheart, if you could take it off, I'd let you. It hurts like a son of a bitch." His mind's picture of her lip bleeding, her unable to touch it, worried about him…it won out over the fact he still saw four of his shoes. She would have been worried. Probably still was. He tried to be hopeful. "What did they hit me with—a sledgehammer?"

"They did hit you pretty hard, but I bet it was whatever they gave you to knock you out all this time. It's been hours. Long, scary hours here by myself."

Whatever they were both handcuffed to rattled as she jerked against it. Maybe something bolted to the floor. Kenderly had to be cuffed and connected to him with a chain or something. She'd moved, and his wrists were pulled. He couldn't be certain and didn't have enough strength in his arms to pull to see if it was a possible escape.

"Remind me to say no to drugs."

"Sure." She sort of laughed and cried at the same time. Then it was just an all-out cry. If he could have seen her, he might have lost his composure. Odds were they were going to die soon, and it wouldn't be easy or as quick as what she'd witnessed when they'd first met.

"It's okay, Kenderly." He was lying through his teeth. These men were going to get ugly and use them against each other. "Look, if you have a chance to save yourself, take it."

Nothing was okay about their situation. No one knew they were missing. No one knew they were anywhere close to here. Tenoreno could have them disappear. Easy.

In pieces.

With his memory returning a little more each minute, he was surprised he'd awakened at all. Tenoreno knew about the flash drive. It was the only bargaining chip Garrison had to try and save Kenderly.

"Sorry." She sniffed. "I'm just so glad you woke up. Now we might have a chance to get out of here."

He wanted to tell her the truth, but what good would that do? Make her spend her last hour crying or hysterical? Okay, she hadn't been hysterical up to this point in their adventure.

In fact, she'd been damn smart about things. She'd been a good sounding board and had come up with a lot of the ideas they'd used. But he still wasn't telling her the truth. Take away someone's hope and that was worse than...

"Garrison?"

"Yeah."

"You wouldn't happen to be able to break your thumb to slide the handcuffs off. Or maybe dislocate your shoulder? No, that wouldn't do anything. What about stepping through the loop of your arms to bring your hands in front of you? We might be able to find something to pick the handcuff lock."

"I thought I was the one who had been drugged." He wished he could do one of those tricks.

"I just thought it was worth a shot. I've been trying to think of something, anything, that would help if you woke up. I mean when you woke up." She shifted again, and his hands were pulled a little farther from his back. "Speaking of shots, how's your arm?"

"Sore. Stiff. Better than my head. Seeing myself hurl twice with this double vision isn't going to be fun. But I'm optimistic." He yanked at the handcuffs.

"Ow, that sort of hurt."

"That confirms that our cuffs are connected by a chain. These things are not coming apart. If I pull, I'm going to hurt you." He was still feeling the effects of whatever drug they'd used on him, so he didn't have much strength anyway.

"I'm not finding a lot of positive in this experience, Garrison."

"Did they question you? What did they want? Do they know about the info?"

"Isabella's murderer—who is more frightening to look at without his mask—asked me a couple of questions. But then he got a call, nudged you with his toe and left."

He couldn't detect any additional shaking in her voice. She just sounded scared. "Do they know about the flash drive?"

"Yes. Do they want to know if we have it? Yes. Do they know what's on it? No."

"Kenderly, you can talk to me. Unless you're upset that I screwed up. I don't have enough words to say I'm sorry. I didn't realize the guy had a partner."

"That's right. I think Isabella's murderer dropped his

pervert of a partner off at your aunt's house to look for something," she whispered. "I heard they don't know what's on the flash drive. They were talking about it when they threw you in here. Apparently you are heavier than you look."

"It's my boots. Why are we whispering?"

"They may be watching us or recording our conversation," she continued with her extra breathy voice.

"You really have watched a lot of crime shows on television."

He didn't think there were any recording devices in the room. No blinking red light or visible camera. No two-way mirror. But he couldn't see all of the room. He knew the door had opened on the wall behind him.

"We live in a very electronic world. Why wouldn't they be listening—" Were her heels scooting against the floor? There was a lot of slack for his arms after the noise. "See. They knew you were awake."

He didn't see anyone or hear footsteps, but needed to get the game going. "Before we get started, fellas, I want you to know that you can let Kenderly go. She doesn't know anything and has been trying to get away from me for three days."

A solitary clap, followed by another, echoed throughout the room. "Nicely played, Lieutenant Travis. But also quite false." Paul Tenoreno walked in front of him.

"Nice suit, fancy ostrich boots, manicured nails—all the signs of a person with money. Should you be visiting the dungeon? Or getting your own hands dirty? That's taking a big chance with your freedom."

He was a short man, no more than five-eight, unless you were sitting on the floor and could only see his kneecaps.

"Don't be absurd. I know all about you, Garrison Travis. You have a twin sister, aunt, mother and what a tragedy, your father was killed when you were a teenager. So don't think you can lie your way out of this. There is no way out."

"Me, lie? Naw, you got that all wrong, pal. I'm a Texas Ranger. We're the freaking oldest law around and handle things the old-fashioned way. We don't need to lie."

His head whipped back on the receiving end of a left cross. He forced his jaw to move from side to side, cracking it back into place. Tenoreno had jabbed him hard. "Dammit. I honestly didn't think you'd do that."

"Come on, Garrison. How do you think I got to where I am today?" He smiled and splayed his hands in an innocent gesture.

Garrison's wrists were jerked away from him. He felt the tug stop and turned his head, attempting to see the scuffle he heard. He saw the murdering bastard who had pulled the trigger held a gun to Kenderly's head. He pulled her by the long strands of multicolored gold and forced her to kneel.

Garrison didn't want to panic. He had to stay calm, keep a cool head, think through what needed to be done. He couldn't. That was Kenderly.

As much as he tried, he couldn't fake it. He'd seen what that scar-faced monster had done to two women. Kenderly's hands were still behind her. Garrison tried to reassure her. The terror in her dark brown eyes spread quickly across her face.

The soulless bastard twisted his fist in her hair, butted the barrel against her temple.

"You see my dilemma. I only need one person to get what I want. We threatened your…health shortly after your arrival. Miss Tyler cares for you and begged for your life. But I believed her when she told us she doesn't possess the information I require."

"We didn't find anything. The jewelry case was empty. Maybe whatever you're looking for fell on to the lawn when we climbed over the balcony. Why not just let her go?"

Tenoreno nodded. His hired thug tugged harder. Kenderly cried out. She was trying to be brave, but the tears streamed down her cheeks.

"We don't have it." He needed time. *Think.*

"That I already know. Where did you hide it?" Tenoreno nodded again.

Garrison's heart stopped as he watched the trigger being squeezed. Kenderly screamed on a long sigh. He shouted no or screamed it himself.

The revolver clicked on an empty chamber.

"Stop. All right." He shook his head, unable to get the image of Kenderly lying dead in front of him out of his mind. "We hid it. But we go together. That's the deal. You want it back? We go together."

When Tenoreno found the flash drive, they'd be dead anyway.

"Tell me what you saw. Prove that I should invest additional time in this venture."

Garrison didn't answer. It went against everything in him. Everything true and right that his father had instilled bounced around in his head, contradicting what his gut told him needed to be done. He heard his mother's voice, too. Begging him to stay alive. Anything he could do to prolong their lives gave them a fighting chance to get away. To jump on a possible mistake.

Staying alive longer...a fighting chance.

Tenoreno looked bored. He flicked a finger, and Kenderly cried out in pain as her head was yanked backward. "Do I really need to have Thomas pull the trigger again? This time it might have a bullet in the chamber. Do you wish to see your friend's brain all over my walls?"

"Garrison?" His name whispered from Kenderly's lips said more than he could express. She didn't have the information that could be given to Tenoreno.

Kenderly's eyes locked with his, pleading for him to say something, to save her life. Her eyes were blacked from the tears ruining her makeup again. Her cheekbone was swollen from being hit. Her bottom lip had been split, and a dark stain of blood trailed across her chin. The revolver's barrel pressed against her had scratched her temple.

The bastard Thomas played with the trigger. His finger tapped it like Morse code. But it wasn't Morse. It was itching to pull it for real.

Garrison strained at his chains. They weren't giving an inch more. He couldn't break away and save her. "Files. Names. Dates. Payments."

"A good guess, but I'm waiting for my proof." Tenoreno crossed his arms and didn't appear patient.

"The deputy first assistant AG of Texas," Garrison blurted.

"That wasn't difficult." He flicked his finger, and the gun disappeared into his man's pocket.

"Dammit, let go of her."

His words had no effect. She was jerked to her feet and then out of his sight.

"Take her to the van," Tenoreno directed, pulling his own weapon from inside his coat. "And send Leonard in here for Mr. Travis."

"Where are you taking her?" Garrison yanked on his cuffs, wishing he could break his thumb and get free.

"Don't worry. You'll be with her. One wrong move while we're retrieving the flash drive, you even blink wrong and she's dead."

"You're going to kill us anyway."

"You know, Travis, I'm not such a bad person. Not as gruesome as you might think. I've got a proposition and a way for your friend to disappear."

"And you think I'll believe you? Why?"

"All you have to do is cooperate. Just follow through on the headlines that are already out there." He leaned against the wall, cocking his head to the side like a big shot, gun relaxed in his hand.

If Garrison were free, he'd take care of this mafia wannabe with one punch.

"Plain speak, if you can. Enough with the riddles. What do I have to do to get you to let Kenderly go?"

"Take the fall, Mr. Travis." He pulled a flash drive from his pocket identical to the one hidden. "I got a ton of these being dropped off at papers and the news programs. You admit that you murdered Isabella and Trinity, and we're done. You go to jail, and she gets a fresh start in the state of her choice."

"It won't work."

"Sure it will. If she opens her mouth, you die in prison. If you don't get convicted, she dies in her new town. I've seen the way she looks at you. She'll do anything you tell her. Course, she stays as my...guest until we're square. She can earn her keep with free haircuts for all the boys."

"It won't work. Nobody will believe I've been working for you."

"People will believe anything." He held his palm toward the door, stopping someone from coming inside. "Especially since you're a lofty Texas Ranger. You're going to take the Rosco family down with you. It's brilliant."

The gun barrel bounced up and down like a presentation pointer.

Was he for real?

Tenoreno might just be crazy enough to believe himself. But Garrison wasn't. If he agreed to this insanity, the Rosco family would have him killed as soon as his butt hit a jail bench.

"What's your answer, lawman?"

There had to be an ulterior motive. Why did he want to involve the Texas Rangers?

Garrison didn't know, but there was only one way to find out.

"I'll do it."

Chapter Nineteen

It had taken the entire two hour drive from Waco to Austin to clear the bureaucratic tape for permission to search the crime scene. When Jesse arrived there were police cars blocking the house and another argument about jurisdiction.

Johnson was on the computer in the car while Jesse leaned on the hood. Three Austin cops stared at him. He wasn't new to how agencies worked together. He'd been with the Texas Department of Public Safety long enough to have experienced his fair share of joint law enforcement.

This was different.

He hadn't been allowed to search on his own. Hell, he hadn't been allowed to stand in the background and look over someone's shoulder while they searched. These officers were treating Johnson and him like suspects. There was nothing relaxed in the posture of the policemen watching him. They looked ready for a fight.

Same as him.

"Any luck, Johnson?"

"No. It's the middle of the night, and no one's picking up, not for me, not for the major." He stood, leaning his elbow on the top of the car. "Oaks pulled through. He's still in ICU with his wife. Guards—from headquarters and the Austin PD—are outside his door. My buddy there didn't know if they were protecting the captain or if they were there to arrest him."

"Something smells like rotting fish." He lowered his voice, nodding to their own guards. "I've got a bad feeling about this."

"Your turn to try the major."

Jesse didn't get it. He'd just said the major hadn't had any luck. So why would he... Once Johnson raised his eyebrow and darted his eyes toward the car, Jesse smartened up. Tensions were high, and Johnson wanted privacy. Got it.

Once inside Johnson snapped his seat belt. "I think we'd be better off leaving for the moment." A police officer ran down the front steps of the battered house. "Now."

Jesse didn't argue. The surrounding officers slowly approached the vehicle, hands on their weapons. He put the car in Reverse and gunned it, weaving backward through police cars and civilian cars parked on the street.

He spun the wheel, threw the car in Drive, praying that his transmission wasn't stripped, and gunned it again.

"Mind telling me what that's all about? And how the hell did you know it was about to happen?"

"Don't stop. We need to find a place to chill for a while." Johnson grabbed his cell from his shirt pocket and began playing a video.

"Is that the news?"

"Yeah. Keep driving."

Jesse listened to the male newscaster. "While this isn't the first time that a Texas Ranger will be indicted or brought to trial, it will be the first time in modern history. WGPN has an anonymous source that evidence has been found linking Lieutenant Garrison Travis to the Rosco family business interests. It's long been suspected that the Rosco family has ties to the drug cartels in Mexico. Authorities are reporting that the rangers in Company F will be temporarily detained until more information is available. Company F is based in Waco where the..."

"What evidence?" Jesse asked.

"Another online source reported a second bank account with payments directly from the Roscos."

"You don't believe that, do you?"

"No. You two haven't been in the company long, but that man bleeds Lone Star red, white and blue."

"You got that right." Jesse hit the main thoroughfare and slowed to blend in with traffic.

"I was at his house yesterday. Remember? If Travis had extra cash, he's not the type who could hide it for long. He'd be living large."

"You think Major Parker is up now?"

Johnson nodded. "You got a place in mind to lay low?"

"We're driving back to his aunt's, taking charge and getting inside. Period. Kenderly Tyler told me to look in the water. I don't think she'd have risked a call before dialing 911 in order to give me false information. We need to find the real evidence."

"Agreed. It probably looks like a normal flash drive. They don't hold up in water so what do you think she meant?" Johnson asked.

"No clue. If being accused of murder wasn't enough, the press accusing him of being dirty will kill Garrison. Is anyone out there on his side?"

"We are," Johnson reminded him matter of factly.

"If Garrison and the woman are still alive, we need to find them. How's that going to happen if we're all in jail?"

"Maybe that's the plan. The evidence that WGPN claimed is exclusive is showing up on multiple sources."

Johnson looked up from scanning his phone. "That's not a coincidence. Someone sent out multiple copies."

"You know these families better than anyone in the state. What's Tenoreno's game plan? What's he trying to do?"

"It looks like he's setting the Rosco family up to take the fall for killing his wife. We have to make that assumption, since they're the ones implicated."

"And why involve Travis?" Jesse asked.

"It sidelines the Rangers. Maybe Oaks was closer to something than we know. We need to find the real evidence." Johnson continued staring at him. "Are you going to force me to ask where you think we should start?"

"The garage. Just makes sense. The two of them found some kind of evidence. He's out of money. Can't risk a call to me. Travis came here for his bike. Transportation to Waco, to the men he trusted to turn himself over to. He knows he's compromised, stashes the evidence nearby. Then heads out hoping to lose Tenoreno's men, can't and then we have an incident at the market that's less than a mile away."

"So you're thinking there's some type of water in or close to the garage."

"Damn straight."

"Now we just have to get it *out* of the garage without being arrested." Johnson shoved his glasses up his nose.

And determine where to find his best friend and the eyewitness. Then clear their names of murder charges. Then save the day. No problem. Typical Texas Ranger stuff.

"Aw hell no," Johnson exclaimed, reading his phone. "They caught him. They just announced he'll be turned over at the county courthouse within the hour."

Chapter Twenty

"This is the wrong way. We're heading south. My aunt's house is north," Garrison whispered. Kenderly had made the same assumption when the tall office buildings of downtown Austin came into view.

They were in the back of a van again. This one had a little more room than the delivery truck of a couple of days ago. It had two small windows high in each back door. They could see each other from the headlights shining inside.

Two armed men sat in the front. The checkered-shirt pervert was driving. The other one pointed his weapon straight at her.

"I wish I could hold your hand or something. Or maybe have you tell me what's going on."

The man in the passenger seat faced forward, and Kenderly twisted closer to Garrison. She didn't know how she managed, but she did.

"Maybe we shouldn't push our luck trying to snuggle."

"Shush. I've been dying to tell you this," she whispered. How did he keep his sense of humor in a situation like this? "I called your friend Jesse when I was in the market office and told him about the flash drive. You don't think that checkered-shirt pervert found it, do you? Jesse will help us, right?"

"If he can."

"What's going on, Garrison? What did Isabella's husband do to you?"

"Damn, you're wonderful."

Had she heard him right? She scooted as close as she could, resting her head awkwardly on his shoulder.

"I mean it," he said, kissing her forehead. "You're just…terrific."

"Oh, golly gee, I like you, too." She answered with old-fashioned sarcasm, then tilted her face to where she could see him. "What is this, seventh grade?"

"Can't a guy give his girl a compliment and tell her he likes her?"

"Here? We're going to share our feelings while handcuffed, in the back of a van taking us to who knows where, with guns pointed at us? And seriously, Garrison… I look a mess."

"Yeah. It'll be a story to remember. Grandkid worthy, maybe."

What?

Lieutenant Garrison Travis, named after two famous Texans, raised his eyebrows as if asking her a question, then winked at her. He kissed the tip of her nose and made her want to cry at the beauty of it. Even handcuffed and probably headed to a grave in the middle of nowhere. His confession was absolutely beautiful.

Even if it did seem like their timing was always off. "I'm really glad it was you who came to rescue me."

"Sweetheart, this is definitely not my best work. Good thing I can't reach more than your nose," he whispered. "Your bottom lip looks like it hurts, and I wouldn't be all that gentle."

She stretched and he stretched, and they met in the middle. He wasn't gentle. The van bumping along made it worse. But since it might be her last kiss ever, she pushed through the little pain and shared it with him.

"You sure do like showing me I'm wrong." He kissed her again. Softly. Grazing her lip with a gentle touch. "Um...you were telling me about your call to Jesse. I assume you left him a message."

She nodded.

"Hey, get away from each other," the checkered-shirt criminal shouted from the front.

"Stay where you are, Kenderly. Go ahead. Shoot us. Then the deal's off. Tenoreno will forgive you. Won't he?"

They hit a bump and readjusted. Garrison ignored the grumblings, focusing his stare back on her.

"What are you talking about? What deal?" She was afraid to ask but had to know.

"The one I made to be the fall guy for a crime boss."

"You did nothing of the sort." She couldn't believe that he'd agree to that. He'd spoken with so much pride about fulfilling his father's hopes and dreams. "What about the spotless Texas Ranger reputation?" Her voice had grown louder, but she was suddenly furious. He had to be doing this for her. Then, in a softer whisper, "You've got a plan, right?"

"To stay alive?" His smile split his face.

It was the smile from when they'd first met. The one she'd been warned about. The one that convinced her he wasn't telling the entire truth. He had a plan, all right. But what if that was what he was stretching the truth about?

"Remember one thing for me, Kenderly. Tenoreno has no intention of letting either one of us live. There's a lot at stake here. He murdered his wife to keep a lid on it. He murdered Rosco's just because she was there."

"But if he's turning you over to the police, can't they

help us? What if we tell the truth? Won't your friend find the flash drive? That proves he's guilty."

"He's already sent a different one framing me to just about everyone in the media. I don't think we can count on the police. Tenoreno's got high-ranking officials on his payroll."

She was scared again. They'd gone from witnesses to murder suspects to confessed killers in less than four days. How could this happen? Bad luck? Would it end with Tenoreno winning? Would they really be dead?

She couldn't question him further. She had nothing to say. No ideas. She wanted to wrap her arms around him and couldn't. She wanted to hold on to him and never let go.

The van turned and slowed to a stop.

"Remember. No one in uniform is going to tell you the truth. They either want you to believe a lie, or they've been fed the lie to repeat. But you can trust Jesse. Get out of here. Find him. Promise me."

"I promise."

She hoped and prayed that he did have a plan and that they'd be running in a few minutes to find someone with a handcuff key.

"Step out of the vehicle. Nice and slow. Get those feet on the ground fast."

Blinded by more flashlight beams than she could distinguish, she couldn't see who was holding them. Then she realized there were flashes a few feet behind them. She heard the whirring of a professional camera.

Both she and Garrison followed the step-by-step instructions exactly. With their hands behind their backs, they were unable to hide their faces. As bad as she looked, the bruises developing on her face would not hide her identity. Even a kick to his head wouldn't hide Garrison's distinctive features.

"Where are we?" she asked once she had both feet on the sidewalk, still blinded by cameras. "What's going on?"

"The county's booking your boyfriend for murder. That's what." The voice belonged to a woman in a police uniform.

"We didn't—"

"Kenderly, don't say a word. You'll be out of here in two shakes. Ignore the taunts and don't answer them— any of them." Garrison was escorted in front of her.

This time the men surrounding him were in different uniforms. There were a couple of men in suits, but none of them wore a white hat representing the Rangers.

"It'll work out," he said, twisting in his escorts' hands. "And remember what we talked about." He was pulled from her and disappeared into the crowd.

The media frenzy gathering for Garrison's arrest was in front of the courthouse. She was still in handcuffs, walking uphill about fifteen feet behind those surrounding him. They continued leading her hero to a podium, but she was held on the outskirts of the crowd. Her body recoiled at the checkered-shirt's hands grasping her arm. The memory of his search for the flash drive made her gag.

Someone spoke at the podium in the distance, but she couldn't focus on his words. Cameras and lights were pointed toward him, leaving her in the dark. The vile checkered-shirt creep turned on a flashlight and pointed it at her face.

"Lieutenant Garrison Travis has a statement to make," the voice she couldn't see announced.

She wished she could swat the bright beam from her eyes. She could only assume that she was spotlighted to remind Garrison she was still in danger. She didn't want to be. She yanked on her arms. Twisted. Tried to fall to the cement. The flashlight wavered. But never dropped.

"I guess by now you all know who I am. I'll be saving the taxpayers some money by waiving my right to council and pleading guilty to the charges."

"No—" she wailed, only to be cut off by a hand over her mouth.

"This is really unusual," one of the voices from the crowd shouted. "Why the makeshift press conference in the middle of the night?"

The blinding light turned off, and she could see Garrison being led away. She was crying at the thought of never seeing him again. Maybe a little because the next few moments seemed so bleak.

"We're taking Miss Tyler to get debriefed," checkered-shirt said.

She didn't know who was listening to him. Her eyes were a bit blurry from the tears, and she couldn't see until she blinked them away. There had to be a place where she could make a run for it.

They walked on a sloped hill, but even then she was so weak she didn't think she could outrun two very fit men—or even unfit men. Emotions and fatigue were wearing her down. They drew even with the van again, and the man from the passenger seat opened the door.

A booted foot kicked out, connecting with his head. The man crumpled to the ground. The checkered-shirt pervert reached for something but let her go.

Kenderly ran. She didn't look back. Her hair blew in front of her face, she flipped it away and darted in front of an oncoming car. She was across the street and ran through an opening in the wall.

Furiously pushing the elevator button, she read that it

was the county jail and courthouse parking. She got on the elevator and rode it to the top floor. She ran in between the only two cars parked next to each other.

"Of all the rotten luck," she huffed. "No one's going to help someone in handcuffs."

Collapsing, she leaned on the tire and sat, forbidding any more tears to come, refusing to let herself panic. She'd gotten this far.

"Maybe I can break my thumb," she mumbled.

"Why don't you come with us instead?" a man in a suit and glasses asked her.

Kenderly bolted in the opposite direction, but within seconds two men grabbed her by the arms. Practically lifting her off the ground they ran down the ramp to a truck parked on the level below.

"Wait a minute. Where are you taking me? If you're going to kill me, just get it over with."

"You don't mean that. You didn't sound like the quitting type. Never give up. Kenderly, do you recognize my voice? I'm Jesse Ryder, Garrison's best friend and partner."

Talking didn't slow him down, but his words certainly did relax her. They got her on the floor of the truck and were leaving the garage in record time. Jesse drove, and the second man took out his keys.

"Let's get these things off you. Can you lift your arms any?" She did and he unlocked the cuffs.

"Is it okay to sit in the seat now?" She rubbed her wrists and rolled her shoulders, constantly looking behind them. No one followed. "They're going to realize I'm gone. Those men—"

"We took care of them. We need to get you out of here."

"Not without Garrison. They're going to kill him as soon as he makes a statement."

"I agree. It's logical. Why else would they have a press conference at this late hour unless that's exactly what they intend to do," Jesse said.

"That's true," the other man stated. "We need backup."

"There's no time. Believe me. They won't risk you or anyone else talking to him. Tenoreno doesn't want any delays." She argued, feeling as if she was an expert on Paul Tenoreno. "Garrison is in serious danger. There's no time. You're the only chance he has to get out of there."

She was about to plead, but one look at their faces and she knew they believed her. Their hesitation made her ask, "What now?"

"Just one problem," Jesse mumbled.

"We show our faces up there, and we'll be arrested," Glasses said.

"What's your name?" she asked. "Don't you have guns?"

Jesse didn't wait at the red light. He turned right from the middle lane, taking her farther from Garrison.

"Bryce Johnson, and yes ma'am, we have guns." He turned in his seat, pulling the seat belt closed, quieting the warning ding sounding throughout the cab.

"Then, why can't you use them?" She sat forward until her head was between the seats, and she could look at both men. "I'll drive the getaway truck."

Chapter Twenty-One

Garrison couldn't see Kenderly anywhere. There was a gun in his side. He was headed into a courtroom that had his name all over it. These guys weren't wasting any time. They were going to tape his confession and get him arraigned.

He doubted he'd make it to a holding cell alive.

No regrets on choosing this path. Neither of them would have made it this far if he hadn't agreed. If he could get these cuffs off, he would have a fighting chance. A slim fighting chance was better than none at all.

Had to be soon or there'd be no chance to save Kenderly.

It surprised him just how much he'd meant it when he'd talked of sharing the stories with their grandkids one day. At this point it seemed like an unrealistic dream. Kenderly was the first woman he'd ever had a thought like that about.

If they got out of this alive, it was worth seeing if the dream could happen.

Pushed, shoved, tripped along the way… He took all of the abuse from law enforcement officers, knowing how he'd feel by a betrayal like this.

Three county deputies propelled him into the courtroom chambers. They stood guard after pulling out a chair and gesturing for him to sit. They didn't speak. He couldn't tell if their looks were honest disgust or dishonest smirks.

Commotion at the back of the room. He didn't care. He calmed his heart rate, preparing to focus the last bit of his energy on escape.

Kenderly needed him.

He memorized the room. Estimated the distance between each guard. Looked to see if their weapons were secured. The deputy farthest from him had his thumb break unsnapped on his holster. He could be compromised, his weapon stolen faster than the others.

Once he made a break, it was useless to try and quiet the other deputies. There was nothing in the room to keep them from yelling. He'd have to run. Take the hallway the judges used, either direction would have a staircase to the bottom floor. He was only one flight up, he could do that in seconds.

The trick would be to get out of the building. Finding a door that wasn't already surrounded, expecting him, with a dirty cop there ready to pull the trigger.

"I don't care if he's refused council or not. The state's attorney's office doesn't want anything called into question. We need a certified signed confession to what he stated earlier. Now, step aside."

He knew that voice and suppressed the urge to turn around to acknowledge Bryce Johnson. Garrison forced himself to remain seated at the table instead of making a move. He waited and made eye contact with his colleague. Then he darted his eyes toward the vulnerable guard.

"Get these handcuffs off him immediately." Johnson directed the guard he'd spotted. He slammed his briefcase on the table, took his glasses off and wiped them with a glass-cleaner cloth.

Garrison had seen him do the same thing in their offices daily, but never with this much determination. A guard slowly approached but unlocked his cuffs without a debate. Grabbing the deputy's sidearm, he knocked him to the ground, dragging Johnson across the deputy's chest.

Garrison pulled the other ranger in front of him. There was video in the halls so he staged it to look like Johnson had been taken hostage. That cover would only last a short time. It wouldn't take long for them to discover his fellow ranger had posed as a lawyer to get near him.

"Don't shoot. Put your guns down, you fools," Johnson screamed like a frightened girl, causing the other two deputies to hesitate. They worked together, backing from the room into the hallway reserved for court staff.

As soon as they were through the door, Johnson spun and led the way to an elevator. "Our ride's on the north side of the building. This way. Ryder's waiting with Kenderly. She insisted on driving the truck."

"She would. The doors will be covered by now."

"Use me as a hostage again."

"No. You're staying here."

"I've got news for you, Travis. All of Company F is being detained. I'd rather my stay be in Waco instead of County. I've put a few of the crazies behind bars here."

"That's it." The elevator doors opened, and Garrison jerked Johnson back and led him farther down the hall.

"I have a better if not riskier idea." He spun the deputy's gun and let Johnson take it. "We're going out the prisoner corridor. There's a second-floor bridge to county lockup."

Johnson fished out his badge and put it on his pocket. "I got you. Prisoner. Ranger. This should work."

JESSE RYDER WAS perhaps even more stubborn than Garrison. He wasn't letting Kenderly drive, and he insisted that she lie on the floor of the backseat, so no one would see her. She wasn't stupid. His plan was safer. She understood completely.

And he was right that Garrison would probably sock him for leaving her alone. Look what had happened the last time they'd been separated.

She'd spoken her thought that it might take more than one ranger to bust another out of jail. They'd both laughed.

There really was something about a Texas Ranger creed or code that Garrison was going to have to explain one day.

"Any sign of them?" she asked.

"Nope. But no one's running out of the courthouse like a maniac is loose with a gun yet, either."

"And you expect that?"

"People running out, cops rushing in. Something like that, yeah."

"So how are they supposed to get out of the building? Think you need to take a look around?"

"Johnson has a phone. When they know, I'll go."

"And I thought Garrison didn't communicate well," she mumbled. Her arms and back were killing her. She was starving and probably dehydrated, to boot. She stretched and relocated to the corner of the seat, keeping herself out of the window as much as possible."

"You really should stay on the floor."

"I can look at what's going on for myself this way, and you won't have to talk at all. You should be happy."

"It's safer."

"Listen, I've been through an awful lot in the past twelve hours. I've been threatened, had a gun fired at my brains—empty, but it was frightening. And I'm worried. I promise to sit here in the corner and not show my face." Not to mention thinking Garrison was dead—more than once. "It's been a hell of a day."

Dawn was breaking behind them. The orange and yellows were reflecting off the windows in the jail.

"What happens now, Jesse? Let's say they do get out, and no one shoots them again."

"Again?"

"Are we all fugitives? Where do we go? How can we possibly get out of this city with the police and the sheriff's department and, shoot, let's not forget the other rangers on the prowl?"

Maybe it was the lack of sleep or everything finally staring her in the face, but she felt kind of loopy. Maybe the bubbling anxiousness starting to shake all her insides was what hysteria felt like. She didn't know and had little control. The feeling wouldn't stop or go away.

"When does Paul Tenoreno and the men he has do his dirty work get his comeuppance?"

"I don't have all those answers, Kenderly. We take things one step at a time. And I promise you. Garrison will be cleared and Tenoreno will go to jail."

She kept her face pushed back in the corner of the seat. Right up to the time the police cars began circling the building. Jesse started the engine, but they cut him off. He immediately began calling his partner's cell. No luck.

With no way out, she watched the ranger switch off the engine and drop his badge and weapon in a compartment under the console. "Kenderly, the officer is coming my direction. If you can get out on the passenger side, you might be able to make it between those parked cars without him seeing you. The other officers are heading to the courthouse. Can you do it?"

"But—"

"No buts. Take my phone and credit card, password's seven nine eight three, and zip code is seven six seven nine nine." The phone and small card holder slid over the console, and she grabbed both. "Got it? Garrison will find you. Remember that. Ready? Go now."

Jesse got out of the truck at the same time she opened her door. As she snuck to the other side of the street, she heard him confronting the police officer, asking questions, raising his voice and being slammed into the front of his truck.

She stuffed the phone in her bra. If it was on silent, she wanted to feel it ring.

Jesse was still drawing attention to himself when she snuck to the next car, and the next. There was construction equipment along the street. She stood up behind it and turned into the parking lot, leaning against the stone wall that separated it from the street.

Her heart raced and her hands shook. She shoved them through her hair and wondered how she could do this on her own. She sank to the ground, unable to keep her knees from buckling.

What if none of them got free? She took a deep breath, then another. Sirens sounded around her. She jumped with the vibration of the phone but pulled it free and started swiping to answer it.

"Jesse?"

"Garrison? It's me."

"Thank God, Kenderly. I'm coming to you. Just tell me where you are."

"Across from the courthouse. Jesse was arrested. Is Bryce okay?"

"Sweetheart, be a little more specific." He was running. She could hear him breathing hard.

"There's construction across the street. I'm against the wall."

"Listen carefully. Do you know how to get to the capitol from there? Johnson said that you and Jesse were on Eleventh Street, same as the capitol. Can you get there?"

"I think so."

"No, sweetheart, you can. We got this. I'll stay on the phone with you. Come on. You walking yet?"

Hysteria or shock was wearing off. She inched her way up the rock wall and saw an exit the direction she needed to go. The police were focused on the opposite side of the street, but she didn't want to risk it.

"What about Bryce?" she asked again.

"He's headed to headquarters to get Jesse out. You know this city. Where can we meet?"

"I'm heading to the west entrance to the capitol grounds. We should be closer to that side. The actual park won't be open at this time of day." She was thinking straight once more. The anxiety that had overwhelmed her for a moment was gone. "Are you okay, Garrison?"

He was still running but answered yes.

"I've met friends across the street from the park on Twelfth, there's a small monument in the greenbelt." She picked up her pace, ready to be back at his side. "I'll wait for you there."

"Sure thing. They didn't get the evidence."

"They mentioned that." So that would be their next move, back to his aunt's house again. "Going there hasn't been very lucky for us."

"I… Maybe you should sit this one out, babe."

"No way. I'm safer with you than anywhere else." And saner. If they lived through this, they could laugh at her going crazy together. "Remember what you said about great stories for the grandchildren?"

"Yeah," he spoke on a marathon breath.

"I'm going to hold you to it, Lieutenant Travis."

Kenderly stood at the statue. Content to just hear Garrison's heavy breathing.

"Don't jump," he said.

She turned around and there he was. She'd never been so glad to see someone in her life. They hung up, and she ran across the street to him, flying into his arms. Not thinking until afterward about his injuries. They didn't seem to matter as he held her to his chest and kissed her as if they'd been apart forever.

"Let's get out of here," he whispered before kissing her again.

Chapter Twenty-Two

Kenderly was quiet and drifted off with the swaying of the cab. Garrison was a lifetime away from relaxing. He couldn't think that she'd relaxed as much as she was just plain exhausted. He'd had a restful drug-induced nap, but she'd been awake for twenty-three hours. The past day had been nonstop action.

If he could think of any place safe, he would have taken the taxi there. He wanted to leave the city with her in his arms and just disappear. As soon as they stepped back on the street, she'd be back in danger again. There just didn't seem to be a path that would keep them out of the line of fire. He skimmed her bruised cheek with the back of his fingers.

It made him choke up just thinking about her begging for his life. Choke up worse when she didn't beg for her own. He hadn't known many women—other than his sister—who could be this brave.

The cab dipped into a pothole, waking Kenderly just as they reached the parking lot near the market. Garrison used Jesse's card to pay, then they took the long way around back. As soon as they turned the corner he saw his bike was still hidden in the alley.

"I didn't think it would still be here."

"Why not?" Kenderly yawned. "It hasn't been twelve

hours since we left. It only feels like it's been a week. Just like it seemed an eternity when you were unconscious."

Kenderly weaved as she walked, but she was still hanging in there. He held on tight to an amazing woman. He hated the thought of losing her again, realizing his fear would stay with him a good long while. For the first time, he came close to understanding what his mother went through after losing his dad and watching both of her children go into law enforcement.

He cared deeply for Kenderly. If their relationship could survive starting this way, it might just survive an average day-to-day life without hiccups.

"How are you going to start that? Didn't Tenoreno's men take your keys?"

"I can pick the storage compartment lock. I have a spare inside. I just need to find a piece of wire. There should be some here in an alley."

"Well, while you do, I'm going to sit down over on these steps and rest my eyes for a few seconds."

The adrenaline had worn off as evidenced by her falling straight to sleep while resting her head against the brick. Garrison found his wire, picked the lock and obtained the key. Everything was ready to kick-start and go, but he sat on the seat and watched her.

His mind hadn't worked past retrieving the flash drive and getting the hell out of Austin. Well, except about staying with Kenderly. That was a given. It had to happen.

So they'd pick up the flash drive and then… What would happen to Tenoreno?

Where could they go that they wouldn't be found? He left the bike and sat next to Kenderly. "I need your help."

"Hmm."

"We need to access the files and see what state prosecutor hasn't been purchased. Or find a judge who's safe to ask for a warrant. Then we can turn over the flash drive and go into hiding until the trial."

Libraries and computer stores wouldn't open for another three hours. There were too many cameras at all-night super stores. So what choice did they have? What were the remaining options?

"Kenderly, wake up. Where's a place we could open the files on the flash drive? I don't want to push our luck hanging around Austin waiting on a library to open up."

"Borrow a laptop," she mumbled before dropping her head on his shoulder.

"Borrow? From who?"

"Don't you have any friends?" she mumbled into his shirt.

"Not here, but you do. Don't you, sweetheart?"

"My friends aren't awake at this time of day." She pushed her hair away from her face and stretched an arm to wake up. "Actually, doesn't your dog walker live across the street from your aunt? Why not email the files from there?"

"It'll all be a moot point if the flash drive isn't in the dang water bottle."

"That is so clever of you." She swatted lightly at his shirt. "I had no idea what you meant when you said it was hidden in the water. I still might be a little loopy, though."

Kenderly stood and shook her head. She walked forward a few steps, stretching her neck and then waving her arms. She bent over and touched her toes. Garrison raced forward and swatted her behind. Things were tense. The city of Austin seemed to be trailing them, but he still wanted his hands on her.

She was working on her last ounce of energy but still had a smile for him.

He straddled the seat, and she hopped on behind him. He pulled her close, very familiar with the shape of her thighs.

"Now that I'm awake, remind me why we need to get the flash drive right this minute. You think someone's watching the house, right? And most of the city is looking for an escaped prisoner—meaning you."

He twisted enough to reach one of her hands. He lifted it to his face and brushed his lips across. He swallowed hard, not wanting to tell her the truth, wanting to protect her from it. But if something happened to him, she needed to know what to do.

"With my confession, Tenoreno brought Company F under serious question. The accusations have brought a halt to all the investigations there. Johnson told me a couple of things that are going to go south real quick if it's not resolved fast."

"I couldn't believe you made that false confession. I know how much it means for you to be a ranger. You trust those men, and they may never trust you again. Why would you?"

To save you.

He couldn't tell her she was the reason he'd do it again in a heartbeat.

"Here's where it becomes our problem. We've got nowhere to go. What if we wait, and Tenoreno's men find the evidence? What if he doesn't take any chances and just burns the place down?"

"If he catches us again…" She brushed his hair, skimming his scalp with her nails. "He's going to kill us this time, isn't he?"

He confirmed with a nod. "Finding the flash drive and delivering it to someone who has not been paid off by Tenoreno is the only way we're going to survive. I think he knows that, too. So his men are going to shoot to kill this go-round."

"All right. I'm ready." She wrapped her arms around his waist. "I'll have you know this is going to be hell on my hair again. I take no responsibility for what I'll look like later today."

He laughed. "Sweetheart, no one's going to notice your hair with that awesome shiner you have."

He gunned the bike to a start while she said a loud "what" in his ear. They could only take the motorcycle so far before the engine would alert anyone watching the house. Having it after as a means to leave town—that's why he wanted it close by.

He pulled up on the sidewalk around the corner from his aunt's street. He rolled forward until they could see the house. Parked in front of the driveway was a cop car, cigarette smoke curling from the open window. He pushed them down the sidewalk, back into the access alley behind a privacy fence and under a low overhanging tree.

"I'll get the flash drive. You stay with the bike."

"Can't I come with? I haven't had much luck on my own."

He kissed her, loving every second he spent with her in his arms. "I'll slip around to the back, jump the fence, get the drive and a bottle of water for you. I'll be back in a shorter time than it takes to make Bear fetch a ball. Easy."

"I'm holding you to that."

He removed the gun from his waist and checked his ammo. Not much. He had to trust this was going to work without problems.

KENDERLY WATCHED GARRISON jog through the alley. He would be crossing the street midway at the next block to avoid detection. So she knew it would take a few minutes. It was a lot more dangerous than his smile let on.

All she had to do was wait. Simple. Sure. Just waiting had nearly gotten her killed yesterday.

The old alley between the houses had tall grass which was wet with the early morning dew. She was afraid to sit, fearing she'd fall asleep as she'd done earlier on the back steps of the market.

So she waited. Impatiently. She checked the time on Jesse's phone about every thirty seconds. The bungle of numbers he'd told her for his password were long forgotten or she would have found what media was saying about their escape. She was just putting the phone in her back pocket again when she noticed a car moving at a snail's pace.

The motorcycle was back far enough it couldn't be seen from the street. The car passed, and she ran to the edge of the fence. It pulled through the stop sign and turned the corner. The familiarity of the man behind the wheel was probably her imagination. She hoped she wouldn't be reacting to all dark sedans with almost black windows that way for the rest of her life.

She kept leaning on the fence when a large man jogged across the street. She pulled back, hiding. It was Thomas. She was certain of it. The same murderer who'd held a gun to her head and pulled the trigger. She'd made peace with God because she'd thought she was about to die.

The nightmares about him would come for many, many years.

Garrison! Shoot to kill.

The words battled in her heart and mind. She was safe where she was. Garrison could be in and out of the garage before Tenoreno's man even reached the house. But what about the cop sitting out front?

She rushed across the yard, pausing at the corner of the house, feeling like a thief. Thomas was slowly sneaking up the sidewalk, acting like a regular person. But he'd never look that way to her. He was a murderer. She couldn't forget the hatred in his eyes or the delight he took pulling the trigger.

He would kill again. She was certain of that. She saw him raise the back of his loose black shirt, pulling a silver gun and pointing the long, black barrel toward the sky. He was going to kill the police officer and then Garrison.

If she watched him kill another person, she wouldn't be able to live with herself. He was almost at the back of the cop car. The sun glinted off the gun as he dropped it behind his thigh.

"Hey! He's got a gun!" came out of her mouth before she'd thought through what to do next. Thomas turned toward her.

The cop's door flew open, weapon drawn, body ready for a fight. He saw Isabella's murderer and relaxed, nodding his acknowledgment.

The fact that they knew each other glued her feet to the driveway she stood on. Thomas was off to his right, running toward the garage. He was soon hidden by a hedge that separated the houses.

The cop was halfway down the street, heading toward her.

She turned, running across the wet grass. She slid to her knees when she turned away from the motorcycle. She couldn't go back there. She couldn't hide in one of these homes or ask for help. Since the police officer was after her, no one would take her word over his.

He was on top of her in no time at all. He covered her mouth with his hand and dragged her back to his car. She fought every inch of the way, but had no real strength left. He threw her in the backseat and locked her in a nightmare.

"Stay inside, ma'am. There's an armed felon nearby."

That would be Garrison. The dirty cop held his gun and pointed toward the house. She didn't hear anything about backup coming to this address on the police radio. If the cop was dirty, as she suspected, he'd let Thomas murder her.

From where the officer's car was parked she could still see him watching the garage from the corner of the house. It seemed such a long time ago that she'd jumped off that porch and into Captain Oaks's car.

She couldn't see Tenoreno's man. Could barely hear anything outside the car at all.

She kicked and pounded and cried.

There was no way she was getting free or out of here alive. No way.

The officer moved to the yard and into the garage. He came out again, shaking his head. That's when she noticed that Thomas was near the car. His hand was on the passenger door. She pushed as far to the other side as possible. He would use her to draw out Garrison.

Her sacrifice would have been worth it if she'd saved someone's life. But she hadn't. And now if she was used against Garrison...

She was a fool.

Chapter Twenty-Three

"Dammit!" Garrison shouldn't have left her alone. Nothing had gone right—almost nothing—so he should have learned his lesson. But he'd left Kenderly on her own again, and there she sat in the back of a dirty cop's car.

Why couldn't they catch a break?

Tenoreno's man, Thomas, had gotten to the garage a minute too late. Garrison was clearing the back fence when he'd heard Kenderly's shout, warning the officer. He didn't blame her. She had to warn him. Just their luck that he was on Tenoreno's payroll.

Pausing in the overgrown hedge between the houses, he watched. Gun in one hand, and in the other was the flash drive still stuck in the water bottle. He couldn't let Kenderly be threatened or touched again. He'd meant every word he'd said in the van. She was wonderful. And strong. How had she not fallen apart after having a gun to her head?

Thomas didn't need permission to shoot today. When he squeezed the trigger this time, a bullet would be firing into Kenderly.

Where could he stash the water bottle? The neighbor didn't have a storage building. No woodpile or trash can nearby. The garage was attached to the house and not accessible. Nothing besides a swing set and a couple of kids' bikes.

The passenger door was pulled open, Thomas would have Kenderly, yanking her out of the car in seconds. Garrison did the only thing possible, he shoved the water bottle into the thick branches of the hedge and pushed through. He could come back for the evidence. Right now, he needed the gun away from Kenderly.

But first things first. He aimed his weapon. He was a good shot, but the line of sight wasn't clear. He could hit Kenderly or... Damn, they actually needed him alive to face the murder charges. He stepped over a bicycle. The image of his aunt's paper thin walls popped into his head. Thomas or the cop could fire and hit one of the neighbors inside their home.

He had to keep the fight in his aunt's yard and somehow not fire his weapon. How was he supposed to keep criminals from shooting? He holstered his gun.

"This should be a hell of a fight," he mumbled to himself. Garrison walked quickly and silently along the hedge. But when Thomas latched on to Kenderly's arm he shouted to get his attention.

"I sure hope you're carrying some ID, you son of a bitch. When we're done, they're going to need to identify the body. Can you handle someone closer to your size?"

Thomas stood, his body still blocking the way out of the vehicle for Kenderly. While swinging his weapon around, Garrison charged the last twenty feet.

Garrison slid feet first, using Thomas's ankles like second base. He popped back up, elbowing the gun from his opponent's thick hands, following it with a left punch to the gut. They danced apart like in a boxing ring, hands up, bodies angled for the first jab.

Thomas roared, dipped his head and charged like a

rhinoceros. He crashed into Garrison, slamming him to the ground. The force took both of them into the neighbor's front yard.

If he could just get up... But Thomas trapped him in the wet grass and punched the side of Garrison's aching head. Garrison punched back, sending two jabs to Thomas's right kidney.

There was another punch to his jaw, and Garrison couldn't get free. He needed Thomas off him, but he couldn't budge him. He drew back his arm, aiming to hit below the belt—

Where was she? He saw the cop creeping closer to his squad car, Kenderly leaning from it to get the gun. "Look out."

The cop jumped forward, pinning her arm under his shoe just before she reached his weapon. The cop leaned down, and she screamed.

"Kenderly?" She didn't answer.

Garrison shoved with all his might. He had to get to her. Finding strength he didn't know he still had, he forced Thomas backward. They both scrambled to their feet. Circling. Ready to attack like wrestlers.

Kenderly was still on the ground. "Get up." The cop nudged her with his boot. She got slowly to her knees, then grabbed the door to help.

Garrison tried to fake Thomas out in order to get to Kenderly, but his opponent planted his feet firmly between them.

The cop tried to lift her with one arm. When that didn't work, he shoved his weapon under her arm and attempted to help her to stand. Garrison caught his breath trying to determine how to get her out of there. She used the outside of the door to pull herself up.

Dammit. He couldn't pull his gun since the cop still had his weapon practically in Kenderly's face.

"Give me the gun and the girl," Thomas growled at the cop.

Behind them he saw Kenderly perk up. Her eyes connected with his. Thank God she was faking it.

The cop reached around her. She shoved the door, slamming it into the cop's arm. He lost his weapon. The gun bounced away from the patrol car, Kenderly went after it but hesitated before following it under the car.

"Dammit, run!" Garrison shouted at her, reaching for the gun at his back. "Get out of here."

Before he could get a firm grip, he turned into a right cross from his opponent. His vision spun with the rest of his head as he fell to the ground. In the blink of Garrison's eye, Thomas had his hands around Kenderly's throat.

The look of desperation he'd seen on her face at Tenoreno's was back as she clawed at the thick hands choking the life from her.

"Where is the flash drive?" he gritted out between his teeth.

Garrison drew on all his strength and rammed Thomas in his side, breaking his hold on Kenderly. They fell on to the rear of the car, then rolled to the pavement on the street. He heard Kenderly coughing, still on her knees. Thomas's hands quickly circled his own windpipe, cutting off the oxygen.

Garrison pulled both thumbs backward, forcing the release. "You. Can't. Win." He fought to say the words between punching and getting punched.

The pavement hadn't grown warm yet, but the sun reflected off metal and into his eyes. The gun. He and Tenoreno's man rolled over and then back again. He'd lost sight of Kenderly. He finally twisted away and kicked his opponent's chest.

Barely an umph escaped. He kicked again, and the guy knocked him on his back. Garrison rolled to his feet and connected with a rib. He remembered how much his head had hurt after yesterday's encounter. He kicked out again.

Garrison was brought back to the ground by another twist and tug on his foot, but this time he lashed out, following with a roll forward. Thomas couldn't pursue Garrison to his feet and wasn't prepared for the boot at his throat or weapon in Kenderly's hands.

"Drop it!" Kenderly shouted at the cop who was reaching for his gun. "I've had a horrible day, so don't tempt me to shoot this thing. I'm probably a terrible shot, but I'm bound to hit something."

Garrison scooped up the deputy's gun, pointing it at Thomas. "That goes for you, too. Don't tempt me." He stood shoulder to shoulder—or as best as he could—next to Kenderly. "You okay?"

"For the moment."

"Let me have that, sweetheart." He took the second gun from her shaking hands, then turned to the cop. "Cuff yourself to the live oak."

Someone in the neighborhood was bound to have called the police about the fighting. Good or bad, they'd be arrested, and Thomas would probably walk.

"Cuff your right wrist. Now around the tree. That's right." Out of the corner of his eye he watched Kenderly direct the cop.

"Get in the car, Kenderly. We need to move it."

"But what about—"

"He's coming with us. Yeah, big guy, let's go. No tricks. Just get into the car." Thomas followed the instructions once both guns were trained on him, and Garrison locked him inside.

Kenderly got close, wrapping her arms around his waist. "I'm so sorry, Garrison. I thought he was going to kill the officer. It looked like he was. I couldn't stand there and do nothing. Not again." Her voice trailed off. He knew what she was remembering.

"It's okay. We've got him. And now we have a laptop."

"The one in the car?"

"Yep. If that won't work, we'll go buy one with Jesse's credit card. All we need is a little time and to verify that none of the rangers are involved. Come on, get in."

He ran back to the hedge, found the bottle and got in the driver's seat, pulling away before the sirens made an appearance from the other direction.

Garrison grabbed Kenderly's hand in victory. "Looks like something finally went right for the good guys."

Chapter Twenty-Four

The files were sent to the state attorney general's office. Kenderly's joyous whoop could probably be heard all the way in Dallas. The relief she felt would have been even greater if Thomas, the murderer, wasn't still in the backseat.

Garrison had spoken to the commander of all the rangers after opening the files. Just as he said, there were no Texas Ranger names on it. The list was very thorough and not very long. Only a few local cops, but numerous attorneys who had been appointed to high positions within the state.

Sometimes just a campaign contribution was listed, but the file contained personal notes from Paul Tenoreno. He was meticulous about meetings and conversations. Right down to the politician's dog's name.

An impartial prosecutor should have no problem going to trial with the evidence against Tenoreno and Rosco. Isabella's notes even said where she'd hidden the handwritten ledger kept by her husband. No wonder he was so desperate to retrieve the flash drive.

"I think we've accomplished the impossible." She was definitely on a victory high, but the feeling was wearing off fast.

"Tenoreno still has to go to trial." Garrison's voice was

somber, bringing reality back. "We still have to testify. It might take a while, Kenderly."

They'd both have to give official statements about what happened. But for now, in this moment, they were safe and could rest. She glanced over her shoulder at Thomas, who looked totally undisturbed by it all. His lack of concern frightened her almost as much as when he was about to kill her.

"Want something to eat? I still have Jesse's credit card." She realized Garrison wasn't serious, but she played along. They could relax just a little. Couldn't they?

"What about him?" She pointed to the murderer in the backseat. "And don't you think that the police will be wanting their car back?"

He playfully hit the steering wheel. "Probably. I prefer my truck anyway."

"Not the motorcycle?"

"Well, the bike does get you close to me. But the truck usually works out as the better date vehicle." Garrison smiled and arched an eyebrow.

"If you're attempting to ask me out on a date…" She pointed toward their prisoner again. "Can we get rid of him first?"

"I think Rangers headquarters here in Austin is an excellent place to do both."

"You are totally right."

The man in the backseat didn't do anything except glare. Maybe he knew the futility of trying to escape, or maybe he had nothing to say. She didn't mind. He stared at her, and the only thing she could do was shut her sore eyes and face forward.

"I'm going to have one whopper of a shiny black eye," she continued. But from the little she'd seen of their passenger, Garrison had paid him back ten times over.

They'd come close to dying so many times. Remembering the ordeal of the past four days left her shaking. She laced her fingers together to keep them still. She avoided looking at anything except the cracked nail painted with her favorite polish.

"You okay, Kenderly?"

"Sure. Why wouldn't I be?"

Thomas Whatever-His-Name-Was laughed. In fact he laughed so hard he sounded as if he was wheezing.

"Why is he laughing?" She turned to the man who had spent four days trying to kill her. "You're going to jail for what you did to Isabella and Trinity. I'm going to make sure of that."

"I'll be out of jail before you can wash the makeup off your face." He lurched toward the plastic window. She flinched, causing him to snicker more. "I'm laughing at you, sweet pea. You think this is all over? You'll never be safe. I'll be out walking around, back working for Tenoreno or somebody else, and you'll be stuck in a dingy hotel room."

"Shut up. Just block him out, Kenderly. Don't listen."

She was glad Garrison knew where he was going. She couldn't concentrate on roads or street signs. He reached across the space separating them and held her hand.

"That's right, honey." Thomas tapped on the window. "Don't listen. But it doesn't matter. I know everything about you. Little that there is. I *will* find you, and then I'll rip your heart out."

Garrison flipped a switch, and the sirens started. He ran red lights and pulled into a parking lot a couple of blocks later. He flew out of the car with his gun drawn and yanked open the back door.

"Out. Get out, so I can—just get out."

Did he think he was going to fight the man again?

Kenderly jumped from the car. Thomas was still taking his time. She was sure the criminal saw the rangers rushing from the building and took his time trying to get Garrison riled.

She didn't want any more fighting and ran to the front of the squad car. By then Garrison wasn't alone. Several rangers took Thomas, cuffed his hands and led him to a different door. Two men she recognized as her rescuers from the night before greeted her and escorted her inside.

"You need a doctor, Kenderly. I didn't realize how badly you'd been hit in all the rush to rescue this one's backside." Bryce stood a little straighter and shook Garrison's hand, who now stood next to her.

"He's not going to make bail. No matter what he thinks, says or begs. I promise you that, Kenderly." She looked up at him. His touch gliding across her skin was as soft as a butterfly's wings.

"Hey, bud." Jesse stuck his hand out, but Garrison pulled him into a bear hug.

"How are my dogs?"

"Fine?" Jesse reached for his phone.

"Are you asking me?" Garrison put his hand over his heart, exaggerating every word and smiling.

"Give me a second." Jesse waved him off and walked away.

Garrison faced Bryce. "He forgot to get someone to feed them today, right?"

"Hey, I'm innocent in all this." He threw up his hands in surrender but grinned before pushing the glasses back high on his nose. "He's right, Kenderly. We're going to protect you. You brought down two of the toughest crime families in the state."

She shook her head. "I didn't do it. Isabella is the one

who had the courage to make her life better. She's the one who deserves to be called a hero."

The men nodded their heads and didn't argue.

"You guys are a mess. We need to get you two to a hospital."

Kenderly sat on the bench, exhausted. Moving another inch seemed way too hard. Whatever adrenaline high she'd received from actually winning their fight with Thomas and the police officer had worn off. It had been replaced with a fear she didn't completely understand.

Bryce attempted to convince them to get checked out by doctors until Garrison held up his hand.

"We're not going anywhere, pal. We've been on the go for days and deserve to sit down for a while. But you could spring for a couple of deluxe breakfasts. And pick up some coffee. Mine's black all the way. Kenderly wants a grande café au lait skinny extra foam." Garrison turned Bryce around and scooted him away from the hall bench. "Are you writing this down? It's extra foam. Bacon, not those flat sausage patties." With both men gone, Garrison took her hand and led her down the hall.

Impressive. He remembered her coffee order. She liked that he could momentarily take her mind off the greater problem of staying alive. But the rush of uncertainty hit her again. What was going to happen with the rest of her life? Would she constantly be looking to see who was behind her instead of planning for a future?

It couldn't be a pleasant way to live. And more than likely was the reason Thomas, the murderer, had finally used his voice…trying to scare her.

Once the door was closed in a small conference room, he pulled her into his arms, snug against his chest. She leaned back, and he caught her lips in a kiss. His fingers caressed her skin. She jumped at the contact but remembered who had her in his grasp. Relaxing in the wonderful feeling of his soft control of their touch, her body went all tingly, wanting more.

Garrison swayed backward, gulping for air, tilting his forehead to hers and dropping his hold to her waist.

Something happened between them. She didn't know if a gradual relationship would have developed this way. Between her mundane life and his exciting one, they may never have survived. But after this long weekend together, she knew she wanted to try.

She wouldn't be scared.

Life was an adventure, and she planned to live it.

"We only have a couple of minutes before they separate us and start asking questions." Garrison's deep voice took on an excited anticipation. "I just wanted to say that…that I…um… I think I'm on the verge of falling for you hard, Kenderly Tyler."

"Don't worry, Lieutenant Travis. I'll catch you." She kissed him quickly, gently. Then whispered, "I'm stronger than I look."

"No arguments there."

A knock on the door made him break away from her. They were joined by several men, all with badges on their belts.

The men gestured for Garrison to leave.

"I'll see you for breakfast."

"Breakfast," she mumbled to herself.

Garrison was the last connection to her past. A part of her life she could never return to. He wouldn't leave her. Not after saying that he…that he what? *Might* fall for her? That wasn't the same as saying he had. It wasn't the same as saying he would.

Panic hit.

Alone. Defenseless. She was just a beautician, all on

her own. If she disappeared, no one would know. She wasn't prepared to take down the Texas mafia. How could any of these men think she could do this?

No! She wouldn't be scared. She would have a life. And when the door shut, everything was different. She would force herself to be different.

The person she'd found hiding deep inside over the past four days would stay strong. The new her had no doubt in her mind what she wanted. She wanted to share her new life with Garrison.

"LOOKS LIKE YOU'LL have your choice of assignments now, Lieutenant. Eventually. We'll need all the hubbub to die down, of course. Your confession is going to confuse our public image for a while."

Garrison felt a hard slap on his back and was not so subtly turned toward an interrogation room by a major he recognized from a seminar months ago. He hadn't caught his name while getting one last look at Kenderly. She'd looked alone and—

It hit him like a truck. No. She looked abandoned, and he was the one deserting her.

"Is there no way we can stay close by? I mean, where she can see me. She looks sort of lost."

His escort just clapped a hand on his shoulder and gestured they sit down.

"We know you're tired, Lieutenant. We'll try to get your testimony recorded as quickly as possible. But you know how important it is to get this down while it's still fresh in your minds."

There was no way around the separate rooms and individual interviews. Garrison had no illusions; it was an interrogation. They'd deliberately brought in a friendly face, but he was almost certain the major had given a talk about debriefing tactics.

Garrison would emphasize the importance of Kenderly's help and the need for her testimony. That they would keep her safe in protective custody. He might not get to see her for a while. Okay, he knew that would be the case. They'd probably keep them separated at least until they could check out their stories.

"Are you going to want a lawyer? Are you certain you don't need emergency care?"

"I'm fine for the moment, sir." Might as well relax and get on with it. "Just hungry like usual, and I'll need a heck of a lot of coffee. It's already been a long day."

"I bet it has. Why don't we just start at the beginning? I've got someone working on that coffee."

The next few days were going to be rough. But the Rangers wanted him in the clear as much as he did. Having one of their own involved with a crime family would call into question a lot of their cases. Clearing him would be the best thing for all involved.

"I'm familiar with procedures, sir. Before we get started, I'd like to go on record regarding the threats the man I had in custody made against Miss Tyler. I believe he's a flight risk, but his threats put her at a high risk. Do we need to wait on a prosecutor?"

"We're reviewing the documents you emailed. We were also able to obtain a warrant which is being served as we speak. Thomas Dimon will not be released on bail. Do you have the original flash drive?"

Garrison's body relaxed. His spine was no longer stiff, and his shoulders dropped. Both physical testaments to the tension he felt regarding Kenderly's safety. He plucked the drive from his pocket and set it on the table.

"My phone has pictures of the murderer leaving the scene Friday."

"Let's start with why you were there."

"On Tuesday of last week, I received a call from Captain Aidan Oaks…"

He told his story, and a doctor checked him out, leaving a bandage around his arm and certifying he was physically fit.

With every mention of Kenderly's name, he thought about the last look she'd given him. He should have told her what to expect, but he didn't want to risk influencing her statement.

He'd arrested his fair share of people. He'd escorted witnesses—from both sides of the law. He'd been on stings, car chases, government details… Sitting on this side of an in-depth interrogation wasn't pleasant but would give him insight to the future ones he conducted.

During each interview, he was asked whether he thought Kenderly Tyler, beautician at the Best Little Hair House in Austin, was legit. Each time he cracked a smile, thinking about their wigs and makeup.

Each time he was asked if he thought Kenderly was capable of the murders of Isabella Tenoreno and Trinity Rosco, he said it was impossible.

The questions didn't stop—breaks were few and far between. He didn't mind. It meant they'd be finished quicker. The men treated him like a hero and were friendly enough, but none of them would tell him about Kenderly. No one answered his one question…was she all right?

Chapter Twenty-Five

"Thomas was right. The motel is dingy," she spoke softly to herself. After a week alone, sometimes she needed to make certain her voice still worked. Dingy and dark, especially with the curtains drawn.

Kenderly paced. She wasn't a pacer, yet…she paced. She'd actually paced more in the past week than she'd thought humanly possible. Then again, she hadn't been outside Rangers headquarters or motel rooms for over a week.

The unknown bugged her. The not knowing where or how long. Everything about starting over. Would she ever be safe? It all bugged her. They had Thomas Dimon in custody, and she'd been assured he wouldn't make bail. They'd indicted Paul Tenoreno, and he also hadn't made bail, which was a huge relief.

But she'd lost control of her life because she had been in the wrong place at the wrong time. At least she wasn't crying about the situation.

But maybe she wanted to, just a little.

She'd thought she'd grown very close to Garrison, and then he'd just left. His last words had been about breakfast. Two days of being deposed or debriefed and feeling alone. She wasn't allowed to call anyone except an attorney. After they assured her no charges were being brought, she didn't need one. She was told time and time again what she couldn't do. Then another week of just sitting, hidden in several run-down motels.

Not one person had mentioned anything about her future. The more they veered away from the subject, the more her brain dwelled on it. And on Garrison.

So she paced.

The men in and out of Company F's headquarters looked like genuine Texas Rangers—boots, jeans, dress shirts, guns and white Stetsons. It was sort of hard to think of Garrison Travis as one of them. He was her personal hero in a curly wig.

But wasn't he the one who put you in a room with strangers and just left?

It was easy to remind herself just how heroic he'd been with each retelling of their adventure to another prosecutor with a video camera. But it was harder to believe when she was alone in a new motel room every night. The prosecutors reminded her how well they'd do with the evidence and testimony. But it was no consolation to walking away from everything she'd built for herself or business.

It just didn't help that she was so completely alone. It gave her too much time to play the what-if game. What if things had been different?

"Blah, blah, blah." Tired of talking to herself again. "It doesn't matter now."

She'd made her decision to honor Isabella and Trinity by testifying, no matter what. She crossed her arms and looked out the window, longing to be outside in the fresh sunshine.

Kenderly stretched her neck from side to side to relieve the stiffness. "How can I be so stiff from just pacing? This is never going away while I'm sleeping in a motel bed."

"I still owe you a back massage." Garrison was in the doorway.

Shiny boots, black jeans, crisp white shirt, white hat and a genuine glad-to-see-you smile that she'd sorely missed. It was so corny to think that she'd missed him more than anything in her life. They'd known each other for so little time, but she did. She couldn't hide how seeing him made her happy.

"I DON'T THINK you'll want it here, though." Garrison loved the unreserved joy on Kenderly's face when she saw him. She no longer looked abandoned, just impatient. "How you holding up?"

It was good to see that she'd come out of this whole thing relatively unharmed. The one conversation he'd had about Kenderly was with Major Parker and Captain Oaks when they'd asked what Garrison wanted as his next assignment.

"I don't suppose reminding you that fraternizing with a witness is against the rules," Oaks had warned.

"What about protecting a fiancé?" he'd asked.

"That, son, is something I can work with." The captain had laughed.

Garrison's short conversation with Oaks had surprised him, but he was comfortable with the decision. As long as Kenderly liked the idea and things worked out. They'd have lots of time to get to know each other while he served on her protection detail.

"Garrison!" She flew into his arms.

"No one would tell me a damn thing until this morning," he whispered. "You should be happy to know they're taking your safety very seriously."

"Well, being safe is extremely lonely." She stepped back when Jesse and Bryce walked in the room.

"Go ahead and kiss her," Bryce said. "No one's coming."

Both men faced the hallway, giving them privacy—of sorts.

Garrison didn't hesitate. He scooped Kenderly to his chest, feet dangling in the air. She tasted as good as he remembered. Her response showed that she'd missed him as much as he'd missed her.

He let her slide down the length of him and kept her close. "Damn, I missed you."

"Me, too. They said it might be months before we go to trial. Will you be able to visit or write or call? Or forget about me altogether?"

"That's never going to happen, and you don't have to worry about visits. I'm going with you." He was more determined than ever. Nothing would keep him from loving her.

"What? No one mentioned anything about you. But wait. Are you sure? I mean, they're talking about months. Are you going to be away from crime fighting the entire time?"

"You don't want me on the detail?"

"Oh no, that's not it at all. I want you to be on my detail for life. I mean…you don't have to, if you don't want to." Kenderly looked so forlorn, yet hopeful.

"Sweetheart, you know what happens if I leave you alone. There's no tellin' what trouble you'd find."

"That is so true." She laughed, making him want to kiss her again.

"I'm not letting you out of my sight." He kissed her

again before any of his superiors marched into the room. "Besides, it'll give us plenty of time to create more of those porch swing stories for the grandkids."

* * * * *

Jon's hazel eyes were close to hers and she could feel warmth where he was touching her.

"I'm going to be right here, okay?" he said. "Your lifeline, like we talked about yesterday. Everybody needs one in this line of work."

Her lifeline. Yes, she needed someone to make sure she wasn't going under. Jon would do that.

As if he could read her mind he said, "I'll be right here. I won't let you go under."

Sherry took a breath and nodded. Okay, she could do this. At least she would try.

"I'm okay."

He kissed her on the forehead. "You're more than okay. You can do this."

"I hope so."

FULLY COMMITTED

BY
JANIE CROUCH

First Published in Great Britain 2016
By Mills & Boon, an imprint of HarperCollins*Publishers*
1 London Bridge Street, London, SE1 9GF

© 2016 Janie Crouch

ISBN: 978-0-263-91895-3

46-0216

Our policy is to use papers that are natural, renewable and recyclable products and made from wood grown in sustainable forests. The logging and manufacturing processes conform to the legal environmental regulations of the country of origin.

Printed and bound in Spain
by CPI, Barcelona

Janie Crouch has loved to read romance her whole life. She cut her teeth on Mills & Boon Romance novels as a preteen, then moved on to a passion for romantic suspense as an adult. Janie lives with her husband and four children overseas. Janie enjoys traveling, long-distance running, movie watching, knitting and adventure/obstacle racing. You can find out more about her at www.janiecrouch.com.

To "my" Jon and Sherry: it has been such a joy
for everyone to watch the two of you fall in love.
A beautiful romance that books—mine or
otherwise—would only hope to imitate.
May you forever live out Ed Sheeran's "Tenerife Sea."
I'll always think of you when I hear it.

Chapter One

Sherry Mitchell was pretty sure she was the only tourist on the beaches of Corpus Christi, Texas, wearing a long-sleeved shirt and jeans to try to help her relax. Especially since the late-afternoon heat was expected to spike toward one hundred degrees on this June day.

Granted, she was under a large, colorful beach umbrella that threw enough shade to protect her from a great deal of the sun's rays and the heat. She was from Houston—a Texas girl born and bred—so was perhaps a little more adjusted to the heat than some of the tourists used to more temperate climates. But she'd still received a couple of odd glances.

She had her bathing suit—a red bikini she'd bought last week especially for this vacation—on under her clothes. Somehow she hadn't been able to force herself to wear just the tiny scraps of cloth just yet.

Not that they were *that* tiny. The suit itself was pretty modest compared to some seen around here on any given day. Not to mention, it was quite attractive on her.

The problem wasn't anything to do with a bathing suit or modesty or appearances at all. The problem was the iciness that seemed to have permeated Sherry's very core recently.

She felt cold almost all the time. As if she would never be warm again.

Intellectually she knew that couldn't be true. She knew this feeling—a chill even in upper-90s weather—was all a product of her mind, her psyche. Her body wasn't really cold. She didn't have some rare disease or unknown illness. It was all inside her head. She'd taken her temperature to make sure.

It had been completely normal.

Nothing was wrong with her physically. She'd double-checked with her doctor. Gone in for a physical. "A couple-years-late, quarter-of-a-century checkup," she'd told him, not wanting to bring up the fact that she had the heater running at her house even though winter had long since passed.

Ironically the doctor had not only declared her completely healthy, but had congratulated her on being more grounded and wise than many people her age who tended to avoid physicals until something was wrong.

Sherry didn't avoid physicals. But it seemed that her mind was doing its best to avoid reality.

She pulled her shirt around her more tightly. It wasn't just the cold. She also couldn't stand the thought of being exposed, of sitting out here with no cover. As if the clothing she wore would somehow keep her insides from fragmenting into a million pieces and flying away.

Icy and *fragmented*. Two words she would never have used to describe herself a year ago now fit her perfectly. She had seen too much, been close to too many people with shattered lives. Had worked for too long without a break, without giving herself a chance to recharge. To heal.

Now her mind was evidently taking over that duty for Sherry. She was getting a break from her work whether she wanted it or not.

Because if she thought the cold was bad on normal occasions, it was downright frigid every time she tried to pick up a pencil and sketch pad.

They both sat beside her under the umbrella on their own towel. She was further from picking them up than she was from stripping down to just her bathing suit and frolicking in the sun.

She missed drawing. Creating the pictures of what she saw in her head. And more recently, creating the pictures other people saw in their heads.

Unfortunately those had turned out to be hideous monsters. A shiver rushed through her and she brought her knees up to her chest, wrapping her arms around them and rocking herself slightly back and forth.

At one time she had drawn every day, all the time. Growing up, she'd drawn or painted or colored on anything she could get her hands on: notebook paper, computer paper, the insides of book covers.

As she'd gotten older and realized there were *actual art supplies* she could buy, she'd rarely been without a sketch pad. Drawing was a part of her. All her friends had learned that Sherry would always be drawing—and usually drawing the people around her—no matter what else was going on. They'd accepted her; had learned that just because there was a pencil flying in her hand and her nose was in her sketchbook didn't mean she was ignoring them.

Her passion had driven her parents—both successful business owners, neither of them with any artistic ability or inclination—a little nuts. Both of them had small companies that could be handed down to Sherry if she would just do the smart thing: go to college and get a business degree. Or even better, a double major in business and something equally useful such as marketing or finance.

Sherry had double-majored, but in what *she* had found interesting: art and psychology. The psychology mostly because understanding what was going on inside the human mind made for more compelling drawings.

For the four years right after college Sherry had found

moderate success in the art world. She wasn't ever going to be rich, but she at least didn't have to wait tables.

Then two years ago she'd stumbled onto what some people in law enforcement had termed her "obvious calling."

Forensic art.

Sherry could admit it was the perfect blend of her natural artistic gifting and what she'd learned with her psychology degree. Once the FBI had learned that she was so good at it, she'd worked consistently—really beyond full-time—for them for the past two years. But if she had known the cost would be her love and passion for drawing, she had to wonder if she would ever have gotten involved with the FBI in the first place.

That seemed like such a selfish statement. She didn't like to think that she would give up the breakthroughs she'd made in cases, the criminals she'd had a part in helping apprehend, just because it made her not want to draw anymore.

But she hadn't even so much as picked up drawing materials for pleasure in more than six months. For the past five months, she'd drawn what she'd needed to for cases, although it had been difficult.

Then last month, after a particularly brutal case, the cold had started. She'd barely made it through her last two cases after that. Her boss at the FBI was glad Sherry was taking a couple of weeks off. It would allow her to "recover and come back fully recharged and ready to do what she did best—listen to a victim, get the picture in her mind and draw it so law-enforcement officers could put another bad guy away."

That was a direct quote. And pretty much the farthest from reality than Sherry had ever felt.

How could she be ready to jump back into forensic art when, even now on vacation, with the vast beauty of the Gulf in front of her fairly begging Sherry to attempt to capture its beauty on paper, she couldn't even pick up a pencil?

All she could do was keep from shivering and flying apart.

It was the third day of her two-week vacation in Corpus Christi. She'd actually made it outside today rather than just looking at the water from her house on the beach, one her parents owned but never used. So maybe she should cut herself a little slack.

She had made it to the beach today. That was enough. Tomorrow she would go a little further. Would actually pull out her sketch pad and draw *something*, even if it resembled a kindergartener's stick figure. And even if she had to put a coat on to do it.

Maybe the day after that she'd actually take off her polar tundra gear and dip her feet in the Gulf. One thing Sherry had learned from working over and over with traumatized people was that you just had to take it a little bit at a time. It was okay to expect that same slow progress from herself.

In a few minutes she'd be driving into downtown Corpus Christi to pick up her friend Caroline. They'd gone to college in Dallas at the same time and had taken a few psychology classes together and then kept in touch. Caroline was a paramedic here in the city.

Sherry would at least slip on a short-sleeved blouse and skirt before meeting her friend. Caroline was already concerned about her. She would be even more worried if Sherry showed up dressed as she was now, particularly in this heat. Sherry hadn't shared what was going on with her—she hadn't wanted to worry her friend. But even without talking about it, she knew Caroline was concerned.

Dinner and margaritas on the back patio of Pier 99, a pier turned restaurant on North Beach, with a good friend and no pressures sounded perfect to Sherry.

No trauma. No stress. No need to force herself to draw. Just margaritas.

JON HATTON HAD a barbecue brisket sandwich—he wasn't ashamed to admit that he'd developed an addiction to the Texas staple in his week of being here—almost up to his mouth when he received the brief text. Another rape victim. Memorial.

Even though it broke part of his heart, he dropped his half-eaten sandwich and stood.

Jon threw down a twenty, more than enough to pay for his meal at the diner plus leave the waitress a hefty tip, and was running out the door less than fifteen seconds after he received the text.

CHRISTUS Spohn Hospital Corpus Christi—Memorial for short—was right smack in the middle of downtown. Jon knew where Memorial was. But not because of any information local law enforcement had provided him, only because of the maps he had studied.

Corpus Christi PD was pretty pissed that Jon, a member of Omega Sector: Critical Response Division, was even here. They had made it clear they didn't find his skills as a behavioral analyst and expertise in crisis management needed or welcomed.

That was just too damn bad because they very definitely had a crisis on their hands. Corpus Christi had a serial rapist on the loose.

Five rapes in just over eight weeks. Actually six now, if the current woman in the hospital was also a victim. The local police, as probably any police force of a city this size, didn't have the resources to deal with this type of situation. People were in a panic and no breaks had been made on the case.

Corpus Christi PD had wanted to handle the situation themselves. But once the story made national news, that option was no longer available.

Omega had been called in and Jon, highly experienced

with situations where multiple skills would be necessary—profiling, crime and linkage analysis, investigative suggestions, multiagency coordination—had been sent.

Jon was good at seeing the overall big picture, at catching details other people sometimes missed. At taking all the individual pieces involved in a case of this magnitude and putting them together so that the whole was more than the sum of the parts.

He was also a pilot, an excellent sharpshooter and could kill a man a dozen different ways with his bare hands. But that probably wasn't in his official dossier.

No matter what list of credentials Omega had provided for Jon's arrival to help with this case, it hadn't made any difference with the locals. Every piece of information was only reluctantly shared. Jon was the last person notified for any possible lead.

But call him Rhett Butler because, frankly, Jon didn't give a damn. He wasn't in Corpus Christi to sit around holding hands and singing "Kumbaya." He was here to stop a predator from victimizing more women.

A particularly smart predator who was too clever to leave behind any evidence so far.

So it wasn't as if the Christi locals could be accused of not doing their jobs properly. Jon hadn't been able to make as much as a single crack in the case himself, despite the time he'd spent in his week here interviewing victims and studying patterns.

It was a frustrating feeling when all he could do was wait for the bad guy to strike again and hope for a mistake. Not a feeling Jon was used to or that sat well with him.

This was the first victim that had been reported since Jon had arrived in town. He planned to make sure there wasn't a next, regardless of how cooperative the Corpus Christi PD was. Or wasn't.

The text notifying him of the victim hadn't come from a member of the police department. Oh, Jon had no doubt they would eventually get around to notifying him of the victim's existence. After all, none of them wanted to be accused of deliberately keeping info from him. But God only knew when that would actually be.

The text had come from Caroline Gill, a paramedic. Jon had met and befriended her and her partner, Michael Dutton, earlier in the week when he'd interviewed them about victim number two, whom they'd also transported a few weeks ago.

Dutton and Gill weren't threatened by Jon's presence here. They had talked openly with him about what they knew, what they'd heard. Jon had even asked them their theories about the case, since they had been the first people on one of the crime scenes.

Perhaps the paramedics' opinions wouldn't amount to anything useful whatsoever. But Jon had been doing this job for Omega Sector long enough to know that a break in a case could often come from unusual sources.

At the very least, his willingness to listen to them had gotten him the text that had him now driving through the city as fast as he safely could.

Jon parked at the closest nonemergency spot he could find at Memorial and jogged to the sliding glass of the emergency entrance door, ignoring the muggy heat that was so unlike the weather in his home state of Colorado. He pulled out his credentials to show the nurse at the front desk, explaining who he was here to see. He was glad when he saw Sara Beth Carreker, the head nurse who had worked in Emergency for years, walk up. Jon had talked to her a few days ago, also, since all the victims had been brought to Memorial's Emergency Trauma Center.

Nurse Carreker's nod was brisk. "I'll show you back

there myself. The patient has been moved into one of the private trauma care rooms." Her lips pinched together.

"I take it that's a bad sign?"

The nurse glanced at him as they walked down the hall. "Medically, it's pretty neutral. Just my opinion, of course. You'll have to ask the doctor for a professional statement." The older woman's eyes argued that she had seen more and probably knew more than a lot of the young doctors around here.

"So, physically she'll recover. That's not why she's in the room." Jon's words weren't questions.

"Yes." Nurse Carreker nodded as they turned a corner. "Emotionally that woman needs as much privacy as she can get."

"Anything you can tell me about her?"

"Young. A local. African-American this time, so that's a little different. But the same type of bruising and craniofacial trauma."

A black female. Jon's jaw clenched. The demographic pattern of the women who had been attacked was widely varied, almost unheard of in a serial rapist. It was one of the reasons Corpus Christi PD had resisted asking for any federal help. Since serial rapists usually had a set type of woman they attacked, the department hadn't thought the perpetrator was just one person.

Nurse Carreker stopped halfway down the hall. "Agent Hatton, y'all try to remember that this isn't a case to that woman. Her whole world has just been destroyed."

Y'all? Just because Jon didn't use the word didn't mean he didn't know what it meant. How many people were here besides him? "Okay, thank you."

The nurse patted him on the arm and left. Jon turned back toward the victim's room. At least half a dozen of Corpus Christi's finest were standing around outside the victim's door. They alternated between glaring at and completely ignoring him as he approached.

Damn, this was going to be a long afternoon.

Chapter Two

Jon noticed that Zane Wales, the detective he'd been working most closely with—*closely* being a very relative term—was busy cross-referencing something on his smartphone with a file in his hands. The younger man made it a point not to make eye contact. Wales should've been the one who had called or texted Jon, not the paramedic.

Jon tamped down his frustration. This wasn't the time or place to get into it with Wales again. Especially because he knew the captain at the local police department all but applauded Wales's attitude. He encouraged any and all negative attitudes toward Jon.

"Hatton," Wales said neutrally in greeting. The man actually wore a cowboy hat all the time. Since they were in Texas that shouldn't surprise Jon, but it was still a little unsettling.

"Wales." Jon raised an eyebrow, but didn't say anything further.

"Doctor's with the victim, so no one can go in yet." Wales put himself between the door and Jon as if Jon were going to barge his way in. Jon barely restrained himself from rolling his eyes.

He looked over at the uniformed officers milling around, half a dozen of them, all male. They all wanted to be here, be somewhere nearby so they could help if needed. While Jon appreciated the gesture, they had to leave.

He turned back to Wales. "A little crowded out here, don't you think, for a woman who's just been brutally attacked?"

Wales looked a little surprised that Jon had said something reasonable. Probably had expected him to pick a fight about not being notified.

"Actually, I agree," Wales said. "The last thing that woman is going to want or need is a bunch of people—men especially, probably—out here hanging around."

The detective's statement reassured Jon on multiple levels. First, he had already been aware of the problem before Jon even pointed it out and would've handled it himself soon, hopefully. Second, Wales might not like him or the fact that he had been assigned to the case, but at least he wasn't going to do something potentially case-damaging such as keep a bunch of unnecessary people there just to spite Jon. The victim was Wales's priority.

So cowboy hat notwithstanding—the jury was definitely still out on that—the young detective had just proved himself to be at least competent and focused.

Jon backed out of the way as Wales went to talk to the uniformed officers and dismiss them. He could hear him reassure the men that they personally would be the first ones called if anything could be done for the victim or if any further help was needed. He was glad to see Wales wasn't a jerk in general.

Just with him, evidently.

After the uniforms left, Wales made his way over to Jon. Both knew it could be some time before they were able to talk to the victim, depending on the extent of the physical and emotional trauma. But sooner was definitely better, while everything was, unfortunately, still fresh in the victim's mind.

They'd have to wait until the doctor came out to give them more information.

"Do we know anything about the victim?" Jon gave it about a fifty-fifty chance that the detective would be forthcoming with information.

Wales hesitated but then responded.

"Vic's name is Jasmine Houze. She's twenty-seven, not married, lives on Mustang Island, which is out near the beach. Works for Flint Hill Resources, an oil company."

Corpus Christi, in Jon's opinion, was a city with an identity crisis: part touristy beach town, part oil/shipping industry. Both businesses seemed to vie for what the city would be known for. There were lovely beaches, but if you wandered too far from them you were right in the middle of oil industry with their buildings and warehouses and machinery. So you had all types of people in the city's makeup.

"Nurse said there was similar craniofacial trauma?" Jon asked.

"I haven't seen her yet or any medical records to confirm," Zane Wales responded. "But, yeah, I understand that's the case."

The extent of the woman's wounds would determine a lot, such as how soon they could question her and to what degree she would be able to coherently remember facts.

It was a full hour later before the doctor, a female, and two female nurses came out. The doctor closed the door behind her in a way that suggested no one would be entering soon.

"Gentlemen," the doctor said in greeting.

"How is she, Dr. Rosemont?" Wales asked. "Is it possible for us to speak with her?"

Jon stayed a half step back. It was better for local detectives to take the lead in these types of cases, he knew from experience. He would only jump in if necessary.

Although the nurses left to complete their other duties, the doctor positioned herself even more solidly in front of the door.

"As I'm sure you can imagine, Ms. Houze is in a delicate state right now, both physically and emotionally." The doctor crossed her arms over her chest.

Jon was glad to see Wales nodding, taking seriously what the doctor was saying. It was important to talk to Ms. Houze, but it was also important to remember that this was the worst day of her entire life.

"We understand," Wales said. "And we want to be sensitive to the situation. But talking to her soon is important, if medically possible."

"Ms. Houze has significant bruising to her face and jaw. The rapist struck her a half-dozen times in rapid succession to stun her. She'll have no permanent damage from those blows, but both her eyes are currently swollen shut."

That was undoubtedly what the attacker had intended, so the victim wouldn't be able to identify him. Jon grimaced. The same thing had happened in the other cases. As a matter of fact, the facial abuse was what had helped alert them to the fact that this was the work of a single man.

"Do you think she'll be willing to talk with us?" Wales asked her.

"I definitely don't think she's interested in surrounding herself with men right now, so only one of you, and that may not work at all." Dr. Rosemont shrugged.

"Then I'll be handling that, boys." The drawl came from behind them.

Jon turned the find the last person he would send into a room with a woman who had been victimized. Senior detective Frank Spangler.

Unlike Wales, who might not like Jon personally, but at least showed promise as a detective, Frank Spangler was the epitome of everything that could be considered bad about law enforcement.

The man had been wearing a badge for too long. He had lost touch with what was most important about his career: namely that he was supposed to serve the people. Spangler was smug and crass and definitely not the person best suited to question a woman who'd just been viciously attacked.

Unfortunately, Detective Spangler was not only the ranking detective, but he was also the Nueces County forensic artist. The *only* one. Jon had already checked.

Jon had seen Spangler's composite drawings for other cases and had to admit the man had some skill with a pencil. But for the current case, none of the victims had seen the rapist's face. They'd all been hit so hard, so quickly, that they'd been completely disoriented and unable to get a clear view before their attacker had pushed them down. So even if Spangler had some drawing talent, gathering any usable intel from the victims hadn't been possible.

But maybe Ms. Houze was different. They had to try.

Dr. Rosemont nodded at the older detective. "That's fine. But under no circumstances are you all to barge in on her at once. My word is law around here, gentlemen. Remember that. Door open at all times and if Ms. Houze says she's had enough, you're to leave immediately."

Jon and Zane both nodded at the doctor. Frank Spangler just gave her a patronizing smile. Her lips pursed.

"I'll check with her and be right out." The doctor knocked softly on the door and made her way inside.

Caroline Gill, the paramedic who had sent Jon the text alerting him of the new victim, joined them in the hallway.

"Hi, Jon. Hey, Zane," Caroline said. She smiled at Jon. But her eyes, he realized, were only for Zane. The detective, on the other hand, didn't really seem to notice the pretty paramedic.

He barely glanced at her from where he was looking over a file in his hand. "Hey, Caroline."

"I'm just getting off work and waiting on my ride."

"Where's your car?" Jon asked her since Zane seemed oblivious that Caroline was here to see him.

"A friend from college is in town and is going to pick me up in a few minutes so we can go to dinner. She dropped me off for my shift this morning so I wouldn't have to find parking."

Wales nodded without even looking up from his file. Caroline's face was a little crestfallen at his behavior.

"Hey, thanks for the text," Jon said to her to change the subject.

Zane looked up sharply at that. He had probably wondered how Jon had gotten here so fast. Well, now he knew.

"Really?" Zane asked Caroline.

Caroline turned toward him and put her hands on her hips. "You know for a detective, Zane Wales, sometimes you're pretty obtuse. So, yeah, *really.*"

Jon swallowed his chuckle.

Frank Spangler cleared his throat and began sorting through items in his briefcase, pulling out some drawing materials. "I doubt this victim will have kept her wits about her any more than any of the others. But here's to hoping."

Jon grimaced and heard Caroline's gasp. Zane's level of obtuse was nothing compared to Frank Spangler's.

"You sure that's the right attitude to go in there with?" Jon asked Spangler. "I'm pretty sure being told she should've kept her wits about her as she was being attacked is not the best way to start an interview."

"Look, I was doing this job before you were in training pants." Spangler sneered at Jon. "I'm not going to say that to *her*, of course. You just stay out and let me work."

It didn't matter if Spangler was going to say it or not. He *thought* it. That was bad enough.

But unless the older man did something illegal or to outright jeopardize the case, there wasn't anything Jon could do. Corpus Christi had been forced to allow him here and give him access to all the information, but it was still their case. From experience, Jon knew that allowing them to handle as much as possible was best in the long run for both the department and the community.

But listening to Spangler's idiocy still wasn't easy. Caroline looked as though she was about to let Spangler have it when the doctor came out the door again.

"Ms. Houze has agreed to see you—*one* of you, like I said. I have suggested she limit the time you're in there to fifteen minutes. She has family on their way. She needs them right now."

"Yeah, well, I would think she would want us to catch the person who did this," Spangler muttered.

"Fifteen minutes, Detective. Tops. I'll be back then." Dr. Rosemont made her way down the hall.

The older officer wasted no time going in, sketch pad and pencil in hand.

"That man is a Grade-A jerk," Caroline snapped.

Jon couldn't agree more.

Zane didn't even disagree. "Fortunately he's only a year from retiring. Plus he's pretty good with composite drawing." The detective shrugged.

They could hear Spangler inside talking to the victim. He'd at least started the conversation by offering appropriate condolences for what had happened. Jon was distracted from listening by the woman who had walked silently down the hall and was now speaking to Caroline.

Blond hair with gentle waves that fell past her shoulders. Slender—almost too slender. A little taller than average height, maybe five foot eight in her knee-length skirt and brown cowboy boots. As with cowboy hats, Jon had never been one for boots, but he could already feel his opinion changing about that. This woman's brown, well-worn ones made it difficult for him to tear his attention from her legs.

Her legs were gorgeous. *She* was gorgeous.

This must be the friend from college the paramedic had mentioned. Caroline walked over with her to where he and Zane were standing.

"Zane, Jon, this is my friend Sherry Mitchell. She's visiting Corpus Christi for a couple of weeks," Caroline told them.

Jon shook Sherry's hand and immediately noticed she was distracted. Her eyes kept darting to the room where Spangler was talking to the victim.

Maybe because it was starting to get a little louder in there.

"Look, I'm your best bet in us apprehending the man who raped you. Do you really want to rest more than you want to catch this guy?" Spangler's voice could be heard clearly.

All the color seemed to seep out of Sherry's face.

"Look, don't cry, for heaven's sake." Spangler continued, his distaste obvious. "I'm a forensic artist. Just tell me what you saw."

"I didn't see anything." Jasmine Houze's voice was soft, slurred, probably from the swelling of her face. "I didn't see him. He hit me and then…and then… I'm sorry." Her crying became louder.

"Nothing?" Spangler demanded. "Nothing at all? Do you not want to catch him? Is that it?"

"Oh, my God," Sherry whispered.

"I'm going in there," Jon said to Zane. "I don't care if Spangler is the ranking officer or not. This has to stop."

"I'm right behind you," Zane agreed.

"No." It was Sherry who spoke. "That woman does not need more men barging in on her and fighting."

Caroline nodded. "She's right. I'll go in. I, at least, have already met her, since Michael and I brought her in this morning. You guys go get the doctor."

"I'm going with you," Zane said to Caroline. "You know

Spangler won't listen to you. He won't listen to Hatton, either."

"Well, for God's sake, shut him up," Jon said. "I'm going to get the doctor."

Sherry had just backed away against the wall. Jon didn't blame her. He'd stay out of this mess, too, if he was her. But she had lost all color and was shivering.

"Are you okay?" he asked, touching her gently on the upper arm.

She nodded without answering, her eyes still drawn toward the victim's room.

Caroline and Zane had already entered. Jon could hear Caroline talking softly to the woman.

Jon looked at Sherry again. "Are you sure you're okay?" He didn't want her to collapse.

"I'm fine," she said. It looked as though her teeth were about to start chattering, but he knew that couldn't be right; it wasn't nearly cold enough in here.

Sherry cocked her head toward the nurses' station. "Just go."

Jon took off running down the hallway to find Dr. Rosemont or Nurse Carreker. Either of them would help put an end to this without damaging Jasmine Houze's psyche further.

He found them both just moments later. Neither woman wasted time and the three of them were soon sprinting down the hallway toward the victim's room, Jon explaining as they ran.

The doctor and nurse, along with Caroline, distracted and comforted Ms. Houze as Jon and Zane both each grabbed one of Frank Spangler's arms.

"Wait, I'm not finished talking to her," Spangler all but screeched.

All three women surrounding the victim turned at the same time and said, "Yes. You are."

Fortunately, Spangler didn't put up a fight; he just walked out, huffing as he went. Jon immediately closed the door behind them.

"You better believe the captain's going to hear about this." Spangler's eyes glared at Jon as if he were personally responsible for him being kicked out of the victim's room. The older man then turned, gathered his things and left.

That was fine. Jon didn't care as long as Spangler wasn't allowed near Jasmine Houze or any of the victims again. And, yes, the police captain *would* hear about this. Jon glanced over at Zane, who just shrugged, shaking his head.

Caroline came out of the room, closing the door softly behind her. "They've given Jasmine a sedative. Her family should be here soon."

Jon looked over to where Sherry had been standing against the wall when he had last seen her. He wanted to talk to her more, to apologize for the craziness, to make sure she was all right.

And to ask her to dinner.

But she was gone.

Chapter Three

The next day Jon was ready to dig a hole and bury himself in it.

For one thing, it was one million degrees outside. He missed the Rocky Mountains of Colorado Springs where Omega Sector: Critical Response Division headquarters was located. He missed the crisp air, often cool even now in June, and the ability to go out and run first thing in the morning or even in the afternoons a lot of the time, and still be pretty comfortable.

Because this face-melting heat of Corpus Christi was probably going to kill him.

Not that he would be going out for a run anytime soon. Why run outside when he could just run in circles inside Corpus Christi Police Department, accomplishing nothing?

He was sitting in Captain Harris's office, along with Zane Wales and Frank Spangler. Spangler was categorically dismissing the complaints that had been called in against him by Jasmine Houze's doctor. He actually called both the victim and Dr. Rosemont "irrational."

Wales had remained silent, refusing to either confirm or deny what had happened in the hospital room.

And while Jon appreciated that the younger man probably didn't want to get Frank Spangler in trouble just before his retirement, Zane's silence was not helping the case. If the Corpus Christi PD wasn't careful, they were going to lose control of the case entirely. One phone call from Jon and this case would be under federal jurisdiction rather than local.

That was a last-resort option and Jon didn't want to do that if he didn't have to. But he wouldn't hesitate if something like that happened again. He'd already made that clear to Captain Harris privately.

"We're going to need another forensic artist," Jon said to the other men.

"Well, that's too bad, since I'm the only one currently licensed in the county. And in our county only people licensed in forensic art are allowed to talk to witnesses or victims in an official capacity." Spangler sat back, secure in his own importance.

"My resources aren't limited to your county, Spangler," Jon said. "And believe me, I would go in there with a paper and pencil myself before I would let you further traumatize another woman like yesterday."

Spangler let out a loud huff. "You see there, Captain? This sort of unfriendly attitude is what we have to deal with all the time from Agent Hatton, all but impeding our investigation—"

Jon resisted the urge to jump out of his chair. Barely. "Are you kidding me? You just had a complaint filed against you from one of the top trauma doctors in the state. And you want to say I'm impeding the investigation?"

"Boys, enough," Captain Harris interrupted in his Texan drawl. "Hatton, please use your federal resources to find another forensic artist."

The captain's contempt for anything federal was evident by the way he said the word with a sneer.

"Fine." Jon's teeth were clenched, but he got the single syllable out.

"Now, if you don't mind, Agent Hatton, I'd like to talk to Detective Spangler alone. Sort through some things."

Somehow Jon didn't think that the "sorting" would involve any sort of reprimand whatsoever. Spangler's snigger and mock salute to Jon suggested the older man knew it, too.

Jon nodded, got up and left. He was afraid if he stayed he would end up punching Spangler, a man who was at least twenty-five years older than Jon's thirty-one. Jon's mom had taught him better than that.

Although Jon wasn't entirely sure his mother wouldn't have punched Frank Spangler herself if she'd been around yesterday.

He made his way over to the desk the department had given him in the darkest, stalest corner of the old brick building. It was right next to the copy machine and cleaning supplies, so it pretty much ensured that Jon dealt with a constant flow of interruptions and had a headache from the chemicals.

Still, it was better than being outside where his shoes would probably melt into the sidewalk. And this was nothing compared to August's heat evidently. That made Jon, a Cincinnati boy at heart, make a mental note to never travel this far south during that month if he could possibly help it.

He sat in his desk chair and spun it around so his back was to the rest of the desks, giving him at least a semblance of privacy. The copy machine wasn't so loud that way, either. He speed-dialed the direct office line for his boss, Steve Drackett, at Omega.

"You bought a cowboy hat yet?" Steve asked by way of greeting.

Jon chuckled slightly. "No. But I'm considering just killing someone on this force and taking his."

"That bad, huh?"

"To say they don't want me here would be a gross understatement. Don't mess with Texas and all that." Jon sighed. "We've got a new victim as of yesterday."

"I heard."

Jon wasn't surprised his boss already knew about Jasmine Houze. Steve tended to know a lot of things about a lot of things.

"I haven't talked to her yet. There was a whole brouhaha at the hospital with one of the senior-ranking detectives. Guy doesn't have bedside manner worth spit and traumatized the poor victim even more than she already was."

"Guy sounds like a problem?" his boss asked.

"Yeah, but he's a year out from retirement, so nobody's going to do anything about him unless he really screws things up."

"You need me to send in help?"

Jon leaned back farther in his chair. "No, I can handle it. I'm not here to make friends. But I guess I should tell you that I gave the police captain final notice about federal takeover." Jon explained exactly what had happened with Frank Spangler and the complaint.

"Well, I've got your back. You say the word and Omega will completely take over. I can have more agents down there in four or five hours." Steve chuckled. "I could have them there in less if you were here to fly them."

Jon smiled at that. "Thanks. It's better for everyone around here if the locals handle it. Good for morale and community relations. If they can't get it together, I'll let you know."

"Any actual progress?" Steve asked.

"Nothing, Steve. That's what kills me. I can't even blame it on Corpus Christi PD. I may not like any of them personally, but they're not inept. This guy is smart. A planner."

"You got a profile worked out on him yet?"

Jon spun his chair around so that he was facing the rest of the desks in the station. The activity and blur of noise actually helped him think.

"He's educated, or at least smart enough to know not to

leave any DNA behind. Not even skin cells. These rapes are definitely acts of dominance, not rage. The perpetrator is in complete control of his emotions."

"I thought reports said the women had been beaten?" Drackett cut in. "That's not anger-based?"

"I don't think so," Jon replied, leaning back farther in his chair. "He only hits them enough to stun them. None of the women has had any broken or fractured noses or cheekbones. If the beatings were out of anger, the facial trauma would've been much greater. It was a deliberate move to keep them from being able to see and identify him."

It was great to let his thought process have free rein with someone who wasn't throwing unnecessary questions or playing devil's advocate just to try to stump him. That was how his conversations with the local detectives had gone over the past week: a constant battle to one-up him.

"Nothing else about this guy is consistent but the craniofacial trauma. His victims are of varied race and age. The times of the attack are all over the place. The locations of the attacks are varied, also—most have been at the victims' homes, but one was at a hotel."

"And no evidence found at any of the scenes?"

"Nothing usable. None of the women got a clean punch or scratch." A single scratch from any of them would've given them trace DNA under their nails, but none of them had been able to do any damage to their attacker. "Each time, as soon as they opened the door, he hit them hard and fast, dazing them and causing swelling in both eyes, effectively blinding them."

He heard Steve's muttered curse. It echoed exactly how Jon felt.

"If that's the case, I'm sure none of the victims has been able to provide any sort of identifying marks or features," Steve said.

Jon grimaced. "No, not at all. But I have to say, if Frank

Spangler has been the only forensic artist available to talk
to the victims, maybe more information can be gathered
from them, if his actions yesterday are anything to go by."

"Were there other complaints lodged against him?"

"No, but even if he wasn't as combative with the other
women as he was yesterday, he still wasn't going to inspire
any confidence in the victims. We need someone else, Steve."

"Omega has a few on retainer, but none in Texas. Let
me make some calls and see what I can find out."

"Okay, I'm heading over to the crime scene. I'm not expecting much, but at least I'll be able to see this one firsthand rather than through pictures like the others," Jon said.

"Good luck. I'll send you the info when I find someone."

Jon ended the call. Steve would find another forensic
artist if there was one around to be had. If not, he'd work
his magic and find someone who *wasn't* around. Steve
always made sure his agents had what they needed. And
God knew Jon needed a better artist than Frank Spangler.

He saw Detective Wales making his way over, cowboy
hat still firmly on his head. "You ready to go check out
the crime scene?"

Jon lifted a single eyebrow. "We're going together?"

The younger man rolled his eyes. "I'm not asking you
out on a date, Hatton. Captain just said Spangler probably needed to stay away from anything having to do with
Jasmine Houze, so I thought we would go together since
we're both headed out there anyway."

Maybe Wales was just trying to make up for not saying anything to the captain about Spangler's true behavior. Whatever it was, Jon would take the peace flag being
offered to him.

The drive from the station to the victim's house was
mostly made in silence except for the country-western
music coming from the radio of Wales's SUV. Honestly

it wasn't half-bad. Maybe Jon should give the genre more of a chance.

Jasmine Houze's home was close enough to the beach to be desirable, but not so close that the price would be in the stratosphere. She was probably a good fifteen-minute walk from the water itself. The neighborhood looked to be in decent shape, certainly not a place where you were afraid to open your own door in the middle of the day.

At least that was what everyone had assumed until yesterday. Jon would damn well bet there was a whole new set of chains and bolts that had been installed on neighboring doors in the past twenty-four hours.

The houses were just far enough apart from each other to afford some privacy. The victim's was one of the four on the street that had large shrubbery in the front yard. Better for privacy.

Unfortunately it made the attack more private, also.

The three front steps leading up to the house had been taped off. Jon could see that the crime lab had already been here: print dust lay all along the railing leading up to the house and the door frame. If this was anything like the other scenes, it would soon be evident that the rapist had worn gloves.

Although Jon and Zane looked around, inside the house didn't yield any more results than outside. They would wait for results from the crime lab, but Jon wasn't holding his breath.

Their next two hours were spent talking to neighbors. Uniformed officers had already taken preliminary statements, but follow-ups were always necessary. Just as with the porch and the house, they discovered nothing. No one had heard anything out of the ordinary yesterday. No one had seen anyone unusual or suspicious walking or driving around lately. No strange cars. Nothing out of place.

Jon was frustrated, but he wasn't surprised.

"I read your preliminary behavioral analysis of the perp," Zane said as they stepped out into the heat after talking to the last neighbor.

He had read Jon's report? That did surprise him. He'd expected it to end up in the electronic trash bin on Wales's computer. He was sure that was where it had ended up in most everyone else's.

"Did you agree with the analysis?" Jon asked.

Zane shrugged and adjusted his hat to settle more fully on his head. "I don't disagree with any of it. Like you said, our guy is smart, focused, patient. The other rape cases I've dealt with haven't been that way. It's been more about rage and dominance."

Jon nodded. "Yeah, most rapists have those characteristics. And maybe our guy does, too, and has just figured out how to hide it."

The detective pondered that for a moment. "I guess what doesn't sit right with me is the fact that he's so smart we're having to sit around and wait for him to strike in order to gather more info."

Jon nodded. He had thought almost the exact same thing yesterday. His eyes tightened behind the sunglasses protecting him from the blazing sun. They were waiting for this guy to make a mistake. And that was not a position Jon wanted to be in.

They were almost back at the station when Jon got the text from Steve Drackett.

Found you a forensic artist. Exceptional recommendations from FBI in Houston. Full file sent.

"Looks like Omega found us another forensic artist," Jon said to Zane. "Maybe this will get us somewhere."

Everyone, especially Spangler, was glaring at Zane upon their entrance into the station. Evidently no one was thrilled with the younger detective's choice to spend time with Jon. Zane shrugged in half apology and left Jon, heading in a different direction.

Jon sighed. So much for making headway with the locals. But as he'd told Steve, he wasn't here to make friends. He grabbed a Coke—not a soda, pop or cola; they were *all* called *Coke* here, he'd been told—and went to his desk, the smell of cleaning agents permeating the air.

He was hot, he was frustrated and he was getting tired of the literal and figurative toxic environment surrounding him.

Most of all, Jon was frustrated that they couldn't get ahead of this bastard.

He sat down to pull up the file on the computer the department had given him—surprisingly one that worked—so he could print the info Steve had sent him on the forensic artist right away.

He took a sip of his soda then almost spewed it out.

Because, damn, if he didn't find the familiar features of Sherry Mitchell staring back at him.

Chapter Four

Sherry was just as lovely in her photo as she had been in real life. It was just a head shot, so unfortunately those legs he'd seen yesterday in the hospital weren't in it, but her long blond hair and clear blue eyes were.

Although Jon could appreciate her attractiveness, he was damn well ticked off at the woman.

How could she have stood there in the hallway yesterday and let Frank Spangler interview the victim? Not say a word about her profession?

And evidently she was stellar at it. If this file was anything to go by, Sherry Mitchell was considered by her supervisor at the FBI to be one of the best forensic artists in Texas, if not the entire Southwest. Her track record was impressive, and it seemed she had a particularly good case history with rape victims.

That just led Jon back to his original question: How could someone who obviously had a talent—having received numerous written commendations from some people pretty damn high up in the Bureau—just choose to do nothing yesterday?

Okay, she'd had dinner plans with Caroline. As trite as that sounded, Jon could actually understand that maybe Sherry hadn't wanted to break her reservation or whatever. But at the very least she could've offered to help at a later time, diffused the situation.

Not just stand there in the hallway shivering as though she'd never seen a trauma victim before.

Somewhere in his mind Jon knew he was being unfair, but he didn't care. He was damn well tired of every law-enforcement agent in the state having some sort of problem with him just because he was outside their don't-mess-with-Texas inner circle. Sherry Mitchell was the last straw.

He intended to let her know that.

The final part of Steve's message stated that although Sherry generally worked for the Houston Bureau field office, she was currently on vacation and her supervisor wasn't sure exactly where.

Jon knew, although not the exact place where she was staying.

But he knew how to get that info, too.

Jon grabbed his phone and called the number from the text he'd received yesterday notifying him of the new rape victim. He knew Caroline Gill would know where Sherry was staying.

"Hello?"

Caroline's voice sounded sleepy. Jon cringed. As a paramedic, Caroline probably worked odd hours. She might have been asleep.

"Hi, Caroline. It's Jon Hatton. I hope I didn't wake you."

"No, I'm fine. I have a shift in a couple of hours. Has something else happened?"

He could hear the concern in her voice. She was definitely wide-awake now. "No, no. Nothing new since Jasmine Houze. Actually, I was calling to ask you about your friend Sherry Mitchell."

"Oh. What about her?"

"I just thought I might stop by to talk to her, if you didn't mind?"

"You found out."

"Found out what?"

"About her being a forensic artist. She's on vacation, Jon. She needs a break."

Was Sherry really so selfish that she wouldn't take a day out of her precious vacation to help the Corpus Christi PD and a woman who had been through a hideous trauma?

"I just want to talk to her, Caroline. I don't want to push or cut into her time off. I'm sure she deserves it as much as anyone."

Jon tried to throw lightness into his tone. Caroline was concerned about her friend. It was an admirable trait even if he didn't see much about Sherry worth protecting if she was as shallow as her actions suggested. Obviously she was good at taking care of herself. She didn't need her perky friend to do it.

Caroline sighed. "She just seems so tired. Maybe that's not the right word, but I don't know exactly what is. She's just…she needs her vacation, Jon. Maybe you should leave her be."

For just a second Sherry's face—devoid of color, teeth almost chattering—flitted through his mind. Okay, yeah, maybe she was more tired or stressed or whatever than he was giving her credit for. But he had no intention of letting a forensic artist of her talent slip through his fingers when she was right in town and there was such a need.

Feeling bad, he shifted his tactics with Caroline.

"I do want to ask her professional opinion, but, really," he chuckled in self-mock, "I'm a little embarrassed to admit this because it's so middle-school-ish, but I was hoping to ask her out. Nothing serious or that would make her uncomfortable, just a meal or something."

That was the truth. Last night, before he'd known how self-centered Sherry obviously was, he had been quite interested in asking her out.

Now he was just interested in Sherry getting past her selfishness and doing her job as a forensic artist.

"Oh." Caroline hesitated, but then finally continued. "Well, that might be good for her. Just, like you said, keep it light." She gave him the address of Sherry's house on the beach. "If she doesn't like you, don't tell her I gave you her address."

"Thanks, Caroline. Maybe we could all go out together. Sherry and I, you and Zane."

Caroline guffawed. That was the only word for the sound that came over the phone. "Yeah, you work on that, Agent Hatton. Let me know how it goes."

The call ended. Jon had no idea what had or hadn't happened between Caroline and Zane Wales, but it was obviously complicated.

Jon had much more important things to worry about than romance between the detective and paramedic.

Right now he had a date of his own to get. And he didn't plan to take no as an answer.

SHERRY SAT IN almost the exact same place she had sat the day before, umbrella up, blocking her from most of the late-afternoon sun's rays.

She had her red bikini on again, but once again had clothes over it. This time at least it was lightweight linen capri pants rather than jeans. Much more appropriate for the beach. Her long-sleeved, button-down shirt was still a little conspicuous, but since it was unbuttoned, not too bad.

Sherry was determined not to let what she had seen—or rather heard—at the hospital yesterday cause her to have a complete setback. To do that, she just had to completely shut the entire incident out of her mind.

It was hard. She had picked up the phone a half-dozen times last night to call Caroline and get the number of the handsome Detective Hatton and tell him that she would at least try to help. But every time she did she'd been racked with a cold so vicious she'd felt paralyzed. There was no way she was going to be of any use to anyone.

Even the cold wasn't as bad as reliving the scene of that poor woman crying as the jerk who called himself a police officer had tried to question her. That was heartbreaking. And knowing Sherry could've stepped in and taken over at any time, if she'd just been able to find the strength to do it, was agonizing.

So here she was, on the beach, putting it all out of her mind. It was her only option.

She had her pencil and sketch pad on her lap in the beach chair she sat in. She'd made random lines, nonsensical shapes to the rhythm of the gulf waves crashing a dozen yards away, but hadn't been able to force herself to do anything beyond that.

At least she wasn't shivering.

She was tempted to try to draw the face of Detective Hatton from last night, since it kept floating through her mind. She definitely remembered his exact features. Dark brown hair, cut short. Hazel eyes. Chiseled, clean-shaved jaw. Confidence permeated how he held himself; intelligence how he studied everyone around him to understand their motives and actions before he responded. The guardedness of his features probably wasn't let down very often.

Even without her talents as an artist she'd be able to remember him clearly. It wasn't a face one was likely to forget. And, Sherry could admit, it was the first time she had felt any heat by looking at a stranger in a long time. Months. Maybe longer.

Then that guy in the hospital room had started belittling the woman and the cold had swamped Sherry again. She'd been almost paralyzed with iciness. It was coming back again now, so she pushed all thoughts of yesterday, even of handsome Detective Hatton, out of her head. She kept her hand on the pencil, but nothing was coming from it.

A few moments later a larger shadow showed up next to her umbrella. Sherry looked over from the drawing she wasn't really drawing and saw casual brown oxfords coupled with dark khakis. Definitely not a bad style, but also not beach wear.

She shaded her face to allow her eyes to travel farther up and found a blue polo shirt neatly tucked into the pants and then the face of Detective Jon Hatton.

Speak of the devil.

"Aren't you a little overdressed for the beach?" he asked by way of greeting.

"No more so than you, Detective Hatton," Sherry responded. She felt at a distinct disadvantage being so far down near the ground with him towering over her. She couldn't see his face well because of the sun, but her brain was more than happy to fill in from memory whatever she couldn't physically see.

"Yeah, well, I'm not on vacation, as you so definitely are," he said.

The use of the word *vacation* seemed almost venomous. His entire frame radiated tension.

"Is that a problem?" she asked.

"Evidently not to you."

It didn't take a genius to see that the detective was mad. And his anger seemed to be directed at her.

"Is there something I can do for you, Detective Hatton? Some sort of problem?"

She could feel her fingers moving with the pencil over the paper, real shapes taking form this time, but she didn't pay it any mind. It wasn't the first time she'd drawn something without giving the paper her direct attention.

Her focus was on Hatton, who was still standing so she had to crane her neck to look up at him. No doubt it was on purpose. The man was too intelligent, too insightful, for it to be anything but a deliberate measure on his part.

It was kind of making her mad. And…hot.

Not a sexual hot, but a regular, healthy, overheated hot because she was sitting on a Texas beach in the late-afternoon June sun in long pants and sleeves.

"Really?" he said. "You can't figure it out?"

God, it felt good not to be icy. Even if it took being around a jerk to do it. Evidently her attraction, or whatever she'd had for him in the first few moments she'd seen him yesterday, was way off base.

Sherry sat straighter in her chair. She wasn't just going to sit here and let him talk down to her, literally and figuratively. She got up from under her umbrella, tucking her pencil behind her ear, sketch pad down at her side.

At nearly five foot eight, Sherry was used to being pretty close to eye to eye with a lot of men, but not to Hatton. She hadn't realized how tall he really was. He had to be at least six foot three, because she *still* had to crane her neck to look up at him. Not something she was used to.

"What is it that you want, Detective Hatton?"

She studiously ignored how the blue in his shirt brought out the blue specks in his eyes, especially in the late-afternoon golden sun.

"What I want is to know why you didn't let me know about that." He pointed toward her waist.

She looked down at herself. Was he still talking about her clothes? "I get cold, okay? It's no crime to have on long sleeves at the beach."

"No." He closed the few feet between them and took the sketch pad that she held in her hand. "This."

He was studying the sketch pad. Sherry felt a flush creep across her cheeks. She didn't want to explain the random lines and doodles that covered her sketch pad. Didn't want to go into the whole story about her drawings or lack thereof. Whether he knew she was an artist or not, she didn't want to have to explain the lack of talent evident on that pad.

"Give it back to me." She reached for the pad, but he took a step backward so she couldn't reach it, still studying it.

"Why didn't you tell me about this yesterday?" He briefly shook the pad in his hand.

That she'd lost her ability to draw?

"Look, it's difficult to explain…"

"Really? What's so difficult about saying, 'I'm a forensic artist. Maybe I can help with the situation'?"

He turned the sketch pad around so what she had drawn was facing her. Sherry was already cringing, preparing to explain, until she got a glimpse of the drawing.

She had drawn Detective Hatton in almost perfect likeness.

Chapter Five

"I guess I'm flattered," Jon continued, holding the sketch pad.

Sherry just stood there, looking at the drawing. It wasn't her greatest work, by any means. Really it was just in the preliminary stages—rough lines and edges—but it was definitely him. It was the first work she'd done that wasn't just absolute crap in weeks.

She'd drawn it subconsciously. Not only was it not bad, but she hadn't gotten any chills when she did it. As a matter of fact, now that she was out from under the protection of the umbrella, she was downright hot. She took off her shirt and tied it around her waist. The sun on her back and shoulders felt wonderful.

But she wasn't quite sure exactly what conversation she was having with Jon Hatton.

"Why are you here?" she asked him.

"Why didn't you tell me you were a forensic artist yesterday at the hospital?"

"Believe it or not, I don't generally make those the first words out of my mouth when I'm talking to a complete stranger." She grabbed the sketch pad out of his hand.

"You saw what was going on with that woman yesterday, how poorly Frank Spangler was handling the interview for the composite drawing, and you did nothing. You ran away."

Sherry's mouth fell open before she closed it again.

What was she supposed to say? It had been all she could do yesterday to just keep it together. The last thing on her mind had been to offer to help.

Yes, she had run away. She wouldn't have been any use to anyone anyway. She'd been shaking so hard she'd hardly been able to get her keys in the car door to unlock it.

But, damn, if she had to explain any of that to him. Jerk.

"Believe it or not, I don't walk around hospitals offering my services to everyone. I was there to pick up my friend. I just happened upon your situation accidentally."

She could tell right away that wasn't going to appease him.

"You were so busy with dinner plans that you couldn't help a woman who had just been through the most traumatic event of her life?"

"You know what, Detective Hatton? There was nothing I could've done yesterday. By the time you got in there and got *your man* out, the damage had already been done. That poor woman wasn't going to talk to anyone, no matter who the artist was."

"He's not my man," Hatton replied.

"Whatever. He's on your police force. Your team."

"No, I'm—"

Sherry held up a hand to cut him off. She wasn't really interested in discussing the idiot who'd further traumatized that woman. As far as she could tell, everyone employed in law enforcement in Corpus Christi was a jerk.

"Who told you I was a forensic artist? Caroline?" Sherry didn't think her friend would say anything, but maybe she had done so.

"No." He shook his head. "I knew we needed a different forensic artist since Spangler has been taken off the case, so I made a call."

"I'm glad to hear that Detective Spangler won't be doing any more damage."

"Me, too. He has no business being around any victims, as far as I'm concerned."

That made Sherry feel a little better. At least Hatton didn't defend Spangler. Sherry turned away and began loading up her beach stuff to take back to the house. She knew she wouldn't be sitting out here anymore today.

"I'm sorry you came all the way to the beach, Detective, if it wasn't to enjoy the sunshine. Because I can't help you. For the next two weeks I'm just a tourist not a forensic artist."

It sounded uncaring and cold even to her own ears. But what could she do about it? Except for the rough outline of Hatton's features—which really didn't count because, first, she hadn't been actually trying to draw him, her fingers had just taken over, and, second, there wasn't enough detail in it to be of any use for any police work anyway—she hadn't been able to draw a face in weeks.

She wasn't trying to be unfeeling; she just couldn't help Detective Hatton. She couldn't even help herself.

JON SWALLOWED HIS ANGER. *Just a tourist for the next two weeks?* That might possibly be the most selfish thing he'd ever heard. Sherry Mitchell might be drop-dead gorgeous in that red bikini top she was wearing, but it was obvious her beauty was only skin-deep.

If it even reached that far. Such a damn shame.

Jon had read in her file that both her parents owned separate successful businesses. Ms. Mitchell had obviously grown up spoiled, and those tendencies had remained when she became an adult.

Normally, Jon didn't mind spoiling the woman he was with. Enjoyed all the slightly crazy nuances that made women the mind-bogglingly lovely creatures that they were. He loved the mental acuity it required to discover what it was they really wanted.

But not in this case. Jon was pissed off at how the woman in front of him categorically refused to assist in a situation where she could really help. Now she was just folding up her chair and umbrella as if it were just another day at the beach. Which evidently it was to her.

No, what really made Jon mad was that he was *still* attracted to her despite her actions. He might think she was completely spoiled, but he knew that, given the chance, he would be kissing every inch of those shoulders and back she'd exposed when she tied that long-sleeved shirt around her waist.

Jon took a deep, cleansing breath. Neither focusing on Sherry's selfishness nor her beauty was getting him anywhere.

He needed to focus on how he could talk her into coming to the hospital and doing her magic as a forensic artist.

Jon had considerable people skills. That was one of the things that made him so good at his job at Omega. He kept a level head. He saw things others missed. He could read people, manipulate them when necessary.

It was time to put his distaste away and focus on getting Ms. Mitchell to do her job.

"It's 'agent.'"

She looked over her shoulder from where she was packing up her beach items. "I beg your pardon?"

"I'm Agent Hatton, not Detective Hatton."

"Agent as in FBI? You don't work for the Corpus Christi Police Department?"

So much for thinking she hadn't wanted to help him because he wasn't a local cop. She'd had no idea. That made him feel a little less hostile. "No, I don't work for the local PD or the Bureau. I work for Omega Sector in the Critical Response Division."

Sherry nodded. "Okay. I've heard a few people at the

FBI field office talk about Omega. Sorry I called you 'detective.'"

"Why don't we just alleviate the problem altogether by you calling me Jon?" He gave her his most charming smile. The one that had always worked on his mom to get him out of trouble.

Sherry paused for just a moment, then nodded. "Okay, Jon. I'm Sherry. But you already knew that, I guess."

Jon kept his smile up. "I did."

"I guess that guy, Spangler, or whatever that moron's name is, really wasn't part of your team if you're not local PD, so please accept my apologies for that statement."

Jon shrugged. "No apologies necessary, but let me assure you that no one like Spangler would ever be on my team, much less be anywhere near a victim."

He could see her relax just the slightest bit and knew he was on the right track with what she needed to hear: that Spangler's actions were inexcusable.

No contest, as far as Jon was concerned.

He walked over and helped her lower the umbrella, which had reopened when she'd turned to talk to him. "Look, I'm sorry if I came across too strong a minute ago. But if you could take a few minutes out of your vacation to talk to Jasmine Houze, the victim, and see if there is anything you can help her remember, that would really be helpful."

Sherry looked at him and then quickly looked away. "Caroline told me none of the women had really gotten a look at the attacker. Is Ms. Houze any different?"

Jon grimaced. "Based on preliminary reports and what she told the doctors, no. It doesn't look like she got a good look at the rapist's face."

Sherry began stuffing all her beach items into a large bag. "Then you don't really need me. I can't help you."

Jon tamped his irritation down again. "All I'm asking

is for you to try. You've got an excellent track record with cases like these, and you're a woman, which might make Ms. Houze more comfortable. Maybe she didn't see her attacker's face, but she might remember something. You're our best shot."

She looked as though she was going to say something but then stopped. Jon frowned as she took the long-sleeved shirt from around her waist and put it on as if she were chilly.

That would be fine if it wasn't ninety degrees outside right now. Jon was already wiping sweat from his face, and he was in a short-sleeved shirt. She was actually buttoning hers up.

"You okay?" he asked.

"Um, yeah. I just caught a little chill, that's all."

Okay, that was odd. She'd been shivering yesterday at the hospital, too. Interesting. An illness?

"Are you sick? Running a fever?"

"No. I just…" She shrugged one delicate shoulder not hidden under her long shirt. "I just get cold sometimes."

Jon wanted to pursue it further, but now was the time to push about the interview, while her defenses were weakened.

"Sherry, Ms. Houze needs you. There is no one else because of the licensing laws in Nueces County. If you don't try, Frank Spangler is the next best option."

Jon didn't say that there was no way that was going to happen, not with him here. But revealing that wouldn't help his argument with Sherry.

"I really can't help you." She huddled farther into her shirt.

"Can't or won't?"

"Does it make a difference?"

"I'm just asking you to try. An hour of your time? If

you can't help after that, at least you tried. You didn't sit here doing nothing."

There was a long pause as she looked at him. She seemed to huddle down farther into her shirt.

"Okay, when?" she finally asked.

"Right now would be best." He didn't want to give her a chance to change her mind or to decide to make other plans.

She looked at him for another long, silent moment. "Fine, Agent Hatton. I will go and talk to the victim. I wouldn't expect anything to come of it, if I were you."

Jon nodded. "Just try. That's all I ask."

Chapter Six

This was not going to be pretty, in any sense of the word. Sherry dropped all her beach items in the screened-in porch attached to the back of the house. She would worry about the beach stuff later. Right now she needed to take a quick shower and change.

She was meeting Jon at the hospital. He'd offered her a ride, but after his pinball attitude toward her on the beach, Sherry knew driving herself was a better plan.

Once he saw she wasn't capable of drawing, she might be stranded in town if she rode with him.

He was pretty much a jerk. Handsome, with cheekbones so sharp you could cut yourself on them, but still a jerk. And if he thought she didn't know that he'd just *handled* her out there—pouring on his considerable charm and bright smile once the intimidation factor didn't work—then he was well mistaken. She knew she'd been managed; it had happened enough times with her parents for her to recognize the pattern.

The thing was, it wasn't that she didn't want to help out Jon or Jasmine Houze—what kind of unfeeling wretch would she be if that was the case?—but she didn't even think she was capable.

She would try. That was all she could do. All Agent Hatton had asked her to do. They'd see if he still felt that way when the pencil wouldn't move because of her shivering.

The thought brought on a bout of cold, despite the fact that she didn't have the air-conditioning running anywhere in the house. Sherry headed to the bathroom and stripped off her clothes, turning the water as hot as it could get without scalding her. She knew she wouldn't be able to stay in there long enough to really get warm—that would take so long, Jon would be in here managing her again—but at least it took a little of the edge off, warming the outside of her body if not the inside.

After her shower she dried her hair, which because of its thickness and length took a long time, but she knew better than to go out with it wet in a situation like this: if she got a chill, damp hair would just exacerbate it. She slipped on black jeans and a long-sleeved dark plum sweater and then pulled on her boots. After a touch of makeup—she wanted to look professional, for Jasmine Houze, not Jon Hatton—she grabbed her sketch pad and a set of pencils, and was out the door.

The drive to the hospital went faster than Sherry would've liked. She focused on a number of different things: the traffic, the scenery, the number of pickup trucks she could count, anything to keep her from thinking about what was coming up. She didn't want to be a shivering mess before she even set foot in the hospital.

Sherry had made it through her last two cases with the cold seeming to permeate her. She could make it through questioning one woman who they suspected hadn't seen anything. But, honestly, whether Jasmine had seen anything would be beside the point. Because either way, Sherry was going to have to walk with the poor woman through the worst day in her entire life.

She sighed as a chill rushed through her. Count pickups now. She'd be dealing with monsters soon enough.

As she found a parking place at the hospital, already having to grit her teeth to keep them from chattering,

Sherry's resolve was firm. She saw Jon standing by the door and she told him, with no holds barred, what was on her mind.

"This one time, Agent Hatton," she said. "I will talk to Ms. Houze today, but that's it. I don't want any further details about the case or the women involved, or anything. You're going to need to find someone else."

His eyes narrowed the slightest bit, but then he nodded. "Call me Jon. And I understand. You're on vacation."

She was pretty sure he didn't understand anything. That he thought she was a spoiled brat who didn't care about anybody but herself. She could admit that bugged her, but she knew she had to take care of herself. Knew she had to find a way of getting past this coldness if she ever hoped to really work as a forensic artist again. Or at this point, to even be able to draw again ever.

Not having her art in her life was not an acceptable compromise.

A little warm, she pushed up her sleeves. At least talking to him had taken care of most of the chill. "That's right, I'm on vacation."

Let the jerk think what he wanted. She brushed past him on her way indoors. She was actually relieved to feel the air-conditioning.

"We need anything that Ms. Houze can give us," Jon told her as they walked down the hall. She noticed he already knew most of the nurses. They waved to him and immediately began whispering to each other. No doubt about the tall, dark-haired, gorgeous agent hallowing their hallways.

Let them have him.

"Anything," he repeated. "A full description of the perp's face would, of course, be optimal. But anything at all would be helpful."

Sherry nodded. "You probably shouldn't hope for too much." From me or her.

Jon grimaced. "I know you don't want to know anything about the case. But we have *nothing*, Sherry. This guy is really smart. So when I say anything Ms. Houze remembers, I mean anything. No matter how small."

"I'll do my best." As they arrived at Jasmine's door, Sherry explained how she worked. "I'm going to leave the door open, but I need you not to come inside. With a case like this, and especially after what happened yesterday with Spangler, it's important for you to stay out. Allow me to build a rapport with her."

"That's fine."

"Even if you feel like it's going too slowly or I'm asking questions that don't pertain to the case, you still don't get to butt in."

He looked a little affronted at that. Good. That was how she felt every time he muttered the word *vacation*.

"What I do takes time, so I hope you brought a *People* magazine or something," she continued.

He rolled his eyes. "How about if I just listen out here and take notes? I don't think a gossip magazine will be necessary."

"Fine. Just don't interrupt unless it's an emergency. No matter if you think I'm off target or missing something."

"I got it. No interruptions. Take as long as you need."

"She knows I'm coming, right? And that's okay with her?" After what had happened yesterday, Sherry wouldn't be surprised if the woman didn't want to see anyone from law enforcement again.

"Yes, we cleared it with her, although I think she is planning to have a family member in, just in case. I okayed it with the doctor, also, just before you got here."

"Fine." She looked at him again. "Just don't expect too much."

"Trust me." Jon's eyes were tight, frustrated. "Anything you can give us is better than where we are now."

"I'll do my best."

"That's all I can ask."

Sherry was afraid her best wasn't going to be anywhere near enough. She straightened her shoulders and walked into the room. This wasn't going to be pretty. But at least she wasn't cold.

THREE HOURS LATER Jon sat in the hallway outside Jasmine Houze's door. Sherry was wrapping it up, he could tell. She and Jasmine were talking about insignificant things: shoes, sales at different stores, favorite place to grab a margarita.

Really more than half of the time Sherry had spent with the woman had been used talking about seemingly insignificant things. Jon understood now why she had warned him not to interrupt. Obviously in the past she had been interrupted by people who thought she should be getting to the root of the issue—the actual drawing—more quickly.

While Jon could see why someone might jump to that conclusion, he wouldn't have interrupted today even if Sherry had never asked any questions about the attack. She very masterfully built a rapport with Jasmine. There had been nothing fake about it. Every question she had asked seemed sincere.

Jon didn't really know how well the woman could draw, but she could question a victim as well as, if not better than, many seasoned law-enforcement officers. Not just ones like Spangler who had no business being around victims. Sherry was excellent at what she did.

No wonder her supervisor held her in such high regard. She had patience, sincerity and an easygoing manner. Jon could tell just from hearing her talk. She knew when to press and when to back off. She'd let Ms. Houze tell her story in pieces, as she was ready, not ever forcing it, but gently bringing her back around to the questioning when they got too far off track.

What Sherry did with so much ease and naturalness couldn't be taught. She had instincts that were right on. As someone who also had pretty good instincts where most people were concerned, Jon was able to recognize it easily in Sherry.

Unfortunately, despite all of Sherry's interviewing abilities, Jon knew without even seeing, there was nothing she would've been able to draw. Jasmine Houze never saw her attacker's face and, despite Sherry cleverly questioning her from multiple different angles, never saw any distinguishing marks or any information that Sherry could've transferred onto paper in a way that would help them find the rapist.

Sherry had listened to Jasmine talk about the attack—details about it that had made him wince, and knew it had to have affected Sherry, also. Listening to such horror, and then subtly asking the poor victim to repeat it, was difficult.

For the first time Jon felt a little bad about how he'd mentally ripped into Sherry about the whole vacation thing. Her job as a forensic artist obviously was hard; that much was clear after listening to her for a couple of hours. No wonder she'd wanted a break from it for a little while as she was on vacation.

Although he knew she didn't want any more details about the case or to be involved in any way, after seeing how good she was today, Jon didn't think there was any way he was going to be able to let her walk away. Maybe if she would be willing to talk to the other victims. Maybe one of them would remember *something* that could lead to a crack in the case.

Hell, maybe Ms. Houze might still remember something. Talking to her again a few days from now would be customary in a case such as this.

Sherry should really be the one to do that, since she'd already built the rapport with her. It would be easier for everyone involved.

Except Sherry, of course.

Jon winced. Perhaps he could get her vacation extended or something. Or—and this didn't sit well with him, but he'd do it if he had to—maybe he could get her supervisor at the Bureau to put pressure on her to help with this case.

Either way Jon knew he needed to keep Sherry on this case with him. No matter what he had to do to make that happen.

He heard Sherry make her goodbyes to Jasmine and the two members of her family who had stayed in the room, wishing them all the best and promising that law enforcement was doing everything in its power to find the person responsible. Wishes and encouragement to stay strong. And to be sure to contact them if Jasmine thought of anything—even the smallest detail—she had forgotten before. To call anytime day or night. She even gave her personal number.

These were things Jon would say if he was in there, but he knew his presence there would just be intrusive.

Sherry backed out of the room, saying one last goodbye before pulling the door closed behind her, still facing it.

"Hey, you did amazing work in there," Jon said. "Honestly. I know she didn't remember anything, but—"

Jon cut himself off midsentence as Sherry turned to face him. Dear God, her lips were almost blue, her entire body completely tensed to keep from shaking.

"Sherry, what the hell?" Jon reached for her as she took a shaky step.

"I'm c-cold," she said.

"I see that. Is this one of your cold spells you were talking about?"

She nodded. He wrapped an arm around her and led her to a bench across the hall. He sat, holding her as close as possible, trying to transfer some of his body heat.

"Let me get one of the doctors to look at you."

"No, it'll pass. I've already seen a doctor. It's…" She trailed off. "It will pass."

"You're sure you're not sick?"

"Not physically." She tapped her head. "It's all in here."

"I don't really understand what you're saying." He was relieved to see her face was beginning to regain color and her shuddering was easing. They sat in silence for long moments as she gathered herself.

"This is why I'm on vacation. For the past few months every time I've done any work at all as a forensic artist, I've been overcome by these cold spells."

"What did your doctor say about them?" he asked, keeping her pinned to his side.

She looked away. "Well, I didn't actually tell him about them. I just had him do a complete physical so I was sure I didn't have a tumor or something. Since he deemed me in perfect health, yet I'm sometimes cold when it's ninety degrees out, I figured it must be psychological."

Jon didn't need to be a doctor to know what was going on here, and was sure her doctor could've figured it out if Sherry had given him all the information.

Sherry was suffering from some form of post-traumatic stress disorder. He had seen it in more than a few of his closest friends at Omega over the years, to varying degrees and with different symptoms. Some not totally dissimilar from what Sherry was experiencing.

Trauma affected the brain. Whether you experienced it firsthand or not, the brain could only take so much before it started taking measures to protect itself. Sherry's mind was trying to stop her from doing further damage to her psyche.

And the time she needed to heal was time Jon didn't have.

Chapter Seven

Two days later, sitting next to Caroline on the beach, Sherry was still considering what Jon had said to her in the hospital hallway. That she was suffering from some sort of post-traumatic stress.

Sherry had never even considered that; had thought that was only something that people who'd been in the military went through. After some research she realized she'd been wrong. Anybody who had experienced or witnessed a traumatic event could suffer from it.

Sherry was positive she didn't have PTSD. That was a serious, very real disorder that affected thousands of people, and she didn't want to take away from the very real trauma sufferers had gone through by comparing her situation to theirs.

But it gave her a starting place about what the heck was going on with her. A reassurance that she wasn't going crazy, but just needed to find some better coping mechanisms when it came to her job.

"So, did you say yes to Agent Handsome when he came calling the other day?" Caroline asked her from where she was perched in the sun.

Sherry had managed to work herself down to just shorts and a tank top over her bikini in the past two days. It wasn't perfect, but it was better. And at least now she felt she had somewhere to start when it came to this blasted coldness.

Whenever she felt the least chill come on, she immediately turned her thoughts in a different direction. Anything that took her away from where her subconscious was going.

The thought of Jon Hatton generally skipped her past warm and straight to hot. Mostly because he was a jerk.

Although she had to admit that when she was so cold after the interview, he'd been very understanding and helpful. Had helped her fight the cold by keeping her close to his body.

Sherry sighed. "I didn't want to, but, yes, I did. He's pretty persuasive. Not to mention I could tell he thought I was the most selfish person on the planet when I resisted at first."

"He thought you were selfish because you wouldn't go out with him?"

Sherry put her sunglasses on top of her head and looked over at her friend. "First of all, how do you know about all this? Second of all, he didn't come by to ask me out, he came by to badger me into meeting with Jasmine Houze."

Caroline let loose a string of obscenities that was totally at odds with her young, sweet look.

Sherry laughed. "I take it you didn't know."

"He asked me where you were staying, but he said it was because he wanted to ask you out."

Sherry thought of how he had helped her at the hospital, kept her by his side until the iciness had passed. Then followed behind her as she'd driven home to make sure she made it all right. No, not a date, but perhaps he wasn't quite as bad as the string of obscenities suggested.

"Well, I think he needed my help more than he needed a date."

"I'm still going to let him have it next time I see him. I was so busy laughing at him when he suggested Zane and I might go on a date with you two that I wasn't really paying attention to anything else."

"What is it with you and Zane? The vibe between the two of you is crazy."

Caroline took another sip of her water, rolling her eyes. "Don't I know it? Zane and I are…complicated. It would just traumatize you further for me to talk about it. Traumatize me, too."

Sherry had told Caroline some of the stuff that had been going on with her: the cold spells and not being able to draw. Caroline was sympathetic and, as a paramedic, she was no stranger to trauma herself.

"How did it go with Jasmine Houze?"

Sherry shrugged. "As good as could be expected, considering she hadn't gotten any sort of look at her attacker."

"Damn it," Caroline muttered. "So you couldn't draw anything, after all."

"Yeah. Glad I didn't even have to try. As much as I'd like to help, I'm not sure I could've done anything useful."

Caroline grimaced. "Somebody's got to put a stop to this guy."

"Yeah, Jon said he's smart."

"So you actually talked to Jon? I thought you said he was a jerk."

"We talked a little bit about the case," Sherry said. "But to be honest, I didn't want any details. He just wanted to make sure I knew that no detail was too small when I was talking to Jasmine."

Caroline nodded. "You know, the crock about asking you out notwithstanding, I've found Jon to be a very stand-up guy. He talked to Michael, my partner, and me about the second victim. Asked our opinions about what had happened since we were first on the scene."

"Is that unusual?" Sherry asked.

"Well, neither Zane nor any of the other local detectives have ever asked my professional opinion, that's for sure.

Too bad I didn't have anything interesting to share with Jon. But he still listened."

"Are we talking about the same Agent Hatton?"

Caroline laughed. "I'm just telling you, he isn't really a jerk."

"If you say so."

Caroline stood. "Okay, I'm off to shower before my shift."

"Okay, I'm going to hang here. Try to face the ol' sketch pad again." Sherry was feeling relaxed, warm. Ready to try. "You be safe out there tonight."

"Will do. Don't push it with the drawing. Let it come when it comes." They hugged and Sherry sent Caroline on her way.

That left Sherry alone with her sketch pad. She flipped to the first page and found the rough outline of Jon's face staring back at her.

Even without trying she had captured his dark good looks. Almost without conscious consent, her fingers took the pencil and began tracing in the details from his face onto the paper. As Caroline said, she didn't overthink it, just let it come.

Fifteen minutes later she had a full portrait of Jon looking back at her. Eyes faintly laced with disapproval, a slight scowl.

Yep, pretty much exactly as she remembered him. Jerk.

She had to admit, at least she wasn't cold. She hadn't felt the iciness grip her bones even once while she was drawing him.

So evidently if she could just go around drawing Jon Hatton, she would be okay. Somehow she didn't think that was going to help her very much.

Her phone rang and Sherry looked at the number, one she didn't recognize. She debated on whether she should answer at all, but decided she would.

"Hello?"

"Ms. Mitchell?" It was a soft female voice, but Sherry didn't recognize it.

"Yes."

"This is Jasmine Houze. I'm sorry to bother you."

Sherry had given Jasmine her phone number at the hospital but honestly hadn't expected the other woman to use it. She figured Jasmine would've called Jon or one of the Corpus Christi detectives before calling her.

Sherry couldn't turn the woman away.

"No, you're not bothering me at all. Are you okay?"

"I'm as well as can be expected, I guess. They released me from the hospital this morning."

"That's good news, right?"

"I'm glad to be out, but I'm not ready to go to my h-house yet."

Sherry's heart broke at the woman's shaky mention of her house. Sherry wasn't surprised she didn't want to go there. She wouldn't be surprised if Jasmine never lived in that house again.

"I totally understand. Do you have somewhere to stay?"

"Yeah, my mom and I are staying at my cousin's house, on the beach. It's not too far from my house. I feel okay there, as long as they're with me." Her words were still a little mushy, undoubtedly injury related.

"That's totally understandable," Sherry said. "You need to give yourself whatever time you need to heal. Don't let anybody rush you and don't allow yourself to get frustrated."

That advice sounded familiar.

"Yeah, the counselor at the hospital told me the same thing."

"That's because we're both brilliant."

That got a laugh, as Sherry had hoped it would.

"I don't mean to bother you, but you said to call if I thought of anything, no matter how small."

"Yes, I was absolutely serious about that. It really doesn't matter how insignificant it may seem."

"Well, this doesn't have anything to do with his face."

That was a little disappointing because, of course, any identifying facial feature would be a wonderful help. But facial features weren't the only things that could assist law enforcement.

"That's okay, Jasmine. His face isn't the only thing you might remember that can help the police. Maybe you should call them."

"I remember part of a tattoo on the inside of h-his arm." Sherry's heart broke as she heard Jasmine begin to cry. "And latex gloves. I don't know why I'm just remembering this now."

"That's okay. More than okay, Jasmine. Really good." A tattoo was something Sherry could draw. "Where is your cousin's house exactly? I can come over there, if you want me to. Draw whatever you remember of the tattoo."

"That would be so great." The relief was plain in the woman's voice. "I just want to get it out of my head."

Sherry very much understood being trapped in one's own head.

"Okay, give me your address. I'll just need to run home and get my car." Sherry had met Caroline on the beach halfway between their two houses so neither of them needed to drive.

She entered the address into her phone when Jasmine gave it to her and was surprised when she saw how close the house was to her present location.

"Actually, I'm only a couple of blocks from you right now. If you don't mind that I'm all sandy, I can be there much sooner if I just walk."

"Sooner is definitely better. I want to be sure I don't forget this."

Sherry was sure Jasmine wouldn't forget the tattoo. It would probably creep into her nightmares for the rest of her life. But there was no need to tell her that.

"Okay, I'll be there in just a few minutes."

They disconnected the call and Sherry began putting her items in her beach bag. Not too much stuff, thankfully: towel, sunscreen, her sketch pad and a few other items. She hadn't brought the umbrella, but she would need to carry her lightweight beach chair.

She categorically refused to think about the possibility that she wouldn't be able to draw what Jasmine described. She marched down the beach, focusing on the picture she'd drawn of Jon. Thinking about him seemed to keep her functional and definitely not cold. Whether that was because he made her mad or for other reasons, she wasn't going to delve into it too deeply.

It didn't take too long to walk to Jasmine's cousin's house, since it was a straight shot down the beach. The beach was mostly empty in the late-afternoon sun, early June being less crowded in the beach town since school had not yet let out. It was a nice walk, and for Sherry, pleasant in the heat.

As she finished the last few hundred yards to the house, Sherry could swear she felt someone watching her. She spun around, but saw no one except for a jogger far away from her headed the other way. She looked up at the houses that lined the street parallel to the beach, but didn't see anyone.

She took a deep breath as she felt cold starting to work its way through her system. She grabbed her long-sleeved shirt out of the bag and slipped it on, then walked more quickly toward the house.

This feeling was all in her imagination, Sherry knew.

But she wished she had walked home and gotten her car, no matter that it would've taken longer.

Right now she needed to keep it together. Someone who had experienced something truly traumatic needed her help. The iciness and imaginary bogeyman watching her were nothing compared to the very real ugliness that made up Jasmine's reality.

Jasmine was sitting in a chair on the second-story deck of her cousin's house. No matter what it took, Sherry was going to focus on that brave woman up there and get through this.

Chapter Eight

Jon pulled up to the house where Jasmine was staying just as Sherry was coming down the outdoor back stairs from the second-story deck. Jasmine was behind her.

He'd been glad when Jasmine's mother called, had told him about Jasmine remembering the tattoo on the rapist's arm. Any identifying mark could help. Not only in finding and arresting the perpetrator, but also in the trial against him.

Maybe if she remembered this, there was hope that she might remember more; that her mind still held some secrets she wasn't aware of yet. Jon hoped so, because even after spending the past two days recombing the crime scene and recanvassing the neighborhood, they still didn't have any leads.

He hadn't been able to get Sherry Mitchell out of his mind. Yes, he wanted her professional opinion and artistic abilities on the case. But more than that, he just wanted to see her again. To see if she was doing any better after that debilitating cold spell she'd suffered at the hospital.

Yet he had known that if he contacted her, his concern would've come across as professional rather than personal. That he was making sure she was okay so she could help him with this case, not because he actually cared what happened to her.

He did have a professional concern for her, definitely.

If there was some way he could help her so that she could in turn use her artist and interviewing skills to help them capture this guy, Jon was more than willing to do that.

But he'd also like to help her because he couldn't stop thinking about her. About her gorgeous long legs, gorgeous blond hair, gorgeous blue eyes.

And the fragility that seemed to surround her. As if she might shatter at any moment.

That was the real reason Jon hadn't stopped back by to see Sherry even though he'd wanted to and desperately wanted her for the case.

She wasn't ready.

If Jon kept pushing—and he knew it was in his nature to do so—then all he'd be doing was creating another victim as a result of this violence. Until Sherry's mind was ready for her to get back to work on the case, Jon didn't want to force it if there were any other options. He already had his boss at Omega looking for other forensic artists. Steve would come up with someone.

Jon was surprised Sherry was here, since Jasmine's mom hadn't mentioned it, and knowing how Sherry felt about getting involved. After seeing the toll working with victims took on her, Jon couldn't have blamed her for just hunkering down under her beach umbrella and never facing anything again.

He'd been wrong about her. She wasn't spoiled; she was protecting herself.

So he already admired the fact that she was here at all. He walked over to where she and Jasmine were talking at the bottom of the outdoor staircase.

"Ladies." He said it while he was still far enough away not to startle Jasmine. He could see how Sherry immediately tensed at his voice.

"Hi, Agent Hatton," Jasmine said. Her face was still

bruised, but not nearly as swollen as it had been two days ago.

"How are you feeling?" he asked her.

The young woman shrugged. "Afraid to go out by myself. Afraid of the dark. Afraid to set foot in my own home. So, not great."

Sherry took her hand. "It's okay to be afraid of all those things. You might always be, and that's okay, too."

"Yeah, well, none of that is as bad as when the doorbell rings. Poor package delivery guy must have thought everybody in the house was crazy. Doorbell rang and I totally freaked out. Then my mom and cousin started crying. All he wanted to do was deliver some shoes my cousin ordered a few days ago."

Jon met Sherry's eye. It was a hard story for either of them to hear. They both knew Jasmine's attacker had rung her doorbell and then forced his way in when she'd cracked open the door.

Jon wanted to comfort Jasmine but knew he couldn't. There was only so much he could do. Sherry, on the other hand, was more easily able to, and reached out to touch the other woman.

"You know what?" Sherry said to Jasmine, rubbing the woman's arm lightly. "Have your cousin disconnect the doorbell. Disconnect it at your house when you go back there. *If* you decide to go back there. Or, if you decide to move into another place, disconnect the doorbell there. Disconnect the damn doorbell at every place you live for the rest of your life. That's *okay*."

"It just seems so cowardly." Jasmine's voice was small.

"No." Both he and Sherry said it at the same time.

"Not cowardly at all," Jon continued.

"You don't ever have to apologize for how you choose to survive," Sherry said. "You need to heal on your timetable, not anyone else's. Taking tiny, little baby steps is still forward progress."

"You're up, outside, talking. That's more than many would be in your situation," Jon said.

"Thanks, you guys. I think I'm going to go in and rest. Describing that tattoo took more out of me than I thought." Jasmine turned to Sherry. "Can you show it to Agent Hatton?"

"Sure, no problem."

Jasmine looked at Jon. "That's okay, right? I just don't want to look at it again right now."

"Absolutely fine. Sherry will go over all the details with me. You don't worry about it."

"Yes, just rest, Jasmine," Sherry said. "If you think of anything else, I'm more than happy to come back."

Jasmine nodded before making her way up the outdoor stairs to where her mother and cousin were waiting. Jon was glad to see she had a good support network. That made a huge difference in the healing process.

He turned back to Sherry. "I realize it was probably difficult for you to come here and that you don't want to be involved in this case. But I appreciate it anyway."

Sherry stiffened. "I didn't do it for you. I did it for that brave woman up there."

"Either way, I still appreciate it. I realize that it still probably took a toll on you, regardless of who you did it for, so thank you."

Sherry nodded. "It wasn't as bad as I thought it might be."

But she still had her long-sleeved shirt on, even in the early-evening heat, so it had been at least somewhat bad.

"Did Jasmine remember anything particularly useful?" he asked her.

"Well, his skin was dark. That's one thing she remembers."

"Like African-American?"

"No, but not fair-skinned. Maybe Mexican or Latin American descent." Sherry brought out the sketch pad she had tucked under one arm. "Basically she remembered his hands. He had on some sort of latex or rubber gloves."

"That's not surprising at all, considering the lack of evidence that has been left at the scenes. If you told me he had wrapped his entire body in some sort of protective gear, I wouldn't be surprised."

Sherry opened her sketch pad to the page she was looking for. There she'd drawn an arm stretched at an odd angle. The latex gloves covered his fingers and hand up to his wrist, but then farther up, peaking through the sleeve hole of a white office shirt, was a tattoo of a skull with two bull's-eyes in the eye sockets. Not big enough to be something overtly noticeable in everyday life, but certainly something identifiable.

"Interesting ink," Jon murmured. "First thing I'll do is have Corpus Christi PD run it against any known gang marks."

Sherry nodded. "I've become familiar with some gang tattoos in my two years working cases in the Southeast and don't recognize this, but my knowledge is in no way exhaustive."

"Does she remember anything else about that shirt?"

"No, just that it was a white cuff, like any normal shirt a man would wear to an office or something, she said. She only remembers it was white because of the thought that his skin was so dark."

Jon looked at the picture again. "His arm seems to be at a weird angle."

"Yeah, that's how Jasmine described it. I walked her through it a couple of times to be sure. I think it is because of how she was thrown on the ground. But it works to our advantage because if his arm had been at a more natural angle, she wouldn't have seen the tattoo."

"That's good. Or as good as something can be in a situation like this." He noticed Sherry was worrying her lip with her teeth, studying the picture. After a few seconds he forced his attention away from her lips. Barely. "Is there something wrong?"

She shrugged. "It's just not my best work. I can see where…"

He waited for her to continue, but she didn't.

"Where you what?"

"Just where I was starting to have my cold spells again. Lines are shaky, not as crisp."

"It looks fine to me."

"In this situation, I think it is okay, since a hand is a hand. If I had been drawing someone's facial features, needing as much detail as possible? Those little errors could've made the difference between the drawing bearing a true resemblance to the perpetrator and just being a generic face that wouldn't do law enforcement any good." She was back to gnawing on her lip.

"Was the cold bad?" Before he could stop himself, he reached up and stroked her lip with his thumb so she wouldn't cause it any harm with her teeth.

Their eyes met for just a moment—a heat-filled moment—before Sherry looked away and he dropped his hand. At least she stopped hurting that soft lip. If she needed anyone to nibble on it, he'd be glad to do that for her.

Although suggesting it would probably not go over well.

She had stopped talking altogether. "I'm sorry, please continue. I just didn't want you to injure that lip."

"Oh." To his surprise, a delicate flush covered her cheek. She continued. "The cold was only bad when I could feel Jasmine's terror."

"That's understandable."

"I tried to focus on her, which was both good and bad. It made it that much harder to hear her story and know she was so frightened. On the other hand, I tried to focus on the fact that I was fine. I am not the one who'd had this horrible event happen to me. The least I could do was man up and listen without freaking out."

Jon couldn't help smiling at *man up*. "You made it through."

"Only because she had very little to remember and it was ninety degrees outside. I don't know what I would've done otherwise."

"I'm sure you would've handled that, too. Woman up'ed. That's one step beyond manning up."

A little of her tension eased. She actually smiled at him.

The beauty of it struck him unexpectedly. Made him want to do things he wouldn't normally consider with a woman he'd only known a few days. Jon liked to think pretty carefully before he leaped into any sort of relationship.

But her smile made him feel that thinking was overrated.

He realized he was seeing her as she was meant to be: relaxed, smiling, easy. Probably how she had been before these panic attacks had started taking over.

She began closing up her sketch pad but not before Jon caught a glimpse of the drawing she'd made of him. He stopped her.

Wow. She'd done a lot of work on this since he'd seen it a couple of days ago on the beach. He had thought it was good then, but this was amazing.

"This is incredible." He didn't know a drawing could look so realistic. She had shaded it in and added depth and perspective. It was almost like looking at a black-and-white photo of himself.

She had truly captured his likeness.

She tried to take the pad from him, but he stepped to the side, still looking at the drawing. "Have you been working on this for the past two days?"

"No, Agent Hatton. Believe it or not, I do have other

things in my life. I did it in about thirty minutes this afternoon."

Oh, great, now they were back to Agent Hatton. But Jon couldn't get past the drawing.

"You did this in less than an hour? From memory?"

"Just give me the damn pad."

She was embarrassed. It was kind of endearing how color stained her cheeks once again. Jon liked it so much better than her face being pinched and pale. She also looked as though she might slug him, so he handed her the sketch pad.

"You're really talented."

"Thanks. Right now it's hit or miss, I'm afraid. I was able to draw this by not focusing on any cases or anything upsetting. That's much harder when you're listening to someone talk about horrific things that happened to them."

"It's at least a start, right? You actually drew something."

Sherry shrugged. "I guess so."

"I don't want to push you to do more than you're ready to do, but if you start feeling able, I'd love your help with this case. Maybe not talking to the other victims, just looking over what Frank Spangler got from them, which wasn't much. See if there's anything he missed. If you think you're up to it."

Chapter Nine

Was she up to it?

Sherry just didn't know. She had made it through the past hour with Jasmine, but just barely. She had drawn that picture of Jon today, but had deliberately kept her mind neutral as she did so.

One thing she knew for sure, she didn't seem to feel cold around Jon Hatton, whether it was anger or attraction.

What wasn't to be attracted to? His dark looks, soft hazel eyes and chiseled chin were etched in her subconscious—she knew that from how quickly she had drawn him. Not to mention height. There weren't many men who made her feel tiny and feminine.

Jon Hatton did. Everything about him made her just want to ease a little closer.

"Just ease into it, you know? As you're ready. Might be good for you, too."

"What?" Sherry had to stop herself from jumping backward. Had she said something out loud about how attractive she found him?

Jon was looking at her funny. "Helping with the cases? Just a little bit at a time?"

Easing into *cases*. Yes. Right.

"Um, yeah, maybe. But right now I've got to get going." Before she did something completely stupid such as tell him how attractive he was and how she very definitely didn't feel cold when she was around him.

"Okay, where's your car?" He reached down to take her beach bag. "I'll put this in it for you."

"I don't have a car. I walked here."

"You *what*?" Jon's tone noticeably deepened.

"I walked from Caroline's house. It's about halfway between where I'm staying and here."

"And you're just going to *walk* home?" If possible his voice deepened even more. And a vein was beginning to bulge a little in his forehead.

"It's only a little over a mile if you walk straight down the beach."

"Are you crazy?"

Now veins were bulging in his forehead and throat. "There's a rapist wandering around Corpus Christi and you think it is okay to just walk home, completely alone?"

Sherry remembered the feeling she'd gotten earlier walking on the beach. As if someone were watching her. Maybe walking alone hadn't been the best plan. "From what I've read, the attacks occurred at houses, not out on a beach in plain sight."

"There's still no way in hell I'm going to let you do something as idiotic as walk home as it's getting dark." His voice wasn't a shout, but it was definitely louder than normal conversation.

The craziness of it all was that Sherry didn't actually disagree with him. She'd be damned if she'd cower just because he was being a jerk.

Again.

"You know if you had just said, 'Why don't I give you a ride home? Now might not be the safest time to be walking alone,' I would've gladly accepted your offer. But now I think I'd rather take my chances alone than be stuck with you."

Jon ran a hand over his face. She could see him attempting to reboot and get the situation and himself under control.

"Attempting to activate normal people mode, rather than jerk mode?" she asked him, aware that she probably shouldn't taunt him. He just made her so mad.

He grimaced but actually chuckled. "Believe it or not, I am actually known for my way with people. I'm a pretty friendly and likable guy."

"That's good to know. So I guess I won't have to suggest personality dialysis."

This time he laughed out loud. "You're a smart ass."

"So I've been told. But not in a long while."

It felt good to be irritated and attracted and warm. For too long she'd felt nothing but cold and fear.

"Why don't I give you a ride home?" Jon repeated her earlier words back to her. "Now might not be the safest time to be walking alone." He gave her a sparkling smile, the dimple in his chin irresistible in the fading light.

"Since I don't want to traumatize the Houze family any more than they've already been by yelling more out here, I accept."

As if there was any way she could resist that dimple.

He took her bag and put it in the backseat, then held the passenger door open for her.

The streets back to her house took a little while longer since there were no direct routes that ran parallel to the beach.

"Personality dialysis." He muttered it under his breath, shaking his head.

Yeah, that hadn't been nice. "Sorry," she said. "Growing up I had a tendency to blurt out whatever I was thinking."

"Trust me. I'll take my chances with your acerbic wit over seeing you suffer through those cold spells any day."

He reached over to grab her hand that was sitting between them in a friendly squeeze. They both felt the heat immediately when they touched. Her eyes met his briefly before he turned back to the road and she put her hands in her lap.

Wow. That had never happened before. Sherry could almost still feel heat running through her fingers where they'd touched.

"Weird," she murmured.

He glanced over at her, but she couldn't read the expression in his eyes. "Yeah, weird."

There was silence for a few moments until she realized he wasn't going in the right direction for her house.

"Do you mind if we go into town and grab a sandwich? I haven't had dinner and have been all but dreaming about this barbecue brisket sandwich I had to part ways with a couple of days ago when called in for the case."

Sherry smiled. She could understand the appeal. "As long as they don't mind me coming in my beach wear."

Jon winked at her. "I'm pretty sure that won't be a problem at this place. They line the tables with newspaper." He made a turn leading them away from the beach. "Did you need anything from Caroline's house?"

"No, I have everything with me. She's working a night shift, so she's not home."

"Okay."

"Plus, she's pretty mad at you." As soon as she said the words, Sherry immediately saw the trap she'd laid for herself and wished she could take them back.

"What? Why?"

Sherry shrugged. "I don't know. Something you said or something."

"When? I would hate to think I've offended her. She's the one who has kept me in the loop when most of Corpus Christi PD has been trying to keep me out of it."

"It's nothing. She's not really mad. Forget I mentioned it."

"No, tell me." His tone brooked no refusal.

"It's nothing, seriously. You just told Caroline you were going to ask me out the other day."

He immediately knew what she was talking about. "Yeah, I told her that to get the address of where you were staying."

Hearing him admit that he'd never had any intention of actually asking her out hurt a little more than it should for someone she'd only known a few days.

She slid a little farther away from him in her seat. "Yeah, well, Caroline figured that out, so you better watch your back."

"Listen, it's not that I didn't want to ask you out. Just at the time, I needed you more for the case."

"And you knew how to work the situation to get what you wanted. How to work her and how to work me. You're pretty good at your job."

Jon glanced over at her, lips pinched together, driving in silence for another ten minutes until they pulled up at the diner. He still didn't say anything as he chose a parking space that was far away from the entrance in a darkened corner of the lot.

He parked and snatched the keys out of the transmission. In the same breath, he turned to her, leaning so far forward that Sherry had to lean back a little so they wouldn't be pressed together.

"You know what I'm good at?" he said. "I'm good at seeing things other people miss. I'm good at juggling multiple problems at the same time. I'm good at helping keep the press at bay and helping keep people from panicking in a situation like this one where it would be justifiable to do so."

He was upset. He didn't raise his voice, his veins weren't standing out in his forehead like when she mentioned walking home, but he seemed to be toeing a thin line with his control.

"You know what I'm not good at?" he continued. "Trying to balance the fact that I need your skills on this case with the overwhelming urge to keep you as far away from it as possible so that you can heal. I'm not good at constantly weighing what's good for the case versus what's good for you, instead of just—what did you call it the other day?—*handling* you to get what I want."

Sherry knew she should do something: get out, crack a joke, tell him to find another forensic artist. But all she could do was stare at him. As if she were hypnotized by his hazel eyes.

"Most of all I'm not good at being able to get you out of my mind. Damned if you haven't been stuck there since the first second I saw you."

His lips were on hers before she could form another thought.

If she thought there was heat when their hands had touched, this was downright explosive.

His mouth was wet, hot, open against hers and she couldn't get enough. Couldn't get close enough.

Forget cold. Within seconds she was *burning*. She forgot everything but the strength and heat of the kiss. It was consuming her.

Her fingers tangled in his hair, pulling him closer. She could feel his at her waist, hips, pulling her to him.

The loud ringing of a phone moments later was what forced them to ease back from each other. Their eyes locked, both downright dazed.

Jon finally reached down into the cup holder and picked up the phone. He looked at it then cursed under his breath. "It's Zane Wales from Corpus Christi PD. I've got to take this."

Sherry nodded.

"Hatton."

He listened to whatever Zane said and muttered another curse. He opened the car door and got out.

Sherry opened her door. It was positively steaming inside the car and for once she needed to cool herself down.

"Where?" Jon was saying. Then listened some more.

"I'll be right there. And for God's sake, make sure Spangler isn't around." He disconnected the call and looked straight at Sherry. "I'm sorry. You can't make an honest man out of me tonight. I've got to go."

"Trouble?" She hoped not.

He nodded, lips pursed. "Another woman has been attacked."

Sherry closed her eyes. When would this end?

"I'll take you home, then head out to the hospital. After what happened last time, I feel like I need to make sure no one upsets the victim in any way."

"I'll just come with you to the hospital. If you have to take me all the way home, it will be over thirty minutes before you get there. Maybe more."

"Are you sure?"

No, she wasn't sure at all. But she knew he needed to get there as soon as he could. "I don't think I'm ready to talk to this new victim, but I do want to help you get there as fast as possible."

He trailed a finger down her cheek. "Thank you. I know just being there isn't easy for you."

"I'll be all right. There's someone who has gone through much worse than me. Let's get you there so you can help her."

Chapter Ten

They pulled up at the hospital and rushed inside. Zane was waiting for them at the door, cowboy hat still firmly on his head, fairly brimming with excitement.

"We've got DNA," he told them without any greeting. "One of the nurses told me this latest victim was able to get a scratch in and there were definitely skin cells under her fingernails."

Jon was excited but surprised. "What sort of injuries does she have? Craniofacial trauma like the others?"

Zane was giddy. "No, just a couple of bruises, from what I understand. Guy was wearing a ski mask or something, so I don't think she got to see his face. Unfortunately."

"A mask? None of the other victims have mentioned a mask," Jon noted as they walked down the hall, Sherry on one side of him, Zane on the other.

"None of the other victims got a look at the perp. This is our lucky break, Hatton."

Jon reserved judgment. There was nothing he'd like more than a lucky break in this case. But he had a sinking feeling that this wasn't it.

Jon found himself back down the same hospital trauma hallway where he'd met Sherry a few days before. She was quiet, but at least this time she wasn't pale and shivering.

"Doing okay?" he murmured to her as they walked.

She nodded, and he reached down and grabbed her hand, giving it a supportive squeeze. She squeezed back before they both let go.

"We're waiting for Dr. Rosemont to come out and give us a report. Captain heard about the DNA and that the patient was conscious and is on his way over."

No doubt the man wanted to be here if there was going to be a big break in the case and press involved. Jon shook his head. He'd be glad to let Captain Harris get as much attention as he could handle as long as it meant they were stopping whoever was responsible.

They could hear yelling from inside the patient's room before they even got to the door. A woman's voice, shrieking.

"Someone thought they could do this to me? Thought they could just throw me down on the ground and attack me?"

Someone murmured something to her, but Jon couldn't hear what they said.

"Yes, I know he had every intention of raping me. But I didn't let him. I just kept hitting and punching."

Jon looked over at Zane with one eyebrow raised. "Sounds like she's not injured too much; not like the other victims."

Zane smiled. "Yeah. Seems like the SOB messed with the wrong woman this time."

"Did he break into her house or building like the others?" Jon asked.

"No." Zane shook his head. "I haven't confirmed this yet with the victim, but I think he was waiting for her at her work. Dragged her out of her car in the back of the parking lot."

Another discrepancy. Jon had to admit, their guy hadn't tended to follow an MO, so maybe it was their serial rapist who'd also committed this crime.

Sherry had taken a step back at the sound of the yelling. Jon stopped to talk to her.

"I'm going get a uniformed officer to take you home."

"No, I'm okay."

"Hey, it makes you uncomfortable to be here, and that's okay." He lowered his voice so Zane couldn't hear him. "I've got to be honest, I'm not even sure we're dealing with the same perpetrator here."

"Really?"

"I won't know until I talk to the victim and check out the scene, but…"

"There are some indications."

"Exactly. And if the attacker was wearing a ski mask, there won't be much for you to draw."

Sherry nodded. "Okay, then if you really don't mind, I guess I'd rather go home. I can call a cab."

"No, there will be plenty of officers that can give you a ride." He took her by the arm and led her toward the nurses' station. "If I need you, I'll call."

"Okay." Her voice was quiet, reserved.

"Actually, I'll be calling you tomorrow regardless. You have to make an honest man out of me before I talk to Caroline again. Have dinner with me tomorrow night, so it's true that I asked you out."

He thought about their kiss and how much more he wanted than just dinner, but that was a good place to start. If she would even agree to a real date.

"No manipulating or yelling, I promise," he said.

She smiled. "And I won't walk through the city alone."

Jon reached his hand out to shake hers. "Deal."

He walked her the rest of the way over to the nurses' station. Sara Beth Carreker, the head nurse from the other day, was working.

"I have to admit, I'm sorry to see you back here again this week, Agent Hatton."

"I'm sorry to see me back here, too, Sara Beth, under these circumstances. This is my friend Sherry. Is it okay if she stays here until one of the uniformed officers gives her a ride home?"

"Sure, I'll be going in with the new victim, but some of the other nurses will be here. And Dr. Trumpold." She pointed at a handsome doctor standing at the counter, going through charts.

Dr. Trumpold shrugged. "I don't think—none of us think—it's very prudent for a male doctor to be in with a sexual assault victim, especially in the first few days."

"I guess that makes your job harder," Sherry said to him.

"It's okay. I understand. Whatever is best for the patients." The doctor smiled at Sherry.

Suddenly leaving Sherry here didn't seem like such a great idea to Jon, but he swallowed that down.

"I'm going to get back down the hall," Jon said and, unable to stop himself, put his arm around her in a sideways hug.

But call it what it really was: a claiming. Jon ignored the relief he felt when she leaned into him and smiled. "If someone hasn't come to take you home in ten minutes, come find me," he said.

Sherry nodded. "It's okay if you need to call me if the victim remembers seeing anything. I can't promise results, but I can at least try," she said.

"Are you a police officer?" Dr. Trumpold asked. "I saw you here the other day, but thought you were friends with the victim."

"No, I'm a forensic artist. Well, actually, I'm just on vacation. Evidently, I don't know what I am doing."

"You're healing, that's what you're doing." Jon reached down quickly and kissed her on the cheek. "The rest…we'll just see. See you tomorrow."

Just that brief touch of his lips—a friendly gesture by most counts—caused heat to flow through both of them. Sherry's eyes met his before darting nervously to Dr. Trumpold, who had politely turned away and started going through files.

"Tomorrow," Jon whispered again, and she nodded.

He turned and walked down the hall. He asked the first Corpus Christi officer he saw to find someone to get Sherry home. He was glad she wasn't staying. She wasn't comfortable. And he wasn't comfortable with her spending too much time with the handsome trauma doctor. Hopefully he had other cases he'd be attending to soon.

Captain Harris and Zane were standing outside the victim's room talking to Dr. Rosemont when Jon joined them.

"Ms. Grimaldi was very fortunate," the doctor was saying. "Especially compared to some of the other rape victims. Although undoubtedly the attacker meant her harm, he was not successful in his rape attempt. Nor did she suffer the same craniofacial trauma as the other victims."

"She was able to scratch the attacker?" Captain Harris asked.

The doctor nodded. "Yes, on the upper arm. The nurse will be out momentarily with the evidence that was collected."

"We'll rush this through and hopefully it will be a hit," the captain said. "Then we'll be able to put this nightmare behind us."

"Captain," Jon interrupted, "I don't think we should be too quick to make any assumptions. Even if you do get a DNA hit, it might not be the same guy as the others."

The captain stood there shaking his head at Jon for long seconds. "You know what we really don't need now, Hatton? Some sort of better-than-you outsider who's playing devil's advocate and doesn't really understand our community at all. People here are in a panic and they need to know immediately if we've caught this monster."

"I agree about people being in a panic." Jon tried to keep his voice level, but damned if he wasn't tired of this *outsider* trash. "I just think it would be prudent to be positive before we make any public announcements about the rapist being arrested."

The captain leaned forward, his lips pressed together in a thin line. "If I can give the people of Corpus Christi a good night's rest for the first time in weeks, I'm not going to deny them that just because you're a bureaucrat who wants to wrap everything in red tape, making it impossible for real police work to be done."

Jon counted to ten silently in his head in an effort not to tell the chief where he could go. Jon's specialty—hell, Omega Sector's specialty—was cutting through red tape, not adding it. Just because Jon refused to jump in to the hooray-we-caught-the-bad-guy party without any evidence did not make him a bureaucrat.

Jon turned toward the doctor. "Do you feel that Ms. Grimaldi is up for any questioning tonight?"

"She's scared, of course, but feels very lucky that she was able to fight off her attacker. I'll ask if she's willing to talk to you." The doctor went back into the room as a nurse came out with a bag of evidence.

Zane took it from her. "I'll go have this run immediately, Captain."

"You tell them to put every rush possible on it, Wales. And leave someone there so that as soon as the results are in we are notified." The captain looked over at Jon, pointedly. "Tonight, if possible."

Zane left, sprinting down the hall. Despite his words earlier, Jon prayed they would get a hit off the DNA and that it really was the serial rapist who had made a mistake with this victim.

Dr. Rosemont returned. "Ms. Grimaldi will see you and seems up for it. In light of what happened last time, I'm going to stay in the room."

Jon wasn't offended. After what had happened last time, the doctor was right to protect her patient. "Thanks."

The moment Jon walked into the room he became convinced this wasn't the attack of the same man. The woman had only one bruise on the side of her face and it was on the lower part of her chin.

The serial rapist had consistently aimed for the eyes first. The blows to the face had been purposeful in nature: to cause his victims not to be able to see or to identify him.

"Ms. Grimaldi, I'm so sorry for what happened to you tonight. If it's okay, we'd like to ask you a few questions?" Jon said.

She nodded and grabbed the hand of the woman—sister? friend?—sitting next to her. "Okay."

Dana Grimaldi was in her early thirties, Jon would estimate. She had blond hair, obviously not her natural color with the dark brown showing at the roots, and was of medium height and build. The serial rapist hadn't stuck to any one MO when choosing the demographics of his victims, so Jon had to admit that she could've fit the bill there.

"I'm Captain Harris from the Corpus Christi PD." The other man spoke up. "I don't normally work cases like this, but I'm here to personally help get this solved for you as soon as possible. Can you walk through what happened?"

"I was working a shift out at the harbor yard. I'm an administrative assistant for one of the companies at the port, so my hours aren't the same hours as the people who work the line, but they're pretty similar. A lot of times I have to walk in and out of the parking lot by myself. In the afternoon, when I get there, it's not a problem, but at night…"

The woman began crying. The other woman scooted

closer and wrapped an arm around her. "You've told them about it. I know you have," the woman murmured.

Ms. Grimaldi looked up at Jon and Captain Harris. "I *have* told my supervisors how unsafe I feel walking out there alone. Where I have to park is usually way in the back. It's isolated from the rest of the parking lot by a line of Dumpsters."

"What did your company say when you told them?" the captain asked her.

It was a good question. Maybe there would be cameras that the company had available. It wouldn't help poor Ms. Grimaldi in what had happened to her, but it would possibly help capture who had done this.

"They said that any of the security guards would gladly walk me out to my car if I wanted them to. That warehouse is huge and finding a security guard sometimes isn't that easy. So I just went by myself." She started crying again, painful sobs. "I was so stupid."

"Hey," Jon said, taking a slow step toward her so as not to spook her unnecessarily. "Just because you walked there by yourself doesn't make this your fault. You could've walked across that parking lot in nothing but skimpy lingerie and that still wouldn't make it okay for someone to attack you. *His* fault. *He's* the one to blame. Not you."

She nodded, tears subsiding a little.

"Tell us what happened next."

"I got into my car. I left the door open once I sat down because it was so hot in the car from sitting in the parking lot all afternoon. I was turning to get my phone out of my purse when the guy reached in and grabbed me." She clung to the other woman.

"He pulled me up out of the car by my shirt, ripping it, and then threw me against the side of the car. He was wearing a mask, so I couldn't see his face."

Jon looked over at Captain Harris. The man had to realize how different this victim's story was than the stories they had heard over the past few weeks. No immediate blows to the face? A mask? At a car instead of inside a building?

"All I could think was about that rapist who was on the loose. We'd all been told not to open our doors to strangers, but I hadn't heard about anything in parking lots. I knew what he was going to do—going to try to do—so I just started fighting like a crazy person."

"You were able to scratch your attacker?" the captain asked.

She nodded. "Yes, although I didn't really notice it at the time. I think it was his arm because that was the only place where I saw skin. I was just trying to scream my head off and get away if I could.

"He hit me when I screamed, right on the jaw, but I just kept screaming and swinging and kicking the best I could. And he just ran away. Some other people heard me and they came running up not long afterward. Called the police and ambulance, and they brought me here."

Her breaths were coming much heavier, but she made it through the story.

"It sounds like you were very brave and did everything right," Jon assured her.

"I was so scared. Now I'm angry, but then I was just scared."

"I can imagine," Captain Harris said. "We're going to use the DNA from when you scratched him and hopefully be able to make an arrest soon. Even tonight."

Jon shook his head. Harris still wanted to run with this being the serial rapist. After hearing Dana's story, Jon was convinced more than ever that—very fortunately for Dana—the man who attacked her wasn't the rapist they'd been searching for.

This was some sort of copycat.

Chapter Eleven

"Ms. Grimaldi, is there anyone that you know of that might want to hurt you in some way? Any ex-boyfriends or husbands or friends that are mad at you? Fights you have had with anyone?"

Harris glared at Jon at the question, but he didn't care. Even though it probably wasn't the serial rapist, Ms. Grimaldi had still been attacked and this was still a case that needed to be solved.

"I broke up with my boyfriend a couple of weeks ago. He was pretty upset. But I know he didn't do this. He's not that type of person."

Jon knew that heartbreak and rage could turn people into someone different. Unrecognizable. He got the man's name and address from the victim. Tony Shefferly.

"Hopefully just to eliminate him as a suspect," Jon told her. Any scratches on his arms would help confirm or eliminate him from their suspect pool.

Since she hadn't seen much because of his mask and the attack, thank God, had not progressed to an actual rape, there weren't many other questions that either Jon or Captain Harris had to ask. Jon turned to leave, but Harris went back, offering his hand out to Dana to shake.

"Your bravery is going to be key in helping us catch this monster who has terrorized our city, Ms. Grimaldi. Thank you for that. We'll be back in touch."

Ms. Grimaldi looked elated at Harris's words. Jon bit his tongue to keep from saying anything. Bringing up the holes in the captain's theory in front of the victim was not a good idea.

As he was going out the door, there was one last thing Jon knew he needed to ask her, based on what Sherry had learned from Jasmine Houze earlier.

"You didn't see any tattoos on the man's arms, did you? About halfway up between his wrist and elbow?"

Dana shook her head. "No, I don't remember seeing anything like that."

"What about gloves? Was the man who attacked you wearing any sort of gloves? Latex or otherwise?"

Dana shuddered. "No, he definitely wasn't wearing gloves. I remember feeling his hands on my arms when he pushed me down on the ground. Definitely no gloves."

"Okay, thanks again for your help. No matter what happens in this investigation, Captain Harris is right, you were certainly very brave."

Jon pulled the door closed behind him when he exited the room to find Captain Harris glaring at him.

"What the hell was that about, Hatton? 'No matter what happens in this investigation.' Are you trying to make me look like a fool?"

No, the older man was taking all the steps to do that himself without any help from Jon. "Captain, I'm trying to be objective here. I don't think this is the same guy."

"What were those questions about the tattoo and gloves?"

"I found out earlier today that Jasmine Houze remembered something. A tattoo on the inside of her attacker's arm. Also, that he was wearing latex gloves."

"You met with a victim without anybody from the department with you?" His nostrils flared.

"No, actually, Ms. Houze called Sherry Mitchell, the forensic artist Omega found to replace Frank Spangler. Ms.

Mitchell met with the victim and provided me with the sketch of the tattoo. I was bringing it in to check against possible gang tattoos when I got the call about Ms. Grimaldi's attack."

That was almost true except for the part where he and Sherry almost set his car on fire from the heat between them. That definitely didn't need to be mentioned to Captain Harris.

"Well, Grimaldi could neither confirm nor deny the tattoo, so that doesn't help us one way or another," Captain Harris responded.

Jon shook his head. "Captain, I respect that you love your city and want to keep it safe. I know you want this guy behind bars so you can assure the people looking to you that the Corpus Christi PD has done its job and has gotten a monster off the street."

"Yeah, so?"

"Part of the reason I was sent here was to help with crisis management. As someone with experience in that area, I'm asking you not to make any formal statements to the press, even if we are able to arrest someone from the DNA findings, until we can definitively link Ms. Grimaldi's case to those of other women."

"Damn it, Hatton…"

"We don't have to link it to all the other cases, just one, and I'll be satisfied." Jon held a hand out in a gesture of peace. "There are too many discrepancies. She was attacked in a parking lot instead of a building. She wasn't immediately struck in the face like the others. The guy wore a ski mask and no gloves."

"None of those things mean it wasn't our perp."

"I agree. But taking all of the facts together gives enough reasonable doubt that it may not be. To report to the press that the suspect is in custody, only to find out—from another woman being raped—that we have the wrong person? As your crisis-management representative, I wanted to tell you that would be a nightmare in terms of community relations."

"Fine," Harris said. "No one will make any official statements about anything until we have evidence linking him to the other cases."

"Thank you, Captain."

"If I'm right, and we are able to link all the rapes to this one guy and the city of Corpus Christi spent more days in worry when it could've been sleeping soundly? I'll expect you to make an announcement to the press that it was the feds' call to do that."

"Fine." Jon didn't have any real concern that would be necessary, but if it kept the captain from making a pretty big mistake, he was willing to risk it.

Captain Harris wasn't mollified. "And it's not like the other part of your job you were sent for—behavioral analysis of this bastard—has been of any use."

Jon didn't have much response to that. "You're right. He's been one step ahead of all of us the whole time. He's made no mistakes. That is part of the reason why this last case, with all its many mistakes, has me thinking it's not the same guy."

Zane Wales came running down the hall. "We've got a hit through the DNA. Perp has a record. Uniforms are on their way over to his last known address right now."

"A serial rapist with a criminal record? How difficult to believe." The captain's sarcasm was obvious.

Jon grabbed the notebook out of his pocket with his notes from Dana Grimaldi. He turned to Zane. "Did the DNA belong to Tony Shefferly?"

Zane stopped midstride, his posture stiffening. "Why do you ask that?"

"That's the victim's ex-boyfriend."

Zane glanced at Captain Harris, then back at Jon. "No, it belonged to Wade Shefferly, Tony's brother."

Chapter Twelve

It had been a long damn day.

Last night Captain Harris still hadn't wanted to admit defeat even when the DNA was discovered as the ex-boyfriend's brother's.

It had taken the man's arrest, hours of questioning through the night and finally unshakable alibis confirmed today for at least three of the other rapes before the captain had admitted Shefferly wasn't the serial rapist they were looking for.

Jon knew after only five minutes of talking to him that he was not smart enough, not controlled enough, not *focused* enough, to be the man responsible for the other attacks.

Shefferly had confessed to what he'd done to Dana Grimaldi. Evidently he'd been angry to the point of hatred at how she'd treated his brother when she cheated on him and broke up with him. He'd thought he could get away with exacting some revenge on his brother's behalf by attacking her in the parking lot. He was hoping the serial rapist would be blamed, although Shefferly swore he'd never actually planned to rape Dana, just knock her around and scare her.

Wade Shefferly would be going to jail—*back* to jail—for what he did to Dana. While Jon was happy about that, it still meant their rapist was on the loose.

If frustration in the police department had been high before Shefferly's arrest, it was twice as bad now. The force had gotten its hopes up then dashed.

"I suppose you want to say, 'I told you so,'" Captain Harris had muttered when Shefferly's alibi checked out for the other rapes.

Jon didn't want to say, "I told you so." He didn't want to say anything but "Let's work together and find the bastard responsible before another woman pays the price."

But he'd been trying to say that since he arrived. Nobody was listening.

Today had been even worse with Jon taking the full brunt of the detectives' and the captain's frustration. In a case of this magnitude, with massive media attention, tempers always flared. People needed somewhere to aim their vexation; Jon's direction seemed easiest for everyone. After all, he was the one who had been called in especially for this case. The one who was supposed to have the expertise needed to get results.

So far, nothing he'd done had been any more useful than anything else.

He knew part of his job as a member of the crisis-management unit was to help the local PD focus its frustration in the right manner, even if it was at him. Damn, if he hadn't had to almost bite his tongue all the way off to keep from snapping back when the men wanted someone to blame.

When Jon had called in to Omega to report the copycat attack and subsequent arrest, his frustration bubbled over. Steve Drackett had tried to assure Jon that Jon was doing everything he could do.

Jon knew he wasn't. He was currently on his way to rectify that.

He needed Sherry.

In his entire professional career Jon couldn't remember

ever feeling so torn. He needed Sherry on this case. Her expertise. Her abilities.

He also had a bone-deep need to just be with her, be near her, protect her.

He was afraid he couldn't have both. That if he pushed for one, he couldn't have the other. That if he made a romantic move, and then asked for her help with the case, she might think he was manipulating her to get what he needed.

Jon knew he should put the case first. Ask for her professional help and step back personally. But as he pulled up in her driveway and saw her open the door and smile at him as he walked up the steps, Jon knew he wouldn't do that.

There was no way he was going to be able to keep his distance from her.

He walked straight up to her and, bending his knees slightly, wrapped both his arms around her waist and hips before straightening to his full height. This brought her neck right up to his face. He buried it in her hair and just breathed.

For the first time all day he felt as though he could actually get air in and out of his lungs without difficulty.

Her arms came around his shoulders and he was thankful—beyond thankful—she didn't pull away. He just needed a minute to clear his head, to be around someone who didn't wish that he would leave town as soon as possible.

Of course, he wasn't even sure that was true with Sherry. She probably thought he was nuts, hugging her like this without even saying hello.

Jon forced himself to release her and set her feet down on the floor. He eased back slowly, afraid of what he was going to see on her face when he looked there.

It wasn't the ridicule or scorn he was half expecting. Just shining blue eyes coupled with her beautiful smile.

"Hey," she greeted him, her Texan upbringing evident in the word.

"Sorry about that," Jon responded. "It's been a hell of a day."

"No apology necessary. I know what it's like to need some sort of lifeline."

Jon imagined she did. "Do you have one? Someone who keeps you grounded when you're doing your work for the Bureau?" He was pretty sure he already knew the answer. Not having someone to help anchor her was part of the reason she was suffering to such a degree now.

"No, not really."

"You need someone. A friend, colleague. Someone. Everybody does."

She nodded. "You're right. Trying to do this alone… The darkness can become too heavy."

"Your supervisor at the Bureau should've provided you with a mentor, or an agent or even the contact info of the FBI therapist. Someone for you to talk to."

"Yeah, I think she meant to. Things just happened fast, crazy fast, when I started working for them. I traveled around a lot, to different field offices, so I wasn't around the same people all the time."

"Still…"

"Oh, I agree I needed someone." Her eyebrows gathered in and she started rubbing her hands together in an absent fashion. "I just thought it was me being weak, letting my artistic nature get the better of me, so I didn't tell anyone how much I was struggling, even when they asked."

Jon grabbed her hands to stop the nervous movement. "Even seasoned agents struggle with being bombarded by the worst side of human nature day after day. And they go through training you never had."

"I guess so." Sherry shrugged. "So, bad day for you, huh?"

"How about if I tell you about it over dinner? Or, if you

don't want to, we don't have to talk about the case at all. Either way, I didn't get to eat any lunch and I'm starved."

"Sounds great to me."

"Maybe we'll even make it into the restaurant this time."

Jon meant that hopefully they wouldn't be disturbed by another call having to do with the case. But as soon as their eyes met and the heat was flashing between them again, Jon knew they were both thinking of the same thing: that kiss last night.

MAYBE WE'LL EVEN make it into the restaurant this time.

It was all Sherry could do not to suggest they skip the restaurant altogether and just stay here at the house. Order pizza, if he was that hungry.

As much as Sherry wanted to explore this heat between them, she wasn't sure that it was the smart thing to do. Her emotional balance teetered so precariously right now, she wasn't sure if she could trust her own feelings.

If she was honest, she wasn't 100 percent sure that Jon wasn't getting close to her just to try to talk her into helping with the case. She didn't think he would deliberately set out to seduce her to get her help or anything like that. But she knew that getting involved with Jon would be complicated.

Plus, she'd decided earlier to try to help him with the case if she could. That is, if she could without completely losing her sanity.

She didn't want to tell him just yet, hadn't really decided to what degree she was willing to offer herself. Or to what degree she'd even be useful if she wasn't able to draw. Offering to help and then being totally inadequate would be worse than not offering in the first place.

She'd deal with that as it came. Right now, dinner. *Not* inside her house. That was too close to the bed.

"Yes, let's go eat. I'm hungry, too."

In more ways than one.

"The barbecue place okay again?" He looked as though he might start drooling over the thought of it, so she wouldn't have had the heart to say no even if she had wanted to. Not to mention she was born in Texas and there just wasn't any way she'd say no to barbecue.

"Sure, let me go grab my jacket."

"Are you serious? It's at least eighty-five degrees out here."

"I never know when I'm going to get cold and sometimes the air-conditioning is too cool in places."

He waited on the small porch while she grabbed her lightweight jacket. When she walked back out he was staring at her legs.

"What? Is there something on my skirt?" She hoped not. It was her favorite denim skirt.

"No. I'm just particular to your legs in those boots."

She smiled at him. "Boots are a Texas thing, mostly, I guess."

"We get them in Colorado, but not as much in Colorado Springs where Omega Sector is located. Despite the mountains, that's more a city than anything else."

He opened her car door and she got in, and then he went around and got in himself.

"Are you from Colorado originally?"

"No, born and raised in Cincinnati. Reds, baby, all the way."

She smiled. "That doesn't sound like a football team. You know in Texas, if it's not football, it pretty much doesn't count as a sport."

"This state is officially killing me." He shook his head. "First, everybody at the precinct hates me and now you tell me baseball isn't important."

"Baseball is your thing, huh?"

"Oh, yeah. I got a full ride to college as a pitcher. Was

actually hoping to go pro—at least the minors. But I blew out my elbow my junior year."

"I'm sorry. That had to have been difficult."

"Yeah, at the time. But it helped me focus on where I needed to be. It wasn't bad enough to keep me out of the FBI, just bad enough to end my pro dreams. I know I'm doing what I'm supposed to now."

"What do you do exactly? Are you a profiler?"

"That's part of it. I get sent in to crisis situations to help local law enforcement that don't have the resources and/or personnel to handle a situation. I'm the last resort before feds come in and completely take over a case."

"That's why everyone at the precinct hates you?"

Jon smiled as he pulled into the parking lot of the restaurant. "Usually, I'm not very popular the first day or two, but normally my charming personality has won over most of the locals by this stage of the game."

Sherry didn't question that. She had no doubt Jon was good at his job and it didn't take long for most people to see that he was about the case, not power hungry or there to get anybody in trouble.

She also had no doubt he was able to figure out what the locals needed and become that person, to a certain degree. They needed a leader? He could definitely be one. A sounding board? No problem. Source of support? Scapegoat?

"So basically you handle them like you handled me the other day. You figure out what to say to get what you want."

He shot a sideways look at her. "Well, not what *I* want. But, yeah, I guess I'm good at figuring out how to get everyone to work together to solve the case. Get the job done."

Sherry could respect that. Sometimes people needed to be managed, especially with cases like the current one. It didn't make Jon a bad person, but evidently the police department didn't agree with her on that fact.

"The locals are giving you a hard time," she said.

"They're frustrated. We're all frustrated. In their defense, I haven't been able to make any real progress in the nearly ten days I've been here."

Now seemed like a good time to tell him. She just hoped she wasn't making a huge mistake. "Well, I was thinking maybe I could help you. Look over the files and see if there's anything the other artist missed. I'm not promising anything, but I could try."

Chapter Thirteen

The next morning Sherry found herself at the Corpus Christi Police Department. It was the last place she had expected to be on her vacation, but she'd committed, so she was here.

Jon had refused to talk about the case last night during dinner, which had been nice. She'd half expected once she'd agreed to help for him to skip dinner altogether—or maybe hit a fast-food drive-through, since he had missed lunch—and head straight in to work.

But he hadn't. He'd nodded at her offer, parked the car and ushered her inside the little restaurant.

Once they were seated at the booth, she asked, "Aren't you going to start bombarding me with details about the case?"

He looked up from his menu. "Shh. I'm on a date with a very beautiful woman. I don't want to talk about work, lest she think that's the only reason I'm here with her."

"That's not why you're here with me? Are you sure?"

Jon set the menu down. "I'll admit at this point, if a three-year-old came up to me and offered to help I would probably accept it. So, yes, I will gladly accept your help. But, no, that is very definitely not why I am here with you."

The way he looked at her had her heating up again. She was beginning to think if she stuck around him she'd never have to worry about being cold again.

"Okay." She managed not to stammer. "I just wanted you to know that you didn't have to do this just to get me to help."

"I promise I'm not managing you, not handling you. I just want to spend time with you. Tomorrow will be soon enough to start on the case."

Over the next couple of hours they proceeded to eat and drink a couple of beers and just relax. Sherry wasn't sure that she'd ever seen someone eat a meal with as much reverence as Jon ate his brisket. "You must be Texan somewhere in your blood the way you love that sandwich."

"The state is definitely growing on me."

That look again. The heat.

She learned that he was thirty-three years old, had three brothers, and his mom and dad still lived in Ohio. That he'd been married briefly when he was younger until his wife had decided marriage vows just weren't for her and left him for another guy.

"Ouch."

He shrugged. "It was painful at the time, but things happen for a reason. Like baseball not working out, my marriage falling apart helped point me in the direction of Omega Sector. I've never doubted that was where I was supposed to be. Was recruited there straight out of Quantico."

He told her more about his life with Omega; some funny stories about some of his friends and how he'd played a part in cracking open the Chicago terrorist bombing a few weeks ago, which had led to the arrest of a US senator.

She told him about growing up as an only child. Of the parents she wasn't very close to and how she had become a forensic artist.

"One of my friends witnessed a hit and run a couple of years ago in Dallas. She got a good look at the driver but was having a hard time describing him to the police accurately. I worked with her and was able to bring the drawing in, which eventually led to his arrest."

"How'd you end up working for the FBI?"

"Someone from the local field office happened to be there when I came in. They saw what I'd done and asked if I could help with a kidnapping case they were working on. For the first couple of months I only worked a few hours a week."

"Then once they discovered how good you were, you suddenly found yourself there full-time."

She shrugged. "Basically. More than full-time."

"And you probably didn't take a break at all for the past two years, did you? A vacation?"

"No. There wasn't time. There was always a case. Helping stop a kidnapper or a rapist or a robber always seemed more important than a vacation."

"Then your mind decided you'd had enough and the stress triggers started." He got quiet for a long moment before continuing. "Then you did finally take a vacation, but along came someone else needing you to help with a case."

"It's okay," she murmured.

He then moved the conversation back to more neutral topics. More stories of his brothers and friends at Omega that kept her entertained.

All in all, it was a thoroughly enjoyable evening. When he took her home the heat between them—which had nothing to do with the temperature outside—was palpable. Sherry thought she had some big decisions to make when Jon walked her up to her door.

He cupped her face with both hands and slid his fingers into her hair at the nape of her neck, tilting her head back so they were looking at each other.

In that moment, whatever he wanted, she was willing. She couldn't remember ever wanting something as much as she wanted Jon right then. As his lips moved toward hers, she raised herself up on her toes to meet him.

But instead of the heat-infused kiss she had expected, like the one from yesterday and the one that had been building between them the entire evening, his lips just briefly, softly, touched hers. Then skimmed over to her cheek.

"I had a wonderful time, Texas," he whispered in her ear. "I'll see you tomorrow."

Then he was gone, leaving Sherry to wonder exactly what had happened.

She was still trying to figure that out now as she was directed back to the desk where Jon could be located here at the station.

He wasn't kidding when he said they didn't like him. Even the uniformed officers working the front desk had sneered when she said who she was here to see. She could see why that would wear thin pretty quickly.

He smiled and stood as she got to the desk the department had assigned him.

"You're like the little wizard who lived under the stairs," she muttered as he pulled up a chair for her to sit in.

"Did I mention that the department was hugely excited that federal law enforcement had been called in to help with the case?"

"They weren't real subtle in demonstrating their disapproval, were they? I guess they couldn't find an actual closet to put you in?"

Jon chuckled. "It's fine. I haven't been here very often anyway. I'm out at scenes and interviews more."

Zane Wales came over to Jon's desk.

"We've got one of the conference rooms cleared so y'all can use it," he told them then turned to Sherry. "Both times I've seen you I've been in a huge hurry. Sorry about that. I'm Zane Wales."

Sherry shook his outstretched hand.

"You're Caroline's…" Sherry wasn't sure what the word was. Friend? Ex-friend? Soul mate? Sworn enemy? Better to stick with something safe. "You know Caroline."

Some emotion flashed across his face too quickly for Sherry to read. Whatever Zane felt for Caroline, it wasn't neutral.

"I do know her. We've known each other since we were in fourth grade."

Evidently, Caroline hadn't been lying when she'd said it was complicated.

They followed Zane into the conference room and Jon set out the files on the table for her.

"I thought you were a forensic artist, not an agent," Zane said.

"She is, but she's just going to look through the files, see if she notices anything we've missed. At this point, any other qualified set of eyes can only help us."

"I don't disagree with you, but the captain and Spangler will throw a hissy fit if they see her in here."

"This is my call, and I stand behind it. Plus, she's a licensed forensic artist in Texas, so neither of them should have cause for complaint."

"That doesn't mean they won't, though," the younger man said.

"Zane, run some interference for us, man." Jon turned to face him. "Let's all start working like we're on the same team. Because since Dana Grimaldi ended up not being attacked by our guy…"

"He's going to strike again soon," Zane finished for him.

Jon nodded. "If everyone here wants to hate me, that's fine. I can take it. But let's catch this son of a bitch before some other poor woman gets raped."

Zane looked at Sherry and then Jon as he walked to

the door. "I'll do what I can. I sure as hell hope you two find something."

"We don't have to do this here if it's going to make everyone mad," Sherry said after Zane left. "I'm not trying to make things worse for you."

"No, I'd rather be here in case there are other resources we need." He walked over to shut the door of the conference room. "Don't worry about anybody else. How do you want to do this?"

She looked at the files, knew the graphic violence she would find when she opened them. Now that it was just the cases sitting right in front of her, Sherry could feel her stomach start to roll, muscles start to tighten. She wanted to turn and walk back out the way she came. Do anything but open these files.

She could feel the chill starting to work its way throughout her body.

She'd made a mistake. She thought she could be of help, thought she could—

"Sherry, look at me."

She couldn't seem to force her eyes away from the documents, from the shattered lives she knew she would find inside.

"Look at me, right now."

Sherry forced her eyes up from the brown folders that had seemed to mesmerize her.

Jon made his way around the table and put both hands on her arms, rubbing them up and down. "I'm going to go through all those files before you even open them. All you need to read is the interview that the other forensic artist had with the victim. You don't need to look at the pictures, don't need the other details. Just the interviews to see if there were any questions you might have asked that were missed."

Jon's hazel eyes were close to hers and she could feel warmth where he was touching her.

"I'm going to be right here, okay?" he said. "Your life-line, like we talked about yesterday. Everybody needs one in this line of work."

Her lifeline. Yes, she needed someone to make sure she wasn't going under. Jon would do that.

As if he could read her mind he said, "I'll be right here. I won't let you go under."

Sherry took a breath and nodded. Okay, she could do this. At least she would try.

"I'm okay."

He kissed her on the forehead. "You're more than okay. You can do this."

"I hope so."

Chapter Fourteen

He'd almost lost her before they even got started.

It hadn't been hard to see her panic when she saw the files out on the table. Jon could kick himself for not thinking it through more carefully. He should've known he couldn't just hand her the documents—complete with gruesome pictures taken after the victims arrived at the hospital—and expect her to just sort through them.

That would be difficult enough for someone not already dealing with a trauma disorder. Sherry most definitely wasn't ready for that. Jon, like her supervisor at the FBI, had treated her as if she were a trained agent.

She wasn't. She was an artist. She might not have any sort of quirky artistic temperament or behavior, but she still wasn't a trained agent. Everybody, including him, needed to remember that if they wanted Sherry to be able to continue to work long term.

He'd caught it in time and, as he'd promised, he would continue to be her lifeline throughout this entire process. To keep her from going under when the darkness was too overwhelming.

Sometimes the job of lifeline wasn't sexy. As now. He'd just sat next to her, within arm's reach, as she went through the interviews in the files. Even though the pictures were now gone, the words themselves, the descriptions of the attacks, were bad enough. Especially for someone who had a gift for visualizing.

They'd been at it all day. She was thorough. Taking notes—pages' worth. Asking questions. Jon was so familiar with the cases he could answer most of her questions without even having to reference other materials.

He could tell when it would become overwhelming to her because she would look up for him, almost as if checking to be sure he was still there. When she would see him, she was able to mentally regroup and get back to work.

But it was painful for her.

He'd wanted to stop it, to give her a break, but except for the brief lunch they'd had, consisting of a sub sandwich he'd ordered in from around the corner, she'd wanted to keep going.

A couple of times he'd forced her to stop. To get up, to stretch, to walk around outside and get some sun. Her work ethic was impressive, but Jon was sure it had gone a long way toward the fragile mental state she was in. She had to learn not to labor herself into physical and emotional exhaustion every time she did forensic work.

As much as he wanted her expertise on the case, he also wanted to stop her and pull her into his lap. He was still trying to figure out why—and for heaven's sake *how*— he'd walked away from her last night. All he'd wanted to do was to stay and give in to the heat that had been dancing between them all night.

Every part of him had wanted to remain. Sensing she'd wanted him to stay had made it twice as hard. No pun intended.

But somewhere Jon had known if he wanted to have any chance of a real relationship with Sherry he could not let the physical side of their connection get out of hand too fast. The blend of their personal and professional relationships was just too entwined right now. If he had taken her inside—taken her to bed—as he'd so desperately wanted to do last night, somewhere in the back of her mind his motive would always have been in question.

He didn't let himself dwell too much on the *real relationship* thoughts that were running through his head because, yeah, that was a little scary, since they had known each other for only a few days and had only really kissed once.

Jon knew himself well enough to know that there was nothing casual in what he was feeling for Sherry. He hadn't felt this way since… Hell, he didn't know if he had ever felt this way about a woman.

But right now she needed him professionally. Her trust in him was humbling and he planned to show her that working on cases under the right circumstances and with someone looking out for her well-being didn't have to be traumatic.

And as her lifeline he realized he needed to reel her in.

"Hey, it's time to call it a day." He reached for the file in her hand and was a little surprised when she let it go. Until he realized she was reaching for another one.

"I just want to go back over something that was written about the second victim."

He took that one out of her hand, too. "And you can. Tomorrow."

"Jon, I feel like I haven't made any progress at all. All I've done all day is sit here and read."

"And make about twelve pages of notes. And ask questions and understand more about the case and the monster who's doing this."

She grimaced. "Yeah, but that doesn't do anything to stop him."

"It might do more than you think."

"This isn't the usual way I'm brought into cases. I don't normally look at files at all, especially not before talking to the victims. So I'm probably much slower at processing this stuff than what you're used to."

He ran a gentle hand down her arm. "You're doing fine. I definitely don't expect you to treat this like you're an agent. I'm just hoping that easing you into it this way might help you with your panic attacks if and when you're ready to talk to any of the victims."

Or, God forbid, if there was a new victim that needed to be interviewed.

"I think a couple of these women might actually know more than they think they do," she said. "There're some questions that could've been asked that might help shed some light. I don't know if they were asked or not."

"Like what?"

"Well, I know they didn't see the attacker's features, but they may remember his general size, how broad he was across the chest and shoulders, giving us an idea about his weight, for example."

"That would be at least something."

"I know it doesn't necessarily help you identify the man specifically, but it could at least eliminate certain groups."

"I agree. And at this point we'll take anything."

"The only good thing about having so many victims is that I can try to use their memories as a collective. Nobody has to have seen everything about the guy who attacked them, but maybe they've all seen enough pieces to give us a framework of the whole."

She paused for a moment. "I'll need to talk to them, Jon." The hesitancy in her voice was evident.

"We can take it slow. Ease you into it."

"We can't take it that slow. You and I both know that."

"Well, I'm not going to let you become an indirect victim. You can only do what you can do, Sherry. I don't expect more than that. Nobody expects more than that."

She looked down at her hands and her hair fell on either side of her face. "I don't even know if I can draw."

He crouched next to her chair. "Like I said, whatever you can do. No matter what, I will be right there with you."

"I'll try." She sighed. "These women have been through so much more than me that I feel like an utter fake even talking as though my problems are important. Line up the interviews as soon as you can."

"Your issues aren't fake, Sherry. And they need to be taken seriously."

She peeked out at him. "You have to admit they're not as serious as the problems these women are facing."

"All that matters is how you handle them. You're trying. That's enough."

She just shrugged.

"But right now we're done for the day." He began putting the files back in the correct order, making sure everything was where it belonged. Sherry stood and began helping him.

"Let's get some dinner, okay?"

"Sure. Can you give me a ride? I caught one with Caroline this morning so I wouldn't have to park."

"It would be my pleasure."

Walking out of the station, Jon could feel eyes on them. Sherry was being branded an outsider merely by her association with him. She didn't seem to notice, or if she did, she didn't care.

Zane had done a good job of keeping the conference room clear today, but when Jon saw Frank Spangler making his way toward them, he knew they weren't going to make it out of the building without a confrontation.

"You may do things differently in your federal job, but here we don't tend to invite our girlfriends to see evidence," Spangler scoffed, stopping their walk toward the main door.

"Spangler, this is Sherry Mitchell. She's assisting us with the serial rapist case." He glanced at Sherry. "Sherry, you remember Spangler?"

Sherry's eyes were cold. "We didn't actually meet, but, yes, I remember you from the other night at the hospital," she said to the older man.

Spangler shifted his weight. "Yeah, well, there isn't much I can do when these women are hysterical."

Sherry took a step toward Spangler, looking as if she might take a swing at him. Although Jon would do nothing but applaud that action, he knew it would just cause them all a bunch of headache in the long run. He slipped an arm around Sherry's waist, lightly restraining her.

"Spangler has been removed from having contact with any of the victims, since his questioning style doesn't seem to be producing any results," Jon said.

The other man's face turned an odd shade of red. "Nobody could get any results from those women. Not a single one of them saw anything or is willing to even try to remember. I'd like to see you do any better."

Jon felt Sherry look over at him and he tightened his grip on her waist before turning back to Spangler. "Sherry's already done better. After talking to one of the victims only once, she was able to help her remember something she saw."

"Beginner's luck," Spangler snorted.

Sherry stepped away from Jon's arm, closer to Spangler. "I'm not a beginner and I stand by my track record. As you will have to stand by yours, whatever that is." Her voice didn't rise, but her shoulders straightened, which made her almost the same height as Spangler. "I don't need to have decades of experience to know that belittling a woman who has just been horribly assaulted is not only bad police work, but would make me a bad person in general. I'm sorry you're near retirement and *still* haven't figured that out."

She turned from both of them and began walking down the hallway toward the exit.

Jon had to force himself not to laugh out loud at the look on Spangler's face. He shrugged at the older man and turned to chase after Sherry, catching her after just a few steps.

"Way to let him have it," he said.

She balled one hand up into a fist. "I was afraid I was going to punch him. What an utter jackass."

He took her fist and began rubbing the knuckles, smiling. "Well, I'm pretty sure your words had a bigger impact than your fist would have. He would've just had you arrested for assaulting an officer."

"Hey, you guys." Zane Wales walked over to them, a file in hand. "I just wanted to give you an update on the tattoo drawing you provided."

"Anything interesting?" Jon asked.

"It's not gang related, at least not of any gang we know of. We're checking local tattoo shops to see if anyone happens to remember doing any tattoos like this. Unfortunately there're so many places in Mexico someone can go to get ink, it may not have been someone local."

"Okay," Jon said. "Thanks for letting us know."

"This is at least progress," Zane said, turning to Sherry. "It's the first breakthrough we've had at all. Thank you for working with the victim."

Sherry nodded. "I'm glad I could help at least that little bit."

Zane tilted his head in the direction of where they'd just had their discussion with Spangler. "You both should watch your back. Spangler is not going to take very well to the comeuppance you just gave him in front of everyone."

"He started it," Sherry said.

"Yeah, but he won't see it that way," Zane said then looked at Jon. "He's close to retirement, and I was protecting him the other day by not confirming what really happened. That probably wasn't the right call, and I'm sorry."

Jon shrugged. "These are your people. Believe it or not, I do understand that. My job here is not to insinuate that the department is inept. My sole purpose is to help you catch this rapist."

"Yeah, I'm beginning to see that. Hopefully the rest of the team will come around soon, too." He grimaced. "But Spangler won't. Especially not now. So be careful."

"Spangler isn't going to be the one who cracks open this case," Jon said to the younger man.

Zane nodded. "I'll get right on this tattoo."

"Sherry's going to be interviewing the victims again over the next couple of days to see if there's anything she can get that was missed before." Jon didn't assign blame. Perhaps there wasn't anything Spangler missed.

"Okay. I wouldn't announce that to Spangler or the captain, for that matter." Zane shrugged. "Easier to ask forgiveness than permission in this situation."

Jon chuckled. "Well, I don't need their permission, but I agree with you. We'll have to use the station, but we'll keep this to ourselves as much as possible."

"Sounds good." Zane turned to Sherry and touched the brim of the cowboy hat always on his head. "Ma'am."

Sherry smiled at him.

Damn it, Jon was going to have to get one of those blasted hats if it meant Sherry would smile at him like that.

She turned to him. "What?"

"Nothing," he muttered. Damn cowboy hats.

A couple of hours later after taking her to another of his newfound favorite places to eat—Sherry laughingly telling him that she was glad he had made friends with the waitresses, since he definitely hadn't made any friends in the police department—Jon drove her back to her place. A storm had come up, so he drove slowly through the rain.

Out of the station, both of them had relaxed and just enjoyed each other's company. The more he was around Sherry, the more he wanted to be around her.

But, damn it, he knew this still wasn't the time. Their working relationship was too new. She needed to know she could trust him to look out for her best interests professionally while they were working on this case.

He rushed around and opened the car door for her and quickly walked her up the steps to her door, covered by a small awning.

"I'll come by and get you tomorrow morning, okay? I've got a call in to victim number one to see if she can come in first thing tomorrow."

She looked at him for a long time as if she was searching for something. Thunder finally crashed and she looked away.

"That's fine," Sherry murmured, unlocking her door and opening it.

Her look—whatever it was, he couldn't quite figure it out—concerned him. "You okay? Nervous about tomorrow? I know it's daunting, but I'm going to be there with you one hundred percent of the—"

His words were cut off by Sherry's lips against his.

A few seconds later he couldn't think of words at all. Could only give in to the heat between them.

She smelled impossibly good.

She tasted even better.

Jon tended to be the one who took the lead in almost all aspects of his life, sexual pursuits included, but he had no problem leaning back against the door frame as Sherry pushed him there. His hands encircled her hips and brought her up close to him. He groaned as she wrapped her arms around his neck, fisting his hair in her hands. They were drowning in the kiss.

Using every ounce of mental energy he had, Jon eased

back just slightly. He wanted to make sure she knew he wasn't using her. "Sherry, I just want to make sure—"

"Jon," she murmured against his mouth. "Shut. Up. You think too much. Just kiss me."

It was all the permission Jon needed. He spun them around so that she was flat against the door frame, cupped her face with both hands and took possession of her mouth. Fire ignited as he stroked his tongue against hers.

Both of them moaned, straining to bring their bodies closer together.

Jon reached down and wrapped his arms around her hips, picking her up without breaking the kiss. He walked them through the door, kicking it closed behind them.

He didn't know where her bed was, and didn't care. The farthest he was going to make it was the couch five feet away. He lowered them both down, loving the feel of her arms and legs wrapped around him.

The storm raged on in the distance, second only to the storm of passion between them.

Chapter Fifteen

Sherry woke up warm for the first time in as long as she could remember.

Not just warm. Hot.

That was perhaps because of the very large man wrapped nearly all the way around her, his chest to her back. One of his arms was stretched out under her neck, between her shoulder and the pillow, and the other was tucked around her waist, keeping her close to him. They had slept that way all night.

At least they had once they'd made it to the bed, *finally*, hours later than they'd arrived on the couch.

Sherry was never going to be able to look at the couch again the same way. Heck, she was never going to be able to look at the bed the same way, either. She was glad she was the only one who ever used this house. Even though they owned it, her parents hadn't vacationed here since she was a child.

She'd never be able to enter this house again without thinking of Jon Hatton.

Who was now beginning to stir behind her.

"Good morning," he murmured as he nuzzled her neck then bit it gently. Chills that had nothing to do with cold ran through Sherry's body.

"Good morning to you, too," she whispered back.

"As much as I would like to stay here all day with you, we have Tina Wescott coming in at 9:00 a.m."

She turned so she could face him. "I'm still not sure about my drawing ability."

Sherry's biggest fear was that they would bring this poor woman in to the station, ask her to recount all the details of the worst day of her entire life, that she would remember something—some feature or characteristic of her attacker—and that Sherry wouldn't be able to draw it.

He used his thumb to rub her forehead, ease the worry lines between her brows. "You drew me on the beach the other day."

"Yeah, but that was different. I wasn't thinking about it."

"Either way, the drawing ability is still there. You haven't lost it. You've just got to figure out how to harness that part of your mind and shut out the other."

Sherry nodded, but she had no idea how to do that.

"We'll just take it one minute at a time. Try not to concentrate on the big picture, literally and figuratively, just on what you're doing at that very minute."

It was good advice and similar to the advice she had given herself before. "Baby steps."

"Exactly." He kissed her. "Now let's go out and get some breakfast so we can get to the station on time."

"Okay, I'm going to take a shower." She got out of bed and headed toward the bathroom. "Someone has kept me in bed, participating in naughty deeds all night." She giggled as his hand streaked out and smacked her on the bottom.

"Wasn't just on the bed," he murmured.

In the bathroom her smiled faded. She turned on the shower, then turned and looked at herself in the mirror, leaning her hands on the bathroom counter. She really was afraid of failing. Failing Jon, failing the victim, failing herself.

The bathroom door opened and Jon came to stand behind her. He kissed the top of her shoulder, looking at her in the mirror.

"Whatever happens, we'll get through it together," he whispered in her ear.

"Okay."

"Right now, a shower."

"Only if you'll join me." She smiled at him, turning around.

"What about breakfast? I want to make sure you have the energy you need."

She put a hand on his chest, walking forward and backing him toward the shower. "I'll eat a huge bowl of cereal."

He reached behind him and opened the shower door. Steam flooded around them. "As long as it's healthy cereal," he said as he pulled her up against him hard.

Every thought in her head seemed to vanish as he moved them both under the hot spray of the shower. As he'd said, she'd just take it one minute at a time. This minute especially.

"FOR THE RECORD, those Sugar-O's do not count as healthy cereal," Jon said as they sat in the Corpus Christi interview room an hour later, waiting for Tina Wescott to arrive.

"I was afraid you would stop if I told you what it was," she whispered.

"Honey, I had you naked in a steamy shower. You could've told me we were eating snails for breakfast and I wouldn't have stopped."

"Snails probably would've had more nutritional value." Sherry laughed softly.

Jon was glad to see the pinched look leave her face at least for a few moments. Despite the comfortable room temperature, she was huddling into her denim jacket and rubbing her hands as if to encourage circulation.

He sat next to her and took her hands in his. They did feel icy.

"Hey," he said. "Remember, one minute at a time. Baby steps. Just ask questions, don't worry about drawing."

Her sketch pad was sitting in front of them on the table. Jon noticed she hadn't touched it once. He wanted to help her, but drawing wasn't something he could do. Unless he was willing to turn the heat up and sweat everyone else to death, he couldn't help her much with the cold, either.

Tina Wescott entered the room and Jon greeted her and introduced Sherry. He was concerned for just a moment that Sherry wouldn't be able to get it together enough to talk to the other woman but then watched as she mentally pulled herself up by her bootstraps.

"Hi, Tina." Sherry shook her hand. "I'm so sorry we're meeting under these circumstances."

Tina had been the first person attacked nine weeks ago. For more than a month her rape had been treated as an isolated incident. It was only after the fourth victim that the police department had realized they were dealing with one single attacker.

Sherry made a little small talk with Tina, about the weather, about Texas A&M's lineup for next season's football team—Sherry hadn't been kidding when she'd said Texas was all about football. The two women could talk more intelligently about A&M's offensive line than Jon could talk about most of the pro teams he followed.

They were still talking about the new quarterback who was coming in when there was a knock on the conference room door. Before Jon could even get over to answer it, it opened and Spangler breezed in. Zane Wales entered behind him, his expression apologetic.

"Mind if we sit in?" Spangler asked. "More heads are better than one, right?"

The rapport Sherry had been building with Tina was

instantly lost. The last thing Jon wanted to do was to make it worse by having it out with Spangler right there.

Jon looked over at Tina, "Is it okay with you if they stay?"

"Sure." Tina shrugged. "That's fine."

Jon wished she had told them to get lost, but he didn't blame her for wanting all the help she could get. "If at any point you're feeling too crowded, we can definitely thin out the room. Don't be afraid to say something."

"I haven't remembered anything else," Tina told them, looking down at her hands.

"That's fine," Sherry said. "I'm just trying to piece together any little bits you or any of the other women remember. Perhaps together, that can give us a clearer picture of the whole."

"Okay."

"I'm just going to warn the officers in here not to interrupt. I'm sure that won't be a problem." She looked pointedly at Frank Spangler.

"I'm just here to observe." He held out his hands in front of him in a gesture of innocence.

"Great," Sherry said with a smile that didn't reach her eyes. "Observing doesn't require any talking. And maybe you'll learn something."

Jon coughed to keep from laughing. Spangler glared at Sherry but didn't say anything, just crossed his arms and sat back in his seat. Zane smiled next to the older man, but was sure not to let him see. Tina didn't seem to notice the tension at all.

Sherry grabbed her sketch pad and opened it without hesitating, obviously something she'd done multiple times before. Good. She was focusing on her annoyance with Spangler, not on freezing up. He might have come in to try to make her feel uncomfortable or to intimidate her, but it was working to her advantage instead.

"Tell me what the weather was like on the day of your attack," Sherry said softly to Tina.

For the next three hours Jon listened as Sherry talked to Tina, often asking her questions that seemed irrelevant. Such as the weather question she'd started with or questions about what had been on the radio that day.

Then Jon realized Sherry was attempting to involve as many of Tina's five senses as she could. Any of them might trigger a memory of something Tina hadn't realized she knew.

Sherry's cognitive interviewing skills matched any Jon had ever seen at Omega Sector or any other law-enforcement group he had worked with. She had a gift. It was easy to see that Tina felt comfortable with her and was willing to answer questions.

Over and over Sherry backed Tina up to about an hour before the attack and had her walk through that time period. It helped Tina's mind to refocus on that day without actually having to concentrate on the attack itself. Then each time Sherry took Tina a little further into the attack, so that she didn't have to describe the entire brutal event all at once.

Baby steps.

Even with Sherry's calm, measured method of asking questions as they got into the heart of Tina's attack, Jon could easily see the toll it was taking on both women. Tina was crying. Sherry was nestling into her jacket.

Although Tina hadn't given her any details to draw, Sherry still had the pencil in her hand. Glancing over at her, he could see her attempt to keep her hand from shaking.

"Okay, Tina, last time, I promise," Sherry said, a slight tremor noticeable. "Let's focus on when you opened the door."

Tina took a shuddery breath. "The doorbell rang. I was

irritated because I couldn't find the remote to pause my TV show. I was trying to hurry. That's why I didn't check the window, like I normally would have."

"That's right. I'm sure that's true," Sherry assured her, trying to keep her focused on the memory itself rather than what she could've done differently.

"I was still listening to the show as I opened the door, so I wouldn't miss anything." More tears flowed down Tina's face. Zane slid a box of tissues to within her reach in case she wanted them. "When the door was ajar just a crack, he slammed it all the way open. I stumbled back a step and he hit me."

Tina began crying in earnest.

"Okay, I want you to stop there, Tina." Sherry reached out and touched the other woman's arm. "Right before he hit you, were you able to see his face at all?"

"No, I'm sorry." She shook her head. "The sun was too bright behind him. And then he hit me too fast. I'm sorry."

"Tina." Sherry's voice was shaky, difficult to hear over Tina's sobs.

"I got all of this before. Why drag her through this again?" Spangler muttered.

He hated to admit it, but Jon had to agree. They already knew Tina hadn't seen her attacker's face. No matter how good a forensic artist Sherry was, there was no way she could force Tina to describe something she hadn't seen.

Jon started to interrupt, but Sherry held out an arm to silence him.

Sherry began again with a stronger voice. "Tina, listen to me. I know you didn't see his face. That's okay. That's not what I want to ask you."

Tina was visibly relieved. "It's not?"

"No, what I want you to do is stand up. Freeze in your mind those first few seconds of when your attacker entered your house."

"Stand up right now?" Tina took a deep breath in and blew it back out.

"Yes." Sherry put the sketch pad down and stood with her. "Okay, now think about the man in the doorway. You were about three feet away from the door when he pushed in and struck you the first time, right?"

"Yeah, that would be about right."

"Okay, so concentrate on before he pushed you to the floor. When you were looking at him in the doorway, what angle did you have your neck?"

Tina looked over at Sherry. "I don't understand."

Sherry walked over to Jon and slipped her hand under his arm to get him to stand. Then she brought him to stand about three feet away from Tina.

"See how you have to crane your neck back to look at Agent Hatton? Was your neck like that?" Sherry went over and grabbed Zane, who was about five-ten, and pulled him around to the other side of the table next to Jon. "Or was it more like looking at Detective Wales?"

Jon realized what Sherry was doing.

"Detective Wales," Tina responded. "Definitely more like Detective Wales."

The men sat. Sherry reached over and squeezed Tina's arm. "That's good. Helpful."

"Really?" Tina looked around the room.

"It lets us know that your attacker was probably around five foot nine or ten," Jon said. "That's good, usable information."

"Thank God." Tina began crying again. "I couldn't stand the thought of being so useless."

Sherry put her arm around her. "The opposite, in fact. Very helpful. I'm going to talk to the other women and we'll continue piecing things together. But that's enough for today. Maybe we can talk again another time."

Tina was obviously exhausted. Zane helped her gather her things and walked her out.

"Why did you stop just when you were getting somewhere?" Spangler asked.

"Knowing when to quit is just as important as knowing when to push," Sherry said as she took her seat. "Memory is a fragile thing. Pushing too hard or for too long can do more damage than good."

"You've got her subconscious thinking down a different path than it was before. She might begin to remember more details," Jon said.

"I hope so," Sherry said. "Because knowing your perp is about average height is not going to help you catch him."

She was withdrawing in her chair, wrapping her arms around her midsection. Sherry had needed a stop to the questioning just as much as Tina had.

"Like you said, it's a detail we didn't have before. We'll just keep adding details together as we get them."

Spangler stood. "Yeah, well, knowing his probable height is not going to stop this guy. So you just put that woman through hell for no reason."

He left shaking his head, Jon and Sherry staring after him.

Chapter Sixteen

Sherry felt a little nauseated, as if she was going to throw up. Was Spangler right? Should she have kept pushing? Had she stopped to spare Tina or to spare herself?

Had she stopped because she knew if Tina did happen to remember something concrete, there was no way Sherry was going to be able to draw it?

Spangler would just have loved that.

"Whatever you're thinking, you need to just cut it out right now." Jon was looking at her from across the conference room table.

"Maybe I should've kept going."

"She'd had enough. Like you said, pushing would've been detrimental."

"Yeah, but I think I actually stopped because pushing would've been detrimental for me, not her."

Jon came around and sat on the edge of the table, his long legs stretched out in front of him, next to her chair. "It would've been detrimental for you both. You made the right call. If you hadn't ended it when you did, I would have."

"I don't trust myself anymore, Jon."

He reached over and rubbed her chin with his thumb. "Baby steps."

Sherry just shrugged. She was afraid baby steps weren't going to get them where they needed to go fast enough.

"Let's get out of this room for a while, okay?" he said.

But out in the detective area where all the desks were visible and everyone seemed to be looking at them, it wasn't any less stressful for Sherry.

"You want to take a walk outside?" she asked. "I need some fresh air." He would never let her walk on her own.

They walked in silence. Sherry appreciated that Jon understood that she just needed some time to pull herself together. The police station was in the more industrial, less touristy, side of town, so it wasn't as nice as walking on the beach, but at least it was quiet.

Last night's storm seemed to have broken the heat wave. It was cooler, in the low eighties, more traditional for weather in June here. The air was muggy, full of the rain from the past few hours.

At first breathing the outside air—even as muggy as it was—was exactly what Sherry needed. Jon's presence in the conference room had done a pretty good job of keeping the cold away, but the last of the chill was vanquished by the coastal heat.

After walking awhile, Sherry started to get the feeling—as she had a few days before when walking to Jasmine Houze's house—that someone was watching her. She stopped and turned but, like then, didn't see anything out of the ordinary.

"What's wrong?" he asked.

Sherry shook her head. "Nothing."

"Not nothing. You were doing okay and then you got all weirded out."

"I just felt like someone was watching us," she said.

"I didn't see anything or anyone out of place."

"I know. It's just me. This happened a couple of days ago, too, when I was walking to Jasmine's house. Plus, I also felt like everyone was staring at me at the police station." She sighed out loud. "I'm pretty sure these are signs

I am either losing my grip on reality or that I am just really, really self-involved."

Jon put his arm around her. "Well, I can officially attest that neither is correct."

"Yeah, I'm not so sure about that."

They turned to work their way back to the station. Sherry wasn't surprised when Jon made her stop at one of the hole-in-the-wall barbecue joints. The man loved his food. Maybe she couldn't make him stay in Texas, but brisket probably could.

Where in the world had that thought come from?

Despite last night, there had been no talk of a relationship—long- or short-term—between them. Sherry assumed Jon would be heading back to Omega headquarters in Colorado once this was over. She'd be staying here, or at least returning to Houston.

The thought didn't sit well with Sherry. She refused to force the "we need to talk about our relationship and where it's going" conversation after only one night with him.

That was one thing she would just have to let happen on its own accord. She had enough on her mind without worrying about their relationship. It would have to be discussed later.

Back at the station, sitting at Jon's desk, looking over the notes she had taken from this morning's talk with Tina, Sherry could feel eyes watching her again. She'd like to draw a picture of the man in the doorway whom Tina had described—even with all the blanks. But the negative looks from almost every direction were damaging her calm. Her calm was pretty damn precarious to begin with.

At least this time she wasn't the only one who noticed it.

"You guys are the talk of the entire building," Zane said as he came over to give Jon a file.

Jon just shrugged. "What's new? They've been shooting daggers at me since day one."

"Yeah, well, Spangler is telling everyone who will listen that you're putting these women through unnecessary hardship—his words, exactly—by bringing them in again to talk to Sherry."

Sherry met Jon's eyes across the desk. Jon shook his head before looking back at Zane.

"He's arguing that Sherry doesn't have the expertise to be working a case of this magnitude. That you brought her here because the two of you are romantically involved."

Sherry's eyes flew to Jon's again. Again, he gave a tiny shake of his head.

"Well, Spangler is an idiot. Because first, Sherry has an impeccable record with the Bureau over the past two years and it will stand up to any scrutiny. And second, my idea of romancing a woman does not involve me bringing her in to talk to people who have been sexually assaulted."

"I pretty much argued those two points with him. So now I'm not on the popular side, either." Zane shrugged.

"If I didn't know better, I would almost think that Spangler is deliberately stalling this case."

Zane shook his head. "I don't think he is. He's just used to being the head honcho around here. Giving up the glory on the last big case before his retirement doesn't sit well with him."

"He can keep all the glory," Sherry said. "I don't want any of it."

"Neither do I," Jon agreed. "I don't care who takes the credit. I just want this bastard caught."

"Spangler is not such a bad guy. He'll come around."

Sherry wasn't so sure.

"I didn't have any luck with tattoo artists in the area," Zane continued. "I've got some men taking the picture around to more shops farther out of the immediate vicinity. I also took it by the hospital this morning to show

Nurse Carreker and some of the other staff and EMTs just before coming here."

"Good, you never know when that will net some results. Nurse Carreker runs a tight ship."

Sherry looked at Zane, who nodded at her before looking down to ardently study the file in his hand. Interesting that he had gone to the hospital to show the tattoo drawing just as Caroline was likely to be arriving to clock in for her shift.

Sherry decided not to bring up that point. Neither Zane nor Caroline ever seemed to want to discuss Zane and Caroline.

"I've got to meet with the captain and the mayor for a couple of hours," Jon said after Zane promised to keep them informed if he heard anything and left. "You want me to take you home or do you want to stay here?"

Really, Sherry didn't want to do either. The thought of sitting at her house alone wasn't appealing, especially given the story she'd just heard over and over from Tina. But staying here at the station without Jon around wasn't particularly tempting, either.

"I don't guess I can talk you into letting me walk on the beach while you're in your meeting."

"Alone?"

Sherry almost giggled at the way his eyebrows raised so high.

"Uh, no," he said.

"I don't want to stay here, Jon. There's enough staring with you here. I'm not sure what will happen with you gone."

"I can ask Zane if he can hang around. Just run interference."

"I don't need to be babysat. Zane has other stuff he needs to do."

"I'm sorry I can't cancel this meeting. It's about strat-

egy with the press. Keeping people calm right now is one
of the best things we can do. Law enforcement is going to
become a lot more difficult if people start trying to take
things into their own hands or see an attacker in any person
who looks at them wrong."

The city had been on the verge of panic for the past few
weeks. Jon's expertise in this area was probably as critical
for the case as Sherry's was with the victims.

"How about if I go over to the hospital? There's a nice
outdoor sitting area with some gazebos. Public yet quiet.
Lots of people around but not any who will bother me."

The hospital was only a couple of blocks away.

"Okay, I'll walk you," Jon said. "Promise me you'll stay
there. No walking alone."

"Promise."

HAVING SOMETHING GO right was a nice change of pace in the
case. Jon left Mayor Birchwood's office feeling as though
for the first time in the nearly two weeks he had been here,
someone had actually listened to him.

Working the press in a case like this was just as important
as the police work. The city was on the verge of
panic and it was now up to the mayor to keep that from
happening.

Captain Harris had tried to skew information to make
Jon look incompetent, but fortunately the mayor wasn't
interested in any sort of imagined rivalry between local
and federal law enforcement. He just wanted what was
best for his city.

When the captain realized Birchwood wasn't looking
for a scapegoat, the three of them were able to work as a
team to come up with a media plan as well as to discuss
the case and what was happening with the investigation.

Either Spangler hadn't gotten to the captain with his

opinion about Sherry yet or the captain felt it wasn't in his best interest to bring it up. He hadn't interrupted when Jon talked about her and what they'd discovered so far about the general height of the attacker and the tattoo.

The mayor had asked for Jon's advice about the statement he was giving on live television tonight. Jon had encouraged him to ask the public to maintain common sense, caution and safety in numbers. Not to open the door to anyone unfamiliar.

"Anything else?" Mayor Birchwood had asked.

"I would appeal to the heart of being Texan," Jon replied. "I've been here two weeks and I already see how people here band together. Remind them that they are Texans. They can take the heat. They're strong."

The mayor jotted down some notes. Even Harris nodded.

"Okay, good. Are we looking at people with previous records?" Birchwood asked.

"Always," Captain Harris responded. "As Agent Hatton will attest, it's hard to pin this guy down to specifics."

Jon agreed. "He's very smart. Genius IQ probably. Very controlled. Knows how forensics works and is careful not to leave any traceable evidence behind."

The mayor grunted. "And that other attack? Not the same guy?"

"No, sir," Harris said. "It became evident that he was just using some basic information from media reports of the attack to try to get away with terrorizing his brother's ex-girlfriend."

"I'm glad you were able to distinguish him from the real rapist before we reported that we had made an arrest, only to discover we were wrong. That would've been a major embarrassment."

Jon very decidedly did not look at Captain Harris.

Harris shifted in his chair. "Yes, sir, it was a team effort."

"What about this tattoo?" the mayor asked. "Should we release that to the press?"

Harris and Jon glanced at each other. That was a tough question. Jon deferred to Harris, since it was ultimately his call.

"I think we should wait," Harris said to the mayor. "Only use it if we have no other options."

"You don't think it might help us find the guy?"

"I just think we might get too many people accusing too many other people of possibly being the perpetrator. Vigilante justice could get out of control."

"I agree," Jon said. "The tattoo doesn't seem to be involved with any gang symbols, but that doesn't mean that our guy is the only one out there with it. We don't want people taking the situation into their own hands."

"And he doesn't know we know about it," Harris finished. "That could possibly give us an advantage. Especially in a lineup."

"Should I mention you're working with this Sherry Mitchell?"

Jon didn't want her name out there and he knew Sherry wouldn't want it, either. "Not by name, definitely. But mentioning the department is working with a forensic artist for details beyond just facial features might help put the public a little more at ease."

"All right," Mayor Birchwood said, standing. This meeting was obviously at an end. "Thank you, gentlemen. I know I don't have to say this, but catching the attacker is of utmost importance. The city is balancing precariously right now. Tourist profit margins are down because no one wants to bring their family where there's a door-to-door rapist."

Jon and Harris both nodded. They, more than anybody, knew what was at stake here.

"Please keep my office posted if anything changes." The mayor showed them to the door.

"I hope your new forensic artist can get more information soon," Captain Harris said as they walked down the hall to the elevator. "Everything the mayor said in there was right. The city is going to blow up soon if we don't get a handle on this case."

"If there's information to be had in the victims' minds, Sherry Mitchell will get it."

"That's not what Frank Spangler is saying."

"Spangler is just trying to save face."

"That may be true, but we're still running out of time."

Jon couldn't agree more. After saying goodbye to Captain Harris, he drove to the hospital from city hall.

He could understand about the city being on the borderline of panic. Right now, without Sherry in his sight, even pretty sure that she was safe, Jon could feel the panic licking at his heels.

If everyone in a city of more than half a million people was feeling this sort of stress about the safety of their loved ones, then, yes, the city was very definitely on the verge of a panic attack.

And had the words *loved one* just gone through his mind in conjunction with Sherry?

He would be the first one to admit that he hadn't been able to get her out of his mind from the moment he'd seen her. Last night and this morning had been possibly the best of his life.

But not to get carried away with the feelings. He needed to think this through further. He *always* thought things through before letting his emotions get involved.

Still, he couldn't deny the profound feeling of rightness,

coupled with relief, when he saw her sitting in the court-yard where he'd left her. Safe and looking more relaxed than she had seemed all day.

Well, almost all day. He could think of a time in the shower this morning where she'd definitely been more relaxed.

"What are you grinning about?" she asked as he walked up to her.

"Um…relaxation techniques." He sat next to her, kissing her on the cheek.

"How did your meeting go?"

"Better than I thought it would. Mayor Birchwood is a pretty reasonable guy. He just wants what's best for his city. How about you? Did you get bored?"

"No, Nurse Carreker stopped by for a few minutes. And Dr. Trumpold."

"That really handsome Italian-looking doctor?"

"Yeah." She all but sighed.

Jon rolled his eyes. "And here I thought I was leaving you here to keep you safe from a serial rapist. I should've locked you up in a cell at the station so you couldn't get into any trouble."

She smiled. "We just talked. Don't be jealous."

Jon snorted. "I am not jealous. He's short. I don't know why women would be into him."

"He's brilliant, successful and probably very rich. Besides, everybody's short compared to you, so that doesn't count." She reached over and put both arms around his neck where he sat next to her on the bench. "Don't worry, he's not my type."

"Humph." Jon turned his head and looked up into the distance in mock offense.

Sherry leaned closer. "How about if we go over to my house and I make you dinner, then prove to you just how much more interested I am in federal agents than handsome doctors?"

Jon glanced over at her without moving his head. "I don't know. I might need a lot of convincing."

"I think I'm up to the challenge."

Chapter Seventeen

Sherry sashayed up the steps to her porch, knowing that Jon was watching from the car. They had decided on the way that if he showed up at the station for the third day in a row wearing the same clothes, people were definitely going to notice. He wanted to take her to the condo where he was staying.

They'd agreed they would stop by her house so she could grab whatever she needed to make dinner, and beyond, before going to his place. Jon didn't offer to come in and Sherry didn't insist. They both knew if he followed her into her house they would never make it back out of the bed tonight.

To make up for the damage to Jon's delicate ego after the doctor comment.

Sherry actually laughed out loud. Jon was going to milk that for as much as he could. And she didn't mind at all.

She was still smiling as she grabbed the things she would need for the meal she planned—fish tacos—and put them in a couple of paper grocery bags by the sink. As she did so she tried to think of the sexiest undergarments she had brought with her on this vacation.

Nothing too spectacular. She definitely hadn't been planning on a romance. But she did have some black lacy things somewhere in her room.

Or maybe she could just change into a sundress and have absolutely nothing on under that.

She rushed from the kitchen into the bedroom, a smile plastered on her face. Jon wouldn't know what hit him.

She smelled it first. Her smile faded as her nostrils were accosted with a metallic scent. Like iron or copper or something rusting.

Had a pipe burst? It was the only thing she could think of that could be rusting.

Her eyes adjusted to the gathering dusk in her bedroom and Sherry saw something on her bed. Oh, no, the roof had leaked during yesterday's storm. She could see the dark stain all over the bed, ruining the quilt. She touched it and was surprised at how oddly thick the water was. And sticky.

She turned the lamp on next to her bed to get a better look and jumped backward, knocking the lamp over but not shattering the bulb.

Blood. It wasn't water, it was *blood*. An obscene amount of it, making a garish stain on her bed's cream-colored quilt.

Right in the middle of it was a note, its white seeming neon against all the red. *Stay out of this.*

Sherry felt she was going to vomit, but she forced it down. Cold descended over her entire body rapidly, uncontrollably. She couldn't stop the shudders that racked her frame; they glued her in place.

Every shadow cast from the setting sun filtering through the window now held a potential enemy. Was the person who did this still in her house?

The thought was enough to jolt her body into taking another step away from the bed.

Jon was right outside. She just had to get him.

She slid her way along the wall with her back to it, eyes glued on the bed. On the blood. So much of it. Once she made it through the door frame of the bedroom, she stumbled as if she were drunk back down the little hall into her kitchen. The iciness in her limbs made movement difficult and violent shivers made her teeth clack together like castanets. Her vision began fading in and out.

She took two steps and leaned heavily on the kitchen island. She saw a bloody handprint there and startled back, until she realized it was from her own hand. Blood, from where she had touched the bed.

Shadows loomed everywhere. She had to get out.

The front door was only a few yards away. She forced her legs to move forward. She had to make it out to Jon. Just a few more steps.

It wasn't safe here.

ONE LOOK AT Sherry's face as she seemed to stumble out the door and Jon knew immediately that something wasn't right. He was out of the car and running up the couple of stairs in seconds.

"What? Sherry, what is it?"

She held up her hand and he felt the air rush out of his lungs as he saw the blood.

"Did you cut yourself? Are you okay?" He looked at her hand but couldn't see any wound on it, only mostly dried blood.

He supported her arms as she grasped his shirt, nearly falling on him. Up close he could see she was paper white, her skin cold to the touch.

"Are you hurt, Sherry? Talk to me, baby."

"N-no." Her teeth were chattering so badly she could barely get the word out. "In…inside."

Jon pulled his Glock out of the holster and turned to face the door, sweeping Sherry behind his back so he was between her and whatever had terrorized her in such a way. "Is someone in there?"

"I don't know." She grasped the back of his shirt to keep him from going forward.

"I'm just going in to check, make sure we're safe. Stay right here, okay? If anyone comes out here, you scream your head off."

Jon didn't want to leave her, but he needed to know what was inside and if it was a threat to them. He turned around and glanced at Sherry.

She nodded. "Bedroom." The word was barely a whisper.

Jon entered the house cautiously, checking all rooms and closets on his way in. He examined all other rooms in the small single-story house before going to the master bedroom.

He saw the blood on the bed immediately. It was impossible to miss, even with the lamp turned over on the floor. But he secured the bathroom and walk-in closet before turning to give the room his full attention.

Confident the house was empty, he returned his Glock to its holster and walked closer to the bed.

The curse that flew out of his mouth was vile at the sight of the blood covering the bed he and Sherry had spent so many hours on the night before. Viler still when he saw the note lying pristine white in the center of the mess.

Stay out of this.

There was no doubt in his mind what that meant. Rage, and not just a little bit of fear, flew through him at the thought of this monster turning his attention to Sherry.

Jon pulled his cell phone out of his pocket and dialed Zane Wales. "It's Hatton," he said without preamble. "I need uniformed officers and a full forensic team out at Sherry Mitchell's place right damn now."

"Oh, my God, Jon. Please tell me—"

"No, she wasn't attacked." Jon cut him off, not wanting

to allow the other man to think the absolute worst. "But her house was visited by him." He gave Zane the address.

He could hear Zane firing off commands to whoever was nearby.

"Not that I don't believe you, but how do you know it was him?"

"He left her a note."

Zane gave an angry curse similar to Jon's. "Do you need an ambulance?"

"No, no one's hurt. At least not at the scene. Just hurry up and get here. Thanks, Zane." He disconnected the call.

Jon was thankful there was no body lying in Sherry's house, but he knew that much blood—if it was from a single person—would definitely mean there was a body somewhere.

It looked as though their rapist might just have escalated to murderer.

Jon didn't touch anything, knowing Forensics could get more from a clean scene than he could get from disturbing it.

Besides, he needed to get back out to Sherry.

She was still on the small portico, huddled down on the ground now instead of standing. Her arms were wrapped around her head as she rocked herself back and forth.

"Sherry, sweetheart." Jon crouched next to her and pulled her into his arms. "It's okay."

He heard her take a shuddery breath, but she didn't look up.

"Is anyone in there?"

"No, the house is empty."

"Is there a bod—" She stopped to take another shaky breath and get though the word. "A body?"

"No, there's no body anywhere in the house. I searched."

She nodded slightly. "But all that blood…"

He pulled her in tighter. "It definitely came from somewhere, but the body is not here. That much I can assure you."

She didn't say anything for a long time, but at least she let go of her head and rested against him. Jon knew the police officers would be here any moment, but he didn't care. There was no way he was letting go of Sherry while she still needed him. Even if they were blocking the door. They could step over them to get inside.

"Did you see the note?" Sherry's voice was tight, hoarse.

Jon kissed the top of her head. "Yes."

"It's him and he knows I'm working with you." Her shaking was coming back.

"Hey, listen to me." He reached down and tilted her chin up with a finger. "Nothing is going to happen to you. I will be with you every minute until we catch this guy. Or if I can't be, I will make sure someone who we can trust is."

He could tell she was still working things through her mind. And it would get worse before it got better. Her home, her safety, had been violated. It would take time for her to come to grips with everything going on.

But what Jon told her was the truth. He was determined to make sure she was safe.

"Do you think we could get you over to my car?" he asked her as he saw blue lights flashing in the distance. "Police are going to be here soon. Forensics. A lot of people going in and out. You might feel better if you're not right here in the door."

She nodded. "Okay. And I can help inside."

"No, absolutely not." There was no way in hell he was letting her back in there, even if there was something she could do, which there wasn't. He gentled his tone. "We need to let the forensic techs do their job. You and I both need to stay out of the way as much as possible."

Actually, Jon planned to be there. He would make sure he didn't contaminate any of the evidence, but he was going to make damn sure this was being handled correctly. Sherry didn't need to experience the scene again. He was quite sure it would already be burned into her mind for a long time.

"Let's get you over to my car." He helped her stand. Her skin was still rough with chills.

"I need to wash my hands," she whispered. "I got blood on your shirt."

He hugged her to him. "Don't worry about that, baby. And I'll get something for you to wipe your hands with until we can get you back to my place and you can take a shower."

She didn't give him any trouble about that, for which he was thankful. She was going to stay where he could protect her himself.

He walked her slowly over to his car and opened the door, easing her in. The uniformed officers were parking and he motioned to them to hold their position.

He grabbed his jacket from the backseat and wrapped it around her. "You stay right here, okay? I'm going to help coordinate what's going on inside, but I'm going to leave a uniformed officer right outside the door."

Sherry nodded, though her eyes were unfocused, staring straight ahead. Being somewhat in shock was understandable.

He knelt next to her so they could see eye to eye. "Hey." He brushed back a strand of hair from her face. "You hang in there, okay? I'll be back as soon as I can and we'll get out of here."

Her eyes focused on him and she nodded. He kissed her forehead.

He stood and closed the door. The sooner he got this finished, the sooner he could get back to Sherry. Jon motioned over two of the uniformed police officers who had showed up.

"You two are both to stay here, do you understand?"

The young officers, one male and one female, both nodded, although neither looked happy about it.

"This is Sherry Mitchell. This is her house. What's in there is pretty horrific and she stumbled onto it unawares. She's in shock, and more than that she's a possible target of the serial rapist."

They were taking the situation much more seriously now.

"I want both of you here, guarding this car, the entire time. If one of you needs to leave, you send someone to get me first. No one, under any circumstances, is to take Ms. Mitchell anywhere, except me."

As he walked away he turned back. "Have someone get her some water. And something to wipe the blood off her hands."

Zane had showed up and walked over to him. They made their way to the front door together.

"What the hell, man?" Zane said in way of greeting. "What is going on?"

They stepped out of the way so the forensic team could get by with its gear, but followed right behind them. Jon pointed them in the right direction once inside the house. "Our rapist stopped by. Evidently he's not too excited about Sherry working with us."

When they stepped into the bedroom, Jon heard Zane's breath whistle through his teeth. "That's a significant amount of blood. There's not a body in here anywhere?"

They stood back, so the forensic team could access the bed without them being in the way.

"No, no body. Just a note saying 'Stay out of this,'" Jon said.

"With all that blood? Has to be a body somewhere."

Jon nodded. "Yeah, my thoughts, also. And that our rapist has escalated to the next step."

"If that's true, it wasn't here that the killing took place," the tech said. "Except for the one handprint, this blood is undisturbed. There's no way a body could've been here and then moved and it look like this. This blood was *poured* here."

Zane glanced over at him, tilting his hat back slightly with his finger. "So it's possible that we don't have a dead body somewhere?"

The tech looked up. "It's possible this isn't even human blood. I think it is, but we'll know for sure pretty quickly once we get back to the lab. The way it was poured, it came in some type of container. So there may not be a dead body, just a wasted donation."

"I hate that this happened," Zane said as they watched the techs continue to work. "But it may be a break for us."

"I agree," Jon said. "And beyond that, there are only so many people who know Sherry has been working with us. Almost all of them are in law enforcement."

It was the reason Jon had *two* people out watching Sherry at the car. As of right now, he didn't trust anybody, especially not with her life.

It was possible that word had leaked out that Sherry was helping them; they hadn't been keeping it a secret. The mayor's office knew, everyone at the department knew, the victims and their families had been contacted, so they knew. Mayor Birchwood might even have included the info in his statement, although not mentioning her by name.

Whoever did this could've heard about Sherry from someone else; then finding her house wouldn't have been that hard.

Jon's gut was telling him it was someone with firsthand information who had done this.

If so, this case had just taken a whole new step into more complicated.

Chapter Eighteen

Jon observed the forensic team for a while longer and then left it in Zane's hands. There was nothing more he could do there and he needed to get Sherry to a safe place.

He was relieved to find her still sitting inside his car with the two patrol officers right where he'd asked them to stay. He released them to other duties and got in next to Sherry.

"Hey, how are you hanging in there?" He kept his tone as soft and even as possible.

She was staring down at the bottle of water and crumpled paper towels in her hand. "I couldn't get all the blood off," she whispered.

She turned her palm around to show him. Jon took her hand in his, which was icy to the touch, and stroked it softly. He knew partially congealed blood could be a beast to remove. "Let's get you to my place so you can take a shower. It will come off, I promise."

She just nodded, still looking down at her hand.

She didn't say anything the entire drive to his condo, which was relatively near the station. He didn't try to talk. What could he said anyway?

He didn't even want to think about what this blow to her psyche meant for the investigation overall. Looking over at her colorless face, he couldn't imagine asking her to just buck up and interview another woman tomorrow.

So although they had narrowed the suspect pool to someone who knew Sherry was working with them, they still didn't really have any suspects whatsoever. And had probably lost Sherry, the person who had been in the best position to help them.

He pulled the car into a spot in the underground parking of the condo unit and went around to help Sherry out. He wished he could've brought some of her clothes, but he knew they were all part of the crime-scene investigation at her house. Maybe tomorrow, if the scene was cleared, he could run by and grab her something. Tonight she'd just have to sleep in one of his shirts.

Once up the elevator and inside his unit on the sixth floor, he took her straight into the bathroom. No point in showing her around; the two-bedroom place wasn't very big, and she was in no shape to process anything.

She was still staring down at her red fingertips and palm. There really wasn't a lot of blood still on them, but the color was odd, as if she'd colored them with a red marker.

"Do you want to take a shower or a bath?"

She looked at him as if she didn't quite understand the question.

"How about a shower?" he continued. It would be better to let all the water ease down the drain.

He helped her out of her shoes and clothes, laying them over the edge of the tub, then turned the water on, almost as hot as he could stand.

Was it really only twelve hours ago when he and Sherry had been laughing in the shower together? Now he led her stiff body into the opening, lovemaking the furthest thing from his mind.

He stayed right there with her for those first few minutes, to make sure she was okay. Slowly he could see awareness come back into her eyes as she stood under the heated spray. She looked over at him.

"You okay?" he asked.

She nodded, then closed her eyes, turning and lifting her face to the spray.

Jon stepped back and closed the shower door. At least she was reacting, rather than standing there just looking so numb.

He went into the kitchen and heated up a can of soup and made some sandwiches. Neither of them had eaten, and although he didn't think she would feel like it, he still wanted to make sure she had the option.

He went into his bedroom and grabbed a T-shirt. It would be more than large enough for her to sleep in.

The shower was still running when he stepped back into the bathroom.

"You doing okay in there?" he asked. "Finally thawed out?"

When she didn't answer, he opened the shower stall door. "Sherry?"

She was scrubbing at her hand with the washcloth. He reached in to stop her, but she snatched her hands away, turning her back to him.

"Sherry, listen to me. The blood is gone, sweetie. I promise."

"My hand is still red."

"Your hand is red now from the hot water and from rubbing it so hard." He put both hands on her shoulders and turned her around gently. "There's no more blood."

He was getting wet from the shower spray ricocheting off her and the walls, but he didn't care. He reached down and took the washcloth from her. This time she didn't fight him.

"Let's get you out of there." He turned off the water and guided her from the shower. He wrapped her in a towel.

"You got wet, too," she whispered then touched him on the chest where he was most wet.

"That's okay. It's basically how I do laundry anyway."

A ghost of a smile. That was good. At least she was now focused on what was going on rather than nonexistent blood on her fingers. He gave her his shirt and helped her slip it over her head.

"How about if you get a little something to eat? Then we can see how you're feeling."

"I don't know if I can eat much, but I'll try."

She managed to get down half a sandwich and half of the glass of wine he put in front of her. He finished everything she didn't eat.

She had one leg bent and her knee propped up under his T-shirt, sitting across from him at the small kitchen table. She wrapped her arms around her knee and laid her head down.

"Do you want to watch some TV?" he asked. "Get on the computer?"

He hoped she wouldn't want to do either, because news of the break-in at her house might already be leaking onto the local news. Not to mention the mayor had given his update around 7:00 p.m., which was sure to be repeating now on the 10:00 p.m. news. Jon would like to know how the mayor did, but that could wait until tomorrow.

"No, not really. I think I just want to go to sleep, if that's okay?"

He reached out and tucked a strand of her hair behind her ear from where her head was resting on her knee. "That's more than okay. It's probably the best thing for you right now."

She nodded and he helped her up, slowing as he led her out of the kitchen. Should he put her in his bed? He wasn't even sure if she would want him in the bed with her. She might just want and need her space.

He would put her there anyway. If she said anything, he would understand and would sleep on the sofa bed in the second bedroom.

"Is this okay?" he asked as he led her to the king-size bed in the middle of the room.

She turned from the bed to look at him. "Is this where you'll be sleeping, too?"

"If that's all right with you?"

"Yes. I don't want to be anywhere by myself tonight."

He wrapped his arms around her and pulled her in to his chest. "You definitely don't need to be alone tonight or any time in the foreseeable future, until you feel like you're ready."

"Thank you for helping me," she whispered into his chest. "I'm sorry I never seem able to handle anything."

"Hey, what happened at your house would spook anyone, even more so someone like you who's already suffering from post-traumatic stress. So no more nonsense about not being able to handle anything."

She smiled, but she didn't believe him, he knew. He helped her get into bed and climbed in next to her, pulling her close.

"I know you probably have things to do. I'm okay."

He needed to make a couple of phone calls, check the progress of the crime-scene investigation and report what had happened to Omega Sector. And he would, in just a minute.

Right now he held her against him.

It didn't take long, much shorter than he would've thought, for her to fall asleep. He shouldn't have been surprised. She had been up most of the night last night, but for very different reasons. She was exhausted, physically and emotionally.

He eased her from beside him and stretched her on a

pillow, then walked around the bed and covered her with the comforter. She never even stirred.

In the kitchen he made the call to Zane Wales first.

"Hey, Hatton. Is Sherry doing okay?" Zane asked after the first ring.

"Yeah, she's sleeping. How did it go at her house?"

"Pretty routine. Lab took everything they needed, including her entire mattress."

That was fine, she would never have been able to get the blood out of that anyway. He couldn't even imagine the emotional chaos that would cause her, given how long she had scrubbed her hand.

"Did they find anything of interest anywhere else in her house?"

"No, it looks like all the attention was concentrated on the bed. Symbolism, I guess. They're running any prints they can find in the house, especially in the master bed and bath. They eliminated Sherry's, of course."

Jon rubbed his forehead. "Mine are going to be there, too. We should probably prepare the lab for that."

"Did you touch something when you initially went into the room?"

Jon could hear the surprise in the younger man's voice. Rightfully so. Disturbing a crime scene when there was no imminent danger would be a pretty rookie move. "No."

"Then why would your prints be—? Oh."

Jon could almost hear the pieces clicking into place for Wales.

"Is there any particular place I should warn the lab about?"

"Living room. Bedroom. Bathroom." Jon was pretty sure he hadn't touched anything in the kitchen, but wasn't completely certain. "Hell, the whole damn house."

"Got it." The young detective was wise enough not to crack any jokes.

"What did they find out about the blood?"

"Definitely human. Good news and bad news there," Zane said. "Good news is a local blood bank truck was broken into sometime today. A few pints of blood were taken. They didn't even notice it was missing until this afternoon."

"So hopefully there's no dead body waiting around for us to find."

"That's what I was thinking. It would certainly be easier to pour blood from donated bags than to collect it from a victim into something and then pour it on the bed."

"All right, thanks for keeping me posted. When do you think they'll clear Sherry's house? I'm not letting her out of my sight until we catch this guy, but she could use some of her stuff."

"I'm sure we can probably get in there tomorrow."

She'd just have to stay in his T-shirt until then, which didn't bother Jon a bit, although he wished it was under different circumstances. He said goodbye to Zane, promising to check in tomorrow, although explaining he would not be there in the morning. Making sure Sherry was all right was his top priority. Then he placed a call to Omega.

It was nearly ten in the evening, so the call was forwarded from the office to Steve Drackett's cell phone.

"I saw the Corpus Christi mayor on the news tonight. He did great. You must have done some coaching with him," Steve said by way of greeting.

"I did. He's pretty levelheaded, willing to listen. Wants to keep the city from becoming any more panicked than it already is."

"What did you think of his speech?"

"I haven't seen it yet."

"Really?"

"We had a situation here, Steve." Jon explained what

had happened at Sherry's house. "Looks like the blood may have been stolen from a local blood bank and isn't from an actual body. So that's a relief at least."

Steve finished Jon's thought for him. "But Sherry is a target."

"Well, I don't plan to let her out of my sight, so he'll have to come through me if he's going to get to her."

"It also sounds like this guy is a little nervous about her involvement," Steve said.

"After seeing her work today, he ought to be. I still don't think any of the victims saw his face, but the way Sherry is able to walk them through the events? She's good, Steve."

"Maybe I need to look into bringing her on full-time at Omega."

That appealed to Jon on so many different levels it scared him. So he just grunted in noncommittal agreement.

He heard a noise from the bedroom. "I've got to go. I'll update you tomorrow if anything new happens."

"Okay. Be careful, Jon. Don't stretch yourself too thin. That's how mistakes happen."

Jon said goodbye, turned out all the lights and double-checked the locks on the front door. He looked in on Sherry, who was shifting restlessly but was still asleep.

After a quick shower, he slipped into a pair of gym shorts. He normally wouldn't wear anything to bed, but he didn't want to panic Sherry in any way if she woke in the middle of the night. Didn't want to trigger anything that might scare her more.

He got into bed and pulled her next to him, relieved when she sank closer to him rather than pulling away. He tucked her to his side and wrapped his fingers in her hair close to her scalp, kissing her forehead. He would do whatever he had to, to keep her safe.

He thought about what Steve had said about wearing himself too thin and making mistakes.

When it came to Sherry's safety, mistakes were not an option.

Chapter Nineteen

Sherry's eyes popped open and she struggled to remember where she was. The predawn light allowed for just enough visibility to see that she wasn't in her own bed. And then it all came rushing back to her.

Her house. The blood.

At least for the second morning in a row, Sherry wasn't cold. She knew that was because of the big heater of a man sleeping next to her, arms keeping her tightly held to him even in his sleep. She wanted to ease away from him, make sure she didn't wake him. But she wanted his warmth more, so she stayed where she was.

She was never going to forget the sight of all that blood. She had to fight the urge to try to rub it off her fingers again, although she knew there wasn't any there. It was difficult to keep the panic at bay.

The rapist had been in her house.

Yesterday Jon had asked if she'd wanted to go home while he met with the mayor. What if she had done that? Would she have walked in to find the rapist in her house? Had he sat there watching her house, waiting to see if she would come home?

Would she have opened her door to his knock and been attacked by him, too, like Tina and Jasmine and the other women?

Would that have been *her* blood on the bed?

Even Jon's warmth wasn't enough to keep out the chill that ran through her system at that thought.

She couldn't stay in the bed any longer. She tried to ease out without waking him, but she'd just barely swung her legs over the side of the bed when his arm reached over and touched her on her hip.

"Hey." His voice was husky with sleep. "You doing okay?"

"Yeah." She glanced at him over her shoulder. He looked tousled but strong and capable. She wanted to ease back onto the bed, into his strength. "I'm not going to freak out or anything. I was just going to take a shower. I'm sorry I woke you. Go back to sleep."

His hand tightened on her hip, pulling her back toward him.

There was nothing she wanted more than to do that. To bask in his warmth, to lean on his strength.

She was ashamed of how she'd reacted last night. Surely Jon hadn't signed on for mass hysterics when he'd spent one night with her. She hardly wanted to be around herself this morning. She couldn't imagine he really wanted to be, either.

He was a good guy. The type that wouldn't turn away from a damsel in distress, so to speak, no matter how much he wished she would pull it together.

So she wasn't going to let herself lie back down and draw from his strength. She needed to find her own strength.

She slid so she was just beyond his reach and she could face him. His eyes narrowed as he withdrew his hand, but she ignored that. One thing had really weighed heavily on her mind, something she had to know right away.

"Did they find the person that blood belonged to? There wasn't a dead body at my house, was there?" The thought that she might have tripped over a dead body did not help with the staying-calm-and-strong plan.

"No, as a matter of fact the forensic lab doesn't think the blood was from anybody being harmed. A blood bank truck was broken into yesterday. Donated blood was stolen."

"So no one was hurt?"

"We don't know definitely, but we are working based on that assumption as of right now."

"Thank God." She felt as if a weight had been lifted from her chest. The thought that the maniac had killed someone to get her attention had been even more traumatic. The blood had been bad enough.

"Yes, it was definitely good news."

He looked so appealing lying there, arms tucked under his head against the pillow. The bed sheet had fallen low on his hips, revealing his chest and abs. She knew he was wearing shorts, but she also knew it wouldn't take much to have those off him.

The desire to crawl to him and kiss her way down that chest and abs—and beyond—was almost overwhelming. But after last night she wasn't even sure that was what he wanted anymore and could admit to herself that she was too cowardly to try to study his face for fear of what she might find there.

Not coldness—she knew he wouldn't be cold or unkind. It wasn't in his nature. No, she was afraid that if she looked in his eyes she would find *warmth* where yesterday there had been *heat*.

That he would gladly be her friend but had enough sense to realize he didn't really want the emotional messiness that would come along with continuing to be romantically involved with her.

She remembered him having to get soaking wet in the shower last night to get her to stop scrubbing her hand. So, yeah, she wouldn't blame him for deciding to firmly park in the friend zone. As much as she'd wanted to make her way over to his mostly naked body with her mostly naked body, she was afraid if she did he might gently stop her.

Then an even more horrifying thought: maybe he *wouldn't* stop her. Just let things continue out of kindness. Pity.

She couldn't stand the possible thought. She slid a little farther away without making eye contact.

"Yeah, I'm just going to take a shower, okay?" She smiled as best she could before walking away.

SEEING SHERRY'S FACE as she had walked out of her house last night after she'd witnessed the crime scene had been disturbing. It was an image burned into his mind that he wasn't likely to forget for a long time.

But, honestly, that tiny fake smile she'd just given him before heading toward the shower was every bit as disturbing.

Jon wasn't sure exactly what was going on, but he didn't like it. He got up and wandered over to the window that looked out on the city as the sun began to rise and it began to wake up.

He didn't expect Sherry to jump into bed with him. Hell, after what had happened last night, if she decided she was sleeping on couches for the foreseeable future, he wouldn't be able to blame her. He definitely didn't expect her to feel all romantic after her house—and her emotions—had just been so brutally violated.

But whatever had just happened a couple of minutes ago? Whatever was going on in that head of hers? Jon really didn't like it.

He hadn't wanted to make any sexual advances because it seemed in bad taste after what she'd been through. Yet

Jon felt he had made a critical tactical error by letting her get up from the bed and go into that shower alone.

The biggest part of him—and other *specific* parts of him—all but demanded he rectify that error by following her in there and making love to her until neither of them was thinking about anything from yesterday.

Mentally he knew he should give her some space. She'd been through another trauma after weeks of already balancing in a delicate emotional state. Yeah, she'd had a little bit of a rough time last night, but the fact that she was coherent and functioning this morning just showed her considerable mental and emotional strength.

The scene of her scrubbing her hand in the shower had been scary, and for a few minutes Jon had thought he was going to have to call in professional help. A doctor-prescribed sedative would not be unheard of in this situation, maybe even advisable.

She had pulled it together, though, had even managed to eat a little bit before going to sleep. She'd had a few bad dreams during the night, he'd been able to tell—whether they were specifically about her house or not he didn't know—but she hadn't woken up sobbing or screaming.

Again, given that her mind was already dealing with the trauma of her work from the past few months, and that she'd been dealing with that *alone* without any sort of support system…last night could've—probably *should've*—emotionally crippled her. But it hadn't.

All in all, she was doing pretty damn good in Jon's opinion.

So what was it that was bothering him so much about their little talk a few minutes ago?

He'd seen her glance over at him, had thought she might instigate something physical as they both sat on the bed. He'd sat back against the pillows in the most casual pose he could muster, wanting her to know she was welcome to ease on over but that it definitely wasn't expected.

He'd been sure she was about to ease. His body tightened now with him just thinking about it.

But then she'd stopped. Shut down. Refused to look him in the eye. Given him that disturbing little smile that didn't come anywhere close to her gorgeous blue eyes, and had all but run for the shower.

Suddenly Jon understood why he was so disturbed with her behavior: she was shutting him out.

Jon turned from the window and walked to the closed bathroom door. Shutting him out was unacceptable. His hand was on the doorknob and he was turning it to open the door when he stopped.

Had she been shutting him out or had she just needed space?

He let go of the knob. If she needed time to mentally and emotionally regroup, he should give her that. But he sure as hell didn't want to.

He walked into the condo's little kitchen to make coffee and think about anything else except her in the shower. And what they had done in the shower yesterday morning. Because that was not going to result in him leaving her alone.

He took stock of what food was in the cabinets. He didn't have much to eat here. He preferred eating out to cooking. He didn't even have Sugar-O's, but he did have some bread to make toast—enough to get them through this morning. They would need to get some real groceries if they were going to be staying here a lot more.

Jon needed to figure out logistically how he was going to manage working on the case. Thinking the rapist might be someone connected to the police department totally put a new spin on things. He didn't want to take Sherry there, not that he expected her to be doing any work today anyway. And he definitely did not plan to leave her alone.

"Hey."

Jon turned as he heard her soft voice from the kitchen doorway. She still had his shirt on but also had put on her jeans from yesterday. She still wasn't quite looking him in the eye.

"Hey. Shower okay?" He kept his distance, leaning against the counter, not wanting to spook her in any way.

"I didn't nearly scrub my hand off, if that's what you mean." Her short laugh was completely devoid of humor.

She was embarrassed by how she'd reacted last night. Was that what this was all about? She was afraid he couldn't deal with the drama?

He all but rolled his eyes. She'd obviously never been around the Omega Sector office before. She had nothing on some of the stuff that happened around there.

Jon walked up to her and put his hands gently on her waist. He didn't want to come on too strong in case his assumptions were incorrect. But he definitely didn't want her standing there looking all uncomfortable, thinking he didn't want her.

Because if she responded to him he wasn't sure they would even make it to the bedroom. He might have to lay her down right here on the kitchen table. And, honestly, he wasn't sure that table would support both of them.

He'd sure as hell like to find out, though.

"Sherry." He pulled her closer to him and hooked a finger under her chin, since she still wouldn't look him in the eyes. "If you need space, that's fine. But if for one second you think that—"

His sentence was cut off by a loud knocking on the door.

Jon released Sherry and ran in to grab his Glock on the bedside table. He pulled her inside the bedroom as the knock came again.

"Stay here."

"Why do you have your gun?" She was looking him in the eyes now, her own huge in her face.

"Because I haven't let anyone know where I'm staying. So nobody should be knocking on my door."

Chapter Twenty

She was seeing a whole different side of Jon. Hard. Physical. Dangerous. He tended to use his mind for every part of the job she'd seen so far. But right now Sherry had no doubt that Jon Hatton, gun in hand, was also a physical force to be reckoned with. Whoever was coming through that door was going to have to make it through Jon.

That was not going to be easy.

Sherry stayed in the bedroom doorway, which allowed her to see what was going on in the kitchen without being in Jon's way.

He stuck his eye up to the peephole then pulled it away quickly, obviously not wanting to make himself a target if someone was waiting with a gun on the other side.

Sherry watched as Jon shook his head and put his gun down on the table.

A knock on the door again. "Hatton, wake the hell up!" From the other side.

As he unlocked the chain on the door, he turned back to her. "I'm sorry for everything that's about to happen in the foreseeable future."

"What?" She took a step closer. "What do you mean?"

Jon opened the door and two men walked in.

"It's about damn time," one of them, the one with brown hair—just a touch too long to be conventional—and giant biceps said, looking at Jon as he strolled in. "I know you like to make sure your skin-care regimen is perfect in the morning, but seriously, leaving us out in the hallway like that?"

"Liam," Jon said in greeting, shaking his head. He shook the hand of the other man—handsome as sin, with some sort of Asian heritage—who walked in behind Liam. "Hi, Brandon. I guess Steve sent you guys."

"You know Drackett. Always afraid everyone is lonely," Liam drawled and then noticed Sherry. "I see that is not the case."

Liam, gorgeous and obviously well aware of that fact, walked over and wrapped his arms around Sherry. She let out a small squeak when he lifted her off her feet in a huge hug.

"Hey there, sweetheart. Why don't you and I sneak away right now, get married in Vegas, and I'll spend the rest of my life helping you forget the horrible time you ever spent with Jon Hatton?"

He kissed her straight on the mouth. She let out another squeak.

"Enough, Goetz," Jon said. "I'm sure Sherry would appreciate it if you would stop molesting her."

Liam winked at her but set her back down. "Some people don't know true love when it slaps them in the face, do they, sweetheart?"

Sherry giggled. It was truly the only option when faced with Liam's outrageousness, which was actually mostly for Jon's benefit, she was sure.

"Sherry, these are two of my colleagues from the Critical Response Division of Omega Sector, Liam Goetz and Brandon Han."

Liam winked at her again. "Introductions are obviously not necessary for me and my true love."

"It's nice to meet you, Sherry." Brandon offered his hand to her.

She shook his hand. "Sherry Mitchell."

Liam went over to pour himself a cup of coffee "Soon to be Mitchell-Goetz."

Jon came over and pulled a chair out for Sherry to sit at the table, then took the seat next to her. "Are you guys here for a reason besides for me to pound on Goetz when he continues to get out of line?"

Liam gave a dramatic wounded face from over at the coffeemaker.

"Actually, yes," Brandon said, pulling out a large stack of files. "Drackett said you mentioned that the police department may be compromised. So he sent us with a copy of all the case files, thinking maybe we can work here."

Brandon turned to Sherry. "Sorry about what happened at your house, by the way."

"Thanks." She turned and looked at Jon. "What do you think is wrong at the police department?"

Jon shrugged. "Zane and I both agreed that whoever did that to your house yesterday might have connections to the Corpus Christi PD."

"Because of the note saying 'Stay out of this'?" she asked.

Jon nodded. "Exactly. People with connections to the department had the most knowledge of you helping us in the case."

"But it wasn't exactly a secret. It could've been someone not directly related, who just heard about it," she murmured.

He took her hand. "Absolutely. I'd rather not take a chance having you at the precinct if we have other options. Like working here."

Sherry nodded. "Okay. We'll still need somewhere for me to interview the other victims."

"No one expects you to do that today. Least of all me." He gave her hand a squeeze. "It's okay to rest, take it easy."

Sherry didn't want to rest. Resting meant too much time to think. To feel useless. To give the attacker more time to plan for his next victim.

"Han is a gifted profiler, one of the best Omega has," Jon continued. "Goetz is more muscle. Actually, I think he might currently be working as a janitor."

Liam shrugged. "Hey, we can't all sit around overthinking everything, like these two. I'm more of an action man myself. You ever get yourself in a hostage situation, trust me, you'll want me rather than Tweedledum and Tweedledee here. And, by the way, we janitors prefer the term 'custodial engineers.'"

Even Jon snickered at that one. He had introduced them as colleagues, but they were much more than that. They were his friends. People he trusted. Even despite the bickering, she could already see an ease in Jon that hadn't been there before.

"Actually, I'm staying to help," Brandon said. "Liam's just passing through on his way to another case."

"Of course, I'm going to try to talk Sherry into coming with me." Liam came over and stood behind her chair and began rubbing her shoulders. "We'll have much more fun than you'll have here with fuddy-duddy," he said in an exaggerated stage whisper.

"You know what?" Jon said, standing and rolling his eyes. "Why don't you go get some groceries while the adults do some work?"

"Only if Sherry comes with me," Liam said.

There was a moment of silence, of seriousness, between the two men. Something passing between them that she wasn't sure she totally understood but knew it was Jon passing her over to Liam.

"If you feel up to going with Liam, to getting some fresh air for a few minutes, that might be a good idea," Jon said to her. "I'd like to run a few aspects of the case by Brandon. Get his opinion as a profiler."

"Yeah, no problem," Sherry said with a chipperness she didn't feel. "Just let me grab my bag."

Sherry felt a weight in her chest and not because she was going to the grocery store. Jon was right, getting out of the condo would probably do her good. This just confirmed that she'd been right: Jon really had decided they were better off as friends.

If he was still interested in her, he wouldn't be sending her off with his handsome, charismatic friend who wanted to steal her away. She knew Liam was just joking in all his grandiose gestures, and she, of course, wasn't taking him seriously. But she knew if the roles were reversed and one of her friends was skirting around, making eyes toward Jon, there would be no way in hell she'd send them off alone for more flirty fun.

Jon obviously did not feel the same way.

"I hear avocados are an aphrodisiac food," Liam said, holding one up at the grocery store a little while later, waggling both eyebrows. "If not, you can still make some awesome guac with it. So a win either way."

Liam had been making similar outrageous comments throughout their entire time at the store. On any other day Sherry would've laughed and gotten into the whole act with him. But she just couldn't seem to work her way past the heaviness in her midsection at the thought that Jon didn't really want her anymore.

"Hey, blue eyes." Liam wrapped an arm around her. "What's going on inside that head of yours? You sad because of what happened in your house yesterday? That's messed up, by the way."

She shrugged as they walked down the grocery aisle. "Yeah, that was really bad. And I kind of freaked out last night." She explained about trying to scrub the nonexistent blood off her hands.

"Doesn't sound too unreasonable to me."

"It's not just that. I've also been having some post-traumatic-type symptoms the past couple of months. Cold spells. Not being able to draw."

Liam nodded. "Having negative emotional reactions—nightmares, insomnia, eating issues, substance abuse—are common problems among agents and officers their first couple of years. So don't feel like you're the only one. Eventually you learn to distance yourself a little from the emotional ugliness. Find some way to ground yourself."

"Yeah, Jon wanted to help with that, and probably could have. But my previous trauma symptoms coupled with last night's little interlude? I'm afraid it's kind of ruined everything between Jon and me. I think he wants to put a little distance between him and my crazy. For which I can't blame him."

"Did he actually say that to you?"

Sherry bit her lip. "Not in those exact words."

Liam rolled his eyes. "Did he say that to you in any words at all?"

"How could he not be thinking it, Liam? I'm one step away from being certifiably committed."

"Hatton? Please, girl. Hatton is the one that keeps us all together back at Omega. If he bailed every time someone went a little crazy, he'd spend his entire life running. Jon lives for the 'help me help you' stuff."

"Yeah, well, you guys are all friends. Jon and I are… well, let's just say we'd spent a grand total of one night together before the incident last night and me dumping my crazy on him. We'd only known each other a couple of days before that, so it's not like we have some friendship to ground us."

Liam stopped walking and smiled down at her. An authentic smile that had nothing to do with jokes. It changed the entire look of his face. "So Hatton finally jumped in headfirst with someone. About damn time. He usually overthinks a relationship to death before getting involved with anybody."

"Really?"

Liam nodded. "If he jumped in with you, it's because he wasn't thinking, he was *feeling*. That's important. I've known Jon a lot of years and have never known him not to overthink a relationship. To just *feel*."

Sherry wasn't convinced. "I saw the look between you before we left. The bro-code look that said, 'Hey, yeah, can you take her off my hands?'"

Liam laughed. "Well, you might need to brush up on your bro-code translating skills, because what that look actually said was, 'Hey, there's a maniac out there, so be damn sure you're watching over her because she's important.'"

Sherry didn't know if she could believe him or not. "Really?"

"Oh, sweetheart, as much as I'd like to steal you away, I could feel his eyes shooting daggers into the back of my skull the moment I touched you in the condo. I've kissed everyone he's ever known, including his mother, and he's never had any sort of reaction. This morning? He was ready to rip my head off."

"He didn't say or do anything."

"Trust me, I know. Han noticed, too, I'm sure. Although he's too polite to say anything about it. Trust me more about this—Jon Hatton can handle whatever 'crazy' you've got to throw at him, although I can tell by talking to you that your crazy is not nearly as toxic as you think it is."

"But—"

"When it comes to Hatton, there are no buts. Once he's decided you mean enough to him for him to help you shoulder your burden, it doesn't matter how big that burden is. He's going to help. He's decided that with you. And the amount of time spent together has nothing to do with the decision."

Could Liam be right?

"Oh, I am always right, darlin'." He answered her unspoken question as if he could read her mind. "Now let's get the groceries and get back so we can put your poor beau out of his misery."

Chapter Twenty-One

"I was looking at these files on the way down. This is a pretty interesting guy you've got here," Brandon said, reading back through the account of the third victim.

Jon knew for Brandon Han to say someone was "interesting" meant they had an unusual perpetrator on their hands. Brandon was a certified genius. He had something like three advanced degrees, could speak a dozen different languages and could run multiple different scenarios in his head at the same time like a computer.

The man was nicknamed "The Machine" because of that, although Jon didn't think people called him that to his face.

When Brandon began really looking at all the angles of a crime, it was a sight to behold—almost spooky. And for him to call someone "interesting" meant the rapist probably had a genius IQ, which wasn't surprising given the complete lack of evidence at the crime scenes.

"There doesn't seem to be any rhyme or reason to how he picks his victims," Jon said in agreement. "The women are different ages, different heights, weights, body sizes, have different hair color, hell, even skin color as of the last victim. None of them knew each other and all are from different socioeconomic backgrounds. Some well-off, some barely making by. One was a student."

"That's what I mean. Interesting. Serial rapists almost always tend to have a type. A pattern or ritual they are following."

"Yeah, well, if he does, I can't see it. I've tried to back away from it, to see if I can spot the pattern if I look at it from a further distance, but, honestly, I've got nothing."

"Maybe it's not the women who are his MO. Maybe it's the situation itself."

Jon nodded. "I thought that, too. There are really only two similarities in all the cases. They all occurred in doorways and they all involved the perp striking the women immediately to stun and effectually blind them, but not hard enough to do permanent damage."

Brandon lined up the hospital photos of all six women next to each other. Their bruised faces placed so closely together were a gruesome sight. "The attacks all happened at different times of day, different days of the week, right?"

"Yes. A week to two weeks between each attack—but no set length of time in between." That had been one of the first patterns Jon looked for. "Most at the women's homes, although one was at a hotel."

"The locations themselves could be an important role," Brandon said. "Especially once the city became aware there was a serial rapist at large. He had to choose places where he wouldn't be noticed or identified."

"Yes, so that has to take some planning."

"Absolutely."

"And the bruising." Brandon pointed to the pictures on the table. "Looking at the women, it's easy to see that this is the same guy. You've got similar bruises in the same location of the face."

Jon agreed. "Guy is controlled. He's not hitting these women out of anger. He has a definite purpose in how he strikes them—it's part of his plan, of what he's trying to accomplish."

They both studied the pictures for a long time, thinking.

Jon leaned back in the kitchen chair, rubbing a weary hand over his face. "Brandon, tell me what I'm missing. You don't have to sugarcoat it or ease me into it to save my feelings. If you see something I've missed, just throw it out there."

"I know you do a lot more than profile and your job here—as it is everywhere—has been multifaceted and complicated." Brandon slapped him on his back. "That's why they sent you instead of me. To deal with all the other stuff I'm terrible at."

Jon rolled his eyes. "Hasn't that been a joy?"

"I wish I could just point out something obvious here that you've missed and say 'nanny-nanny-boo-boo, moron, now go arrest the bad guy.'"

Jon chuckled. "But you don't have anything obvious to point out."

"All I can give you is my opinion, which is no more or no less valuable than yours."

"I'll take it."

"This guy is all about the planning. I think the rapes themselves are almost secondary. The thrill for him is figuring out the who, when and where he's going to do it without getting caught."

Jon nodded. That made sense.

"This is very much about not getting caught. That's why he got so angry about you guys using Sherry. He's afraid she'll be able to help the victims remember something about him. I also think he feels like it's cheating of some sort on your part to bring her in at this stage of the game."

Could that be possible? It made sense in a twisted way.

"You're dealing with a bored genius. He knows how law enforcement works. He knows how forensics works. He knows how the human body works."

"Why do you say that about the body?"

"Like you said, he hits the women just enough to suit his purposes—making it so they're dazed and can't see him. That sort of control? You'd have to know a lot about your own strength and how the bones of the face are made up. None of those women have broken noses or cheekbones. That's deliberate."

"I definitely agree."

"Even more than that, I think it has to do with bruising on his hand. If he hit them hard enough to fracture cheekbones, it would leave marking on his hands for days that would be impossible to miss."

"That would explain why there are different amounts of time between each attack." Jon had to admit that made sense.

Brandon shrugged. "Don't know for sure, but waiting for his hand to completely heal would be a logical reason."

They studied the pictures.

"He wants a challenge," Brandon continued. "He's probably highly successful in whatever line of work he's in, which would definitely be white collar."

"Victim six, Jasmine Houze, thinks he was wearing a white office shirt. So literally white collar."

"I wouldn't be surprised if this guy is a CEO or something. He's used to planning things to the minutest detail, a habit that translates into his crimes. The rapes are his newest challenge, since he's probably bored in whatever field he works in. Although highly successful."

Brandon sat back, crossing his arms over his chest. "I think you're dealing with a bored genius who wondered for years what crimes he could get away with and then finally started putting them into practice."

Jon got the distinct feeling that concept might have struck just a little too close to home for Brandon. The man was a loner. Jon couldn't recall ever seeing him casually hanging out with anyone.

Not that he was a rapist or about to commit any other crimes. But the bored genius part? That was definitely Brandon.

"Jon, I wouldn't be surprised if he escalates. To use poker terms, you anted up, and he's calling. You brought Sherry into this, so he'll do something to counter."

"Speaking of Sherry, where the hell are they? It's not like we need groceries for a month."

"You worried about her safety or you worried about her with Liam?" Brandon asked.

"Safety, of course. Goetz is a putz."

A putz that women went gaga over. If he kissed Sherry again, Jon would have to see how good *his* knowledge of the human body was, because he'd definitely be trying to break Liam's nose.

"Maybe I should call them and make sure they're all right."

"If you're truly worried about safety, you know no one is going to get the drop on Liam. But if you're worried that he might be talking her into running away with him to a tropical island…" Brandon chuckled.

Liam was his friend, and Jon knew he didn't have to worry about him really trying to steal Sherry away. But all Jon could see was that pitiful smile she'd given him as she'd eased out of bed this morning, the one that had suggested she thought he didn't really want her.

He reached for his phone. He'd be damned if she'd turn to Goetz—who Jon was sure would be more than willing to comfort her—because she thought Jon didn't want her.

They needed to get back to the damn house. Right damn now.

He was looking up Liam's contact info when the door opened.

"Kids, we're home."

Liam was carrying two large bags of groceries. Sherry

followed behind him, looking at Liam with that bemused, utterly charmed smile women tended to have around him.

Jon didn't think about what he was doing, he just grabbed Sherry and pulled her to him, kissing her soundly. He heard her startled gasp before she melted against him and wound her arms around his neck.

He didn't care about the other two men in the room, didn't care that they were sure to give him a hard time about this. All he cared about was making sure Sherry knew that *hell, yes* he still wanted her.

"Ahem, excuse me, I'm going to have to ask you to get your hands off my woman." Liam's words eventually penetrated Jon's mind and he stopped kissing her, reluctantly, although he kept her pinned to his side.

Liam wasn't actually even paying them any attention since he was putting groceries away. Brandon was studying the case pictures again.

Jon smiled down at Sherry. "I'm glad you two made it back okay and that this clown didn't talk you into eloping."

Liam sighed dramatically from across the room.

"Well, here was where I wanted to be." She smiled up at him, stealing his breath.

He trailed a finger down her cheek. "Here is where you're wanted."

"I'm sorry about freaking out last night."

"No apology necessary. You never have to be sorry for choosing to survive something. You said that to Jasmine, and it's just as true for you. Anytime I can help you do that, carry some of that burden for you, I'm glad to do so."

Sherry looked over at Liam, and Jon looked up in time to see him wink at her from where he was opening a box of cereal. Evidently the two of them had discussed Jon and freak-outs while they were away.

She eased away from him and walked over to the table, looking down at the pictures.

"Here, let me put those away," Jon said. "There's no need to look at them."

"No, it's okay." She put out an arm to stop him. "I'm done letting fear get the better of me. There's work to be done."

"Do you see, Jon?" Liam said as he shoveled a spoonful of cereal into his mouth. "Do you see why I'm so in love with her?"

Jon could definitely see why *he* was falling in love with her. Liam be damned.

"Sherry, it says here you project that the rapist is probably around five foot nine or ten?" Brandon asked, seemingly oblivious to everything else being said in the kitchen.

"Yes." She nodded. "That's based on the neck angle of victim number one—Tina Wescott—when he first entered her doorway. Hopefully I'll be able to confirm that when I talk to the other women."

Brandon looked over at Jon. "The rapist being that height—pretty short for a man—would fit the profile we were discussing earlier."

Jon held out a chair for Sherry and then sat in the one next to her. "He's probably tried to overcompensate for his height his whole life. It may be why he chose rapes as his crime—because he's always felt like he had something to prove with women."

"Exactly," Brandon agreed. "The tattoo is interesting. It's placed on his body somewhere where you only see it if he decides to show it to you."

"I wouldn't be surprised if he has others," Jon said.

Brandon nodded. "Me, either. Honestly, I wouldn't be surprised to find he has tattoos commemorating his victims."

"I'll send locals out to tattoo shops to see if there are any repeat customers coinciding with the attack dates." It was a long shot, Jon knew, but was at least something. Although a man that smart probably wouldn't use the same shop more than once.

"I want to talk to the other victims," Sherry said. "We can't wait any longer. You'll just have to help me get through it."

Jon stretched his arm around the back of her chair and squeezed her. "Okay. I'll set them up. But I don't want to do it at the police station. I still am not sure one of those guys isn't the attacker."

Brandon shrugged. "Any number of law-enforcement officers—especially high-ranking or ones on the force for a long time—could fit the profile. They'd know how to hit. They'd know what to look for in a location where they wouldn't be seen. They'd know about forensic evidence and how not to leave any."

That was what Jon was afraid of. And he definitely wasn't going to keep working in their building if he was basically hand-delivering all the information the perp needed to keep successfully committing crimes.

"I'll go to their houses or wherever they're staying. That's probably better for them anyway," Sherry said.

"Are you sure?" he asked her. Yeah, things were becoming more critical. But Jon didn't want to lose sight of the fact that Sherry was still in a delicate emotional place. He wanted her help with this case, but he also wanted to make sure she was going to be able to function after it was over.

"I can do this." Her voice was stronger, more assured, than it had ever been when she was talking about the case. "Just don't let me go under."

"I won't." He kissed the side of her head as he stood to go make the calls.

He wondered if this bastard knew that by bringing the fight directly to Sherry's doorstep he would awaken the warrior in her rather than cause her to cower. It had been the wrong move on his part on multiple different levels.

And it was going to be the reason why they caught him.

Chapter Twenty-Two

True to her word, Sherry spent the next two days interviewing the other women. She worked with them tirelessly. She laughed with them, cried with them. She knew the most intimate details about their lives by the time she finished.

She was obviously much more comfortable—or at the very least much more focused—than she had been when interviewing Tina Wescott at the station a couple of days ago. Although there hadn't been any facial descriptions to draw, Sherry had been ready with her sketch pad. She'd been ready to work through any of her emotional walls and draw, if they did think of something.

For each interview she sat the woman facing a blank wall. And, as with Tina, walked them back to an hour before the crime. She would start by asking them for general descriptions, and then rewind and start again, each time focusing on different sets of details.

She was able to confirm that the man's height was no more than five foot ten. More than one victim felt that he had darker skin. Not African-American, but highly tanned Caucasian or perhaps even of Mexican or South American descent. One woman remembered his shoes with vivid clarity.

Unfortunately, Nike sold a few hundred thousand pairs of those types of athletic shoes any given year.

Jon and Brandon had been with Sherry for each interview, although usually out of the way. Liam had left yesterday for his other case.

"She's really very good at what she does," Brandon
observed.

"I know."

"She doesn't hold back, she gets right there into the
moment with them. It's one of the reasons she's so good."

"It's also one of the reasons why she's suffering from
post-traumatic stress," Jon said.

"Yeah, she'll have to find a way to protect herself better emotionally."

Jon had made sure he was always nearby in case the
debilitating chills came back. A couple of times she had
stopped and taken a break from an interview and sought
him out.

Usually after he'd pulled her close, or they'd taken a
walk, or a few deep breaths, she'd been able to pull herself out of the dark place she'd been heading.

"She's learning that taking a break for her own sanity is
just as okay as the victim needing a break," Jon said. "She
had the drawing skills and she had the obvious interviewing and people skills, so the Bureau scooped her right up."

"But nobody made sure she had the emotional resources
to cope with what she was doing."

"Exactly."

"She'll get there."

"I plan to make sure of that." The more Jon knew her,
the more he hoped being around to help keep her grounded
would become a permanent job for him.

"Have you heard anything that seems to conflict with
our profile?" he asked Brandon as Sherry finished talking
to victim number four and was now making small talk.

"No, nothing."

"Anybody at the precinct fit the role?"

Brandon had been spending his spare hours at the Corpus Christi Police Department under the pretense of looking over the full case files, but really to get a read on possible suspects there.

"Only a couple."

"There are enough people there who seem to have impeded forward progress on this case to make me suspect them."

Brandon nodded. "Fortunately for them, being a jerk isn't a crime, otherwise we'd definitely be arresting some people."

"I was thinking that if someone knew we were looking for that particular tattoo he might try to cover it up, either with makeup or a shirt."

"Yeah, we can't legally ask everyone to show us their arms. Might make this investigation a whole lot easier if we could," Brandon said.

Jon's phone buzzed in his pocket. It was a text from Zane. Jon read it, then rubbed a weary hand across his face. "That was Wales. We've got another victim at Memorial."

They had all known it was coming, but had hoped they'd be able to get far enough ahead of the guy to stop him.

Brandon muttered an expletive.

"My feelings exactly," Jon said. "I've got to tell Sherry."

NOTHING SHE'D BEEN able to do had been enough. It was the thought that kept running through her head as she sat in the backseat of the car that raced toward the hospital.

"You don't have to go if you don't want to," Jon said, making eye contact with her from the rearview mirror. "I'm sure Brandon will take you to my place."

"I will," Brandon said. "Truly, Sherry. If you feel like this is too much for you, Jon and I would be the first to support you on that."

Sherry thought about it for a moment but knew she

could do this. The past couple of days had been tough, but she had handled it. Hearing what these women had gone through—over and over—had threatened to trigger the debilitating chills, but when it had gotten to its worst, Sherry just called for a break.

Actually the first few times, Jon had seen what was happening and *he* had called for a break. But then Sherry recognized the pattern herself and had started doing it. For two years she'd been interviewing victims, careful to watch for when they needed a break and when they needed to stop altogether. Because at some point more harm than good could be done by continuing to push.

Why she never realized the same was true for herself was beyond her. As a forensic artist, Sherry was not only responsible for the mental and emotional well-being of the people with whom she spoke, but was responsible for that in herself.

She felt as though a choir of angels should be singing or something at her grand epiphany.

She knew it would change everything in her career. She looked down at the sketch pad in her hand. It was now full of drawings she'd made of the past two days. Nothing important to the case, but it at least meant her mind was freeing itself to draw again.

She trusted when the time came for her to draw a face for actual police work, she would be able to do it. That might be right now at the hospital.

So, no, she wasn't going to go home and hide and feel as if it was too much for her.

She reached up and touched Jon's shoulder. "Truly, I'm okay. I can do this, if I'm needed. If not, I'll just stay out of your way."

Jon reached up with his own hand and squeezed hers, then put it back on the wheel.

They pulled into the hospital lot and rushed into the

trauma unit. Sherry silently hoped this would be the same as the last time they'd rushed here—a false alarm, so to speak, where the woman hadn't actually been raped.

But she knew when she saw the full magnitude of both the police and hospital staff fairly hovering in the hallway that they wouldn't be that lucky.

It was Zane who met them halfway in the hallway. For the first time Sherry had ever seen him, he had his cowboy hat in his hands rather than on his head. She was absently wondering why he would hide such a gorgeous head full of hair under that hat, and then she noticed his face.

Haggard. Stricken. Completely devoid of color.

This was a man hanging on by a thread.

"What, Wales? What is it?" Jon asked when Zane couldn't seem to get any words out. "Is it definitely the same guy? Same facial trauma?"

Jon looked toward the hospital room, highly focused on the case and not really noticing what was happening right in front of him.

"What, Zane?" Sherry reached out and touched him on his arm. "Was someone killed?"

Jon's attention refocused on the man in front of him. "Just say it."

"It's Caroline. Caroline is the victim."

Sherry took a step back, reeling into herself. No.

"Oh, my God." She felt Jon's arms come around her almost from a distance.

Bubbly, feisty, little Caroline? She couldn't be the victim of this monster.

"I—" Zane seemed lost. In shock. "I—"

Brandon made eye contact with Jon, then took over.

"Hey, man." Brandon put a guiding hand on Zane's back. "Why don't you come sit down over here?" He led Zane to some chairs, where he slid bonelessly into one, staring blankly ahead. Brandon sat with him.

"He's not okay," Sherry whispered.

"No, he's definitely not," Jon answered, his arm still around her. "None of us are okay, but Wales may never be okay again. I'm going to get someone to take you home."

"No!" Sherry leaned back from him. "She's my friend, Jon. I'm not going to go boo-hoo at your house while my friend is in there and needs support. My emotional state takes a backseat to what she needs right now."

Jon tugged her into his chest tightly. "Okay."

"I know you have stuff you need to do. I'm okay. Just get me in to see her as soon as you can."

"Are you sure?"

"More than positive. I'll sit with Zane while you and Brandon go work this situation." She looked at all the people milling around outside Caroline's door; they were almost like zombies. "Those people need somebody to lead them and tell them how they can best help."

She knew without a doubt Jon was the man for that job.

Jon turned to do his job, and Sherry walked over to the chair, relieving Brandon.

"Are you okay?" Brandon asked.

"Yes. I'm going to sit here with him. You go do your job."

Sherry wrapped an arm around Zane as she sat.

"Caroline is the strongest, most feisty gal I know," she said. "We will help her get through this."

"I should've been there," Zane said, sliding his hat in circles in his hands centimeter by centimeter. "I was supposed to have been there."

"Zane—"

"Caroline isn't stupid. She wouldn't just open her door to anyone when there's a maniac out on the loose. I was supposed to go to her house this afternoon, but decided not to go. Decided she wasn't what I wanted. Again. Like the dumb ass that I am."

Sherry wasn't sure what could be said to comfort the man. "Zane, you can't blame—"

Zane turned and looked Sherry in the eye. "She opened that door this afternoon thinking it was me. I know that with every fiber of my being. But it wasn't me. It was a monster."

Sometimes there weren't any words that could be said. Nothing would fix this. She rubbed his arm. "I'm so sorry."

"I'll have to live with that every day for the rest of my life." He crushed his hat with his fingers. "She's in a coma, Sherry. The trauma was much worse than the previous victims. Dr. Rosemont isn't sure when she'll wake up. *If* she'll wake up."

Sherry could feel tears pouring down her cheeks. "She's strong, Zane. A fighter."

"I should've been there."

Chapter Twenty-Three

"Are you sure Sherry is going to be okay?" Brandon asked as he caught up to Jon walking down the hall. "Caroline is her friend, right?"

Jon glanced at Sherry over his shoulder where she sat with Zane. "That woman has shown a measure of grit in the past forty-eight hours that is truly remarkable." Jon had seen seasoned agents crumple under less pressure.

"No arguments from me."

"I'm beginning to think there isn't anything that Sherry can't handle. She might have to work her way through some bad points initially, but she gets herself there."

It was downright impressive.

He realized Brandon was staring at him. "What?"

"First Derek, now you."

Derek was a member of Omega's SWAT team who was currently on his honeymoon or he would probably be here right now helping with this case. "First Derek what?"

"Nothing." Brandon slapped him on the shoulder, smiling. "You'll figure it out. You're smart."

Jon shook his head, turning his focus to the case at hand. The hospital hallway was crowded, even more than it had been with Jasmine Houze a week ago. Jon knew why.

Caroline was one of their own. The desire to stop this bastard had just shot through the roof. It also made for a very explosive *Texan* crowd that would need to be handled appropriately.

First he needed all the details from Dr. Rosemont about Caroline's condition. She was still in there with Caroline, but Jon spotted Dr. Trumpold, Sherry's "handsome" doctor—although Jon decided not to hold that against him this time—and cornered him to ask some questions.

"Dr. Trumpold, I just arrived. Can you give me any sort of update?"

"Agent Hatton."

Jon was a little surprised the man knew his name. That meant there had been too damn many victims brought in.

"I haven't been in there, of course. Dr. Rosemont and I have agreed that it's best for all male personnel to stay out of any of the victims' rooms unless they've been given express permission."

The man shrugged, hands in his lab coat pocket. It wasn't difficult to see he felt frustrated for being left out of the loop.

"But from what I understand, Ms. Gill is in a coma," the doctor continued. "Evidently the craniofacial trauma was much greater this time."

Jon looked over at Brandon. "He's really escalated, then. Sick bastard."

"If you'll excuse me, gentlemen, I have to attend to some other patients. Dr. Rosemont should be out shortly."

Jon and Brandon turned back toward the door.

"A coma," Jon muttered. "That's not good. Maybe she saw something and he's trying to keep her quiet."

"It's possible. But with this guy, I think he would've finished the job and killed her outright. Made sure there was no chance she could identify him."

Jon agreed. This guy wouldn't leave loose ends.

"I think this has to do with Caroline's connection with Sherry. Pointing out that he knows things about her—who she's friends with—and that he isn't afraid to punish her for her continuing to help the police."

Jon could feel rage flow through him. He was more determined than ever to keep Sherry out of this madman's hands.

"That anger you're feeling? Everybody in this hallway is feeling the same thing," Brandon said as they looked at the twenty or thirty people standing around. "I know you think someone in the department could be the rapist, and I'm not discrediting that possibility. But everyone here is furious for what has happened to one of their own. And they're feeding off one another."

Jon agreed. They needed encouragement and they needed to be dispersed. He wasn't sure they were going to listen to him. He was still the outsider.

But he had to try.

Jon got their attention. "People, I know Caroline Gill appreciates your show of support here, but we're going to need everyone to leave."

There were some loud murmurs of disagreement. The men and women were angry and Jon had just given them a target at which to direct their anger: him.

"Look, I know you all care about Caroline, have worked with her, are friends with her. But right now you are needed elsewhere, doing your jobs."

An angry voice from the crowd shouted, "That's easy for you to say, you don't really know Caroline at all."

Jon took in a deep breath. "I know I don't. Not nearly as well as you guys. This is what I do know—when word gets out there has been another attack, the city is going to be tempted to tip over into panic. Each one of you is needed to stop that from happening."

"Do you think you know our town better than us?" A different voice this time.

"No. I do know that we need to work with the evidence

we have. We need to hit the tattoo parlors again for information about the one piece of visual evidence we have. We need to be hitting the streets, seeing if any contacts—old, new or otherwise—have heard or seen *anything* to do with the attack. Most of all, we need to be a visual presence in the city, helping people stay calm."

"Why should we listen to you? You don't really care about us."

He wasn't getting through to them, Jon could tell. They were too incensed.

"No."

Jon was surprised to hear a voice from behind him as he tried to figure out what he could further say.

It was Zane. Cowboy hat back on his head.

"That sort of talk needs to end right now," Zane told them, his tone brooking no refusal. "Agent Hatton—Jon—has worked tirelessly on this case and it's time we all start treating each other like we're on the same side.

"There's a real bad guy out there," the detective continued, his voice breaking just slightly at the words, "and it's not Jon, or any member of the feds. It's time we pull together and stop this bastard."

People were nodding, responding to Zane the way they couldn't to Jon.

"So go do like you've been directed." Another voice this time. Captain Harris. "Do what Agent Hatton told you to do. We solve this, stop this, as a team. The city needs to see you right now and know you're there, like Hatton said. He may not be from Texas, but he's close enough in my book."

The leadership from these two men made all the difference. The officers and hospital workers began to disperse, a few even coming to shake Jon's hand. He promised to keep everyone updated.

"Thank you," he said to Captain Harris and Zane.

"I'm done messing around," Harris said. "He attacked one of our own. He's going down."

"I couldn't agree more."

SHERRY SPENT THE next thirty-six hours next to Caroline's hospital bed. Most of that time Zane sat there with her—when he wasn't pacing up and down the hallway. Sherry had at least gotten a little bit of sleep on the couch in the room. Zane hadn't even considered it.

The doctors still had no definitive answer for when Caroline might wake up. She did have brain activity. That was the most important thing.

Jon had been in and out, willing to leave Sherry at the hospital as long as she promised to stay put and not leave alone under any circumstances. She knew Jon had other things to do besides babysit her: the crime scene, not to mention advising the mayor on further media issues.

Especially now that everyone was willing to listen to him, thanks to Zane's and Captain Harris's words at the hospital.

Caroline's face was hard to look at, the trauma so much more extensive than the other victims. Her nose was broken, cheekbone shattered. She would need reconstructive surgery, but they wanted to wait until she was out of the coma first.

Dr. Rosemont said Caroline might be able to hear what was going on around her, so Sherry tried to talk to her as much as she could. She even read to her from the local gossip magazines. Her voice was starting to get hoarse.

She was pretty sure Zane sat there and whispered in Caroline's ear when Sherry was sleeping. He was determined to let her know she wasn't alone.

Sherry hadn't seen much of Brandon. Jon said he was wandering around the police station and the mayor's office, anywhere that might have known about the connection between Sherry and the department.

"What is he doing?" she asked.

"Looking at people's hands," Jon said with a shrug. "The damage to Caroline's face couldn't be done without there being some sort of telltale sign on the perp's hands and knuckles."

She and Jon were sitting in the hallway outside Caroline's door. His arm was around her and she had her head on his shoulder. It felt good to be like this; to be close to him. Plus, it allowed them to talk, since Zane had finally fallen asleep sitting in the chair, his head propped next to Caroline's arm on the bed. Sherry didn't want to wake him.

"He's a mess. He blames himself," Sherry said.

"Yeah, I know. He's going to have to work through this in his own way."

"It's not his fault."

"Yeah, but nobody in the world is going to be able to make him believe that except him. Or maybe Caroline. I doubt even her."

They sat in silence for a while, just holding on to each other. She knew Jon probably had other things he needed to do.

"Do you have to go?"

His arm tightened around her. "Eventually. But not right now. Right now I'm not going anywhere."

Sherry snuggled in deeper.

A few minutes later Dr. Rosemont and some of the other hospital staff came running down the hallway and into Caroline's room. Sherry and Jon both jumped up.

"What's going on?"

Zane came out of Caroline's hospital room. "She woke up."

"Is she okay? Is she talking?" Sherry asked.

Zane smiled for the first time since Sherry had arrived at the hospital. "She told me I needed to take a shower."

The man then covered his face and started crying.

Sherry rushed up to put her arms around him. "She's going to be okay, Zane. She's awake. She's going to be okay."

"I know. I'm all right." He pulled himself together, then gave an embarrassed look at Jon. "Sorry."

"No need to apologize to me," Jon said, slapping him on the back. "Tears aren't weakness in a situation like this."

Jon knew Zane couldn't handle any more kindness than that, Sherry realized. Jon's ability to *handle* people maybe wasn't such a bad thing, after all.

"Caroline wants to talk to you two. She says she saw the man who attacked her."

As soon as the doctor let them through, they were by Caroline's side.

"Hey, sweetie," Sherry said. "I'm so glad you're awake."

Caroline grimaced. "I'm not. It was much less painful when I was sleeping." Her words were mushy from the swelling.

"We're going to up your pain medication, Caroline," Dr. Rosemont said. "There's no need for you to fight the pain right now. There will be plenty of time for that."

"Not yet," Caroline said. She turned her face toward Sherry and Jon even though she probably couldn't see out of either eye very well. "I saw him."

"That's what Zane told us, honey. Do you remember anything?"

"As soon as the door burst open, I knew what was happening. I knew I only had a second to get a look. I could see his fist coming toward me."

Caroline's breathing became more labored.

Dr. Rosemont took a step closer. "Let's stop for right now, Caroline," she said. "You can tell us this later."

"No, now." Caroline was adamant.

"Sweetie, we can wait." Sherry leaned close and murmured, "It's okay."

"No, you have to stop him now." She took a breath. "I didn't see his face because of the sunlight, but I did see his hair."

"His hair?" Sherry asked. "Tell me." She wished she had her sketch pad, but she wasn't about to leave to get it. She felt Jon put something in her hands. A notebook and pen.

It wasn't a sketch pad, but it was enough. Thank God for that man and his ability to see everything that was going on.

"He had long blond hair," Caroline whispered.

Sherry glanced at Jon. He had the same confused look on his face.

Long blond hair was weird. Or at the very least highly distinguishing, given the man's dark skin.

"Caroline, I don't mean any offense by this, okay? But are you sure about the hair?" Sherry asked as gently as she could.

Caroline tried to nod but then groaned in pain. "I *know* I saw his long blond hair lying against the side of his cheek when he turned to the side. Straight. Long—shoulder length. Yellow blond."

"Okay." Sherry sketched out a picture, leaving the face blank but with straight hair flowing on the sides.

"I knew what was going to happen. And I knew I had to keep this clear in my mind. It was the only way I could fight." Caroline's voice was getting weaker.

The doctor gave Sherry and Jon a pointed look.

"You did great, Caroline," Jon reassured her. "We're going to go now and get this info out to every officer in the city. You've done your job. You rest now."

"Okay." Caroline's voice was tiny. Heartbreaking.

"I'm staying here with her," Zane told them as they walked out. "Do you think her intel is correct?"

Jon looked over at Sherry.

She shrugged. "Memory is fragile. Contaminated within seconds. But Caroline was aware of what was happening, and is trained to be aware of what is going on around her. If she says the man had blond hair, I believe her."

"I do, too," Jon agreed. "I'm going to have Sherry draw something up and, like I told Caroline, we're going to get it out to every damn officer in the city."

Chapter Twenty-Four

Things moved faster than Jon could've dreamed. Especially now that the Corpus Christi PD had decided they were all on the same team. When he and Sherry arrived at the precinct, someone had already gotten all the materials out and ready for Sherry to draw her sketch. Sherry just sat and began working.

She drew a composite sketch based on the details she had gathered from all the victims. She based the facial size on averages of men around five foot nine. Put in generic features based on his possible Latin American or Mexican heritage given the skin tones Jasmine Houze recognized. Then she added the long, straight blond hair.

She handed it to Jon, shrugging. "It's the best I can do with the info I have right now."

Jon looked at it. To be honest, he didn't really think it was going to help. The features were too generic and the hair was too specific.

But he was willing to try. So he showed it to Captain Harris and they sent it out electronically to every officer in the city. They agreed to wait to see what happened before putting the drawing on the news, knowing that would probably trigger the man to change his appearance if he hadn't done so already.

Under other circumstances the sketch might not have helped at all, but the locals were determined to find justice for Caroline. They were beating the pavement looking for the guy, working extra hours without pay for her.

One uniformed officer—the man deserved a medal in Jon's opinion—had gotten the sketch to his cousin who owned a chain of barbershops, feeling that the first thing someone like that would do was try to get rid of the identifiable hair.

Two hours later they had a call. Someone matching the description had come in asking for a haircut.

And he had tattoos on his arm.

The barbers had been instructed to stall him for as long as possible without cutting his hair, but to begin to slowly cut it if it looked as though the guy would leave.

Jon and Brandon had provided backup for the uniformed officers who had gone in to make the arrest.

The suspect had been getting his hair washed by the barber at the time. It went down as one of the most bizarre arrests that Jon had ever seen.

And just as Caroline had said, the man had long blond hair. He was around five-ten, a young, tanned punk who had dyed his hair blond to stand out; to be cool.

Well, his need for cool was going to cost him the rest of his life in prison.

He was confident, cocky. Playing off the whole thing as if he had no idea what they were arresting him for. Sending sly looks in Jon and Brandon's direction.

"He's younger than I would've thought," Brandon said.

"Yeah, maybe we were dealing with a young, bored genius rather than someone established in a career," Jon responded, watching the officers walk him out to the car in cuffs.

Brandon shrugged. "That still works with the profile, I guess."

The skull on his arm was what had convinced them

both. It wasn't exactly what Jasmine Houze had described—there were diamonds drawn in the eye sockets rather than targets—but as Sherry had said, memories were fragile. Given the circumstances, Jasmine's memory was pretty damn close.

The smile the guy gave them was malicious to the core. Jon felt relieved to have him off the streets. He wanted to see if Captain Harris would let Jon talk to the guy; see what he could get out of him. The blond hair and tattoo were pretty damning, but a confession would be the best way to make sure he went to prison for a long time.

THEY'D GOTTEN HIM. The excitement around the station was palpable. Evidently the guy had been getting his hair washed at the time of the arrest, which made everyone snicker. It was important to look pretty on your way to jail.

Jon had texted Sherry that he wanted to interview the suspect himself, which didn't surprise her at all. And it was fine. Sherry wanted to let Caroline and Zane know the good news face-to-face.

Maybe now Zane would be able to start forgiving himself.

She knew processing and questioning the suspect would take a long time. She just jotted a note for Jon to let him know where she was going and left it at his desk rather than disturb him with a text. She ended it with "You, me, celebration tonight. Naked. So tell Brandon to make other plans."

She folded it and wrote his name on the outside. Somebody might read it, but Sherry no longer cared if anyone knew about her and Jon.

Of course, he would be heading back to Colorado soon, now that the case was finished. Sherry wasn't going to think about that right now. Right now she wanted to share the good news about the arrest with her friends.

Caroline was sleeping, but they woke her to tell her. She tried to stay awake to talk to them about it but couldn't manage.

"She has a long path to recovery," Sherry told Zane.

Zane nodded. "Yeah, but catching that bastard was a big step."

"Let's just hope he confesses. That would make everything easier when they go to prosecute."

They talked for a few more minutes before Sherry stood to get back to the station.

Zane stopped her. "Sherry, do you mind going by Caroline's house and picking up a few things for her? You know, stuff that might make her feel more comfortable here? A gown and whatnot. I don't want to leave her."

She touched Zane's arm. "Sure. That's a really great idea. I'll just need to borrow your car."

"No problem. And her house is still a crime scene, so don't go near the front door area." Sherry could tell he had difficulty just forming the words.

Zane dragged some keys out of his pocket. "Here're the keys to my SUV and Caroline's back door. If there's a uniformed officer there, just have him call me for clearance."

Sherry drove to Caroline's house and got inside, avoiding the front hallway area altogether. She got the items she thought her friend would want—some pajamas and other clothes, her own pillow, the book on the bedside table—and put them inside Zane's SUV.

The big yellow Do Not Cross tape at Caroline's front door was difficult to look at. Sherry wondered if Caroline would ever be able to live here again.

Sherry decided it was time for her to face her own crime scene of a house. Although Jon had gotten her some of her own clothes, she hadn't been back there yet herself.

It was time to face that so she could move on. Better to do it now without an audience, even though she knew Jon would gladly have come with her. If she was going to have a breakdown again, she wanted to do it on her own.

She decided to walk. Her house was only a few blocks away if she walked along the shoreline. She took off her shoes and rolled up her jeans.

Sherry breathed in the heavy air of the storm that would be rolling in in the next couple of hours. The waves were crashing higher and the beach was empty of almost everyone. Just how Sherry liked it. She smiled at a couple she passed as they strolled hand in hand, enjoying the roughness of the weather just as she was.

Now that the case was winding up, she and Jon had things to talk about, decisions to be made. Their relationship was something special, she knew. Something real. And she knew Jon felt the same thing. He had mentioned the possibility of her working for the Omega Sector: Critical Response Division more than once.

It did sound as if she might be a better fit there. That her needs would be considered in a way they hadn't been at the Bureau office. And of course…Jon. She couldn't help smiling at the thought.

Another brave walker came toward her as she was about to make the turn off the beach for the road leading to the house. She smiled and waved when she realized it was handsome Dr. Trumpold from the hospital, the source of all Jon's jealously.

"Hi, Sherry," he said, smiling as he passed her.

Sherry was shocked he knew her name. Wait until she lorded this over Jon's head. She smiled at the thought.

But the truth was, no matter how handsome or successful Dr. Trumpold was, he still was no Jon Hatton.

She turned around for one last glance of the handsome doctor. He had stopped about fifty yards from her to look out at the sea. A gust of wind picked up and he slipped on the hood of the yellow sweatshirt he was wearing.

From this angle, the hood made Trumpold look like Fabio. As if he had long blond—

Sherry felt her stomach drop as a chill that had nothing to do with the wind settled over her. She suddenly knew that whoever Jon had arrested today was the wrong guy.

Caroline hadn't seen blond hair in the quick glance she'd gotten of her attacker, although Sherry could very easily see why she would think so. What her friend had seen was the hood of a yellow sweatshirt pulled on the rapist's head.

Dr. Trumpold's head.

He turned and looked at Sherry, his smile eerily friendly.

Sherry dropped her shoes and ran toward her house, knowing he was following her.

Chapter Twenty-Five

It didn't take Jon and Brandon long in the interview room to figure out they had the wrong guy.

He was a punk, no doubt, with attitude to match his ridiculous hair. But someone with a high IQ, not to mention an understanding of how forensics worked so he didn't leave behind any DNA? Definitely not this guy.

And his hands certainly didn't match the profile. No swelling, no bruising, no marks whatsoever. Jon supposed that he could've used something else to inflict the extensive damage on Caroline, but she had mentioned his fist, so Jon didn't think so.

Jon wouldn't be surprised if this guy was guilty of a number of crimes, but he was not the monster who had committed the rapes.

They talked to him for a few more minutes, then left.

"Damn it." Jon considered attempting to put a fist through the cement wall, but he knew the wall would win.

"There's no way that is the guy," Brandon agreed, his frustration clear. "They'll run DNA. I wouldn't be surprised if he's not responsible for some other crimes."

"I've got to talk to the captain, let him know. Based on my experience, that's not going to be pretty."

Brandon nodded. "Yeah, as hard as it is, we don't want people letting down their guard, thinking everything is safe if it's not."

Jon felt as if a hundred pounds had been placed on his shoulders. An arrest in this case, giving the people of Corpus Christi what they needed to feel safe, justice for Caroline and Jasmine and Tina and the other women... Jon had known he wanted to do that, but he'd had no idea how much he'd *needed* to.

Right now he needed to put his arms around Sherry. Just breathe her in.

He should be surprised by how much that need seemed to trump everything else but he wasn't. Although he would give anything to have it the other way around, at least arresting the wrong guy meant he had a few more days with her here. Days he'd be spending trying to convince her to move to Colorado Springs and take that job at Omega.

The captain could wait five minutes. Jon needed to see Sherry.

It didn't take long for him to find her note. He smiled. No, they wouldn't be celebrating tonight, but he still planned for there to be nakedness.

"What's that smile about?" Brandon asked.

"Nothing," Jon said. "Sherry. She went to see Caroline. Telling Zane and Caroline the news about this guy is going to be just as hard as telling Captain Harris."

"How about if I talk to the captain and you go tell them? Face-to-face might be better."

Jon agreed and tried calling Sherry on the way to the hospital, but it went to her voice mail. When he walked inside and found she wasn't with Zane and Caroline a little feeling of panic set in. He and Zane went out into the hallway to talk.

"I asked Sherry to go pick up some stuff for Caroline, to make her feel more comfortable," Zane said. "I gave her a key for the back door so she wouldn't disturb the crime scene in any way, although Forensics is done there."

"That's not what I'm worried about."

He tried Sherry's number again. Voice mail. He left a message this time.

"Hi, baby, it's me. It's very important that you call me the second you get this message, okay?"

"Jon, what's going on?"

"The suspect we have in custody is not the right guy, Zane." Jon put his hand on the other man's shoulder. "I'm sorry. I was really hoping he was the one."

"You're sure?"

"Positive. I'm sorry," Jon repeated, knowing the words weren't enough.

Zane's curse was ugly. Jon couldn't agree more.

Jon's phone buzzed in his hand. Sherry. Relief coursed through him. "Hey, where are you?"

"Jon."

He could barely understand her over her labored breathing.

"He's right outside. I know he's going to kill me."

Jon was running down the hallway toward his car before she got to the second sentence.

SHERRY WASTED NO time running as fast as she could toward her house. If she was wrong and Dr. Trumpold wasn't the rapist, she would apologize profusely later.

But she knew she wasn't wrong. Too much of it made sense. He knew her, knew she was helping the police. And he was definitely smart enough to try to get away with it, as Jon and Brandon had profiled.

She had a good fifty-yard head start on him and knew that her survival depended on her reaching her house before he caught her. She yelled for help as she ran, but the wind drowned out her voice.

She thought of stopping at another house. Of pounding on a door for help. But if she chose a house where no one was home, that would be it for her—he'd be on her. She wouldn't have the chance to try a second house.

She had to make it to hers.

She could see her house now and dug her key chain out of her pocket as she ran, ignoring the pain of running on asphalt in bare feet. She turned sharply into her driveway, then up the three stairs of her small porch. She saw Dr. Trumpold out of the corner of her eye come sprinting into the driveway. She only had seconds.

She took a breath and focused on the keys. If she fumbled or dropped them now, he'd catch her. She sobbed in relief as the lock turned and she let herself in, slamming the door behind her and locking it. She heard Trumpold crash into it just a second later.

She knew she still wasn't safe. Too many windows… ways to get in.

She called Jon.

He answered after just one ring. "Hey, where are you?"

"Jon." She tried to get her breathing under control but couldn't. "He's right outside. I know he's going to kill me."

"Where are you, Sherry?"

"My house. He's here. I saw him on the beach. It's Dr. Trumpold. He's the rapist." She heard a loud thump against the door as Trumpold slammed himself against it. "He's breaking through the front door."

She heard Jon curse. "Sherry, get in your bedroom. Pull the dresser against the door. I'm on my way. Stay on the line with me."

The beating against the door stopped for a moment. "Sherry, I just want to talk. Explain why I did what I did. Open the door." Trumpold's voice sounded so reasonable from the outside.

"Sweetheart, get in your bedroom. Right now." Jon's voice on the phone drowned out the one outside the door.

Sherry did as Jon said. Immediately she could hear the pounding start on the door again.

"Okay, I'm in the bedroom. He says he just wants to talk."

Jon's bark of laughter held no humor whatsoever. "Fine. He can talk to you through the bedroom door. I'm ten minutes out."

They both knew Trumpold would be able to get into her bedroom before then.

Sherry rushed over to the dresser chest and pushed with all her might to move it in front of the door. At first it wouldn't budge, so she turned and put her back to it, pushing with her legs.

Instead of moving it fell over. But it still blocked the door and that was what counted.

"What happened? Are you okay?"

"Yes, I pushed the chest of drawers in front of the door."

"Good girl."

She couldn't hear Trumpold pounding on the outside door anymore. Was he already inside? Had he given up?

Her bedroom was almost unrecognizable to her, between the fallen dresser and her bed mattress completely missing. It looked as if it had been through a tornado.

"I don't know where he is," Sherry whispered to Jon. "It's quiet now. I'm scared."

"I know, baby. Stay focused. Look for things you can use as weapons if he gets in. Things you can throw. Hit him with. Candles, a lamp, hair spray to spray him in the eyes."

Sherry nodded and started gathering items. She was facing the door, waiting for Trumpold to start pounding.

And was totally unprepared for when the large window broke behind her and he came leaping through.

She was able to throw only one candle at him, which caught him on the shoulder before he was on her. Her cell phone fell to the floor and shattered into pieces.

"Everything law enforcement does tends to be so predictable," Trumpold said, grabbing the lamp that she tried to swing at him and throwing it across the room. "For example, barricading a door. SWAT 101."

Had she really ever thought he was handsome? Now all she could see was a madman. "I thought you said you wanted to talk."

He shrugged. "I admit that wasn't the truth. I'm naughty." He laughed at his own joke. "It was worth a try, you know? You never know when someone is going to be stupid enough to just throw open the door."

He took a step closer to her and grabbed her by the hair, jerking her closer to him. "Like all those women. Especially your friend Caroline. How stupid was she?"

"She thought you were someone else," Sherry snarled, wincing as he pulled her hair again. She knew she had to keep him talking, but she also felt an ingrained need to defend her friend.

"Actually, I know that." Trumpold laughed again. "I overheard her talking on the phone to that cop love-me, love-me-not boyfriend of hers. 'Tomorrow. Three o'clock. Be there, Zane. You know you want to.'" He said it in a falsetto voice, mimicking Caroline.

He tugged on Sherry's hair again, bringing tears to her eyes. "The drama between those two. Seriously, it's like a soap opera. I waited to see if he would show up and he didn't."

He brought Sherry's face right up to his. "I did."

Sherry thought she might vomit.

"When I heard about the blond hair thing, I knew it was time to retire the yellow hoodie. Oops. That could've been a mess. But I'm so glad you were able to figure it out first."

Sherry knew he was going to kill her. There was no way he would let her live knowing what she knew. She began struggling in earnest.

He released her long enough to backhand her. She fell to the floor. He picked her up by the collar of her shirt.

"It's okay, because I realize now this whole punching with my fists thing is getting old. It hurts when you punch someone, you know? I've had to hide my hands for the past couple of days." He held them out where she could see his bruised and swollen knuckles. "Not an easy thing to do when you're a doctor."

He hit her again and Sherry spat blood, falling back to the floor.

"I've been bored with medicine for a while now, so leaving that behind and going to ground won't be a problem. I've been preparing for that contingency for months, in case law enforcement ever caught on to me. I'll pop back up somewhere else."

Sherry cringed away from him as he crouched to get close to her, straddling her hips. "You've shown me that it's infinitely more exciting to pursue and capture someone who *knows* me. Who *knows* what's going to happen. It means I have to kill them, but I think that's just the next step for me, don't you?"

Sherry just tried to control her terror to breathe enough air into her lungs and wait for a chance to get away.

He pulled out a wicked-looking, long-bladed knife and pointed it at the side of her neck. "Now, this is overkill, I know. It's, like, Crocodile Dundee big, right?" He chuckled again. "But I like it. It's kind of sexy. Knives are really a natural choice for me, since I've used scalpels for years at the hospital. I can kill quickly and painlessly or slowly and much less painlessly."

Sherry could feel the blade slide into her neck, the sharp sting. She stopped fighting. If she fought now he would just slice the blade across her throat.

"I'm sorry I don't have time to play with you longer."

He kissed her cheek. "But I estimate the cavalry will arrive in about two minutes and I need to be gone before then."

Sherry felt the knife slice her deeper and tried to make one last desperate jerk away as Trumpold's body suddenly flew off hers.

Jon.

He had come in silently through the window and tackled Trumpold. Sherry brought her fingers up to her neck as she slid herself out of the way of where they were fighting. Her hand was soon soaked with her own blood.

That wasn't good.

Jon and the doctor were rolling on the floor. Jon had him in height, but Trumpold was strong and had the knife. Sherry winced as the Crocodile Dundee knife cut Jon in the biceps. Then she slumped against the dresser, feeling dizzy.

Jon got in a couple of good punches to Trumpold's face and Trumpold fell to the floor. Jon kicked away his knife and left him there on the floor, rushing to Sherry.

He pulled off his shirt.

"I don't think I can have sex right now," Sherry said. Her vision was getting a little fuzzy.

He pressed the shirt against her neck. He put his face right in front of hers. "Hey, you stay with me. I want a rain check on that offer, okay?"

Where he pressed against her neck hurt and she wanted to sleep but tried to stay awake.

She saw Trumpold get up behind Jon with that damn knife. She tried to form words but couldn't. She flung an arm out instead.

Jon turned and threw up his arm, stopping the knife from slicing into his back, although it cut deep into his arm. Trumpold raised the knife again. Jon shielded Sherry with his body, but she realized it was going to cost Jon his life. She weakly tried to push him out of the way as the knife sped toward his back again, but he wouldn't budge in his protection of her.

Then the doctor flew backward, away from them both, as a shot rang out from the window.

Sherry heard Zane's voice. "You're never going to hurt anyone again, you son of a bitch."

And everything fell to black.

Chapter Twenty-Six

Between the two of them they had eighty-six stitches.

Although Sherry's cut was deeper and she'd lost a lot more blood, Jon actually had the most stitches. But stitches wouldn't have helped either of them if Zane hadn't showed up when he had.

He'd followed Jon, with Caroline's prompting, and if he hadn't, both Jon and Sherry would be dead.

Jon had known he couldn't take the pressure off her neck wound without the danger of her bleeding to death, so stopping Trumpold's attack at his back would've been nearly impossible.

Zane's shot to Trumpold's chest hadn't killed him, unfortunately, but he'd be in prison for a long time. Sherry hoped that would give all the women he'd attacked a little peace. And she hoped Zane's role in stopping him would help the detective find some self-forgiveness, as well.

Sherry never planned to tell Zane what Trumpold had said about Caroline's attack. Of how he'd waited for Zane to arrive and seized the opportunity to attack Caroline when Zane hadn't showed up.

Of course, she didn't have to tell Zane what Trumpold said. Zane had already been telling himself that since it happened.

Sherry's hospital room had been filled with Omega agents all day to the point where Dr. Rosemont finally had to kick them out. Brandon had been there, talking with her, asking questions, wanting to understand how Trumpold's brain worked. Liam had come back through town and crawled into her hospital bed with her, wrapping his arms around her as if they'd been lovers for years. Everyone else in the room had pretty much just rolled their eyes and ignored him.

Steve Drackett, director of the Omega Critical Response Division, had even made an appearance himself. He was checking on Jon, meeting with the mayor, but also wanted to make sure Sherry knew that she officially had a job waiting for her at Omega anytime she wanted to take it.

They were all gone now, but Jon hadn't left her the whole time. She'd woken in the hospital, fine once they'd been able stitch the wound and replace the blood she'd lost. He'd already gotten his own stitches by the time she was moved into a private room from the trauma unit. But she didn't need to stay. They were releasing her tonight.

Except she didn't really have anywhere to go. The beach house was a crime scene. Again.

"Are you about ready to go? Nurse Carreker said we're free whenever you're ready."

Most of the hospital was still reeling from the fact that Dr. Trumpold—a trusted doctor at their hospital—had been the rapist. Many of them had worked with the man every day for years.

"I don't really have anywhere to go. I guess I need to check into a hotel."

He put an arm around her as they walked down the hall toward the exit.

"That won't be necessary, if you don't mind staying with me for a few days."

"At the condo?"

"No, that was rented by Omega for work. I've gotten a different place."

He didn't offer any more information, so Sherry just walked with him as he led her to the car and then began to drive. It didn't take long to realize they were headed toward the beach.

"Is this okay?" he asked when he realized she understood where they were going. "I got a place. It's on the south end, not near your house or Caroline's. But I know you love the beach, and I wanted it to be a place that held good memories for you. For both of us."

Sherry nodded but didn't say anything. Honestly, she wasn't sure.

He drove in silence until they arrived at a tiny little cottage just a couple of blocks from the waterfront. He put the car in Park and turned to her.

"You are owed two weeks of vacation, which starts now. The last week you worked for Omega, which they'll pay you for."

"But—"

"Director Drackett's orders, not mine. I had nothing to do with it."

Okay, she could handle that.

"I'm also taking two weeks of vacation and would like to spend it here with you, if you'll have me?"

She smiled at him and waggled her eyebrows. "Oh, I'll have you. Believe me, I'll have you."

"Good, because I had somebody go by and get your stuff from the house. It included that red bikini. I hope you will spend almost every hour of the next two weeks in that or less. Except for maybe your cowboy boots."

Sherry laughed and they opened the car doors. The sun was shining in grand Southern Texas fashion. She held her face up to it as she got out of the car. Jon came around to close the door behind her.

He backed her up against the car. "Just want to forewarn you, Ms. Mitchell, I also plan to spend the entire next two weeks convincing you to take that job at Omega. Because I don't think I can go back there without you."

Sherry wondered if she should tell him she already planned to take that job. Nah. It'd be more fun keeping him in suspense. "It sounds like you plan on handling me, Agent Hatton."

"Oh, very much so, Ms. Mitchell." He breathed soft kisses from her mouth along her jaw to her ear.

"I hope you'll do that correctly, Agent. Not overthink the situation too much."

"The only thing I'm in danger of overthinking is how to get you to fall in love with me like I am with you." He worked his lips back up to hers, then eased back so he could see the beautiful blue of her eyes.

She smiled. "No thinking necessary. Already falling."

She leaned in to his addictive warmth. She didn't think she'd ever feel too warm next to him. She loved the heat they generated.

And she knew. This house. This time. They were exactly what she needed.

He was exactly what she needed.

* * * * *

MILLS & BOON®

INTRIGUE
Romantic Suspense

A SEDUCTIVE COMBINATION OF DANGER AND DESIRE

16_MB518

MILLS & BOON®
The Billionaires Collection!

This fabulous 6 book collection features stories from some of our talented writers. Feel the temperature rise with our ultra-sexy and powerful billionaires. Don't miss this great offer – buy the collection today to get two books free!

Order yours at
**www.millsandboon.co.uk
/billionaires**

MILLS & BOON®

Let us take you back in time with our Medieval Brides...

The Novice Bride – Carol Townend

The Dumont Bride – Terri Brisbin

The Lord's Forced Bride – Anne Herries

The Warrior's Princess Bride – Meriel Fuller

The Overlord's Bride – Margaret Moore

Templar Knight, Forbidden Bride – Lynna Banning

Order yours at
www.millsandboon.co.uk/medievalbrides

MILLS & BOON®

Why shop at millsandboon.co.uk?

Each year, thousands of romance readers find their perfect read at millsandboon.co.uk. That's because we're passionate about bringing you the very best romantic fiction. Here are some of the advantages of shopping at www.millsandboon.co.uk:

✴ **Get new books first**—you'll be able to buy your favourite books one month before they hit the shops

✴ **Get exclusive discounts**—you'll also be able to buy our specially created monthly collections, with up to 50% off the RRP

✴ **Find your favourite authors**—latest news, interviews and new releases for all your favourite authors and series on our website, plus ideas for what to try next

✴ **Join in**—once you've bought your favourite books, don't forget to register with us to rate, review and join in the discussions

Visit **www.millsandboon.co.uk**
for all this and more today!